Nicholas Blincoe

Nicholas Blincoe was born in R.......................s
through welding..ted a
PhD in contempo..Warwick
University. He...................................ovels: *Acid
Casuals*, *Jeli*..nich won a
CWA Silver Dagger Award, *The Dope Priest* and *White Mice*.
He is also a critic, screenwriter and journalist and is married
to the filmmaker Leila Sansour.

'Blincoe handles both the period setting and the metafictional fun with flair and assurance . . . provoking and engaging.'
Sam Thompson, *Guardian*

'Blincoe evokes the turbulence of these terrible months of siege, hunger and bloodshed in Paris exceptionally well . . . [a] clever, ambitious and demanding novel.'
Allan Massie, *Scotsman*

'Two sieges, an impossible love in two separate epochs, and re-enactments of urban violence. Blincoe does not push the parallels too hard and lets the reader make the connections . . . *Burning Paris* works inventively on several levels. It is an engaging chronicle of human interaction and a docudrama firmly rooted in carefully observed social history. The Palestinian sieges are graphically evoked in the style of vivid front-line journalism . . . [Blincoe's] observation of modern life in cosmopolitan Paris is sharp, shrewd and graphic, qualities which also describe his sprightly style.'
David Coward, *The Times Literary Supplement*

'Blincoe works [his] two worlds with clever and subtle humour, drawing intriguing similarities between each situation . . . a clever blend of historical detail and present day reality painted on a back-drop of war and impossible circumstances.'
Big Issue

'To some extent, *Burning Paris* is a novel of ideas but it wouldn't work without plenty of action . . . Here, there is a love pentagon, a city under siege, and all the tuches-saving intrigue that develops when a national war becomes civil'
Tom Payne, *Daily Telegraph*

'A searing, epic tale of love and war'
Attitude

Nicholas Blincoe

Burning Paris

SCEPTRE

First published in Great Britain in 2004 by Hodder and Stoughton
A division of Hodder Headline

A Sceptre Paperback

1   3   5   7   9   10   8   6   4   2

A CIP catalogue record for this title is available from the British Library

ISBN 0 340 73469 8

Typeset in Monotype Sabon by
Palimpsest Book Production Limited
Polmont, Stirlingshire

Printed and bound in Great Britain by
Clays Ltd, St Ives plc

Hodder Headline's policy is to use papers that are natural, renewable
and recyclable products and made from wood grown in sustainable forests.
The logging and manufacturing processes are expected to conform to
the environmental regulations of the country of origin.

Hodder and Stoughton Ltd
A division of Hodder Headline
338 Euston Road
London NW1 3BH

For Tom Hurndall and Rachel Corrie

1904, *Dartmouth Naval Academy*

Yesterday's sensation was the new battleship, twelve-inch cannons bristling from its hulk like crystals from black quartz. Throughout class, the cadets' eyes were pulled towards the windows by the monster in the docks below. But today it was forgotten, and they were obsessed with the training exercises for the SMLE rifle. They wanted to know whether Brunel would be going down to the beach in the afternoon to watch.

Brunel wiped the day's grammar off the blackboard as he said, 'I'll go for a short time'.

Seventy-four-year-old Mons Brunel, the Mons short for Monsieur because he taught French to naval cadets, the youngest of them only twelve. Mons had begun as a pet name but after thirty years at the academy it had come to seem like a description of a geographical feature. So high you wouldn't get over it, so low you couldn't get under it. Brunel used to be five foot eight; he was smaller now. He wore his beard as short and as neat as did the English officers that surrounded him, and dressed in a dark blue coat that could be mistaken for a uniform. Yes, he was a civilian, and a foreign one at that. But he had not always been a civilian and if he appeared to follow naval discipline it was because it came naturally to him.

The class was over and Brunel was talking to a group of his boys in one of those informal moments between the end of classes and the beginning of mess. The boys valued these times, partly because there were few informal moments in their day and partly because, as Brunel knew, he was far more interesting when he spoke of battleships and weapons than when he taught French.

'What's happening, Mons Brunel? Why are you only going for a short time?'

'I am going to London to talk to a journalist.'

'A journalist? Are you in the news?'

Brunel shook his head. 'They want to ask me about an old friend.'

'What's he done?'

'She,' Brunel said. 'She was accused of burning Paris down.'

'Did she do it?'

'No. It was me.'

'Really? Why?'

'It was pissing me off.'

The short-magazine Lee-Enfield was introduced as a result of the Boer war. Brunel had seen a rifle that had been sporterized, as the Boers called it: the wooden stock cut away to leave a naked steel barrel. It made the rifle easier to manoeuvre on horseback and less bulky when crawling through bush. The short-magazine Lee-Enfield took account of this innovation; it was lighter because it was shorter. Brunel found the name confusing because only the rifle was short. The magazine was fairly large; it held ten rounds.

The training exercise took place on the wide sweep of beach to the west of the naval docks. It was a demonstration rather than an exercise, conducted by experienced marines. They ran from the low tideline in staggered waves against enemy positions in the dunes. The enemy was imaginary: the rounds were live. Brunel's boys loved it, the noise and the sprays of sand as the rounds bit into the dunes.

The senior officers and civilian observers were gathered together a little further down the quay. Brunel recognised a number of his old pupils but discretion had long ago become a habit with him and he was careful to stand back, behind the current crop of cadets. One of these old boys was plying an adjutant with questions, while sketching the marines' path with his finger in the air. As he followed this line from the shore to the quay, he noticed Brunel and pulled up, turning his pointed finger into a casual salute.

Brunel, who walked with a stick, limped over. Once he was safely balanced, he saluted back. He only saluted his boys.

'Commander.'

'I'm not a commander any more. I joined the family business full time.'

'I'm sorry, sir. How do I address you?'

'Your Royal Highness.'

'*Bien.*'

They turned back to the beach. The marines were demonstrating a new offensive manoeuvre: running in small packs, supported by covering fire. Once the leading men found cover, they would commence firing as those to the rear broke forward. In this way, the men attacked in relays, shouting commands to each other as they went.

'Have you come across anything like this before, Mons Brunel?' the prince asked.

Brunel nodded. The manoeuvre might have been rediscovered with the Boer war, but Brunel had seen it back in the 1860s with the first appearance of breech-loading rifles. The speed of loading meant that a competent soldier could fire twelve rounds a minute, though because of overheating and the need for accuracy they tended to be restricted to eight rounds a minute.

'The broken formation is a harder target,' Brunel explained. 'If they had marched up the beach like the old red line, they would be slaughtered.'

'I like the idea of men working in small teams, the *esprit de corps.*'

'Maybe you shouldn't. A battle like this is controlled on the ground by non-coms and junior officers, not by generals on hills.'

'And if there are no generals, then no princes.'

'No, sir.'

*   *   *

3

Brunel reread the journalist's letter in his hotel room on the Strand. He had chosen the Savoy because he hoped the room would be comfortable. He could afford it – he barely spent what he earned at the naval college. But each time he read the letter, he felt the beginnings of palpitations and the room was suddenly too small. The phrases that caused all the excitement: the journalist had a surprise, he would be bringing along a comrade, an old friend – a sister! – from M. Brunel's days in Paris.

Brunel left his room for the bar. Once in the lobby, he changed his mind, hovering for a beat before veering towards the door. He refused a cab, he had decided that he needed to buy a gift, and set out looking for a perfumery among the still-open shops. He circled Covent Garden before heading towards Regent Street, moving as briskly as he could in an attempt to outstrip the tremors that ran across his chest and from his hand to his stick. As he returned through Leicester Square, perfume bottle gift-wrapped in the pocket of his overcoat, he decided that he needed to eat. He got a supper table at the Criterion, and a large brandy.

It was a mistake. Not to eat, but to choose a place that was so full of life. From his table against the wall he was looking directly at a party of six people, three women and three men. The women were smoking enthusiastically, their cigarettes bobbing like batons to the rhythms of their conversation and laughter. The men were entranced: they were admirers. The women, perhaps, were actresses. Brunel lifted his menu above his eye-line and sought out the most sleep-inducing item on the menu. He settled on poached haddock, hoping that it would not keep him awake, reminding him of its cold fishy presence at four in the morning.

The journalist was an idiot. Few people like surprises, soldiers don't like them at all. He would anticipate the meeting all night, playing through scenarios, and it would not matter what he chose to eat or drink, he would not sleep. Worrying about everything from the suitability of his gift to imagining how, now that arthritis had weaselled into his hip wound, they would cope together in bed. Brunel had already pulled back the sheets – and he was barely through his entrée in the restaurant. He had hours left to imagine that.

She would be sixty-three-years-old. Almost ten years younger than him. Brunel assumed that men and women of their age often made love. Why wouldn't they? Whenever he was caught out by desire, perhaps on waking on a morning when the sun was bright, the sheets were clean and his mind disorientated, he could feel her close and would wait to be filled by her feel and taste. And when it failed to materialise, and he realised where he was, all he could do was get out of bed and get on with life. What was he doing when he was wide awake, giving in to his dreams? They had not seen or spoken to each other for more than thirty years; could they really recapture anything of their past?

As he was leaving, a man leapt to his feet, as though to attention.

'Sir. Mons Brunel.'

Brunel nodded in recognition, but without speaking. He didn't want to misremember the boy's name; rather, the name of the boy that this forty-year-old man had once been.

'It's Cavendish, Mons Brunel, sir.'

Brunel smiled and said, 'Cavendish. Good to see you.' Now he remembered that the boy had left the naval academy after contracting meningitis. By the time the disease had run its course, the boy had spent so much time alone reading that his parents had decided he was better suited to a conventional education. 'Did I hear that you joined the diplomatic service? I always thought you would work abroad.'

'My current job keeps me here, sir. But what about you, what are you doing in London?'

'I'm here, I think, because of a mistake. A journalist asked to interview me and I agreed.'

'Anxious that he will ask too much, sir?' Cavendish grinned. 'If you wanted to give me his name, I could ask my own questions.'

'No. Thank you.'

For Cavendish to have made the offer, he must have access to intelligence files. Evidently, that was the job that kept him in London. No doubt spies are necessary, but Brunel knew that if his own story were to begin over again it would have a very different end. He had slipped into Britain a long time ago, in the days when groups like the Anarchists and the Fenians were still regarded as cranks and novelties, rather than terrorist threats. He could not today arrive from nowhere and apply for a post at the Royal Naval Academy. He certainly would not get the job on a misunderstanding, an assumed relationship to the more famous Brunels, the family of engineers.

The Naval Academy had kept Brunel alive by keeping his brain active. He had his work and his pupils, and he was constantly absorbed by the latest technological changes, the rapid improvements to the ships, the ordnance, the new radio telegraphy. He had that kind of mind, and although these were exactly the things that would interest a spy or a terrorist Brunel was neither. He was an ex-marine, a soldier who lived among sailors because he believed that, too often, a landlocked and slow-moving army was nothing more than a glorified police force. He strongly believed that, considering everything, he was fortunate to be able to spend the remains of his life among naval cadets. He knew that his students appreciated the respect they received from this old Frenchman. He did not presume to think that they loved him, but they did. It was true; he was a poor language teacher, but a mind that could bring the science and application of warfare to life was not necessarily the best at giving life back to his own language, once it had been reduced to irregular verb tables, grammatical rules and vocabulary tests.

Brunel remembered that Cavendish had been good at French as a twelve-year-old, a talent that must have stood him in good stead in the espionage business. But he blushed when Brunel rejected his clumsy offer to vet the journalist and changed the subject, proving, at least, that the British were reassuringly incompetent spies.

'If you're still in London tomorrow, sir,' he said, 'there's a reception for a French military delegation.'

'Is this a party invitation?'

'I can certainly get you one.'

'To meet a French military delegation? No. I think you know I'm a wanted man in France.'

Cavendish blushed again. 'Yes, sir. I believe we know that.'

Brunel's leg gave him trouble all night. He should not have walked back to the hotel, but that was not the reason that he didn't sleep. He twice sent down for brandy and moved from the bed to a chair by the window, covering himself with a blanket he had found in the wardrobe. Sitting upright, he finally began to doze. Dreams can bring a new perspective to one's anxieties, but they never do it conveniently, at a time that suits. Brunel dreamt about the new SMLE rifle. It kept overheating in his hands, and his hands kept slipping towards the barrel as he fired. He could not work out how he was managing to fire and grip the barrel at the same time.

He had arranged to meet Joseph Harold Beddoes, the journalist, at ten o'clock. Brunel arrived in the salon early and settled on a group of three high-backed chairs, the bottle of perfume placed on a small table to his left. While he waited, he tried to read *The Times* and failed to digest the devilled kidneys he had chosen for breakfast. Kidneys for the blood and iron, for the sake of his strength. Over the next forty-five minutes, he would read across the width of a column and let his eyes travel on, across the newspaper and out to the hotel lobby. He noticed the large young man, like misshapen dough, the moment he entered the salon, even before he stopped the waiter and asked for Brunel by name. Brunel reached for his stick, preparing to stand and make himself more visible, but then he saw the woman following behind and suddenly wanted a moment to compose himself. He tried to isolate all the things that struck him as odd, both about the woman and the scene. Perhaps the air of shabbiness about her black clothes, the black hat squashed on to wiry grey hair. And why was she walking behind Beddoes? Brunel could not believe that she would be so deferential. Or that it would not occur to the journalist to be more chivalrous.

As they approached, Brunel was surprised to see that she had grown so thin and stooped. And then realised it wasn't her after all. It was that crazy Anarchist.

'Louise Michel.' As Brunel stood, he let his newspaper fall to the table to cover the bottle of perfume, with its ridiculous name: Jicky.

Louise Michel pursed her lips, nodding seriously so that her chin disappeared into her bony neck to simulate an Adam's apple. Yet Brunel could tell that she was pleased to see him, even as she greeted him with a clenched fist and the salute: 'Comrade General.'

Brunel now understood why the journalist had hurried ahead. It was impossible to know how to behave around Louise Michel, to imagine what kind of behaviour would be appropriate. Brunel certainly wasn't going to return her clenched salute.

He stepped forward and kissed her, first one cheek and then the other. 'It's very good to see you.' Suddenly he meant it. 'Sit down.'

The journalist was a narrow-shouldered, fat-hipped young man whose eyes blinked and bobbed behind his spectacles. Brunel could see how excited he was to have arranged this meeting. There was his story, right there, bringing the pair of them together. Louise Michel, the most infamous of the Paris Commune's woman revolutionaries, and Paul-Antoine Brunel, the Commune's general, the man responsible for torching the Hôtel de Ville and razing the Tuileries Palace. Beddoes flapped open his writing pad and twisted off the top of his reservoir pen, blinking all the while. He would probably have liked either

Michel or Brunel to have fainted dead away. Instead, he asked if they had seen each other since 1871.

They shook their heads. No, they never had. Louise briskly recounted her life. Brunel knew that it had been almost a year after the siege before she was tried and finally transported to a prison island in the Pacific. He now learnt that she had been repatriated eight years later in the amnesty of 1880 and since then had been imprisoned another three times for revolutionary activities. All Brunel could say in return was that he had lived in Britain almost continuously since their defeat. Nor was he active, at least not in Louise Michel's sense of the word. He said only that he had been living quietly by the English seaside.

'The issue here,' the journalist said, 'is the story of the female arsonists, *les pétroleuses*.'

'The myth,' said Brunel.

'Exactly. And the genesis of that myth, insofar as Mlle Michel represents the model of the female firebrand and you provided the story with its foundations, through real acts of arson.'

'It wasn't arson. I was providing clear fields of fire for my artillery.'

Although Brunel spoke dispassionately, Beddoes grew even more excited. His watery-blue eyes swam around behind the frames of his glasses.

'Yes. Exactly. The military reasons; if a building was in the way, you removed it. Burning Paris was not the vindictive act of an Anarchist; it was the ruthlessness of a military commander.'

Now the journalist had offended Louise Michel. 'Why vindictive and Anarchist? Why both terms together? Anarchism strives for a society based on mutuality. It is never vindictive towards the old order. I can assure you that it is the other way around, always and without exception.' She leant forward to prod at the table with her finger. 'The state is an entirely vindictive entity.'

She underlined each word by driving her finger into the table top. She had not changed at all. Brunel had a theory: that the differences between men and women are never so marked as when they share the same ideology. He did not include himself in this theory, primarily because he did not believe he maintained any form of ideology. At the end of the four-month siege of Paris, when the Prussian forces entered the city, Brunel had refused to accept that France was defeated. His opposition to the government's surrender led him to make common cause with the city's revolutionaries, without ever sharing their ideas. But as he fought beside them, Brunel came to realise that there was one kind of radicalism appropriate to men, and another that only manifested itself in women. And although the feminine variety might be rarer, it never burnt itself out because it so rarely contained the softening tints of hypocrisy or self-interest or ambition. The cartoon image of Louise Michel had always seemed fair comment. She really was the Red Virgin, married to her cause.

And Brunel was called the Burner. That was less fair.

'I can't do this interview,' Brunel said.

That brought the journalist up short. 'What? Why not?'

'As you said, the story of *les pétroleuses* is a myth. If it's a myth, then it's not news. So there is no point.'

Brunel drove down on his stick and pulled himself upright.

The journalist began blinking faster, knowing that he had little time left. 'But the persistency of the myth, the way that the government manipulated the truth for propaganda purposes, that is the story. That is a real issue.'

'I don't see it. But I am grateful for the opportunity to have been reacquainted with Mademoiselle Michel.'

Brunel turned to wish Louise Michel *au revoir* as he simultaneously tucked his perfume gift into his pocket.

Now the journalist was on his feet, taking Brunel by his arm. 'If you don't do the interview, then no one will hear your voice. And I cannot be sure that my interpretation of your character would be fair – or how it would be received by your employees at the Royal Naval Academy.'

Beddoes had resorted to blackmail.

Brunel said, 'Let go of my arm, or you'll be pulling my stick out of your backside.'

The journalist dropped his hand. Brunel never let his gaze wander. Their eyes locked until the journalist sank back into his chair.

'I might have been susceptible to blackmail once. But these days, I don't care. I'm too old.' Brunel looked down at the young man. 'Though obviously not frail enough for you.'

Brunel's past life, at least its vague outline, had become apparent over his thirty years at the academy. There would be a change in the air as staff and officers brushed against the question of his military experience, and then chose to brush right on by. If it was never talked about, then it could never become a problem. Brunel was grateful for their silence, and he kept quiet. But when he received the journalist's letter, he had forgotten his caution. Because he had been in love, had remained in love through a lifetime's separation, the possibility that she might be willing to see him again overrode every other consideration. Risk didn't come into it, only the desperate hope that she had sought him out. Brunel had never even asked the journalist the name of this woman. When Beddoes coyly spoke of 'his sister, his comrade', Brunel saw only one face.

Not that lunatic Louise Michel. God bless her, but no thanks.

He waited in the lobby until the journalist and Michel had left the building, then followed them on to the Strand. They separated almost immediately, Beddoes turning right towards Fleet Street and Michel heading in the opposite direction. Brunel caught up with Michel before she crossed the road.

'Forgive me, Mademoiselle Michel. Do you know what happened to Babette Hébert?'

Louise Michel squinted and smiled. 'Oh, Comrade. No. I'm sorry, I don't.'

'She was not on the court lists, as far as you know?' Brunel had read the accounts of the trials without ever seeing her mentioned. 'Perhaps under an assumed identity?'

'I don't think Comrade Babette could have hidden behind a false name, do you?' Michel took his hand. 'I only wish I could help you. But all I know are rumours and I would not like to repeat those.'

'Please do.' Brunel folded his fingers around the hand that held his, warming Michel's brittle sticklike fingers. 'Whatever you know, I would be grateful to hear it.'

'Very well. I believe she cut a deal just as Paris was falling. She was said to have escaped, to have become a housekeeper somewhere. That is what I heard.'

Michel had no other information, but it was enough to make Brunel waver. He had intended to take the lunchtime train but, instead, stayed one more night at the Savoy. When Joseph Beddoes waddled into work next morning, Brunel was waiting outside his offices, ready to help with his story of the Burner Brunel. Better than that, Brunel was prepared to give the journalist the diaries that he had begun during the last months of the Franco-Prussian war, when the citizens of Paris were beginning to starve, and which he had kept throughout the civil war that followed, when those who rejected the surrender ended up fighting their own government. Some days later Beddoes received the diaries, and the love letters that were pressed between their pages, and he wrote back to Brunel to assure him that he would soon start work.

He never did.

Joseph Harold Beddoes was my great-grandfather, a middling journalist whose work, where it survives, limps along in an uninspiring, rigid style. I have no idea why he did nothing with Brunel's journals. It has taken me three years fully to understand why I took them up.

Brunel's journal is the story of a love affair as much as a war. Lieutenant Brunel's company had fought one of the most desperate actions in the battle of Sedan, the decisive engagement of the Franco-Prussian war. After the victory of Prussia and its allies (although Germany did not yet exist, the war was fought as a German-speaking coalition under Prussian leadership), Brunel became one of thousands of French prisoners of war. The Emperor of France, Napoleon III, surrendered at Sedan on 2 September 1870 and went into exile, followed by his wife, the Empress Eugénie. The rest of the war against the German forces was conducted by a hastily improvised Republican Government under the presidency of General Louis Jules Trochu, the Governor of Paris. Given that the new Republican Government was composed exclusively of Parisians, under the leadership of the man responsible for the vast defences around the capital, it was perhaps inevitable that the war stagnated into a siege of Paris. There were battles in the provinces. The Minister of the Interior, Léon Gambetta, a young lawyer, escaped from Paris by balloon in early October and managed to raise an army, establishing a centre of resistance at Tours in the Loire valley. But it was always clear that the fate of Paris would be the decisive factor in the outcome of the war.

Paul-Antoine Brunel, having escaped his Prussian captors, slipped through the siege lines and entered Paris on 26 October, carrying a secret communiqué for President Trochu. It was in Paris that Brunel met his lover. In the civil war that ensued, they campaigned side by side on the barricades. Among Joseph Beddoes' notes for the book that he never wrote, I read Brunel's protestations that *les pétroleuses* were a myth. Yet his mistress did enough to establish the myth; she was female and she was an arsonist. When I first began wondering whether I could take up Brunel's history, I realised that I would be attempting a love story. I was set back some months by the thought that I might end with a novel in which a war was simply the picturesque backdrop to a romance. The problem was that I was unclear about what attracted me to Brunel's story. My motives would remain hazy until I, too, survived a war.

When I began this book, I was nervous of historical fiction. I kept writing and rewriting my descriptions of London in the early twentieth century. I worried whether I had any flair for the re-creation of history: the sights and the smells. Brunel lived in Dartmouth, so it is possible that he would have been struck by the crowds in London, or the smell of the river behind his hotel, or the quantity of horse dung strewn about the streets. If horse dung was strewn around the streets. It must have been, where else would it be? But would Brunel really notice, wouldn't he take it all for granted? The challenge, I thought, was to give the reader surprising details, but in non-obtrusive ways. My father once told me that the biggest change during his lifetime was the Clean Air Act of the early 1960s. He said that it was impossible to believe just how dirty things used to be. If he went walking on the moors, his trousers would be black from the knees down, because the grass was so filthy. Even in my own lifetime, I remember how black the big public buildings used to be, the churches, the libraries and town halls. At the time I thought it was natural, but my own son, born in the mid 1980s, would have difficulty even imagining that deep, death-star black. There was a boom in the sandblasting business in the 1970s, and in a few short years all the churches had turned a honey yellow and stayed that way. The only building I know that retains its polluted colour is the Garrick Club in Covent Garden, and the black is falling off that. Soon it will be merely grey.

I was advised that stories are told through sparse details. I considered having Brunel trail his hand over the façade of Covent Garden market ('*his white opera gloves turned black; embarrassed, he put them in his pocket*'). Or, walking through the market, step in a pile of manure ('*a woman approached him, a flower girl or a prostitute. Rather than refuse her, Brunel stepped off the pavement where his boot found the soft pillow of fresh horse dung*'). I led him around the outskirts of Covent Garden because I had a vision of Eliza Doolittle skipping around the pillars and I worried that I would end up describing the whole of *My Fair Lady*, or *Pygmalion*, whichever is lodged most firmly in my mind.

As Brunel reached Leicester Square, I tried to think my way into the past, Stanislavsky-style, by singing the First World War song 'It's a Long Way to Tipperary' ('*Goodbye Piccadilly, farewell Leicester Square . . .*'). But I kept seeing the Warner Village cinema and the crowds of foreign students huddled around the buskers, trying to buy ten-pound lots of grass. I chose the restaurant at the Criterion for Brunel's supper because it is Europe's oldest cocktail bar and I thought I would have him drink one as a cute surprise for the reader. In the end, a glass of brandy seemed a better idea than a banana daiquiri. For all I know, Brunel didn't go out at all the night before he met my great-grandfather. But I suspect that he did; it is clear from his journals that Brunel was a worrier. Not in a neurotic way, but he did worry, and through worrying he would develop reasons for every course of action he took.

I was particularly concerned that writing historical fiction would tempt me into irony, and I would be unable to resist leading my characters into declarations that we know to be useless or stupid. I am not convinced that we can assume a better knowledge of historical events than the men and women who lived through them. Do we really believe that hindsight is twenty-twenty? We might be as mistaken about past events as current ones, our shared knowledge nothing but half-truths and clichés. It does seem that by the start of the First World War, the generals had forgotten the lessons of earlier wars and allowed their men simply to march into barrages of enemy fire. Yet perhaps they were genuinely afraid of allowing non-commissioned officers to determine the shape of battles on the ground, preferring to pore over their maps, miles away from the front, pushing around battalions of model soldiers.

So there could be room for dramatic irony as Brunel discussed battle tactics with the future George V, supreme commander of the Empire forces in the First World War. George V is said to have suffered lifelong doubts about his intelligence, but he was smart enough to know that if total war demanded the full commitment of the nation, it also required a king capable of communicating with his people. The royal family is often caricatured as a bunch of Germans who got lucky, but on the outbreak of war George V surrendered all the family-owned land and titles in Hanover, dumped the name Saxe-Coburg and began calling himself Windsor. I could have made Brunel responsible for that decision, the rebranding of the monarchy. I didn't, but as I thought through all the possible ways I could tell Brunel's story, I began to realise that I was interested in dramatising a new way of thinking.

Brunel's interest in the business of warfare and his sensitivity to the way that military technology would change society touch upon important modern ideas. Perhaps the most important. He had a profound optimism that war can herald a fairer society, because the rank and file, rather than the generals, would be the ones to assume control of the battles. With this one extreme idea, I believe Brunel was thinking beyond modernity. He was thinking for the future.

With every improvement in field artillery, commanders have moved further and further from the battlefield. The new Prussian guns used in the siege of Paris could lob a shell six miles, from behind the siege lines into the heart of the Left Bank. The German princes and generals set up their court in Versailles and when they were so far from the field of action it must have seemed possible to imagine a time when these elites would disappear altogether. The Anarchists were proclaiming an end to God, kings and masters, and Brunel seemed to share something of this vision. He recognised that the new breech-loading rifles, as well as the howitzers and mortars, could be extraordinarily powerful in the hands of the ordinary soldiers. They allowed small, light forces to seize the initiative and take control of battles on the ground. And if the ordinary soldiers had this power, then surely they could control the world!

Long before I saw a real war, the idea of warfare had begun to fascinate and trouble me. I used to be an economist. I almost completed a Ph.D., provisionally entitled 'Town or Market: which came first?' A neat title, but the real question was this: is our notion of a liberal democracy primarily an economic idea or a political idea? Who built our civilisation: politicians or merchants? It was phrased like a version of the chicken-and-egg question but it was a fashionable topic when I began writing, at the end of the 1980s, and the answer seemed self-evident: economics took precedence over politics. Margaret Thatcher's maxim – 'You can't buck the markets' – had been proved true. Free-market economics had defeated Communism, and economics could now bring democracy to the rest of the world. But somehow, as the 1990s wore on, everyone lost confidence in the project, and I lost confidence along with them.

I gave up the Ph.D. At the time, I joked that abandoning my thesis was proof that you never could buck the markets; my girlfriend and I had a young son and we were struggling to live on my student grant. I started work as a professional economist, spending much of the next ten years with the World Bank. Eventually I broke up with the mother of my son. When I started this book, I was going through another life change. I had begun to reconsider my Ph.D. thesis and, with distance, saw that the subject seemed less and less like a chicken-and-egg argument and more like a game of stone-scissors-paper. The years after the Second World War saw an enormous burst of faith in the state and, thus, in politics. This ended in the 1980s with a renewed interest in free-market economics. If we were willing to take risks, then we were free. It was just like the game: scissors cut paper, economists beat politicians. The years 1985–92 were a great time to be an economist. It is difficult to convey our optimism now, the absolute conviction that only we understood the world, we economists. History had come to an end and put economists in control.

But things changed. The collapse of communism, the break-up of old states and the emergence of regional conflicts, the war on terrorism – whatever the reason, the reign of the market came to an end. The new argument went that we lived in a world of violent chaos. In this world, our lives would be determined by our ability to determine 'security'; that is, to wage war.

I saw this quite early, not because I was psychic, but because I was working for the World Bank. By 1997 I was living in Jerusalem, helping to fund civilian projects in the Palestinian territories but, for the most part, living with Israelis and under Israeli rule. And I knew many people who would put forward this argument: we offer peace for peace, but in this neighbour-hood, in this world, you know, war never ends.

Well, now I have seen a war up close. In retrospect and thanks to hindsight, that faulty machine, I finally know why I was so interested in Paul-Antoine Brunel: he was capable of running a war. He looked forward to a world where war is constant, promising warriors the freedom to determine their own lives, just as long as the conflict never ended. Stone beats scissors. It seems to me that this game is now reaching its end. The era of Machiavelli was swept away by Adam Smith, who allowed the entrepreneur to win his freedom from the closed world of the courtier. In our new world, the warrior shatters the illusion of a level playing field, where we compete on merit alone, in fairness and transparency. The truth now is that only power and the willingness to use it matter.

The black battleship in the docks, at the opening of this introduction, was supposed to suggest the dreadnought, although it wasn't black, and was not launched until 1906. That was a cheat, but the arms race was in full swing and the game was battleships. Jicky by Guerlain was created in 1889. George V was taught French by Brunel, but he learnt nothing; he spoke no language except English, which is a very English characteristic. Perhaps the entire future course of Britain was changed because Brunel was such a poor teacher: fluent in the language but incapable of sharing its logic.

This reminds me of a quote by Clausewitz, the great theorist of war. He argued that wars have grammar but not logic. It is an affecting phrase; Clausewitz is saying that when we study a war, we can break it down into actions and study battle tactics, but we cannot ascribe any logical shape to its overall sweep. The more I thought about this insight, the more chilling it seemed: the idea that an expert, a professional like Clausewitz, has never made sense of war; the idea that we can become expert at waging war, but we will never make war work for us. Like language, war has a grammar. Unlike language, it never makes sense. Each war fractures the world, throws the pieces in the air and spreads disorder.

If Clausewitz is right, I would be unable to explain the workings of Brunel's mind, or the shape of the life he made for himself. And the truth is: Clausewitz is right. But fortunately I have more stories. I have my own.

James Joseph Beddoes
Begun London, May 2001; revised Coventry, December 2003

Part One

October–November

Wednesday, 26 October 1870

When Brunel crossed the Prussian lines at night, carrying his communiqué for President Trochu, his journey was lit by the guns from the marines at Fort Rosny. It was strange for the French marines to be so far inland but they had been ordered to defend the Parisian forts as though they were on board ship.

Brunel whistled to the sentry from out of the dark, before stepping forward to identify himself. As the sentry escorted Brunel to the captain's quarters, the man admitted he was getting used to finding men wandering around in the night. There were the local farmers who had refused to be evacuated and who came to the fort after dark to sell food, and there were the Parisians who sneaked out of the city to recover rabbit traps or look for mushrooms in this no-man's land. 'Then they wonder how they got lost, mushrooming in the pitch black. The thing about Parisians, they're pretty stupid.' He took a fresh look at Brunel as they reached the light of the courtyard and added, 'But the worst of them, they don't look as bad as you, sir.'

Brunel had an idea how he looked: he had been on the road for two days, walking most of the way, and before that he had been living in farmhouses and barnyards, mostly barnyards. He had chosen to enter Paris via Rosny because he knew the captain of the fort. As he greeted his old companion in the warmth of his quarters, with a fire in the grate and a bottle of cognac already open, Brunel had to say, this was the closest to luxury he had experienced in a long time. In response, there being a rivalry between the Marsouin – the name that the marine infantry went by – and the gunners, the captain asked why it had taken Brunel so long to get back from Sedan; was he the slowest swimmer among the Marsouin?

The carafe on the table rattled to the sound of the French guns. The return fire from the Prussians was light. As Brunel had reported to the captain, the enemy's lines were sparse and patchy, the bulk of its forces lying much further back, bedding down in the villages they had occupied. The captain joked that the Prussians weren't up to much if they were driven indoors by the autumn rain, but both men knew that the enemy was quiet because it was preparing its own heavy artillery, the steel Krupp guns that had recently arrived from Prussia. The captain wondered if they were so much better than his bronze guns but shrugged before Brunel could answer, saying that anyway they would soon find out for themselves.

The captain telegraphed Paris with the news that Brunel was carrying a message for the President. Brunel left for the city at dawn, travelling on a munitions wagon with a junior officer who was working as a messenger for Admiral de la Roncière. Their route took them by deserted villages and estates on roads that had been churned up during the building of the earthworks and were now softening into mud. On the way Brunel found out a little about his companion, a seventeen-year-old *aspirant* named Barclay who had been stationed in Algiers almost from the moment he joined the marines. Barclay said that he regretted that his battalion had returned to France too late to fight at Bazeilles. Beyond that, he was respectful and, for a while, rather quiet. Once Paris came into view, he pointed through the rain mist to the mines and the electric detonator cables that ran towards the city walls, asking Brunel: 'Is the city impregnable, sir?' Brunel was impressed, and said so. The pair of them bumped along, discussing the defences, and entered Paris through the open gate at the Porte de Bagnolet. A lookout from the National Guard heard them rumble across the moat, got off his haunches and peered up at them as they passed. Just inside the gate was a wooden platform serving the train that ran within the city walls. A few more Nationals could be seen sleeping beneath it. Barclay mimed a tippling action and said, 'How about that? Do you think we're impregnable now?' Even in their sleep the men looked pretty drunk.

With the dawn, there was reveille. Bugles and drums sounded from Belleville, answered by other bugles across the city. Paris was waking. They passed along the northern end of Père Lachaise cemetery and on to Château d'Eau, which was beginning to show signs of life. Barclay spotted a café opening across the square. They had eaten breakfast at the fort, but Barclay was hungry again.

'Do we have time for a coffee, sir?'

Brunel looked around. It was first light, and they were less than half an hour from Trochu's offices at the Tuileries. He doubted they were keeping the President waiting so he agreed. He had last had a decent cup of coffee, he remembered, on 12 August, the day his division shipped out for Sedan.

Brunel went up to the counter while Barclay took a seat by the door, so that he could keep his eyes on the wagon. Château d'Eau stood on the outskirts of Belleville, where the factories of Paris crowded hard on the tenement blocks, and Barclay explained that he was nervous of leaving the wagon unattended – though there was nothing in the back apart from empty crates and sacking.

There was no sign of the waiter, and when Brunel got tired of staring at the curtain behind the bar, he rapped on the counter-top. After a short wait a face appeared and took the order for a cold platter and two coffees. Brunel sat down next to Barclay and for the next ten minutes explored his beard, persuading himself it was lice-ridden. It had begun to itch so badly he could not believe there was nothing wrong with it.

The waiter swung around his counter, carrying Barclay's second breakfast and their coffees.

'Everything all right, officers?'

'Not so bad,' said Brunel, looking at the wan liquid in the

bottom of his cup. 'But splash a little milk in the coffee, will you?'

'You want a splash of milk? A big splash or a little splash?'

Brunel could tell the waiter was a joker, he just couldn't tell what the joke was.

'I tell you what, bring out the milk and start splashing. I'll tell you when to relax.'

The waiter looked at Barclay as though to ask, 'Who is this clown?'

Barclay touched Brunel's arm as he told the waiter, 'Forget about the milk. We're fine.'

As the waiter moved away, Brunel said, 'What was that about?'

'How would you know? There's no milk in the whole city, sir.'

Brunel remembered the hundreds of thousand of cows and sheep he had seen, back in August. The Bois de Boulogne had been cut down for timber to shore up the earthworks, and the animals that replaced the trees seemed to cover the entire space, spreading out as far as the eye could see. It was impossible to believe that only ten weeks later there was no milk.

'How's that? There must be milk.'

'Don't ask me. Everything about this place is crazy.' Barclay was peering over his shoulder, staring at the curtain behind the bar. 'Where did that guy go? Did you see?' Brunel heard the note of anxiety in his voice, muffled only because Barclay was trying to fold a piece of sausage around a chicken leg so that he could suck the whole thing into his mouth as quickly as possible. 'Are you ready to move? We should get out of here.'

'What's the problem?'

'Nothing, sir. But when they're all so screwy, we don't want to start another spy scare.'

Barclay pulled out a few coins, trying to guess how much the food might be, and once he had settled on a sum he cleared the pavement with a couple of strides and hauled himself on to the box of his wagon. Brunel leapt up beside him. He knew it was nothing to do with his demand for milky coffee, but the streets had grown busier. The square was half full of kids, running around and waving sticks.

'They're going to think I'm a spy because I didn't know about the milk shortage?' Brunel asked.

'I don't know, sir. But I don't want to hang around and find out.' Barclay shook out the reins. 'I keep saying, this place is crazier than you can imagine.'

'I'll tell you what's crazy: yesterday, I drove a cow all the way through the Prussian lines.'

'Fuck me. Is that true, sir?'

Brunel nodded. 'I even sold milk to them.'

'You'd get lynched, for sure, if anyone heard about that around here, sir.'

A group of boys were pawing at the back of the wagon. It was nothing serious, but the street din continued to grow, and by the time they had got moving there was no mistaking the sound of boots on stones and the clatter of metal from the street to their right. Brunel recognised the sound of men trying to load their rifles as they ran. Barclay said, 'I wish you'd kept the cow, sir. Because we could really do with it now.'

'It's out there somewhere. I abandoned it just before I got to Rosny.'

A horse reared up ahead, blocking their path. Barclay had to struggle to halt the wagon, but Brunel's hands were free. Barclay heard Brunel pull back the hammer on his pistol, and when he looked down Brunel flashed him a sight of the Remington, cocked and cradled in his lap.

Brunel assumed the horseman was an officer from an irregular unit. He was wearing a green braid jacket similar to one of the North African regiments. The man was tall, too tall for it be an illusion caused by the height of the horse, and he had a grand bony head, the shape exaggerated by his long and thinning hair. He spun the horse around in the street, as much to entertain the crowd of local boys and the Nationals that had appeared behind him. It made quite a show, with the glitter of a jacket that had twice the embroidery of any Brunel had seen before. But the real surprise was the man's skirt; it was white and pleated, and it flared out with each pirouette.

'Are these the Prussian spies?'

The waiter from the restaurant appeared at the side of the wagon. 'That's them, Flo.'

'You are outnumbered, comrades,' the man said, reining his horse around one more time so that he could get a closer look at Brunel's pistol. 'So why not put down your weapon?'

'Tell your men to put down their rifles,' Brunel replied, adding: 'I'm a marine lieutenant.'

'Really? And is that a Prussian gun, Comrade?'

'It's American. Is that a French uniform?' Brunel paused, before adding, 'Flo.'

'It's my French uniform.' He straightened in his saddle: 'Gustave Flourens, commandant of the Belleville battalions.'

There were five hoops embroidered on his arm, one too many for a commandant. When Brunel pointed out that he was a little overdressed, he said, 'I've been promoted.'

'To what? Shepherdess?'

'It's Greek, my friend.' He brushed at the pleats with his hand. 'A tribute to the warriors of Sparta.'

Flourens' men had gathered around him. As a bunch, they looked little different from the drunks at the Porte de Bagnolet, their National Guard tunics paired with ordinary trousers. Apparently none loved their commandant enough to wear a skirt.

'He's not a spy, sir,' Barclay piped up. 'He's a Marsouin.'

'Fresh from the sea? Because, I have to say, something stinks.'

Beneath the layers of grime, Brunel was wearing coarse cotton trousers, a jersey and an old army greatcoat that he claimed to have stolen off a French corpse whenever he was questioned by a German cavalry patrol, though the coat was his own.

'Let's not antagonise each other,' Brunel said, his voice as calm as he could keep it. 'That's not going to see any of us safe out of this situation.'

There had to be five or six hundred people around the wagon, clamouring for a glimpse of the spies and Commandant Flourens on his horse. Flo's small unit of Nationals had taken to crowd control, trying to keep a space clear so neither Flourens nor the suspects were jostled.

'Why not be sensible, then? Surrender to me and I promise I'll undertake your interrogation personally.'

Brunel did not need to think the suggestion through. 'No. President Trochu is expecting me. I'll wait until he can see me.'

Flourens compromised, sending word to the Prefect of Police. It took less than twenty minutes for the return message: he was told to do nothing to harm the man. As they waited for the police to arrive, Flourens gave every appearance of being comfortable, lounging in his saddle, one hand resting on the cavalry sword that nestled between the pleats of his skirt. He threw casual comments down to his men or made oblique cracks to Brunel. But his eyes rarely left the pistol and Brunel knew he was only waiting for his concentration to lapse. It never happened.

A cadre of policemen arrived with their own corps of Nationals, from a unit more loyal to the police than to their comrades in the Belleville battalions. It was a quick lesson in the politics of the city and Brunel learned it watching the stand-off before the negotiations began. Flourens had two demands: he wanted Brunel carried to the Prefecture inside a police truck and he wanted to lead the convoy that took him there, both conditions being necessary to prove that he had arrested the spy and delivered him to the government. The negotiations took place inside the café, leaving Brunel and Barclay exposed on the box of the wagon. There were shouts of 'traitor' from the crowd, picking up in intensity as Brunel agreed to climb down from the wagon and allow himself to be escorted aboard the steel-clad police wagon. There was only one further reason for delay: Flo had mislaid his horse. But soon enough they set off.

As they rode out of Château d'Eau, Brunel peered through the grilles of the truck, catching glimpses of a Paris that had grown greyer since he last saw it in early August, when his division had arrived from Brittany. Travelling down the rue du Temple, they were overlooked by the headquarters of the big national companies, although most were closed and shuttered, leaving business to the smaller shops. The further they went into the heart of Paris, the thinner the procession became, the crowds melting into the queues outside shops or slipping back to Belleville. It was the kids who kept up the pace, running all the way to the Hôtel de Ville and over the Seine to the Île de la Cité. As the truck swung into the Prefecture, the police had to shut the gates against their swarm. There was a fearful racket off the cobblestones, with the wheels of the carriages and the hooves of the horses amplified by the Prefecture's high walls. But over this noise, Brunel heard Flourens proclaiming his decisive role in the capture of the prisoner. The speech lasted five minutes, but finally he wheeled about and the gates of the Prefecture swung open again. Brunel heard someone mutter, 'What an arsehole.'

Then, a moment later, 'Get that guy out.'

Edmond Adam, the Prefect of Police, was an unprepossessing man in his mid-fifties. He stared across his desk to Brunel. Barclay stood right beside him, but the Prefect spoke only to Brunel.

'What's your name, sir?'

'Lieutenant Paul-Antoine Brunel, sir. Third Marine Division.'

The Prefect looked over his shoulder, checking that one of his men was taking notes. Satisfied, he turned back to Brunel. 'Where did you fight?'

'With the 12th at Bazeilles.'

'I heard the villagers got a raw deal.'

'Is this the debriefing, sir?'

'Not at all. Welcome to Paris.' When the Prefect stood and stretched out a hand, Brunel thought he was supposed to take it like a civilian, before realising that he was being offered a cigarette. 'It's an honour to meet you, Lieutenant. I'm only sorry about the reception you got in Belleville.'

Right behind the Prefect, a policeman was laying out Brunel's pistol, with the two extra cylinders and the bag that held the caps and balls. Adam continued talking.

'Trochu was sent word of your arrival. We assume he's expecting you, but at the moment he cannot be found. He's the bloody President, he's not supposed to just disappear.'

Brunel was beginning to feel dizzy. He knew he felt too sick for the cigarette and tried to wave the case away. This time it was Prefect Adam who mistook the gesture, taking Brunel's hand and giving it a firm, dry shake.

'What's this message you've brought? You carried it through the German lines without mishap?'

'It's not a message, sir,' Brunel said. 'It's information. That's to say, I'm carrying it in my head.'

Barclay leaned over and took a cigarette from Adam's case. Adam smiled and sparked up a light for him, rapping out a semi-distracted, 'Pleasure,' before turning back to Brunel. 'This information, is it sensitive?'

'I would say so, sir. Yes.'

The brevity of the response must have alerted the Prefect, because he asked, 'Are you feeling all right, Lieutenant?'

Brunel nodded; of course, he was fine and, when Adam asked if he had eaten, replied that he had had breakfast at the fort at Rosny. Adam looked at the office clock.

'Well, you could probably eat again. At least to rebuild your strength after what you've been through.' He turned to Barclay. 'What about you? Are you hungry, son?'

Barclay admitted he could eat. Quite happily. But as the Prefect stretched out his hand again, this time indicating the door they should take, Brunel tried to focus. He knew that he needed something other than food. He only needed to articulate it. His hand went up to his face and once more he felt the itch of his beard, a persistent itch that was buried deep in the grease and the dirt.

'Perhaps a shave, sir.' He tried to think what else he needed. 'A shave would be good.'

'A shave?' Adam paused for thought then suddenly brightened. 'Shave. Food. I know the perfect place.'

Chez Babette lay on the rue de la Paix, the street running north from the Place Vendôme up to the unfinished opera house, which stood criss-crossed with scaffolding and shrouded against the grey sky. Brunel rode in Edmond Adam's own carriage, Barclay following in the wagon. On the short journey, the Prefect sang the praises of the chef, the fabulous Babette, but Brunel scarcely heard him, more concerned with finding an explanation for the weakness that had affected him earlier. He had not slept in the past thirty-six hours, except maybe for an hour by the fire in the captain's quarters as Barclay readied the wagon. If the lack of sleep was to blame, Brunel was certain a wash and a shave could revive him. However, when the carriage stopped at the restaurant door, ornate as the frame of a Venetian mirror, he thought it a strange place to find a barber.

There was no sign that the restaurant was open nor that it ever would be. The windows were covered by thick red curtains. But when Edmond Adam knocked, the door was opened by a young girl who instantly tried to pull him inside. He practically had to restrain her before he could explain that he had an appointment elsewhere, he could not come in, but had a favour to ask. He pointed towards Brunel, explaining that the man was a hero.

Barclay was whispering, 'How about this, sir? Can you believe our luck? They say this is the best place in the city and just look at that girl.'

Prefect Adam waved them forward. 'Murielle will look after you. Get a shave, get some rest. I have to go but the moment I discover where President Trochu's hiding, I'll send a policeman to collect you.'

The Prefect climbed into his coach with Barclay's thanks ringing in his ears. Brunel was still dazed enough to miss his cue. Moments later, the Prefect was gone and this young girl was winking at them and beckoning, 'This way.'

Brunel almost wondered if they were in a brothel. There was this fresh girl out front, and the woman's name, Babette, over the door. There were the suspicious drapes. But if it was a brothel, it was an odd one. The tables were surely unnecessary. Who would come to sit? Above all, there was the decoration, which, though luxurious, was far from abundant. Brunel had never seen an understated brothel before.

'Who's that?'

Brunel turned when he heard the voice. A woman was standing at the entrance to a passageway. Her hair was tied back beneath a bandanna, emphasising the dark oval of her face and eyes so dark and fierce that they could not have had more of an impact if she and Brunel had been standing nose to nose. Although she was leaning against the door frame, and her voice was slow and quiet, there was nothing relaxed in her manner. She had an authority that bordered on the severe.

Murielle replied quickly, 'It was Monsieur Adam. He asked if we would feed these men, madame. And that one . . .' she pointed at Brunel, '. . . that one needs a shave.'

'More than a shave, I would say, by the look of him.'

Brunel touched a hand to his army greatcoat. The material had a thick dirt sheen that stayed on his fingers and made it impossible to touch anything in the room. And Flourens had already warned him that he smelt.

'I would be grateful, Madame Babette.' Brunel had taken a guess that this was the chef that the Prefect had praised so highly. Clearly he was correct.

The woman nodded and before disappearing said, 'Send a message to Zizi. Tell him he has a client.'

There was a staircase at the back of the restaurant. The girl led Brunel to an upstairs room and left him. A bowl and jug were laid out by a clean towel. Brunel placed his hand on the jug; it was scalding. He reached beneath his jersey, unhooked the Remington from the cord that hung around his neck and placed the pistol on the chair. He threw the jersey on top, along with the filthy blouse that had originally come from a country church. He was grateful to the people who had supplied them, but he wished he didn't have to put them on again. As he turned to the water jug, he rubbed at the angry red line left on his neck by the weight of his pistol.

There was soap by the bowl. Soap and two bottles of perfume: one flask-shaped with a sword design on the front, the other fancy, embossed with the imperial bees. Brunel took a sniff at each before settling down to wash himself.

The water in the bowl soon acquired a dark scum. Brunel added a few more drops from the jug. Economical, little by little, he was becoming cleaner. When the door opened behind him, he assumed that it was Murielle. He turned to ask her if he could have more water and found that he was staring back into the hard dark eyes of Babette.

'Do you know, I spend half my day trying to source fresh cream and butter. If you ask me how much milk is worth today, I would say, litre for litre, that I would swap my finest burgundy for it. The situation is grave.' As before, her voice was so slow and quiet that it was almost a drawl. Yet he had no doubt that there was real anger in it as she said, 'So imagine how I felt when I heard that you had a cow and you threw her away.'

'I didn't throw her away.'

'No. You gave her to the enemy.'

'Okay. You tell me, how do you drive a cow through a mine-field?'

'You walk ahead of it.'

Brunel dunked his head in the washbasin and blew bubbles into the water. He was slow, too slow to tell whether this was sardonic humour or something more serious. As he lifted his head, he heard her say, 'They brought in a quarter of a million sheep and forty thousand bullocks with no idea of how to feed them. But they forgot to bring cows.'

Brunel had not realised that among all the animals he had seen on the Bois de Boulogne, none had been dairy cows. But what startled him was that figure: a quarter of a million. It still had enough resonance to sound unimaginably huge. But because he had actually seen the bullocks and the sheep, all corralled in one place, it was only the idea that sounded unimaginable. The figure itself was becoming easy to grasp, as well as others even bigger. Half a million men on a battlefield. It was possible; Brunel had seen that, too.

A boy appeared at Babette's shoulder, carrying a leather case and with a strop draped over his shoulder. Presumably this was Zizi or his apprentice, come to shave him.

As Babette moved sideways to allow the boy to enter the room, Brunel told him, 'Put the shaving equipment down, there, beside the bowl and give me five minutes.'

The boy shook his head. 'I only just managed to get away. I have to get right back.'

Brunel became stern. 'I'm in the middle of a conversation, boy. Put the razor down and come back when I call you.'

The boy turned white, looking to Babette for guidance. She nodded. 'Go on, Christian. It's all right.'

Once the boy had gone Brunel said, 'I'm sorry about the cow. But I can't bring it back.'

'You could go looking.'

'Maybe I will. How about you giving me the shave?'

'Are you offering a deal?' she asked. 'Because if you are, sit down.'

The idea – either a dare or a wager – had just come to him. He was not sure how, only that he wanted to test this woman.

But as she walked towards him, rolling up the sleeves of her blouse, he had to wonder if he had gone too far. Her arms were a warm brown colour, but covered in welts and scars so evenly spaced that they looked like the markings on a ruler. They seemed deliberate enough for Brunel to imagine they were the result of a ritual. But then he remembered that he had seen cuts like that before on the arms of a naval cook, who would work through all but the worst weather, pulling dishes in and out of an oven as the ship rose and fell, oblivious to the scorch of flesh as the top of his arms met the hot oven shelves. This woman was a cook and this was her restaurant. He took a deep breath and made sure he smiled as she sharpened the razor.

Her fingers were so long that she seemed to hold his face in pincers as she turned it from side to side. Brunel realised that if she was a cook and if she had never worked at sea, then the scars on her arms suggested she might be the clumsiest woman alive. But he remained seated as she twisted his head left and right, ending by running her hands roughly over his face, through the thicker hair beneath his lips and along the moustache.

'Are you keeping the moustache?' Babette was holding a razor.

'As you like.' Brunel kept his eye on the razor as it approached his face. 'Aren't you going to soap me up first?'

'Maybe.' She waved the blade under his nose, then said, 'Of course I am.'

She scooped water out of the jug and slapped it on his face. It was dirty, Brunel told her. She told him to shut up. Her hands were neither soft nor gentle. Brunel would have complained but staring into her eyes he began to get the idea that, if he could see through this shave, he might get something else later. His penis thickened inside his trousers, reminding him of its existence. Something he had barely thought about in weeks.

Then the blade touched his face and the desire went. The blade felt dull against the thin film of soap.

'Ow. Damn.'

'Shut up.'

'Have you . . .'

He wanted to ask her if she had ever even shaved a man before but she had grabbed hold of his nose and pushed his face to one side. He kept his mouth closed and his face still as the razor hacked at his cheeks.

She splashed more water onto his face. Brunel lowered his eyes, noticing the crucifix around Babette's neck for the first time, then continued his gaze downwards to the floor where bloody water was beginning to pool. He knew he had to say something.

'You mentioned someone called Zizi?'

'Yes – my husband. He's a barber, he would have done a much better job than me.'

Brunel put his hand to his face. He felt bumps under his hand and the sting of his fresh cuts. His palm came away freckled with blood.

Brunel said, 'Listen. Shave me properly and I swear, I'll find you another cow.'

Rue Marcadet, September 2001

I spent months poring over Paul-Antoine Brunel's two small brown notebooks, trying to pad out his sparse and underwritten diary entries. I must have half known, from the beginning, that they were never going to carry me through an entire novel. But I kept persevering. I found a police photograph of Brunel in an on-line historical archive, a picture of a man with hard cheek-bones and a strong gaze. I stuck it up on the board above my desk, hoping that it would meld with the photographs of my family and friends and help me get inside the man. If anything, it had the opposite effect. The desperado in a police mugshot did not fit alongside anyone I knew.

Then I began to wonder: perhaps my real problem was not Brunel but all the other people in my life. I had been talking about Brunel's diaries for years and too many of my friends knew what I was doing. Not only my friends, but also my son and his mother and both sets of our parents. Everyone knew. In the early days, it had seemed a good idea to talk up the novel and build the momentum that I needed to get moving. But now that I had resigned my job and was always at home to answer their telephone calls, they were doing a poor job of disguising their anxiety. They tried to be supportive, but the unspoken thought was always there: perhaps I had gone nuts.

I had real and serious commitments, yet I was earning no money. I had savings and had negotiated a decent severance from work, though it was hardly a fortune. As I worked away in my London apartment, I began to worry that I had locked myself into a project that was outside my experience and way beyond my talents. But when I spoke to a sympathetic friend, he urged me to ride it out – Ben said I was simply going through a seasonal readjustment, a necessary downgrading of expectations in a period of uncertainty.

Ben and I met when we were working at the World Bank. He is still in the field, though he was talking like a financial analyst as a joke. We were at a party; in fact, we were at Ben's own party, so I was lucky that he spared the time to listen. He had hired the restaurant and booked the DJ and still he had time for my problems. Better yet, he came up with a solution.

Ben offered me his apartment in Paris for six months. He was so excited by his idea that he kept on selling it long after I had accepted. He told me how difficult it was to move to France, describing the wall-to-wall bureaucracy that meant the telephone and all the utilities take weeks to sort out. This was perfect: an opportunity to slide into the city without all the friction. I could find a tenant for my place in London and make a fresh start, rent-free, in the City of Light. He was flying to Colombia in the morning, he had no time to organise a sub-let. I would be doing him a favour, and me, too: I would be able to soak up the atmosphere in Paris, getting colour for my book. What about it? The external pressures, the money, the responsibilities, all put to one side – the far side of the English Channel. What did I say? I was already yelling, thank you. I practically snatched his hand off. I loved the idea. And, given the chance, I knew I could also love his Parisian neighbour, Flavie, who was flitting around the party and charming everyone who moved into her orbit.

Three weeks later, I moved into the rue Marcadet with a suitcase of handwritten notes and the one and a half chapters that I had managed to complete. Any apartment within spitting distance of the rue de la Paix is wildly expensive. The rue Marcadet is nowhere near there – it's way up in the 18th arrondissement, an area filled with immigrant families and single French people living in tiny apartments. It was the middle of September, almost exactly a hundred and thirty-one years too late to get accurate colour. But I thought it was perfect. I had a six-month breathing space, just as Ben had promised. And next door I had a possible model for Babette.

Flavie rang my bell the day after I moved in, insisting that neighbours could not be strangers and asking if I would like a drink. I gabbled something, I'm not sure what. I remember smiling, bobbing my head up and down, transfixed by her wide beautiful eyes and the frown mark that hung between them. As she stood there, asking, 'How about it, James?' she looked just as she had at Ben's party, the frown still hinting at the best kind of seriousness: kind of playful, kind of caring, but not too much. As Ben said, he had brought her to guarantee a little *je ne sais quoi*, and not rely on our *je ne sais fuck*. Seeing Flavie again, I had to admit, she still had it and I still had the other stuff.

We stepped across the hall to her apartment where a half-bottle of dessert wine and a chocolate cake stood waiting on the table. I dithered over the choice of seats, either a battered chaise longue or an upright chair. Flavie pointed to the chaise longue and we sat together; she rather prone, me rather less so.

I knew that Flavie owned a hair salon. Ben had toured the party, asking everyone how they liked the leaving 'do that Flavie had given him. Later, we had got talking at the bar and I learned that Flavie was the co-proprietor of a salon in the quartier behind the rue St Denis. She had come to Paris as a teenager and, after getting a start in a family-owned hairdresser's, had trained in an upscale salon in the Marais. After a few years working her way up, she was on the point of buying her own franchise in an international chain. That was when she decided that she preferred to run her own shop. Right from the start, I began to imagine that she represented a route into the world of haute couture, perfumers and stylists, not to mention the gourmets and the grande cuisine, the whole Paris appeal that really began during Napoleon and Eugénie's Second Empire. It might sound like a huge leap – Flavie only owned a half-share in a small salon – but in essence her story was close to that of Babette and her husband, Georges 'Zizi' Hébert. It sparked my imagination and I needed it to be sparked.

Flavie wears her dark hair mid-length, brushing against her shoulders. Since the party, a warmer blonde streak had crept in, framing the edge of her face. I told her I liked it like that, like an easier version of those girls that grow up loving Brontë novels and listening to Goth music.

'Easier? What are you saying: I'm easy?'

I probably blushed. I told her I was raving and scrabbled around for a fresh comparison. Out of nowhere, I remembered an old photograph of Maria Callas with a similar hairstyle and suggested that.

Now she burst out laughing. 'Callas? That's just camp.'

Flavie spoke in good, accented English, with one hand touching her newly coloured hair, the other swooping cake off the table and up to her mouth. All I was thinking was, could this be a prelude to sex? The dessert wine. The chocolate cake. The chaise longue. It's an involuntary reflex – I click into fantasy mode whenever I'm with a woman I immediately and desperately fancy. But because this was France and the French have their sexy reputation, I was more hopeful than usual. I read French novels almost as eagerly as English or American ones. I watch any French film that gets a halfway decent review in the newspaper. Yet most of my preconceptions about French culture come from American films and sitcoms like Chevy Chase's *European Vacation* and the long-running storyline in *Cheers*, when a Frenchman cheerfully and cynically tries to steal Woody Harrelson's girlfriend and even borrows money from him to do it.

Flavie didn't jump me and I didn't jump her. There was no embarrassing, rebuffed pass. I managed to keep my cool and talk about Ben, explaining that we knew each other slightly at university but only became friends when we started to work together. We agreed that he was brave to take a six-month contract in one of the most precarious parts of Latin America. Flavie thought it must be interesting to immerse oneself in such different cultures. I shrugged, *maybe*, still thinking of Chevy Chase and Woody Harrelson. I know from experience that economists do not immerse, although Ben could always be tempted to dip a toe into something. Actually, not a toe: just something into something.

Flavie wanted to know if she remembered right: did Ben say I was a journalist? Ben had agreed to keep quiet about my book, but because he had told me Flavie could be inquisitive we had concocted a cover story: I was now a financial journalist. I had always done some journalism, and a friend who ran the financial pages of a British newspaper had promised to buy any articles I wrote on the run-up to the European single currency in January, so long as I adopted the pessimism his paper favoured.

Flavie said, 'I think Ben's London party was even better than his Paris party.'

'I enjoyed it.'

'It was so funny for me. So funny. So *hétéro*.'

Which was the moment that I realised that Flavie was gay. It ought not to have been a surprise. Ben is gay. All of his French male friends are gay. It was at least a possibility that he would have female gay friends, too. Flavie had seemed to be single when I met her at the party, so I had let my imagination get the better of me. But the purpose of moving to Paris was to start again, with a clear head. Flavie and I were unlikely to start an affair. Okay. I resolved to get over it, treat it as a warning that I should deal with facts and not wishful thinking.

I said, 'I don't remember, did I meet your girlfriend at Ben's party?'

'No. She wasn't there. We were in the middle of a fight that weekend, but we are always between fights. Big fights, big make-ups. Tonight, we plan to make up.'

'Good luck.'

'Thank you. I have my fingers crossed.' She held up her hand.

'We are going to eat at a very fine restaurant, move on to a cocktail bar and, finally, shake our booties at a club. Every moment absolutely filled with glamour or excess. So maybe it's a good thing that I look like Maria Callas.'

Flavie has her own brisk style, but when she appeared at my door a few days later she was briskness unbound. She offered to make coffee and within seconds she had cleaned out my espresso pot, dumped the spent grounds in the pedal bin and even sealed the plastic bag ready for the chute. After a trip to the bathroom, I discovered that she had rearranged and refolded the towels. I was flattered that she was improving my domestic ambience and so it was a while before I realised that she was upset; this was not ordinary briskness, it was too hectic. Eventually she told me that her girlfriend was a big problem and they were no longer an item. I brewed some of the camomile tea that Ben had left behind and, slowly, Flavie shifted down a gear. Rather than touch everything, she began simply to look at the objects in the apartment, finally asking me if I always travelled so light. The only things she had never seen before were my laptop, a few notebooks and a suitcase. Everything else, from the tea to the towels to the CD collection to the various vases and the rest, all of it belonged to Ben.

I told her she'd got me wrong; I travelled heavy. 'I've got so much stuff, I'm having it shipped in from London. It arrives tomorrow.'

Flavie might have taken an interest in me out of loyalty to Ben. But I was there when she needed a distraction from heart-break, and that gave our friendship some space to grow. There was no prompting of confessions or lending of ears; I don't have the skills. I function more along the lines of: what do you think of runny cheese? or hip hop? or Osama Bin Laden? Flavie managed to get more out of me, asking questions that seemed innocuous but always ended up with me revealing more than I had intended. As I spoke about my own life and relationships,

I wondered if she was trying to nudge me into a rally. Perhaps I was supposed to respond with my own questions so that she could tell me about herself and her girlfriend Elise, and Elise's specific big problem. If I was, I disappointed her. But I soon got unmediated experience of Elise anyway.

I think Elise is absolutely fine. She is good-looking, big and tough-minded. Her major problem, from Flavie's point of view, is her temper. Her infidelity is almost secondary. Elise goes absolutely ballistic whenever Flavie refuses to forgive her flings. And despite Flavie's insistence that day that the whole cycle was finally over, soon enough they were an item, *encore*.

It was around the time that I met Elise that I became an overnight success as a financial journalist. It was a strange turn-around and it happened by accident, or catastrophe. I moved to Paris only a few days after the 11 September attack on the World Trade Center and as a result few American journalists were prepared to fly to Europe. I certainly didn't blame them; who would want to fly after that? An event people were already preferring to talk about in code: 9/11 and Ground Zero. Soon, of course, the focus would shift from the fear of air travel to the three thousand and more dead, but in those first few weeks everyone was alert to a fresh attack on an equal scale. It was hardly even a matter of being scared. It was, odd to say, the depressing fact of air travel, itself; the idea that, at any moment, it might become our entire horizon, in all of its cramped, dog-eared laminate detail. Anyone who travelled regularly by air weighed up their future and what they saw were check-in queues, luggage slumped on conveyor belts, piss-weak coffee drunk in too-small seats, plastic-tasting alcohol from tiny bottles. After that, it was just insane death.

I was a success because I was on the spot when so few other journalists were. As 9/11 affected the market, there was no shortage of work. I could pick and choose assignments. In fact, I was on my way to an assignment when I finally met Elise. It was in a bar for gay girls and I was Flavie's guest. As the lone man, I was treated with perfect manners, even polite curiosity. When Flavie's friends asked why I was in Paris, I told them I was interested in economic integration within the Euro-zone and played up the few glamorous aspects of financial journalism, like the fact that I was heading to a champagne reception at the Élysée Palace.

I found out later that Elise had waited for me to go to the loo – the unused and redundant Gents – and then demanded to know why Flavie was tolerating such a lech: did she enjoy being slavered over by sleazy heterosexuals? Flavie thought it was hilarious; she and I were just friends. In fact, Flavie claimed, she had thought I was gay until I started talking about my son and the end of my relationship with his mother. I was at least semi-gay, she said. I was Ben's closest friend and I loved Maria Callas. Once Flavie had convinced everyone I was a failed hetero-sexual, hanging on the fringes of homosexuality, that was it. Soon, Elise was offering to accompany me to the Élysée Palace.

It was the next day that I discovered Flavie had thought I was gay. She had come round to the flat and was drinking the ordi-nary English-style black tea that I had taken a fortnight to buy, while she pounded out a tom-tom beat on a cardboard box and demanded to know when I intended to unpack. I had a headache, a hangover, and I wanted to ask her to stop her drumming but I couldn't. I couldn't even meet her clear-eyed gaze. The boxes were piled on top of and underneath my dining table, forcing guests to sit on orphaned chairs with nowhere to rest a cup or chocolate biscuit.

She said, 'You should be ashamed, living like this.'

'I feel ashamed.'

'So how did you and Elise get on?'

'Good. Fun. I think Elise enjoyed it.'

The reception had been organised in honour of European bankers, a lavish affair to celebrate a future under a single currency. I had hoped Flavie would accompany me but she said she was too tired, and when Elise volunteered I had said, sure. The fact was, I was feeling insecure and I suspected that Elise would give me kudos. She is so striking-looking: very tall, with broad shoulders and big breasts. She weighs only about twelve pounds less than me and carries it well, without looking remotely overweight. It is unusual for a French woman to be so *built*, so I wasn't surprised to learn that her father was Dutch.

'You enjoyed it too?' Flavie asked.

'Are you kidding? All the champagne and finger food. I got too drunk because I'm English and stupid and the champagne went down too easily.'

'Because it was free,' she said. 'You don't look so good.'

I wasn't about to argue: I didn't feel healthy. It wasn't simply that I had a hangover. Not even the queasy feeling that comes from a week of late nights. On top of everything, I also felt stressed. It was bothering me that I had been in Paris a fort-night, yet I had got side-tracked already and had written none of my novel. I was still looking at cardboard boxes. Ben's apart-ment wasn't a studio, strictly speaking, but it was pretty small and the tower of boxes at its centre created its own bijou black hole. I could never escape it, certainly not in the bed-sized alcove where I slept.

Flavie said, 'Maybe you will feel better if you unpack – or let me help you.'

She produced a six-inch knife from behind her back. It was my kitchen knife.

I told her, 'I'm only letting you do this because I'm so weak.'

'You think you can stop me?'

She began sawing at the sticky tape as though there was a bomb inside and she only had thirty seconds to defuse it. She was right; I couldn't stop her. She had too much energy and I was definitely too weak to fight, especially with the stress-induced tight pains that ran across my chest. I watched from across the room, hunched on a chair with my arms in a body-hugging fold.

'*French–English Dictionary. Time Out Guide to Paris.*' She took the first two books out of the box.

'I could have used those.'

'You should have unpacked earlier.' She was hauling out the rest of my books. '*The Fall of Paris. The Women of the Commune. The Debacle.* What are these? Are you going to write a history?'

'I'm just interested.'

'No one's that interested.' She held up a picture book entitled *Men-at-War*. It had detailed pictures of the uniforms of the French imperial troops.

'Woo-woo. Soldiers.' I did a camp gesture with my hand, before remembering that it is sailors, not soldiers, that are supposed to be queer and, more importantly, that I was talking to a queer woman. 'Sorry. Okay. I'm writing a novel.'

'About Paris?' She flicked through my Penguin copy of *The Debacle.* 'Like Zola?'

'Not word for word. I haven't written much of it yet.'

'Will it be a love story?'

'Kind of. Love and war.'

'Hey – you could write the gay *Dr Zhivago*.'

'Why would I want to do that?'

'Two men, either side of the historic divide . . .'

'It's not what I'm planning really.'

'Their hot breath mixing with the smell of gunpowder, their firm bodies like steel, pressing against the barricades.'

'I'm not here to write gay porn.'

She laughed. 'I'm only messing with you, James. You know, it's so funny. You won't believe, I thought that you were gay when I first met you.'

I was shocked. 'Why would you think that?'

'What? You think there's a problem with being gay?'

'Apart from kissing men? I don't see you doing any of that.'

'Don't get clever with me,' she said. 'I'm holding a knife.'

She waved it at me, a duellist's parry that seemed to leave a

47

mark in the air. It was her attempt to break the tension. I smiled weakly but simultaneously shrank deeper into my chair.

'You look terrible,' she said. 'Are you feeling ill?'

I babbled something about unusual stress levels. I half believed the pains in my chest were the warning signs of an incipient heart attack.

Flavie asked, 'Are you having breathing trouble?'

'I can certainly feel it when I breathe. My chest gets tight as it expands.'

'And it's been like this all day?' she asked. 'Then it's a mystery.'

I had paid little attention to the speeches at the party. If anything important was said I told myself I could crib something from *Le Monde*. And then I returned to the champagne.

On the Metro back, Elise was at least as drunk as me. She had a sudden idea that she wanted cocktails, so we leapt off at the next stop and found a bar that she remembered liking. A few more cocktails, a skipped meal, and we were on the street, running for the nearest hotel. We were drunk and we were hot. I knew that I was betraying Flavie, and why? She would still be gay; now she would be a gay woman betrayed by her friends out of jealousy and inadequacy. Somehow, this seemed fine. Elise and I were celebrating our baser selves, and our baser selves were getting it on, making each other horny.

Despite all the drink, once we were alone in a cheap hotel we managed to scare up a mood of awkward embarrassment. We bumped knees and legs at every turn. Elise got her head stuck in her pullover and then I managed to turn her tights and knickers into a single thick cord that got wrapped around her thighs. She was pretty trussed up before we decided to calm down and do this with cool precision. She joked that we had to expect a little awkwardness. She was a lesbian and rarely slept with men. And, as I am now aware, she had been led to believe that I was a closet queer. Certainly, nothing I did proved I had any experience at all. Yet the sex wasn't really so bad, at least not the next couple of times. It was actually kind of lusty, very physical, making full use of the bed area.

So that was what happened, before I woke with chest pains. I was trying to keep cool, hoping that Elise would keep shtum about our hotel tumble. Now that I was sober, I was ready to do everything possible to ensure that Flavie never found out.

'It could be stress. Either stress, or perhaps you lifted something heavy,' said Flavie, looking around at all the boxes in the apartment. 'You have to be careful.'

I was about to shake my head but stopped. I suddenly realised exactly where the pain had come from. She was right; it wasn't stress. It was entirely muscular. Elise must have weighed seventy kilos and that's a lot to lift, all night long.

After Babette finished shaving him, Brunel's face was a patch-work of raw flesh and coarse bristle, topped with a lopsided moustache. She had scraped away half his confidence together with his skin and when he returned, head down, to the restau-rant, he was unable to explain how it had happened. So he kept quiet. Murielle brought him a plate of soup and he gave it all his attention, although that wasn't easy when the girl remained standing behind Barclay's chair, shaking with laughter.

'Madame made a mess of you.'

The soup was good. But anything would have tasted good after weeks crawling through fields. It wasn't so great that Brunel could ignore Murielle or forget the flayed skin across his cheeks.

Barclay finally spoke up. 'Listen, sir. You can't go and see President Trochu looking like that.'

'I don't have a choice, do I? Anyway, she promised she could fix it.'

'Fix what? Fix your face?' Barclay said. 'How's she going to do that, sir? She was the one who cut you up.'

Brunel kept his head bowed, spooning the soup to his lips. 'She told me her husband would know what to do. She's gone to speak to him.'

'She's bringing her husband in? I mean . . . hell, sir.' Barclay lapsed into incoherence, waving his hands as though he was shaking two giant sponges. 'I don't get it. At least, couldn't you have stopped her sooner, sir?'

He could have. But then he wouldn't have had her pressed against him, cross-eyed with concentration as she hacked at his beard, the tip of her tongue visible between her lips. He had to admit there was no rational explanation.

'I didn't realise how bad it looked,' he said. 'It was my fault, anyway. I told her to do it. I insisted. Now I'm going to have to trust her.'

Brunel and Barclay were sitting at the back of the restaurant, by the corridor that led to Babette's kitchen. The heat and the noise carried down the passageway, a muffled fury, like the engine room of a steamship heard from on deck. Babette's staff were somewhere back there, preparing everything for a party that night. Because of it the restaurant was closed, and Barclay and Brunel had only been admitted as a favour to Prefect Adam. As the only customers, they got all of Murielle's attention: good news for Barclay, not so good for Brunel.

The girl bent low, squinting as she asked, 'What's that under your lip?'

It was what they called an *impérial*, after the type of beard favoured by the Emperor. Brunel reared back in his seat as Murielle flicked at the bloody tuft. Everything the girl did caught him by surprise but he found it hard to read coquetry. As Murielle cleared away his empty bowl, she teased him and flirted with Barclay, speculating on everything, from the soup to the shave to the coming party. She theorised that if Madame Babette had taken to hairdressing, perhaps Zizi could make his debut as a chef. How about that? She was howling with laughter: over Brunel's bloody face, Babette's savagery and the thought of this man Zizi attempting to cook a meal.

The soup was followed by pheasant with ceps. Brunel imagined Babette sending teams out to collect mushrooms in the fields between the two armies. Or to shoot pheasant.

He had promised to find her a cow.

He wiped his mouth and sat back. Then a pause before he asked, 'How long have Babette and her husband been married?' He wondered if a straight question might dissuade her from asking further questions. It didn't.

'Why? Have you got your eye on Madame Babette?'

How could he answer, when he wasn't sure of the game or its rules? He lifted his hand in the air, as though preparing to juggle the giant sponges that Barclay had abandoned.

*   *   *

Babette appeared from the street just as Murielle was serving coffee. She said she had spoken to her husband and he could see Brunel in ten minutes. Murielle brought an extra cup and Babette smiled her thanks as she joined the men at the table. The coffee settled as dark pools but it poured like burnt caramel. Like Babette's hair: thick and dark behind the broad bandanna, a loose tress electrified with a warm orange light. Babette pushed the strand back behind her ears.

Murielle hovered with the coffee pot. 'What can Monsieur Hébert do, madame? I mean, look at him. He's beyond salvage.'

'He's not so bad. And anyway, we all believe Zizi can work wonders.'

Brunel spoke. 'Where is your husband?'

'At work, across the road. Worth has seen how they turn out cannons in the factories in Belleville. Now he plans to automate the beauty business.' She saw the look of incomprehension on Brunel's face and backtracked: 'Zizi is in partnership with the dressmaker, Freddie Worth . . . Charles Frederick Worth. You must have heard of him?'

Brunel was not sure he had. But he knew what a dressmaker was.

'The Comédie Française is staging a grand performance for the war fund tonight and Worth has reopened his salon for the occasion. The women are coming in shifts of twenty and thirty, yet Zizi has promised to look at you and try to undo all of my damage.' There was something in Babette's eyes, perhaps even concern. 'We can't let Trochu see you like this. Better that you look like a hero. You are a hero, aren't you?'

'No.'

'Well, I suppose that's what a hero might say. But it's not promising.'

Barclay couldn't let this pass. 'Lieutenant Brunel fought at Bazeilles, madame.'

'Which was our one glorious defeat, after a run of the inglorious kind. Does that sound flippant, Lieutenant? I'm sorry, when I hear Freddie and Zizi together, their style of talking begins to infect me.' She stood.

'One other thing. I asked Freddie if he would clean and repair your uniform.'

'I don't have a uniform.'

'You have a coat. As for the rest, you can take his.' Babette turned her eyes towards Barclay. 'You wouldn't mind lending your uniform to the lieutenant, would you?'

'He doesn't mind,' said Murielle.

The House of Worth stood in the Place Vendôme, a private mansion until it was bought by Charles Frederick Worth.

Babette led Brunel through the marbled lobby to the staircase. The hum grew louder with every step, without ever separating into its component voices; it was just a single, ascending pitch of . . . as far as Brunel was concerned, it sounded like hysteria. and it unsettled him. Then he was pushed through a double door into the salon and he was in the middle of it, a mass fitting for the aristocracy of Paris.

Five heavily padded sofas were staggered around the room, a formation that only allowed the women on them to speak if they twisted to their right or their left. They spoke continuously, spinning one way and then the other until the noise swirled about the building. And rolling through the salon like a shipyard bully was Charles Frederick Worth: a big Englishman in a turban, working the room and keeping it all moving. Nor was it pure intimidation; the man was an entertainer, bringing warmth as he moved from sofa to sofa. But whenever he paused, the temperature dropped and the sound would dip slightly as

Monsieur Worth asked a woman to stand and led her away to her fitting.

Babette put a hand on Brunel's chest. 'Wait here.'

She pushed him back on to the landing and disappeared down a corridor with Barclay's uniform tucked underneath her arm. Left alone, Brunel distracted himself by looking down to the foyer below and up to the high grand ceiling, before turning back to the salon. Worth was now standing by the balcony windows, conferring with a thin, officious woman. Worth accepted her assessments with a nod before returning to his performance.

Through the door to a smaller salon, Brunel glimpsed the young boy he had met at Babette's and sent away. The boy buzzed around, folding towels. A moment later, he was holding a broom and sweeping up hair. Brunel shifted his weight and caught sight of a woman reflected in an enormous mirror. Behind her, tending to the curls that framed her face, was a man. He could only be Zizi. Who else? His hair was swept back to emphasise the slash of his eyebrows above widely spaced eyes. Strange that the eyebrows were so dark when his colouring was so pale. Zizi was holding a zinc spray can, squirting his customers' hair with a fine mist. Looking up, he caught Brunel's eyes in the mirror and flashed a smile of recognition to show that he knew about Brunel, and was expecting him.

Brunel stepped out of the sightline of the mirror.

When Babette caught his arm, he protested that he could wait at the Prefecture. She simply said, 'You're staying. The laundry woman says the uniform will take at least an hour. Monsieur Hébert, Zizi, is certain that he will have finished with you long before then.' She bustled him down the corridor to a panelled room that had been fitted with a bathroom suite. At the foot of the bathtub was a chair.

'I'm sorry I have to go. But good luck.'

She held out her hand, which he took in a gentle grip, unable to think of lifting it to his lips. He applied the slightest of pressure, for the smallest fraction of a second, and then Babette took her hand back.

'Thank you,' he said.

'You don't need to thank me,' she said. 'You promised me a cow, remember?'

After she had gone, Brunel stared at the plumbing on the bathtub, and listened to the laughter and the arguments from the salon.

When the young boy, Zizi's assistant, entered with a towel over his arm and a bag in his hand, Brunel assumed that he was fetching and carrying so did nothing but nod at him. But the boy walked over and stared at Brunel's face, then took hold of his chin. Brunel was so surprised that it was a moment before he jerked free.

'What's your game?'

'I'm supposed to fix you up, sir.'

'And that's too difficult to explain?'

'I . . . I thought you knew, sir.'

'I didn't. I thought I was getting this guy Zizi. What's in the bag?'

He had scared the boy, who shook as he opened his bag and showed Brunel a series of bottles: creams and perfumes.

'How old are you? And are you any good?'

'I'm fourteen. And I know what to do with you.'

Brunel chewed at his lip. It hurt. It was cut. He decided that the kid couldn't be any more clumsy than Babette. 'Fine. Get to work.'

The boy did seem to know what he was doing. Brunel didn't ask any more questions – not even the length of his experience. He got his name – Christian – and then lay back to savour the scalding heat of the perfumed water, to feel the creams sink into his skin, soothing the grazes and softening the beard. Then came the deep warmth of the towels as Christian wrapped them around his face and turned his attention to his hair. Inside this darkened cocoon, Brunel felt the kid's fingers on his scalp, massaging the soap in a circular movement. It was so soothing that Brunel was sorry when the kid whipped the warm towels off his face and began the shave.

He asked, 'Is this usual?'

'What, sir? A shave?'

'No. Everything – the dressmakers, the barbers, the women. Is this the way things are?'

'We usually go to the ladies' mansions. But this is easier. It was Monsieur Worth's idea.'

Christian's blade reached Brunel's lip and paused. He asked if Brunel wanted to keep the *impérial*.

'I don't know. How does it look?'

'It's your decision, sir.'

The boy held up a mirror. Brunel stared at his reflection and wondered if Babette had given him the beard as a political statement. What a family: a woman chef married to a ladies' hairdresser. As he touched his finger to the tuft, Brunel decided he was going to keep it. If she liked it, it would stay. If it proved no help, it could come off. After catching sight of her husband, Brunel had decided he needed all the help he could get.

He asked the kid, 'Christian, what's this Zizi like?'

There was a silence.

'How are things between him and Babette?'

The boy still would not answer. Brunel could feel that the ground was dangerous, but he pushed on.

'I know he's your boss.'

'He's my father. They are my parents.'

'Oh.'

The rest of the session passed in complete silence. They didn't even speak when Christian held up the mirror for Brunel to examine the back of his neck. Brunel simply nodded. It was only as the boy was leaving that Brunel decided the situation was stupid. If he could speak to his men, he could speak to this boy.

'I offended you. I am very sorry.'

Christian still refused to speak. He gave a curt bow and left the room.

Brunel was told that he would meet His Excellency President Trochu at the theatre. Although the President had decided it was important to attend the performance, he had no intention of watching the play. He commandeered an office inside the theatre; after the briefest appearance, he would slip away to continue his work.

Night came in a dark cloud and settled. Then just before eight o'clock, the street lights fluttered into a glow. Someone had made the decision to turn on the gas, although only in the 1st arrondissement. Brunel was escorted to the theatre by young Barclay, and as they turned on to the rue de Richelieu the building blazed ahead of them: an incendiary orange, bursting through a frost of glass. Who would have thought light could seem so luxurious, that it could overflow a building like that? The carriages were drawing up outside, spilling out the powerful and the wealthy of Paris. Another three or four thousand citizens on foot stared from behind police lines and cheered as they recognised members of the arriving audience.

Among those who received cheers were Dorian and Nadar, names that meant nothing to Brunel. Barclay explained that Dorian was the Minister of Works and had set up the munitions factories in Belleville, while Nadar was responsible for the production of the carrier balloons inside the city's railway stations, the only buildings large enough to accommodate the balloon sections. The two men paused on the steps of the theatre and lifted their hats to the crowd. President Trochu also got a cheer, although not as loud. And he didn't pause, he just swept up the steps, barely visible in the midst of his Breton bodyguards. Victor Hugo proved the best value, wearing the kepi of the Nationals and milking the crowd by roaring insults at the Prussians.

Brunel left Barclay on the pavement and had made it as far

as the theatre lobby when Gustave Flourens arrived, provoking respectable shouts of 'Flo' and 'Florence', although he had brought a detachment of his own men to cheer for him. He dismounted in a flurry of skirt and leg kicks, democratically hugging his men before leaving them to guard his horse. He spotted Brunel as he entered the theatre but made a show of pausing and staring before he spoke.

'Good God, man. This is unbelievable. I arrest you as a spy, and a few hours later you turn up steam-cleaned and pressed. Did the police do this to you? Because if they did, they are going to get all my laundry.'

Brunel looked at his reflection in the door glass; it showed a marine officer in good order. Babette's son had made a good job of his face; he looked as though he might have been pulled through brambles but not, at least, skinned by Chinese torturers. After he had been waiting for almost three hours, one of Charles Frederick Worth's seamstresses had brought him a set of clean and folded clothes that was eight parts Barclay's uniform. The beret, with its pompom, had been replaced by a kepi embroidered with the red anchor insignia, which had been copied from the collar patches of Brunel's overcoat. The coat, itself, was a miracle. Brunel was baffled as to how two months of filth could disappear so completely – even if he had been kept waiting three times as long as predicted. The only problem lay in the braiding on the sleeve of the tunic; by some accident, the seamstress had promoted him to captain. But as long as he kept his greatcoat on, Brunel would not have to explain the mistake.

The orchestra's first tunings were beginning to filter through the lobby walls; the programme was almost under way. Flourens parted with a show of regret: 'I must away to my box.' As the audience took their seats, and the mezzanine thinned out, Trochu's temporary office was marked out by the cadre of sullen Breton Mobiles outside the door.

The theatre seemed to contain all the glamour of the Second Republic, and Brunel had time to savour it as he waited for

Trochu to see him. All the key figures of the city's new Republican administration were there. As they were called to the general's office, Brunel stood by, passed over as though his news from the outside world was of no importance. He saw the balloonist Nadar again, but as for the rest their faces meant nothing to him. In frustration, he approached Trochu's body-guards, catching them by surprise by speaking Breton. Brunel had spent long enough in and out of the port of Brest to know that French-speakers were rare in Brittany, so he had learnt their language well enough to get by. The Mobiles told him that the President was investigating the downing of one of the city's balloons. Trochu was a methodical man, they said, and it would take him some time to arrive at a conclusion. If Brunel wanted to wait inside the auditorium, they would fetch him when he was ready. Brunel accepted the offer.

The performance – *The Misanthrope* – was brisk, if rather abrupt. After ten minutes, he realised the cast were performing extracts. It was hot and the auditorium was full. Brunel could only stand at the back, staring over the heads of the audience. He made himself comfortable by taking off his coat and draping it over the partition at the rear of the circle. The evening had reached a plateau, filled not with Molière but with Victor Hugo. The old man was still wearing his kepi, and demanding applause for 'the divine, the Divine!' young actress who was the last to leave the stage. Once Hugo was satisfied that the audience was ready for him, he began blasting through a poem written specially for the occasion. Brunel thought it was good. At least, a good performance, involving a lot of vigorous bellowing. Yet it wasn't enough to keep his mind in the auditorium.

Brunel was thinking of Babette and her son. The boy was fourteen years old and his mother looked barely thirty. It was possible, of course, but it didn't seem plausible. Hugo's poem was long; Brunel had plenty of time to devote to his calcula-tions, until he was interrupted by the clatter of boots and rifles in the theatre lobby.

A party of Zouaves were starting up the staircase, two steps at a time, in their red pantaloons, fez tassels swinging. Brunel slipped out of the circle door in time to see Trochu's Bretons block their way. The two sets of soldiers were eyeball to eyeball, jostling and hissing insults. But behind them, a figure was calmly clearing himself a passage. Brunel recognised him as General Auguste Ducrot. Brunel had last seen him on the day that the general was arrested. At the time Brunel was on a route march with thousands of other men being taken to a prison island on the river Meuse. They had passed by General Ducrot as he was being led away to imprisonment in Prussia. Now he was here; like Brunel, he had somehow succeeded in making his way to Paris.

General Ducrot smiled at the Bretons as he asked, 'Which one of you cunts speaks French? Take me to your leader.'

Brunel was called to the office less than ten minutes later. General Ducrot sat on one side of the room. Opposite him, stormy and grey, was the oldest of the French generals, Joseph Vinoy. Between these two was His Excellency President Trochu with his kepi on the desk in front of him and his high bald head shining under the gaslight.

'Kept you waiting half the day, must apologise.'

Trochu acknowledged Brunel's snapped-out salute, adding the word 'Captain' to his short apology. Brunel was a fraction too slow in realising that his overcoat was still hanging at the back of the circle. Trochu had taken the false three stripes on the sleeve of his tunic at face value.

'We've been in crisis meetings all day. We have lost our first balloon.'

Trochu lit a pipe and sucked at it noisily, speculating that the balloon may have been shot down, or sprung a leak or may have been sent heavenwards with a faulty valve. Brunel tried to interrupt the flow by saying 'Sir' as a prelude to his own apology and explanation, lifting himself on to his toes and stiffening as he spoke. Trochu misunderstood, simply ordering him to stand at ease.

'Of course, the inclement weather may have forced it down. There's a lot of uncertainty surrounding the performance of coal gas at low temperatures. Dorian says the scientists are perplexed, but they continue to experiment. Whatever. The Prussians have the balloon, along with all of our recent communiqués.'

As Brunel waited for the President's next pause, and his next chance at an explanation, he found his gaze straying into a tic-toc swing from one side of the room to the other. General Ducrot was sitting smoking a cheroot. At the other, General Vinoy was glowering from behind his whiskers. It was evident that the men were rivals.

'So a shame about the balloon, if the news is confirmed. And it will be. The Prussians sent a runner under a white flag to bring us the news. Gloating, I suppose. They even knew the name of the balloon, which they certainly could not have seen from the ground. The Montgolfier; I expect they appreciated the irony.' Finally: 'Captain, at ease, at ease, I say. Please, take a seat. You know I have a great fondness for the marines.'

This was his chance. 'Sir, if I could just say . . .'

'You assume it is flattery. It's not. As a Breton, I grew up surrounded by marines. My earliest memories. My earliest memories. You know Brest?'

'Sir, yes. I was stationed at Brest.'

'Wonderful men, the marines. A source of great pride. You know you are the first person to have entered the city in a month.'

'So I was told, sir.'

'The Prussians send us other crumbs: Metz will surrender. What do you know of that?'

The casual switch in Trochu's conversation belied the importance of this news. There was a French army of one hundred and sixty thousand men, commanded by General Bazaine, under siege in the city of Metz. Brunel could confirm that Bazaine was on the verge of capitulation.

'That is what I came to tell you.' Brunel had travelled through enemy lines to bring Paris this news. And to urge Paris to act before it was too late. 'Marshal Bazaine will surrender in the week. It is certain.'

Trochu looked right and left, at his two generals. 'It seems, then, that the Prussians are again telling us the truth. If this latest source is also dependable.'

Brunel was quick to defend the French militiamen who were risking their lives to continue the resistance around Metz. 'Sir, it comes from the local Francs-Tireurs. They intercepted a carrier pigeon, and they also have an informant in the Prussian camp. In both cases, the details are the same: the food supplies ran out last week and there is typhoid in the city. Marshal Bazaine has no plans for a break-out and has spent the last month offering himself as a conduit for a peace treaty between the Prussians and the Empress Eugénie.'

Trochu gave a melancholic nod. 'It is treason, of course.'

Auguste Ducrot spoke up for the first time, repeating Trochu's word with much greater confidence. 'It is treason, sir. You are the President.'

'Am I? I am still the Governor of Paris, that is certain. But as for being the President – I cannot even contact the rest of France. I speak through balloons and pigeon post.' Trochu sucked at his pipe; it made a gurgling, tarry rasp and he stared at it forlornly, as though he had expected better of it.

General Ducrot broke what could not quite be called silence. 'If you came all this way with bad news, Captain, what do you recommend we do?'

Brunel had practised this speech. He spoke clearly and, he hoped, with force: 'The siege at Metz has tied up two hundred thousand of the best Prussian troops. When the city surrenders, those troops will head south and reinforce the siege here, around Paris. That will prove decisive. All of our best fighting men are locked inside the city. This will be their last chance to break out. If we don't seize it, the only army in France capable of fighting the Prussians will be rendered useless.'

'That is true,' General Ducrot said. 'We can break out. We have almost two hundred thousand professional troops stationed here in the city. But, mark you, if they go, then we would be leaving Paris in the hands of the Belleville Nationals.'

'Exactly.' Joseph Vinoy spoke for the first time, with the force of a man who had struggled to remain silent at all. 'We would be surrendering our capital twice over, to the scum and to the hun.'

'Nevertheless, we do not have a choice. We must break out,' General Ducrot replied.

In that moment, Auguste Ducrot won Brunel's loyalty and, as was clear from the reaction at the far side of the room, he guaranteed Vinoy's enmity.

The Solicitor's Letter

My chest pains were entirely the result of a bout of hotel-room gymnastics. If Flavie had hinted at the slightest suspicion, I would have confessed to the whole, heavy night with Elise. But what would I have said then, assuming she chose to stay for an explanation? I could have asked: how often are people unfaithful? Women sleep with their sisters' boyfriends. Men sleep with their friends' wives. It's not uncommon. Does every betrayal automatically torpedo a relationship?

No amount of facetious squirming would have helped me out of the situation. But I do wonder how much we really disapprove of infidelity. The French seem peculiarly tolerant but don't we all bend towards complicity? Don't we forgive it among our friends? We keep quiet for them, we cover their backs. We read books that explain infidelity and we watch films that celebrate it. And even on the few occasions when we disapprove, we recognise that infidelity is a constant temptation, and that it cannot be allowed to become the end of the world. It's only when it affects us personally that we see another side; infidelity might tempt us, but when we act upon it, it is never out of naked desire. Beyond instinct, it's all calculation.

When Flavie suggested my chest pains were muscular, I honestly thought she had me rumbled. But she asked out of concern, thinking of the number of boxes we had to unpack, and the amount of Ben's belongings that needed carrying to the lumber room beneath the stairs, three floors down. What could I do? I attacked the boxes with so much speed and was so ruthless in putting Ben's belongings into storage that I think I took her breath away. The moment she left my apartment, I telephoned Elise so that we could get a joint story together. For some reason, this took more cool self-containment than the whole of my charade in front of Flavie. Elise was expecting my call. She sounded distant, and I assumed she was angry, thinking perhaps she had transferred all the blame on to me. But that wasn't the case at all.

She said, 'You know, I'm meeting Flavie later tonight. If I come by a little earlier, we can use the time together.'

'*Use?*' I knew exactly what she meant. 'I'm not sure that's a good idea. Really.'

'You don't think so? What's changed?'

'But Flavie lives right next door to me. She's my neighbour. She's your girlfriend.'

'But that's the fun. It's not as though you were so good in bed. Only the danger makes it worth while.'

'Not for me.' And once again I tried to rationalise what had made it seem worth while, the previous night. Why was I so keen to prove that I had a restless and reckless dick? And, having proved it, why was I so desperate to suppress the facts? I told Elise, 'We can't ever let Flavie know anything.'

Elise left me waiting for an answer. I only knew that she was still on the line because I heard her click her tongue before finally saying, 'If that's what you want. But it is difficult if you see so much of Flavie. It would be better if you were not so close. Not so close, and definitely not hanging around wherever she goes. What do you think?'

She put down the telephone.

Elise had manipulated the situation so successfully that, five minutes after the call, I hardly trusted my own recollection of our conversation. The whole thing left me so dazed, I almost forgot to wallow in misery and self-pity for the rest of the day. It was the most bizarre thing: I was forbidden from seeing Flavie. When I did get angry, it wasn't on my account. Elise didn't exactly force me into the hotel at gunpoint. I paid for the room with my already-stressed credit card.

The days passed and I kept my distance, as I had been told to do. But I saw Flavie all the time. If she was with Elise, then Elise would always cast an eye in the direction of my apartment. More often I saw Flavie on her own, either outside on the pavement or inside, standing at her kitchen sink. Our apartment block is built around a central light-well and it is just possible to look from my living room, across the chasm, into Flavie's kitchen.

I felt I was spying on her. I was.

My bedroom window stands directly above the front door to our apartment block. Flavie knows half the neighbourhood so, more often than not, when she stops to punch in the door code, someone will walk up and start chatting. As soon as I hear Flavie's voice, I stop what I am doing and take a sliding leap across the futon to look out of the window. I tell myself that it helps punctuate the day. I spend most of my time either reading, writing or transcribing interviews. By the time Flavie returns from her salon, I am desperate for a break. I could lurk at the spyhole on my door and, as she comes up the stairs, casually appear in front of her. Carrying a knotted bag of rubbish as an alibi. I tried it once. Flavie smiled and said, *Hello, stranger*. I told her, again, that I had been very busy recently and regretted that I never had the time to go out.

The other day I was in the kitchen when I heard Flavie's voice rise up from the street. She was early, it was only lunchtime. I dropped everything to jump across the futon and watch as she talked to Nawar, the girl from the bakery opposite. Flavie was carelessly swinging a bag of groceries against her leg as she talked. The weather was good for late October, and I remember thinking that it was nothing like the weather I was trying to conjure up in the Brunel book. Although the weather is the least of my problems. Brunel's diaries provide only an outline for the character of Babette, and the process of colouring in that outline has been long and difficult. There is no doubt: Flavie is becoming less and less use as a model for Babette – just as she is becoming a grander obsession in my life.

As I stared down at her, at the sway of her arms as she held the shopping bag, it was a few moments before I saw that it contained a baguette. Nothing strange about a shopping bag and a baguette. Nothing, except that Flavie was talking to a baker but the bag proved she had bought her bread elsewhere. It was a sign of a rare relationship that worked without jealousy or intrigue. A relationship straight out of the economic textbooks, both non-exclusive and civilised, free and open. In an ideal world, every market would work like that, although it never could in England. We are mortified if our hairdresser suspects us of seeing anyone else. If we switch doctor, dentist or dry-cleaner we happily crawl on our stomachs below their windows to avoid being seen.

Flavie is not like that. Not like me. And she has nothing in common with Babette. She is open where Babette was secretive. She is at ease with her choices where Babette could never take anything lightly. Flavie is liberal. Babette was not.

Yet Flavie is so vulnerable and she doesn't even know it. Babette was so much tougher.

The sun cast shadows on Flavie's arms, showing up the definition of the V where the muscle of her shoulder met the biceps. Our age appreciates a shapely turned arm the way previous generations valued ankles. I stood in my window admiring the sweep of the line, until the moment was spoilt and I remembered that Flavie didn't get her muscles down the gym; she got them from humping her enormous girlfriend.

I leapt back across the bed and returned to the kitchen. My sandwich was spread out over the counter, waiting to be assembled. When I heard Flavie's feet on the stairs, I held my breath. As I always do.

This time she knocked on the door.

I breathed out.

She was holding a sheaf of letters. I couldn't make out what they were; the elastic in my mind spasmed and for one second I thought she was returning the love letters I had never written.

'You have a lot of mail downstairs.'

Does that sound too much like a joke? Should I have cast my eyes towards my maleness downstairs? What I actually did was stare at the letters in her hand. Finally, I realised they were addressed to me, redirected from my flat in London. Evidently, my new tenant was the kind of idler who waits until he has a good big pile of letters before forwarding them.

'So,' she said. 'Are you very very very busy?'

I made a noise, 'Uhn-huh,' that was about as non-committal as vocalisation could get. And yet Flavie remained hovering. She seemed nervous, although I was scared to read too much into her mood. I had been sending out such mixed signals over the past three weeks – cold shoulders and puppy eyes – that I doubt she knew where she was with me. But she was still standing there.

Then she glanced over my shoulder and caught sight of the food spread over the working surface.

She laughed. 'Is that your lunch?'

'It's a cheese sandwich.'

'Let me see.'

She slipped past me, taking up a position in front of my sandwich and standing, staring, a finger pressed to her lips until she was ready to speak.

'You know, the way you organise your kitchen is so fascinating. This must be how anthropologists feel when they study gorillas. If I study you closely enough, I will discover you have your own tools, your own way of doing things, all of it different to us.'

'It's just a cheese sandwich,' I said, staring at the bread, cheese, chutney and the pepper mill laid out assembly-line style.

'No one else makes it that way. You freak.' She smiled, and finally said what was on her mind. 'I didn't want to ask you, because you always tell me no, no, no these days. But you remember Jean-Luc and the guys?'

Here it was, the new terrain. In fact, some abandoned terrain from my first weekend in Paris. Flavie had introduced me to Jean-Luc soon after I arrived, but as we hated each other on sight she had never tried to put us in the same room again.

Now I found myself saying, 'Really? Jean-Luc. He's an interesting guy.'

'That's odd. Because Jean-Luc was also asking after you. He remembered a conversation you had with him. Big politics. The Middle East. A lot of shouting. He wondered if he could get a chance to talk to you again.'

'That would be . . .' I could not believe I was saying this '. . . that would be great.'

'What about tonight?'

A month ago, I would have dislocated my fingers one by one to get out of an evening with Jean-Luc and *ze guys*. I preferred hanging out in lesbian bars where everyone was pleasant with me, or at least condescending. Now that Elise had cast me out of that peculiar Eden, I was grateful to find any space where Flavie and I could continue our relationship, no matter how dreary and confrontational.

To celebrate I rifled through Ben's CD rack for something upbeat to accompany my sandwich, my coffee and my pile of mail. In the pile was a letter that I had been expecting for the last four months. It read:

Lindt and Partners
Lawfirm
Copenhagen

Dear Mr James Joseph Beddoes
Re: Karen Blixen (Isak Dinesen) – Babette
Thank you for your letter of the 23rd ultimo asking for permission to use the character of Babette in your book.

It is our view that Babette is such a special part of the work of Karen Blixen (Isak Dinesen) that we are not inclined to give our blessing to your use of that character in your work. We feel that it would be encroaching upon Karen Blixen's work if somebody else were to use her creation. I therefore regret to say that we cannot help you.

Yours sincerely

Peter Lindt

Fuck.

This took the shine off my celebrations. I had accepted that Flavie could not be the inspiration for the Babette of my book; now I was even further from fleshing her out. I could not find a model in life and I was forbidden from drawing one from fiction. It was an hour before I calmed down and searched my hard drive for my original letter. I had written to Karen Blixen's estate in June or July. As I reread my request, I wondered what would happen if I were a lawyer; could I find a way to weasel between their words and mine?

We were riding the Metro when Flavie told me that there would only be two of the guys there tonight. I wasn't surprised that Jean-Luc had driven the rest away. He is a radical lawyer, happy to harangue a crowd wherever he happened to find one: his table, the room, the Metro carriage, whatever.

I shrugged, telling Flavie the fewer people the better. But I must have sighed as I said it because Flavie asked if I was okay.

'If you keep making those noises, I am going to feel guilty I dragged you along tonight.'

'It's nothing to do with you, Flavie.'

'If that's true, why are you always distant? I think you really do have a problem with me.'

Her concern was so genuine that it cut through me. I was convinced that she would soon discover that Elise and I had betrayed her, yet she was worrying that she had upset me.

I said, 'I got some bad news today.' And I told her about the letter and my feeling that my whole project was now in jeopardy.

'But then you should definitely talk to Jean-Luc, he's a lawyer.'

'I'd prefer not to.'

'Come on. Do it.'

'No.'

'Fuck you – yes.'

'Fuck off – no.'

She was laughing. Then she grabbed hold of my arm and she was serious again. 'I haven't told you the truth, James. I really need you to be nice and intelligent to everyone tonight. I was trying to impress someone and I claimed I had this big expert as my friend.'

'Me? What am I an expert of?' I paused, realising this wasn't the first question in my mind. 'Who were you trying to impress?'

'I should be honest. It was not really Jean-Luc who wanted you to come tonight. It was me.' She blinked in apology. 'There is a woman called Marguerite, who works with Palestinian charities, and I told her my friend was such an expert that he had even lived there and he knew everyone.'

'Me?'

Flavie nodded.

There were very many things I could have said; the best, perhaps, to disavow any expertise on Palestine. But I didn't.

I said, 'But if you are attracted to this woman, what about Elise?'

'Elise doesn't really take our relationship seriously, I think because we are two girls. Marguerite is different. She is very serious, but that's good. We should be serious, and show the world our relationships matter just as much as any other commitment.'

She was right. Elise did not take their affair seriously and neither did I. I saw two girls together and thought it was light-weight. A switch in my head had clicked off: the gravity switch.

Now I had a second chance.

My first night out with Jean-Luc and the guys was an evening lost among jabbering Parisians, all of them smoking faster than any Englishman, while drinking far, far slower. This second night was different. There were no guys. It was just Jean-Luc and a tall thin woman with unruly red hair named Marguerite Galperin, a schoolteacher in the *banlieues*.

As we walked into the café, Jean-Luc stood and said, 'James, my friend. It's been a long time.' He slapped my back and shook my hand before turning to Flavie. He might as well not have been there at all. Flavie and Marguerite Galperin were smiling at each other, their heads slightly tilted to the side, agreeing how good it was to see each other again. I was surprised to find Marguerite such a tall and gawky woman, with no real sense of assurance behind her loose-limbed shrugs and toothy smile. Her effect on Flavie had led me to imagine a more commanding figure.

I first met Jean-Luc in the immediate aftermath of September 11, soon after *Le Monde* had run the headline WE ARE ALL AMERICANS. The mood had been shifting ever since and the feeling in Paris was that Britain was determined to be the most American. At that meeting, Jean-Luc had questioned me all night on Tony Blair, as though I had a direct line into his thoughts. He took up the same line on this occasion, rather more aggressively, wanting to know Blair's reasons for supporting an American President with very different views to his own. I tried to argue that the relationship between the UK and America was too important for one man or one party to jeopardise. Tony Blair understood that the alliance with the US was a key long-term strategy, allowing the British to punch above their weight. Jean-Luc mused on this, before saying: 'And that's more important than dignity? You know, I saw your Prime Minister on TV last night. What country was he in: was it Egypt or Syria or Saudi or Pakistan?'

'It was Gaza. You know what Yasser Arafat looks like? He was the gnome-like guy standing next to him. I thought we were here to talk about Palestine?'

'That's right, that's what we are talking about. Excuse me,

it's just that Blair's itinerary makes me dizzy. Maybe he gets dizzy, too. He has a kind of glassy look, you know? Kind of ticcy. What do you think?'

Marguerite leaned over the table, cutting off my eye-line with Jean-Luc. 'Thank you for coming, James. Do you mind if I tell you a little about my organisation, the Civil Mission to Palestine? Then maybe you will be able to tell us if you can help or not.'

I had no idea what to expect. But I said, 'Please. Tell me all about it.'

Over the next hour, Marguerite launched into a painstaking description of the work of her group and its aim to protect the everyday life of Palestinians. The phrases 'ordinary people', 'everyday life' and 'grassroots' figured heavily in her presentation and, despite all the moments when my attention wandered, I understood that she wanted to work directly with civic bodies in Palestine, bypassing the Palestinian Authority. If I was feeling more feisty, this could have irritated me: the idea that there is a notional group called the 'people', which remains submerged and unrepresented by the parties they join and the leaders they elect. I could see why Jean-Luc might wish to believe this; he wore the enamel pin of a tiny French Marxist party and would not accept that its failure at the ballot box proved its detachment from 'ordinary' people or, indeed, reality. I say that I could have become irritated, but I also sympathised with Marguerite's position. As long as the Palestinian Authority was under direct assault by Israel, anything that her group could do to protect and preserve the institutions that made normal life possible had to be a good thing. I realised that Marguerite was Jewish, not only from her surname but also from her concern for justice for the Palestinians, a concern that is far from unusual among Jews, even (or especially) in these dark times.

Marguerite needed me because, although she had extensive contacts with all kinds of Palestinian charities from schools to religious trusts, she was putting out feelers, trying to find a way to work with people on the government payroll: from the utilities like gas and electric and especially water, to state schools and hospitals. She did not actually use the phrase 'put out feelers', and when I said it she did not understand me. I rephrased, telling her I would look at my old files and try to find contacts within the Palestinian civil service who might be able to help her.

Flavie sensed that business was over. She nudged me and said, 'Ask Jean-Luc to help with your problem.'

'You have a problem, James?' Jean-Luc had been quiet through much of Marguerite's presentation, adding only amplifications and expletives. The silence seemed to have dulled his brain, but now he was ready to wake up. 'Come on. Tell Jean-Luc your problem.'

I shot Flavie a glance. 'That's fine. There is no problem.'

'I think you are hiding something, James.'

'You would be wrong to pursue that thought, Jean-Luc.'

'Come on, my friend. What's the matter?'

'Nothing.'

I was lying. In that moment, I realised that my depiction of Gustave Flourens had grown out of my first meeting with Jean-Luc. Perhaps these cross-fertilisations are inevitable. On the Metro earlier, a woman had been reading a profile of Alexander McQueen, who had fallen out with his employees during the recent Paris fashion week. I had deliberately followed McQueen's story, looking for ways to flesh out my depiction of Charles Frederick Worth, the original English couturier in Paris. Here were two parallels from life, and there would be more.

I could not keep worrying about the Danish lawyers so I made my decision. There was Karen Blixen's Babette, of the story 'Babette's Feast' and its film version, which, to be honest, I saw long before I ever read the original story. And then there was mine, or at least the enigmatic B, referred to by a single initial throughout Lieutenant Brunel's journal. These were two different people, two different creations entirely.

The Party Chez Babette

Fifty metres from the theatre, Brunel stepped out of the bubble of light into unlit streets. This was where the night began, in the wet mist that hung in the gullies between buildings. There was a little moonlight, just enough to make the sky seem brighter than the streets below – as though a grey-blue cover had been placed on a dark bowl. Somewhere beyond this space, Brunel could hear the heavy guns, but in the echo between the sky and the ground it was impossible to tell which direction the shells came from, which fort was under attack or how near to the city walls the fighting had come.

The Second Army was based at Porte Maillot, out along the Champs Elysées. The designation was misleading; the Second Army comprised virtually all of the regular troops left in France, and it had been a deliberate policy to keep them isolated on the western outskirts of Paris, away from the temptations of the city and the politics of the Parisian volunteers. If Brunel had ridden out with General Ducrot's Zouaves as he was supposed to, he would have been asleep in camp by now. But he was on foot so it was nothing to turn right and walk back to the Place Vendôme, past the giant gunmetal column that stood at its centre. A squad of Nationals stood outside the National Guard headquarters. They approached him, saw the marine uniform and waved him on, snapping out salutes as he passed by, on to the rue de la Paix and Chez Babette.

Brunel let his feet fall. Tiredness curdled in his body. Though he knew why he had taken this detour, he had to keep asking himself why he thought it was a good idea. Hanging around outside her home wasn't going to help, unless he wanted to be mistaken for a coachman. A line of coaches stood on the far side of the road, the drivers talking in a loose group, warmed by the pulse of light and heat coming from the restaurant.

A rider approached from the south. Brunel paid no attention, not even when the man swung down and hitched his horse to the line of coaches. But then he appeared right beside Brunel, slapping his gloves against his skirts. It was Gustave Flourens.

'I heard you charmed all the generals at the theatre. That's good going, for your first day in Paris. But why aren't you at Porte Maillot?'

Brunel had no excuse to hand so he said, 'I have a message for the owner.'

Brunel had no intention of telling Flourens the truth: that he believed there was a spark between him and Babette, and he had to see where it would lead. Until then, he could not sleep. As he searched for a plausible lie, Flourens continued badgering him.

'Come on, friend. We got off to a bad start. Why not make amends: help me out. There's a woman at the party who absolutely needs to see me. All the way through the play, she was wiggling her tongue at me.'

'You're too late. I've already delivered the message.'

'Already? You're done? Ah well.' Flourens grinned. 'Bad luck for me. But I'll brazen it out. I've crashed better places.'

Brunel watched him stride towards the door. As he disappeared through it, Brunel ran for the side of the building, down a passage and into the stable yard. As he pushed at the kitchen door, he caught a blast of warm steam. The steam cleared, and he saw the kitchen staff desert their stations and run for the corridor that led to the restaurant. As Brunel expected, Flo's entrance was providing the diversion he needed.

He slipped through the door.

He felt the heat like a slap on each cheek. The ovens were stoked so high that he could have been walking into a foundry, but instead of the dry blast, the powdery dirt underfoot and the smell of acid and steel, there was a sticky heat and the taste of soupy beef. As he became accustomed to that one sensation, it dissolved into others. Into onions, some treacle-sweet, some acrid and raw. Then the fragrance of herbs, sage and thyme, basil that smelt of raw cat piss one second and was sweet and fresh the next. Brunel took a step forward and was struck by another searing blast of heat. Each corner of the kitchen had its own climate: winds that were so hot and moist they slipped across his face, as viscous as egg yolks; steams that seemed to rise from the floor and condense as sweat beneath his shirt; cooler winds that lapped his feet and sudden pinpoint-accurate darts of steam.

The kitchen staff were returning. Someone was driving them back to their stations and they came in a spill, five men and two women, falling over each other's feet and laughing among themselves. As they swept by, Brunel set his face in the expression of a man who was supposed to be exactly where he was. He pushed through them without a glance, his eyes on the corridor ahead. And suddenly she was in front of him.

Babette wore a white blouse, a bandanna around her neck, another holding back her hair. Her blue skirt was gathered in a broad band at the waist, and in that band she had tucked a number of cloths, each in a blue and white check. The cloths might have seemed festive, if any had been clean. There were spatters of blood, knife-edge streaks, dark smears, as well as handprints and flashes of red wine. Her blouse was clean, though; white, if not crisp white. The heat of the kitchen had dissolved the laundry starch and now the cotton clung to her damp skin.

Brunel could not take in all of this detail at once, but he noticed small things: where the sweat pooled along her upper lip and in the indentation at the heart of her neck. He saw the pale glaze of shadow beneath her eyes, where her kohl had melted and spread. He saw her nostrils flare and imagined that she was smelling the same things as him, inside this airlock between the kitchen and the restaurant. Her own scent, flesh rubbed in hot butter and mixed with spices, cloves and peppers and sumac. Smells that inflamed his nostrils and sent the blood pulsing under his skin.

She was in a rage. Perhaps it was because she was heading up a busy kitchen and had a banquet on her hands. Her staff were so easily distracted. Perhaps Flo's intrusion had lit the fuse. But the truth, he knew, was that she was mad at him. She reddened, the heat flush burning into pure anger.

'You! What did you say to my son?' She pushed at him.

'What do you think I said?'

'Do you want me to spell it out? You creep.' She pushed again.

Brunel took a step back. 'I'm not, I swear.'

'No? You just crept in here . . .'

She had forced him almost to the kitchen door. Now she looked across to one of her sous-chefs, the biggest man in her kitchen, and called out, 'Peter? How did this man get in here?'

Peter looked up, shaking his head. He was holding a cleaver twenty-five centimetres long.

There was no time to win her over. Brunel tried, however. 'Can we talk?'

She was not even looking at him any more. 'Throw him out.'

As Peter tried to take his arm, Brunel shrugged away, holding out his hands to show that he was unarmed. Then he turned and quietly left the kitchen. Peter remained right behind him every step of the way, the cleaver hanging by his side, the blade so sharp that it crackled with light.

Outside in the stable yard, Brunel turned to Peter and said, 'You're going to regret this.'

'Yeah? When's that?'

Brunel swept the big man's feet away and dumped him on his arse. 'Now, you fat fuck.'

Peter was so dazed that Brunel just took the cleaver straight out of his hand. He considered blunt-siding the guy across his head. Instead, he waved it under his eyes as a threat. Then he re-entered the kitchen.

Babette took one look at the cleaver and was out of the kitchen so fast that he barely had time to drop the blade. He ran after her, into the restaurant.

The party at the central table was about ten strong. Charles Frederick Worth was there, opposite the skinny bossy woman from his salon. Murielle was there, too, waiting on the table. But Brunel's eyes were drawn to Babette's husband, leaning towards the fellow next to him and laughing. He pulled away as he saw Brunel enter, looking at him with an arched eyebrow.

The Prefect, Edmond Adam, stepped through the door from the street. Another familiar face, though the two policemen behind him were not. They were slapping their hands together, making a big show of getting rid of rubbish.

Babette was at Prefect Adam's side. 'I'm sorry about this, Monsieur le Préfet, but can you throw this man out, too?'

'Lieutenant Brunel? Why? What's he done?' Adam looked from Brunel back to Babette. 'All right. If you insist.' He waved his men forward.

Brunel would have tried a last appeal to Babette, but she was already heading back to her kitchen, as though she cared so little that there wasn't even any pleasure in watching his humiliation. So he decided to go quietly. When Prefect Adam saw this, he stopped his policemen as they were grabbing Brunel's arms. At the door, he whispered, 'What's up? Are you and Flo forming a double-act?' Brunel could only shake his head and apologise for ruining the Prefect's supper.

Flourens stood across the road, wiping at a muddy smear on the back of his skirt. It was clear that the policemen had used much more force when they expelled him. But Flo was still smiling, and as the restaurant door closed he approached Brunel and said, 'You're not welcome either? What kind of restaurant is it, anyway?'

Brunel offered a thin smile. 'If neither of us is welcome?

Probably a good one. Do you know where I could find a cow?'

'In the middle of the night?'

'Yes.'

'Actually, I do.'

Flourens did not seem to find anything wrong with stealing a cow. It amazed Brunel, who knew exactly how insane the idea was. If he could have thought of another way to impress Babette, he would have taken it. He had felt so overwhelmed in her kitchen. The heat was so oppressive, he had felt so weak. When Babette appeared, she might have stepped out of another world.

Flo's horse clattered behind them as they led it into the streets north of Les Halles. It had begun to drizzle again, and the cold was seeping into their clothes. Flo was complaining.

'I hope she appreciates this.'

'I doubt she will. Which building is it?'

Flo pointed to a baker's shop. 'It's been closed since the siege began. But someone noticed this butcher named Roos coming and going at night. So they wondered, why does he have the keys?'

'Why does he have the keys?'

'He's got a cow hidden there.'

'Are you sure?' Brunel looked at the steps leading to the basement of the patisserie. 'We should make certain before we break in.'

'Some kids saw Roos' daughters coming up with milk churns.'

'That sounds promising.'

'And then there's all the mooing.'

'Let's go.'

The building looked empty. But if cows were so valuable, the butcher would not leave his unguarded. Brunel stared hard through the windows, trying to penetrate the darkness of the empty shop. He took a step back into the street and looked at the upper windows; though it was doubtful that any guard would sleep up there. He would need to be as close to the cow as possible.

Flourens was testing the hammer of his gun. He said, 'Why so shifty? We kick in the door, spinning our pistols. Who's going to stop us?'

'How long do you think it will take to get a cow up a narrow flight of steps? This isn't a smash-and-grab raid.'

Flourens nodded, admitting the point. 'Maybe we need more men.'

'The more men, the more noise.' Brunel started down the steps to the cellars. 'Let's do it my way. Quietly.'

The door had a window, but it was covered with bars. Brunel couldn't see much of anything. He motioned to Flo to stay at the top of the steps.

'Keep your gun on the door, but don't shoot unless I say.'

Brunel used the butt of his pistol to break the glass. In a moment, there were footsteps on the cellar's stone floor and a boy of about eighteen appeared, a lamp in one hand and a rifle in the other. The light was so weak that Brunel was worried the boy wouldn't even see the pistol in Brunel's hand.

'Stop there,' he whispered. 'Look at me.'

The kid lifted his lantern higher.

'You see the pistol?'

The boy nodded, his rifle too heavy for him to level and take aim one-handed.

'Fine. Just open the door and let me in.'

The boy shook his head. 'I'm not doing that.'

'You think I won't shoot you?'

'How will you get in the door if I'm lying dead?'

'If I shoot you in the leg, you'd still be able to crawl over and open the door. And believe me, you would crawl, just to save the other leg.'

The boy thought about it. Then he opened the door.

The smell was horrendous. The boy had been shovelling the cowshit into the old coal cellar, but it was so liquid that even with a couple of sandbags across the doorway the shit ran back into the main cellar. The cow was at the back, in the shadows.

You didn't need to be a vet to tell that this was a deeply sad creature, living with its bin full of hay, its stone bed and no sunlight.

Brunel asked the kid, 'How do we get it out of here?'

'Why are you stealing it?'

'We're commandeering it. For France.'

'Really?'

He sounded almost hopeful. Brunel looked at him and said, 'How did you even get the cow down the steps?'

'We made a ramp.' The boy pointed to a staircase at the back of the cellar, leading to the ground floor. The boards for the ramp were leaning against the wall, next to a stack of galvanised milk cans. The stairs had two flights, with a small landing between them. Brunel and the boy laid the boards on the first flight and then fell to arguing with Flourens about who got to pull the cow and who got to push at its backside. Flo was adamant, he was going nowhere near the shitty end.

The cow couldn't seem to get any traction with its hooves, which kept slipping on the boards. The problem was eased after they put sacking around them but it still took half an hour to get the cow up the first flight, followed by an awkward ten minutes on the landing as they manoeuvred the boards around the cow to make the second ramp. Just as they conquered the second flight, they faced a new problem.

The kid said, 'She's leaking.'

'What do you mean, leaking?'

'Leaking. Can't you smell it?'

Brunel looked down – the kid's arm was already coated. Brunel tried to get a grip higher up, as far from the leak as possible. At the same time, he warned the kid not to loosen his grip; they didn't want to have to go through this again. Flourens lashed at the rump of the cow, which reared and bolted upstairs of its own accord.

Brunel watched it skid around the tiled floor, crash against an archway and disappear into a salon.

'I thought cows couldn't climb stairs?'

'They can't climb down,' said the kid. 'We hadn't tried to get it up.'

They cornered the cow in a window alcove and got a rope back around its neck. With the cow under control, Flo took a look at the kid. He seemed sorry for him as he said, 'We can take it from here, son. You go and wash up.'

'I'm not staying here. Roos is going to kill me when he finds out I helped steal his cow.'

Flourens said, 'Do you want to join the Belleville Nationals, son? I'm looking for good men.'

The kid hesitated. He turned to Brunel. 'What's your regiment, sir?'

'I don't have one.'

The kid turned to Flourens. 'Looks like it's your bunch then.'

Flo wasn't insulted. He wasn't even listening properly. He told the kid to come and see him in Belleville in the morning and helped Brunel lead the cow through the empty streets to the rue de la Paix.

They were almost at Chez Babette when Brunel asked Flo how he had known about his meeting with the President, General Ducrot and General Vinoy. Flo grinned, bragging that nothing happened in the city without his knowledge. 'Trochu has to brief us on his plans if he wants to keep us behind his government.'

Something about his confidence that convinced Brunel he was speaking the truth. He chanced a question. 'Can you tell me how Auguste Ducrot arrived in the city? I thought he was a prisoner in Berlin.'

'That's easy, it's barely even a secret any more. Ducrot gave his *parole* to the Prussians that he would retire to his estate and take no more part in the fighting. Then he broke his word and headed straight for Paris.'

'He broke his word?'

'Why not? What's it worth – to him or to us?' Flo asked. 'But what did you think of him?'

Brunel was wary of speaking his mind. So he simply said, 'Ducrot's a soldier. I can work with him.'

'Really? I thought he was responsible for getting two thousand marines killed at Bazeilles.'

Jean-Luc and Me

Jean-Luc and Elise, both in their different ways, are fast wearing me down. Elise uses the telephone to force her way into my life and ask me to spy on Flavie. Jean-Luc comes by motorbike.

Elise called early to ask what I was doing. I told her, truthfully, that I was hoovering the louvres of my blind. There is not a chance in hell she understood me but she said 'Yeah?' and briskly switched the topic, following her own agenda.

'Listen, James, do you know if Flavie came home last night? Was she on her own?'

Flavie ditched Elise a week ago. Elise accepted the news with something approaching calm and Flavie insisted the break-up was amicable. Then the telephone calls began and Elise set me straight: 'Amicable, is that what she is telling you? If you want to know the truth, I say it's only temporary.'

Elise was trying to recruit a network of spies. When she called this morning, she had already spoken to her source at Flavie's salon.

'You know that Flavie has not arrived at work yet?'

'I'm not getting involved in this, Elise. Why do you think I have any talent for lesbian intrigue?'

'Listen, you can see into Flavie's kitchen from your apartment. I want you to take a look, that's all. The people at the salon are worried, it's the truth.'

The rest of the fifteen-minute conversation was one long struggle to tell Elise nothing. There was nothing to tell: Flavie was home, alone and only a few minutes late for work. But nothing I say will ever discourage Elise from calling me, and I knew she would try again.

Jean-Luc arrived in the afternoon, announcing his arrival with two rapid slaps on my door. He long ago memorised the security code to the street door so there was no line of defence: he could walk straight up to the apartment door. His first visit came a few days after the meeting with Marguerite Galperin, asking for the list of Palestinian contacts that I had promised. But he continued to visit even after I had provided it.

The typical scene: Jean-Luc would stand smoking at the window, complaining about the cold while I reminded him that it was his idea, his compromise. I would have preferred him not to smoke anywhere in the apartment. He would then tighten his scarf, blow smoke into the central light-well and continue to interrupt the flow of my thoughts.

While he dangled into the light-well, I would sit across the room at my laptop, trying to look like a man who could only spare a few moments. Jean-Luc knew I was working as a business journalist; perhaps if he had also known about the novel, he would have shown more respect. We spent hours talking, but despite all his accusations and charges, my defences and rebuffs, we only had one thing in common: Flavie. Our whole relationship was founded on a single shared interest, a shared weakness.

One day, Jean-Luc saw a brightly wrapped package on my desk and immediately asked, 'A present? For Flavie?' I had to tear away the store-wrapped parcel and show him the papiermâché cow that I had bought for myself as a mascot. A work mascot: a Jersey cow with happy black splotches.

'You bought yourself a paper cow? Why would you do that?'

'I liked it. Why would you think I bought it for Flavie?'

'Well, she's a charming woman, why not buy her gifts?'

Yet despite such moments, Jean-Luc seemed determined to put our relationship on another foundation. He loved the idea that I had been an economist, and though I told him it was all in the past, he insisted that we had the basis of an ideological understanding: two professionals, the man of law, the man of the market. We could see through the bullshit. He asked, 'Who believes this is a war on terror? It's about trade, money, oil. George W. Bush set up a business with Osama Bin Laden's brother, you know that?'

Of course I knew it. The whole world knew it. It was in every magazine profile on either man, and the subject of a million conspiracy sites on the internet. I pointed out that as there were something like a hundred and fifty Bin Laden half-brothers, everyone in the world could find a degree of connection to the family. Jean-Luc ignored me and continued: 'This isn't war. It's economics. And economics is war by other means.'

I told him that this was, and always would be, pure crap. Economics belongs in one sphere and war belongs in another. In a war, you blow up your neighbour's home. In a free market, you buy his tomatoes. Of course, war and economics can co-exist. People have to eat; there will always be markets within wars, regulated by governments and supplemented by racket-eers and smugglers. But the idea that the market trader or the butcher is doing the exact same thing as the soldier is nonsense: there is no point of comparison between an exchange of goods and an exchange of fire, and this should have been obvious even to Jean-Luc, though his ideological spectacles are thicker than his motorbike goggles. Jean-Luc relied on a very clear, even simple, idea of the modern world as a vertically-integrated oligarchy, a single huge corporation that dealt chiefly in oil and weapons and paid its stooges to sit in government. The current American administration certainly made Jean-Luc's view seem plausible, with its oil men and its security advisers. And so, while I tried to argue my corner, he would confidently tell me I was naive. He said, of course economics is war: it is class war, it is the military-industrial complex, it is neo-imperialism or whatever jargon he favoured that day. He told me that I had to read economics treatises with suspicion: I had to see that they were all about conflict. That was the context, that was the subtext.

Jean-Luc had convinced himself that the war in Afghanistan would last for ever. Now that it seemed to be over after a month he was perplexed and sought economic reasons. But the fact was, everyone else was just as confused: our friends, the newspapers, the people on television, the world's politicians. When events move so fast, there is an excess of energy, almost too much momentum. No one knew how the momentum from Afghanistan would be used, or where it would take us. The war had left an abstract space that was yet to be filled with any concrete ideas, and though there was talk of a new peace initiative in the Middle East, there was also the possibility of more war, perhaps in Iraq, perhaps in Sudan.

Jean-Luc did not just talk about Afghanistan. He talked about my apartment block. He saw the light-well as a multi-level aquarium, stacks and stacks of viewing tanks that give him an insight into another world. His apartment, in the 5th arrondissement, had been in his family for generations but as he spoke to me he claimed to prefer it here, in the 18th. He looked down at all the windows that face into the light-well, in raptures with his insight into urban domesticity. White or black, Arab or European or Vietnamese, everyone spent their time cooking and hanging out their washing. In another situation, I could have imagined Jean-Luc attacking any ostentatious display of home-making. It's not as though he ever cooked or washed, favouring restaurants and dry-cleaners. Yet ever since he agreed to stand by the open window when he smoked, he had adopted a proprietorial position, like an impresario proud of his performers. He stood, waving his hand and flicking the ash away from his cigarette. Leaving burn marks on my neighbours' washing, for all I knew.

I could have let Jean-Luc rant, let him speechify or eulogise, just as he liked, hanging out of my living-room window. I didn't have to listen to him. But I was on edge that day. The phone call with Elise had set me on a bad track. So I told him, 'Can you just be quiet for five minutes, Jean-Luc. I'm trying to finish some work.'

'This is thinking. Talking is thinking: it is dialogue, the most pure kind of thought since Socrates. Come on, this is your specialist field, money, business, power.'

'It's not my field. I told you, I quit.'

'Why did you do that? I never understood.'

'It's the wrong question. The question is, why did I get into it in the first place? I lost confidence in my doctorate but I had to do something to earn money. I started to work for the World Bank because my girlfriend was pregnant.'

'I didn't know that.'

This really got under my skin. I took a deep breath and, rather than calming down, found myself losing my temper. 'Why the hell should you know it? I don't hand out digests of my life story to everyone I meet. We barely know each other.'

He put up his hands. 'Okay, okay. So you have a child, James? I didn't know that.'

'I've got a son.' I felt a tight vein of anger, beginning in my temples and running straight through my core, surrounded by a flabbier feeling of embarrassment. I could feel my face going bright red. I decided to apologise. 'Look, I've been working too long. I'll get some fresh air and buy a litre of milk.'

'Do you want me to go?'

'No. Stay there. I'll be back in twenty minutes.'

There is a Chinese grocer a little way up the street from the apartment and an ordinary supermarket on the parallel road. I drifted through the Chinese shop to look at the dried fish. I had no idea how to prepare them but they were so spooky, I found them compelling and wanted to learn. I needed to improve my kitchen skills, to master techniques that I could project on to Babette. Though Chinese cookery was not, perhaps, the best place to start. I drifted out again, making for the supermarket. My blow-up with Jean-Luc had left me dazed. Flavie could tease confessions out of me, but for the most part I preferred not to talk about my personal life. Isn't that a normal thing, to keep a little fence around the things one considers private? This had never before been a problem with Jean-Luc because he had no small talk whatsoever; our conversations were usually safe and non-intrusive, though incredibly tiring.

But as I walked, I found the thing that niggled me was not the personal stuff. It was Jean-Luc's reaction to the speed of the war. Why was everyone so surprised when Afghanistan moved so fast? Surely that's an interesting fact in itself. The US is the most powerful nation the world has ever seen. And we were all guilty of wishful thinking: we were hoping that it was not quite as powerful as all that.

Power is not something that exists in degrees, to be measured and compared. It's either there or it isn't, and America has it. It has all of it. I could tell Jean-Luc this. Then I could ratchet the discussion up a notch by telling him that I am writing about the siege of Paris, four long months in which France learned that it was defenceless. France would never again fight a war and win, except as an ally of the United States. After 1871 France would always be powerless, as insignificant as a Pacific island republic or a Himalayan kingdom, if it did not have nuclear weapons.

The French have two words for power. This is a strange enough occurrence in itself. English can provide a synonym for virtually every word in the language, but it is rather rare in French. So, why the two words, when they are indistinguishable in so many ways: *pouvoir* and *puissance*? One can say *le pouvoir paternel* or *la puissance paternelle*, for instance, and they mean the same thing: paternal authority. I know that French philosophers have used the two words to distinguish between different kinds of power, noting that *pouvoir* is more active, the *can-do* word, while *puissance* is more about potential, the charge inside the battery, the power to be unleashed.

I used to have a slightly different view: that *pouvoir* is military and *puissance* economic. But if the economic age is coming to an end, then so are all the possibilities it named. Since the Enlightenment, we have maintained our faith in humanity's potential, in human dreams and desires. In the market place, we speculated on the potential of companies and saw these speculations fulfil themselves or fail. We invested our hopes and our dreams and our pension funds with confidence, believing the returns would grow and that humanity would flourish. But this faith in our future is ending. The idea is fast catching hold that it was all hogwash and whatever we are – humanity! – we are nasty and brutish. We ought no longer to encourage human dreams. We ought to get out the guns and build the stockade.

Forget about potential. I might have the potential to write a decent book. I might, potentially, find a heterosexual woman who has the same effect on me as Flavie. These are both possibilities, both dreams. There are others. I could, conceivably, have returned to my apartment, taken hold of Jean-Luc's ankles and tipped him out of the window. It was a possible threat, though as remote as the possibility of him transforming into a feather and floating to safety. Elise tried to ruin my friendship with Flavie. She conjured up a world where Flavie and I might have had a love affair and took a pre-emptive strike. She was crazy.

The French may have two words for power but, really, they only need the one. It's all any of us needs. One word for power. Lots of words for powerlessness in all its gradations: weak, feeble, neutered, impotent, enervated. A word to describe the stateless refugee, another for the ineffectual European diplomat. Another for spoilt thirty-somethings, unhappy in love. Open your own thesaurus and welcome to a world where everyone feels so helpless that they comfort themselves with dreams.

When I returned, Jean-Luc was still hanging out of the window. His only interest in visiting me was to spy on Flavie.

It had taken me so long to put it together, although it had been happening right in front of my eyes. I dropped my shopping bag and leapt across the room.

He had taken up a position where he could see into Flavie's kitchen and through it, via a hall mirror, to her bedroom. I pulled him back by the collar of his shirt. As I choked him, he managed to splutter out, 'Wait, she has Marguerite with her. I think this is it.'

I stared. He was telling the truth – Marguerite was in there. She appeared even thinner and paler than the last time I saw her, with one long bony arm stretched up and over to scratch at the space between her shoulder blades in the way that only gawky, rangy people can manage.

'How long has she been there?'

'She arrived soon after you left. They have been standing so close, but I have not seen them kiss, yet.'

We crowded at the window, leaning out together. Marguerite was reaching for a cardigan, either because she was cold or because she was leaving. Flavie moved in close but she slipped to the side, shaking her head.

'What was that?'

Jean-Luc did not know. 'She pushed her away, I think.'

I rushed to the front door and put my eye to the spyhole, Jean-Luc right at my shoulder.

'What do you see? What do you see?'

'Shush.'

The door opened and Marguerite came out, pale as cooked spaghetti and as spiky and fragile as the dried stuff. She turned, allowing Flavie to hold her hand. But then she broke away, giving a weird little wave as she disappeared down the stairs.

Jean-Luc elbowed me. 'What's happening?'

'Hush.'

I watched Flavie crumple, rebuffed.

'She rejected her?'

'I think she rejected her.'

Marguerite ran down the stairs without looking back. Flavie remained in the doorway, looming large and round and desolate in the fish-eye lens of my spyhole. This morning, it was just me, Elise and Jean-Luc: the three losers. Now we are four!

Captain Brunel of the Marsouin

The army camp lay outside the city walls, where the Seine curved around Paris to form a natural defence along its western front. Then, where the river turned again to continue its route to the sea, the fortress town of St Denis provided another defence. This secure strip of land, with the Seine as its horizon and the city walls as its backbone, was almost a city in itself, but a movable city, a city in flight.

Brunel got some idea of the camp's size when he reached it in the early hours of the morning. But it was only when he was summoned to see the commander of the naval and marine forces, Admiral de la Roncière, that he truly grasped its size. The old man had commandeered an attractive villa in the suburbs on the outskirts of the camp. Brunel looked out from the first-floor salon to see a tight grid of tents stretching right across the Bois de Boulogne. The last time that Brunel had seen the Bois, hundreds of thousands of sheep had been grazing between the stumps of felled trees. Now it had changed again. The sheep were replaced by this chequer grid of tents. And at the centre lay General Ducrot's war room, a pavilion built to send a message to the half-million men camped around him: that he was in charge, running the war under canvas. Brunel was surprised to learn that Ducrot even slept there at night. Admiral de la Roncière said he thought this was laudable, especially when General Vinoy continued to live at home, in his Parisian mansion.

'But it's almost certain, now,' the admiral said. 'General Ducrot will be made Commander of the Second Army. He's even had the huge scale model of Paris brought from the Tuileries and erected inside his tent, which keeps the men's eyes on their job. Although some might find it a little flashy, fighting the war like a draper, decorating his shop window.'

They were standing by the salon window. The air was so heavy that morning that it rolled across the camp in a wave, flattening the canvas as it went. The admiral wiped his eyes with a cloth, squinting as he searched for the area where the marines were camped. The Marsouin were an amalgamation of those who had fought at Bazeilles and the two thirds that had returned to France from Algiers and the Pacific, too late to join the battle. Four thousand men in total, with another three thousand marine gunners scattered around the forts. When the admiral asked Brunel about his impression of the men, Brunel had to confess he had no idea. He had only arrived back at three in the morning and it was now just eight o'clock.

'Well, find out. General Ducrot wants you to make a report.' The admiral touched Brunel's sleeve. 'The odd thing is that he referred to you as Captain Brunel, but now I see how he made that mistake. Can you sort that out, do you think?'

Embarrassed, Brunel placed a hand over the braiding on the cuff of his tunic. 'I am sorry about that, sir. I will clear it up immediately.'

'Oh, let's wait until after we've eaten.'

They turned back to the warmth of the salon and the buffet from which the admiral took his breakfast. Brunel had refused the offer to join him; he had managed no more than a couple of hours' sleep and felt he could not stand, eat, hold a conversation and balance a plate of food at the same time. As he answered the admiral's questions, he kept his movements and his words short and crisp. If he looked bright at all, it was only an illusion created by coffee and cigarettes.

The admiral calculated that the marines were only 2 per cent of the strength of the army. The gunners had to be discounted as they could not be moved from the forts. 'Four thousand men sounds small enough,' he said. 'But Ducrot knows how much he needs them. They are his best troops and crucial to his planned break-out. The problem is that he believes the marines hate him.'

'The general didn't seem the kind of man who depends upon good opinions,' Brunel replied.

'Auguste Ducrot is a realist. The marines do hate him, and after the mix-up at Bazeilles I don't think anyone blames them.' The admiral waved a chop at Brunel. 'But you, you have attracted his eye. And he thinks that you may be the man to overturn that opinion. He wants to bring you on to his staff, as his ambassador to the marine battalions. What do you think? Do you think you can sell General Ducrot to the Marsouin?'

Brunel was frank. 'I don't know, sir.'

The admiral waved the chop again; it flapped between his fingers and he seemed to lose his thread. 'I believe I recognise this chop from yesterday. Is it going to keep reappearing until I eat it? Sorry, what did you say?'

'I doubt I can make the marines love General Ducrot, sir.'

'A tough job, so better to start right away. The only problem is that I have also received a message from Edmond Adam, the Prefect of the Police. And he, too, wants to see you urgently.'

Brunel blinked.

'Do you know what it's about?' the admiral asked.

Brunel could only assume it was because of the cow. 'I may have an idea. A dispute with a Parisian butcher, sir.'

'We're in the middle of the war. I don't want my officers picking fights with civilians.'

'Nothing like that, sir. A genuine misunderstanding.'

'Do you want me to deal with it?'

'No sir.' Brunel snapped out the response. He had stolen a cow out of a coal-hole. The fewer people who knew the story, the better. 'If I speak to the Prefect, I know I can clear it up in an hour.'

'Get over to Ducrot's tent. Then worry about Monsieur le Préfet,' the admiral said. 'But first, at least I can make one of your problems disappear. Let us concoct a plausible story of how you might have become a captain.'

Brunel waited for General Ducrot inside his great pavilion. The model of Paris lay before him, bristling with the spires and towers of the city's churches, crowned at the top by the heights of Montmartre and bisected by an optimistic grey-blue arc representing the Seine, criss-crossed by bridges and filled with tiny replica gunboats and *bateaux-mouches*. The model, at least five metres long and four metres broad, stood on its own enormous table. Off to its north-west side, another smaller table held a model of St Denis, surrounded by walls, its cathedral towering at the centre.

General Auguste Ducrot appeared from the depths of the tent, asking, 'What do you say? Can you persuade the marines I didn't fuck up at Bazeilles?' before Brunel had even finished his salute.

Brunel had not expected the general to be so open about the problem. But when he had met the general the night before, they had been in a conference. Today they were alone.

Brunel said, 'I have just come from the admiral's quarters, sir. We discussed it.'

He might have added, without coming to a conclusion, though they did manage to construct a story of Brunel's battlefield promotion, from lieutenant to captain, as Marsouin officers were cut down or lost in the retreat.

All Brunel could say, in truth, was, 'Bazeilles is still an issue, sir.'

General Ducrot had ordered the retreat from Bazeilles. The marines had defended the village through hours of bitter fighting, helped by villagers who were either fighting on the front lines or working to keep supply lines open under brutal fire. The defenders of Bazeilles, Marsouin and villagers alike, had barricaded themselves in attics; they were crouched behind garden walls or upturned carts; they had dug themselves into drainage ditches. In this haphazard way, they formed an impro-vised line that stretched across the village.

Abandoning these positions was almost as hard as keeping them. When the marines followed orders and broke cover, running for the open road to the rear of the village, they left behind the men and women who had trusted them. This was why Ducrot was so hated by the Marsouin. Not because he got their comrades killed, but because his orders led to the deaths of hundreds of villagers, executed because they were fighting out of uniform, without the protection given to troops by the new Geneva rules.

At the heart of this massacre there was, as there always is, a nugget of stupidity, the rubber bladder that only needs squeezing to turn a debacle into a farce. Marshal MacMahon, the commander of the forces at Sedan, had named General Ducrot as his replacement after being hit in the arse by a frag-ment of a shell. Ducrot was commander for less than three hours. He had just enough time to order the retreat from Bazeilles before MacMahon's authority to appoint his successor was questioned and Ducrot was forced to step down.

The result was that the Marsouin received counter-orders: they were to retake the village. Bazeilles lay behind them, pounded by shells and filled with the smoke of burning build-ings. During the retreat, the marines had hardly dared look back at it. But when the orders came, they turned and ran back into the inferno. The battle was desperate, but they were impelled by guilt as much as revenge. They fought for the villagers as well as for the friends they had lost.

Brunel wondered what he would have said if he had met General Ducrot that day. Now, he was cooler. Standing in the calm of this tent, he took in the general's neat grey beard, his plain uniform with only the lapel insignia to show his rank. It was exactly how Brunel would wish an officer to look. A modern general, rather than a scarlet-hosed clown, straight out of the pages of an illustrated children's book. Yet, at the same time,

Brunel recognised it was a political front. Here at the camp, the general aimed to look like an infantryman, planted solidly between the models of future battlefields. Yet when he rode into Paris he used Zouaves as his outriders.

It all came down to one issue: did Brunel trust the general?

'What about you, Captain?' The general seemed to be reading his mind. 'Do you believe I was wrong about Bazeilles?'

'We could never have held the village without reinforcements, sir.'

'Is that your answer? I should have sent reinforcements?'

Brunel shook his head. 'Why would you waste another man, sir? You made the right decision, we had to retreat.'

'I've made tough decisions in battles. But this was never one of them. I was the second-in-command on that front, I knew exactly what the marines had achieved. Getting into Bazeilles was a miracle in itself, let alone holding it. I was receiving your reports, I respected the arguments. But none of it mattered. We were being swept away all along the valley. If we had tried to hold on to any one point, it would have become a pivot for the whole German advance. We had eight hours before they would be swinging round our necks. After MacMahon was wounded, I pulled you out.

'Then I was countermanded. I was told the Emperor needed a victory. The son of a bitch – he wanted a victory when he didn't even have a retreat.'

'We were in the pisspot, and it was raining shit.' Brunel quoted the words the general was reported to have used at the time.

The general answered with a grim smile.

'You were right, sir.'

'I hope you can get that message across to your comrades. Only a victorious army can afford to hold on to land. We need the freedom to move. Bazeilles threatened to take that away from us. And Paris could do exactly the same thing.' The general was standing between his two giant models; now he spread out his arms, one towards Paris, the other to St Denis. 'This is where

99

we begin our break-out, right where I stand. From here, we smash a line all the way to Normandy. Once we have our liberty and a port, we bring in guns and supplies from Britain and America and we change the whole shape of the war.'

He turned slightly, holding the space between the two cities.

'Through this gap, between St Denis and the Seine. All I need is a wedge to keep the door open. This is why I need the Marsouin, Captain. To place themselves where I stand now.'

'I promise, the marines will not let you down, sir.'

But first, he needed to speak to Edmond Adam.

Brunel headed back to the Prefecture on horseback, though he would almost have preferred the police wagon again. Riding across the Pont Neuf, the cobbles slick with rainwater, his eyes drifted to the gunboats, the real ones, lining the quayside just as they did on Ducrot's model. As he stared downwards, his horse stumbled. He might have fallen if a passer-by had not grabbed his reins and steadied him.

He believed that he could straighten out the affair once he had spoken to Edmond Adam. Cattle rustling could not be so great a crime – not in the city. The fact that the cow had been hidden, that had to be as embarrassing for the owner as for the thief.

It was embarrassing enough for the thief.

Brunel had never faced a firing squad, never even taken part in one. But this is how the situation struck him as he stood against a blank wall in the Prefecture, his hands hanging loosely at his front, covering his testicles. It's how he imagined he would stand if he was being shot. At the moment, he was only having his photograph taken.

The young photographer was so huge that he made the process seem like a great physical enterprise. As he ducked back behind his camera he said, 'Come on, man. You must have had your photograph taken before.'

'Not in a police station.'

Brunel had begun to realise how seriously the affair was being taken as he was searched. His small cache of bills, his pocket knife, the pouch of caps and balls for his Remington – all these were removed and placed in a tin box. When Brunel asked to speak to Edmond Adam, he was told that the Prefect was fully aware of his arrest. And he was led through to this bizarre, white-walled room with its stench of photographic chemicals.

The photographer was big in body and face, with broad shoulders and wild hair that he had to push back with his hand as he stared over the camera at Brunel. He said his name was Raoul Rigault and insisted that he was a civilian, not a policeman. Two policemen stood by the door, out of the picture.

'It's a new initiative: an entire photographic record,' Rigault said. 'Imagine the possibilities: we could photograph the whole city, *en face*, left and right profiles, and store all the records in a single room. Have to be a bloody big room, but it's within the bounds of possibility. Ready?'

The room flared white, then cooled to grey. Blue plankton scrolled across Brunel's field of vision before fading away. Raoul Rigault reappeared from beneath his camera's cape.

'How did you even get into Paris?'

'I hitched.'

'That's your best story? And you wonder why you raised suspicions,' Rigault said. 'All right. Sideways now.'

Brunel shifted a quarter-turn. The room flared up again. As the glare dissolved, all Brunel could think to say was, 'I didn't really hitch. That was supposed to be a joke.'

'It's not the way Trochu saw it.' Rigault walked out from behind his camera and handed Brunel a tightly rolled paper tube. The tube was a newspaper, entitled *Le Combat*. Brunel straightened it out and read the headline: METZ FALLEN.

'What's this?'

'The reason you're here. President Trochu says you invented the story. He's calling you a traitor.'

The newspaper carried the day's date. The story about Metz seemed accurate enough, if you skimmed the rhetoric about turning tides, brewing storms and the uprising of spirits. There was also a cartoon that showed the senior French soldiers as waiters – President Trochu, Marshal Bazaine, Generals Vinoy and Ducrot – all serving up Metz to the enemy on a plate.

'Our President's claiming it's all lies – spread by you, a Prussian spy.' Rigault took the newspaper out of Brunel's hands and rearranged his shoulders. 'Straighten up, man. You have to stand tall so we get an accurate idea of your height.'

Brunel said, 'Is Trochu crazy? Why's he saying this?'

'He claims that you cooked up the entire story, then you sold it to Flourens and Flo got the story published.'

'Are you serious?'

'Look around. Doesn't this look serious?' Rigault leaned towards him, one hand resting on the whitewashed wall so that he cloaked Brunel with his body. 'Listen, you can tell me the truth. Did you leak the information to Flo?'

'I didn't tell anyone except President Trochu – in front of Vinoy and Ducrot.'

'But it is true? Metz really has fallen? Because if Trochu and all his generals can only bring us defeats, some people might say it's time for a new government.'

My Home Life

My mother rang asking about my plans for Christmas. With a tenant in my London flat, I no longer had a base in England and nowhere to put up my son during the holiday week. In the circumstances, it made sense to stay with my parents. Evan would see his grandparents, I would get to see my whole family together. My mother was keen and I had agreed in principle, promising to call in the next week and confirm the details.

It was nine o'clock. I had bought a new dressing gown from La Samaritaine and was wearing it, post-shower, surfing the apartment. I was winding down, learning to drink herbal tea rather than coffee. I had three separate books open and on the go, one on the kitchen worktop, one on the futon, one lying on top of a speaker cabinet. The truth was, I was fidgety as hell and even the shop-new fabric of the dressing gown was giving me the itch. I pulled a chair over to the window and picked the copy of Émile Zola's *The Ladies' Paradise* off the speaker. My gaze slipped down the page and over the edge, continuing along the metal rail that was set across the casement. I stood and leaned out, holding on to the rail. Just to see how far I could lean, if I could lean even further than I had five minutes ago.

Three weeks previously, I had bought the second series of *The Sopranos* on DVD. Flavie and I had a standing date to watch it together, two episodes every Wednesday. Tonight, she had cancelled on me. That was fine. Yet the moment I opted for an early night, I began sensing her beside me, her soft feet on her apartment floor, padding around in time to the cerebral French disco music that was seeping through her wall. Then about eight o'clock, Elise arrived. Flavie had given no explanation for cancelling our television date, but I had never thought that Elise could be the reason. Elise had not been around in weeks. The moment I heard her voice in the corridor, I rushed to the spyhole, catching her just as she disappeared into Flavie's apartment. Now I was twice as attuned to any sound through our shared wall. The fact that it was all so subdued made it all the stranger. Elise is the anti-subdued, she has decibels tattooed on the back of her scalp.

I couldn't see anything. Not in the kitchen. Not in the mirror that reflected a sliver of the wider apartment. Then the telephone rang.

I reared back from the window as though I had triggered an alarm. Even when I saw my telephone vibrating on my desk, I had to take a deep breath and collect my thoughts before I answered.

It was Jean-Luc, speaking so quickly I had to make him repeat himself.

'I said, you have to turn on the TV in ten minutes' time and catch me on CNN. My court case is making news in America.'

Jean-Luc had taken a high-profile case, defending a young McDonald's fry cook accused of sabotaging a restaurant in one of the Parisian *banlieues*. There had been several such saboteurs recently, the most famous of which was José Bové, a former left-wing activist who had retired to run a small cheese farm. He was now the leader of a radical farmers' union, waging a campaign against mass-produced foods. It made a potent bundle; Bové was opposed to globalisation, but he also represented much, much more than that: a hippy love of the countryside, a bourgeois love of food, a nationalist love of French produce, and a general opposition to the crappiness of modern life. He came over as left wing, right wing, anarchist and common sense all at once. And when he trashed a McDonald's restaurant close to his home village, the whole country embraced it as a legitimate piece of political theatre, rather than vandalism.

Jean-Luc was unlucky – his client was the vandal, but he was intent on making the best of it.

He said, 'CNN sent a crew to interview me outside the court. Promise me you'll tape it. And call round on Flavie, I want her to see it, too.'

The apartment had satellite TV, from a dish inexpertly strapped to a sprocket by the bedroom window. Flavie did not even have cable. But while I could promise to tape the news for Jean-Luc, I was reluctant to knock on Flavie's door.

I explained that she and Elise were in there together.

'Not Elise. Fuck.' This brought Jean-Luc up short. 'You have to split them up before that bitch gets her claws back into Flavie. Knock on the door now, tell them that Jean-Luc is on TV.' Jean-Luc sounded despairing. 'Go on, knock on the door now.'

'I don't know about this.'

'Listen to me, Flavie and Elise were poison. They were poison. Flavie and Margeurite Galperin, on the other hand, they have a real future. The only thing standing in their way is themselves, they don't see it yet. So drag Elise out before she destroys everything. Knock on the door. Throw her out.'

Jean-Luc's passion was out of character, at least because his aim appeared selfless. I did not like the idea of Elise and Flavie getting back together either, but Marguerite Galperin played no part in my thinking.

I tightened the belt of my dressing gown, stepped out into the hall and counted out three raps on the door. My rhythm was firm, brisk and not in the least anxious, or so I hoped. I heard a hand grab the internal lock, followed by the tell-tale pause to look through the spyhole, then Flavie opened up, but only by the width of her head.

'Hello, James. Did we decide we would miss *The Sopranos* tonight? I thought we did.'

'It's not that. I'm sorry to interrupt.' I could hear sobbing over the sound of the dance track on the stereo. Elise was crying, and with that realisation I began to lose all confidence in my mission.

'Is something the matter, James?'

'Nothing. Jean-Luc told me to tell you he is on television, that's all. I'm taping it, anyway. So . . . I'll leave you and we can speak tomorrow.' Elise's sobbing seemed to be growing louder. I was halfway back inside my own door now. But just before I shut myself away, I said, 'If you need me or want me, I'm just six feet away.'

'Thank you, James. Good night.'

We nodded at each other. And we closed our doors in unison.

The news had started, though by my watch there was another five minutes before Jean-Luc would appear. I was fingers and thumbs unwrapping the cellophane from a new VHS tape but I got it inside the machine before the item began.

Jean-Luc called again to ask if Flavie was watching the report. I told him, no, I was on my own.

'What are you saying? You left them together?'

'You don't understand. Elise was crying.'

'No. No. You don't understand. So what, she's crying? You have to separate them, my friend.'

I don't know how persistent Jean-Luc would have been if I had not turned to the television and seen his head loom above the presenter. I only had to say, 'You're on,' and he whooped and got off the line.

The on-screen Jean-Luc was standing outside the court, saying: 'We will argue that it is not my client's responsibility to explain his actions, it is McDo who must explain theirs. They must explain their vandalism towards a whole stratum of society: the industrialisation of man's highest pleasure. Where is the love of food when it is reduced to an etiquette controlled by buzzers? Can they justify this, can they speak of its humanity? If they cannot, we must ask how this inhumanity played on the mind of Tareq.'

Jean-Luc was hamming up his Frenchness to annoy an American audience. He did not mean anything malicious by it. But the humour was misplaced; two people were badly injured in Tareq Imad's arson attack on his local McDonald's, an attack motivated by his dismissal earlier in the day.

I moved back to the window as the interviewer thanked Jean-Luc for his time. I had not thought to wonder why an attack on a Parisian McDonald's should be an issue on a global TV station but as the picture switched from the court to the CNN studio I caught sight of the graphics behind the newscaster's head: 'The Rise of Anti-Americanism'. I wondered how Jean-Luc would react to being held up as the chief symptom. I knew he did not regard himself as anti-American; he wore a cowboy hat as ordinary leisure wear and rode a retro-American motorcycle. But his love of America was selective, and the motorcycle was made in Japan.

I thought I could still hear crying. I used the remote to turn down the volume, watching the green matchsticks diminish across the screen. The crying was so clear, coming in huge wet gulping sobs. As though Elise was suffocating, the tears squeezing out the oxygen. I peered through the window, leaning as far out as I could.

Elise was leaning from the other window, and she was staring directly at me. I darted inside, just the length of time it took to register how stupid I looked, then leaned back out. Elise was still there, smiling confidently. She gave me a big, showy wink.

I heard the flush of a toilet and then Flavie appeared, evidently straight from her bathroom. Elise started gulping again and disappeared back inside the kitchen. I watched as Flavie folded her into an embrace. Elise towered above her, but rested her head on Flavie's shoulder. Flavie soothed her by patting her on the back. She was completely unaware that it was a performance and the tears were fake.

The Prisoner of the Île de la Cité

Brunel had taken off his army greatcoat and wrapped it around his body as he struggled to keep himself warm and dry in his cell beneath the Seine. Whenever a face appeared at the slot in the door, he demanded an interview with the Prefect, but the faces appeared so rarely, perhaps only three times over the two days he spent there. He was too feverish to be certain. It was Sunday morning when they came and led him to a suite of rooms on the second floor of the Prefecture. They gave no explanation, but Brunel assumed that Edmond Adam was finally ready to see him.

He was led to a divan by the fire. The fire took all his attention, so it was a few moments before he realised he was being asked a question.

'I must have your word, sir, that you will not leave these rooms.'

Brunel looked up, blinking, to focus on this young man, the Deputy Prefect. When he repeated his question, Brunel asked, 'What's the problem? Is the war over?'

'No. We are still at war, Captain. And now we are on the verge of revolution, too.' The Deputy tugged at his ear lobe. 'Under the circumstances, the Prefect wishes you to be comfortable and regrets that it is not possible to release you. Do you understand?'

'No.'

'The Prefect has placed this suite of rooms at your disposal. He is asking you to rest here, Captain Brunel. And he asks you to trust him.' Brunel paused, then gave a quick nod. The Deputy seemed relieved; at least, he ceased pulling at his ear. 'Is there anything I can get you, sir?'

'Get me a doctor. I feel terrible.'

The police surgeon prescribed nothing more than hot soup and the warmth of the fire. Brunel fell into a sweat-drenched, daylight sleep on the divan couch, rolling in and out of consciousness to the constant mournful note of a bell from Nôtre Dame Cathedral signalling another defeat. But when he eventually began to take stock of his surroundings, his mind was agile enough to start questioning the dramatic change in his situation. He could find no obvious explanation.

He wrapped a blanket around his shoulders and staggered over to the windows, which gave a view down to the Seine where sailors were working on the *bateaux-mouches*, converting the pleasure boats into floating ambulances. Then he crossed the room and poked his head out of the door. One of the Prefecture servants sat on a chair, reading a newspaper. The man leapt to his feet when he saw Brunel and asked if the captain required anything, adding, 'The doctor prescribed a bath, sir.'

'Was he a real doctor?' Brunel pulled the blanket tight. 'All right, I'll take the bath.'

The salon had a washroom leading off to the side, a square empty room with two doors. There was no plumbing, but Brunel was asked to wait just ten minutes. Within that time a steaming bath appeared, floating with all kinds of shrubbery. He asked the servant what the greenery was for, and was told that the doctor had recommended herbs to be thrown in the water.

There was something hypnotic about the bath. Brunel sat, knees to his nose, in a restful daze. The city grew dark but Brunel did not bother lighting the lamps, content with the glow of the fire. After his bath, he wrapped himself in a gown and stretched out on his divan. This was how Edmond Adam found him when he entered. Brunel did no more than glance in the Prefect's direction. The Prefect offered no salute and took no offence. He just collapsed on a chair.

'Do you want to know what's happening in the city?' Edmond Adam was a plump man. He spoke with a wheeze, as though he had been running, and his bald head was covered in drops of sweat that glistened in the firelight. 'Or should I just thank you for being so patient?'

'Tell me what's happening. I heard the city is on the brink of an explosion, and I must remain here.'

'It's official, Metz has surrendered. The confirmation came an hour ago, so Trochu can no longer claim the story is a Prussian ploy designed to sap our will. I think this could spark a full-scale rebellion against his government.' The Prefect almost had his breath back. He lifted a bottle of wine that he seemed to have produced from thin air and rolled it around in his hands as he asked: 'Do you want to share this with me?'

'You are happy to drink with me, but scared to release me? Am I supposed to be a traitor or a Red?'

'I know Trochu lied about you. He'd been holding briefings with his left-wing ministers. It was he who told Louis Delescluze.' The Prefect named the leader of the left-wing bloc in the Republican Government. 'And God knows why, but Delescluze told Gustave Flourens, who told the editor of *Le Combat*, who printed the news. It was only when Trochu realised the effect it would have on the Belleville battalions that he tried to deny the story was true.'

'So he branded me a spy?'

'Yes. And he's the President, so I had to believe him. If it's a comfort, General Ducrot is so angry at the way Trochu has treated you that he's barely coherent. At my guess, I will be able to release you by tomorrow evening.' Edmond Adam pulled the cork from his bottle and held the bottle to his nose. 'So let's drink to that.'

'Why can't you release me now?'

'Here's the irony. It's impossible and, again, it's all the fault of Gustave Flourens. He's demanding your release – and it's no time for us to be seen giving in to demagogues.' The Prefect poured two glasses of wine. 'Flourens seems to have taken quite a shine to you. Have you got any idea why that might be?'

Brunel took a gulp of wine. 'Is this anything to do with a cow?'

The firelight played across the Prefect's face. He was smiling for the first time since he arrived in the room. 'What was the idea of giving Babette Hébert a cow? You know the butcher would have got you arrested if Trochu had not beaten him to it.'

'It's generally known, then?'

'I'd say it's rumoured.' Edmond Adam was clearly beginning to enjoy himself, spinning out Brunel's exploits. 'Don't worry. I warned the butcher that he was better off keeping quiet. If he kicked up a fuss, people might start wondering how many other animals he has hidden around Paris. He took my point and Babette allowed him to reclaim the cow. But only after she had squeezed the poor beast dry.' The Prefect wiggled his nose in his handkerchief, snuffling back a burst of laughter. 'Cheer up, man. You seem more worried about being branded a cow thief than a Prussian spy.'

'Why not? I really am a cow thief.'

'True. But out of the most romantic of impulses. It's so auda-cious, it might even work on her.'

'It won't.' Brunel's eyes drifted back into the fire. 'There's more to the story. Before I knew who he was, I upset her son.'

'You might have upset him – but so what? Everyone knows the marriage is dead.'

The photography clerk's face came grinning around the door, hair like black corkscrews almost filling the frame. The gap between his front teeth gave him a look of cunning as he said, 'Remember me? Raoul Rigault!' Brunel had been awake for less than an hour. He nodded to Rigault out of recognition, not in greeting. But the man swam into the room, his shoulders rolling.

'What is this? This is luxury. They are terrified of you, my friend.'

He made his progress around the room, entirely unembarrassed as he wandered through the side door and shouted, 'Fantastic. Look at that bath. You could stage an orgy in there.'

'Are you here for a reason?' Brunel suspected the man was just sightseeing.

'I'm bringing greetings, my friend. Gustave Flourens is thinking of you.' Rigault reappeared back in the salon. 'He wants you to know that you are not forgotten. The word is out. A new spirit is growing.'

Brunel's breakfast lay on the sideboard. Raoul Rigault alighted on it, grabbing a drumstick in his paw. 'Who's got the money for chicken? No one I know. The times we live in, hey? When the struggle throws up these kinds of anomalies. The more dangerous the man, the better they provide for him.'

Over the next half-hour, Rigault filled his patter with asides of this kind, as well as praise for both Flourens and Brunel, and declarations on the imminence of great changes. On the surface, it seemed that Rigault was enjoying the comedy of the situation: that he was freeloading off a prisoner, eating better food than he could afford on a clerk's wages. But there was a dark edge to his performance. Brunel suspected that not only was Rigault more angry than he seemed, but that behind his empty phrases he also knew more than he was saying. Yet the only significant information that he brought to Brunel was that President Trochu was holding crisis meetings in the Hôtel de Ville while outside, a great demonstration was building.

More news of the demonstration came in the afternoon, and from a far more welcome source. Babette Hébert visited Brunel in his suite and although she sat as far from him as she could, she revealed a warmth he never suspected she possessed. Even her account of the growing unrest in the city was filled with good humour. She told him how she had met the Prefect in the Place Vendôme, smelling a battalion of Nationals in order to gauge their loyalty.

'The Prefect was smelling the troops?' Brunel was a step behind her throughout the tale, too busy trying to work out if her decision to visit him was proof of a romantic interest. She had taken more care handing her coat to the servant than she had in greeting him. However, the coat was drenched, and surely the fact that she had walked to see him in a rainstorm meant something. 'What did he think the smell would tell him?'

'He said he was sniffing out hotheads, on the assumption that only cool heads bathe.' Beneath the coat, Babette was wearing a simple dark dress and a Spanish-style jacket. Brunel assumed the jacket was to cover the scars on her arms. Its length emphasised the trim symmetry of the span of her shoulders and the width of her backside. 'You know each quartier raises its own battalions, and votes on its officers. Edmond Adam only trusts the ones from the most fragrant districts.'

'How did they smell?'

'Rank. They stank to high heaven. But without gas, only the older buildings with wood-burning stoves have spare hot water, so it's not exactly an accurate indicator. He might have been better asking them to turn out their pockets and seeing which ones came with money and which ones had brought their hunger.'

She smelled stinging fresh, of lemons and lavender. He had caught it as they touched hands, as they greeted each other. He caught it again when she raised herself up and looked over his shoulder at the divan.

'Are you feeling unwell?'

The divan was made up as a bed, the blankets turned back on the sheet. Brunel had told the servant not to clear the bedclothes away. It seemed a mistake all of a sudden, and he groped for an excuse. 'I caught a chill on my first night.' This was not going well, presenting himself as an invalid. He paused and tried a different tack, waving a hand around the salon. 'If I look uncomfortable, it's just that I've never entertained anyone in so much style.'

'You should get arrested more often.'

There was coffee on the table, served in china cups and accompanied by Madeleine biscuits. The salon had two windows, floor to ceiling, and even in the heavy rain the room seemed light and airy. Whatever could be furnished, was. Whatever could be polished, shone. The situation was so obviously crazy; he could not see why it had not resolved itself yet.

'Is the city really about to blow up?' he asked.

'I don't know. There are thousands demonstrating in the middle of a rainstorm, which is hardly a good sign, but I saw no sign of any planning. Though what would I know? Edmond Adam's the expert, he's the one with the spies.'

Abruptly, Brunel said what was on his mind. 'Forgive me, Mme Hébert. Why did you come?'

'Because . . . I wanted to apologise for having you thrown out of my restaurant.'

'No one invited me. You have nothing to apologise for.'

'I also wanted to thank you for keeping our wager. I don't think I've ever appreciated a prize more.'

He spoke without thinking: 'I didn't realise I'd hit on anything so romantic.'

'I'm not looking for romance.'

Brunel was standing at the table, the coffee pot in his hand. He nodded at Babette, showing that he understood her. Then he cast his eyes down to the tray, replacing the coffee pot and turning it slightly so that the handle lined up with those of the cups. He looked up again. He said, 'Madame, I'm not looking for romance either. I didn't come to the city to improve my social life. I came to fight. Nothing has gone to plan. The city is a madhouse. I've been arrested twice, I've been accused of spying and inciting revolution, I've found myself promoted, assigned to the staff of General Ducrot, and I've been branded a traitor by President Trochu. That's not the worst, though. The worst is that I'm no better than anyone; I've gone mad, too. I've been pursuing you and doing it so crazily that I dread to think what effect I have had on you. I think I might have done better if I had been trying to scare you off.'

Even this attempt at a grand speech was running off its rails. He added, 'I have no idea what I'm even trying to say.' Somewhere behind him, Brunel was conscious of a knocking but he ignored it, convinced that if he didn't keep plunging forward he was going to regret it later.

'Something is persuading me to act out of character. And if I am having trouble explaining what it is, it's because it's new to me. I've never before felt driven into acts of . . . of . . . I don't want to say insanity.' He paused. He searched. He found the word. 'I want to say passion.'

'I'm not looking for passion.' Babette tried to cushion her words with a smile. A goodbye smile.

Brunel was fast losing the urge to speak. Behind him, the knocking had been replaced by a tapping sound. He turned and saw the servant standing inside the room, but tapping at the door jamb, as though he was still asking permission to enter.

'Sir, the Prefect's wife demands to see you. Monsieur le Préfet has been taken hostage.'

Gustave Flourens had taken advantage of the demonstrations outside the Hôtel de Ville to launch an insurrection. He now held the Prefect, the President and a good number of his ministers hostage. The Deputy Prefect confirmed the details when he appeared; he had insisted on preceding Mme Adam because she was in such a desperate state, he said, she was not thinking clearly. When she had learned that Babette and Brunel were in the building together, she had drawn her own conclusions about the rebellion. A conclusion that was not entirely lucid.

This became clear when the woman stalked into the salon, turning on Babette with cold burning anger. 'This is Gustave Flourens' revenge. Since you got Edmond to rough him up, he's been biding his time. He has his perfect moment now. He has Edmond at his mercy.'

Brunel recognised Mme Adam as one of the diners at Chez Babette on the night that the Prefect had escorted him from the restaurant.

Babette said, 'I doubt that Florence seized the government out of vengeance on your husband, madame.'

'You doubt it, do you, Madame Babette?' The Prefect's wife put a sour twist on a name everyone else used affectionately. 'What is it? A feeling? A presentiment, perhaps? Do you want to know my feeling? I feel Flourens is going to drag Edmond down to the cellars and put a bullet in his head.' She turned on Brunel. 'And you. You think I've forgotten? You dress like a soldier, but have the swagger of a street thug. Wouldn't you love to see Edmond dead?'

'I barely know your husband, madame. But I do respect him.'

Mme Adam had no retort; instead she picked a biscuit off the plate on the table and threw it in Brunel's face. It bounced off his forehead.

Eventually, Mme Adam's fury subsided and she collapsed on to a chair. Yet as she sat, waiting for news from the Hôtel de Ville, she kept twisting her thumb in her other fist as though winding herself up for a fresh attack. The Deputy Prefect attempted to contact the rebels by telegraph, but they appeared to have no-one at their end capable of monitoring the equipment. So then he had spies placed in the square outside the Hôtel de Ville, and they brought back reports of Gustave Flourens' speeches, which were frequent and intemperate, yelled from the windows of the building.

Brunel saw no reason to remain a prisoner in the building. He and Babette slipped out of the room together, leaving Mme Adam in the care of the Deputy. It was still raining. Sheets of water fell on the courtyard at the centre of the Prefecture. As they stood in the lobby, collecting Brunel's confiscated belongings and waiting to discover what had been done with Babette's wet coat, the Deputy Prefect reappeared at their shoulder. And now he did have news.

'There's a group of Nationals heading down the quay. Perhaps seventy strong.'

'Are they coming here?' Brunel asked.

'I think so.'

It was Babette who saw the guards give way at the main gates. She heard the commotion coming from the street and reached the window as the gates swung open. Brunel reached the door in time to see the rebels flood into the courtyard. There were indeed about seventy men, all armed. They were led by the imposing figure of Raoul Rigault, marked by the width of his grin and his black hair that, with the weight of the rainwater, now hung below his shoulders.

Someone let out a cry, which brought a swift retort – the rebels fired a round into the air. The gunshot echoed through the Prefecture.

Raoul Rigault strode up the steps to the entrance hall, his men clustered behind him, filling the portico. Rigault was breathless but exultant, flushed with excitement and all but ready to take up a champion's pose.

'Gentlemen. It's my pleasure to inform you we have a new government.'

He turned his head so that all those gathered in the lobby could share his smile, share his moment. Seeing Babette for the first time, he added, 'I beg your pardon. Gentlemen and ladies . . . and Captain Brunel.'

Brunel was holding his revolver, hurriedly grabbed from the policeman who was returning it. 'What are you doing here, Rigault?'

'Surveying my fiefdom. I have been appointed the new Prefect of Police. I welcome you all. Please be so kind as to give your names to my deputy here.' He nodded to a smaller man at his side, a crushed copy of himself.

Brunel said, 'Who made you Prefect, Rigault?'

'His Excellency the new President, Gustave Flourens.'

Brunel attempted to keep his voice flat, the tone convincing as he said, 'I don't think so. Flourens appointed me . . .' He paused, letting the lie sink in. 'I received the telegram almost an hour ago.'

'Why would he appoint you?'

'Why would he appoint a fucking clerk? We're not having an argument here. If you have a problem, take it up with Flo.'

Brunel brought his pistol up to waist level, letting Rigault's men see as he cocked the hammer, although he kept the barrel aimed at the floor.

Rigault's grin was twisting around his face, the red flush fading to a pale anger.

'That fucking cretin.' Raoul glared at Brunel, but the blast of anger was followed by a moment of lucidity. 'How do I know you're telling the truth?'

Brunel levelled his pistol at Rigault. 'Do you want to read the telegram? Why not step up here and give your name to one of my deputies.'

Rigault looked at the men at Brunel's side. It was clear that the policemen were gaining their resolve. Brunel had given them backbone.

'I'll give you three seconds to make up your mind, Rigault. *One.*'

Rigault's men had arrived as a phalanx and were now strung across the courtyard in disarray.

'*Two.*'

All around the edges of the yard, policemen were coming out to see what was happening, some armed, some not. Rigault's men were nervous, but also dazed that they had lost the initiative so quickly.

'*Three.*'

Raoul Rigault held up his hands. 'I'm going to speak to Flo.' He turned, shouting from the portico, 'Get around this wagon, everyone. We're on our way.'

Brunel whispered to the Deputy Prefect, 'What's he doing?'

The Deputy had remained silent throughout the attempted

putsch, although he had stood resolute at Brunel's side with the wit not to give him away. Now he tried to decipher Raoul Rigault's antics in the courtyard. 'It looks like he's stealing a wagon.'

The rebels had formed a ring around the wagon, which picked up speed as it approached the gates. Its tarpaulin caught as it scraped through, catching on the edge of the gate and pulling free. The wagon's cargo was revealed: cartons. Raoul Rigault grinned over his shoulder, making an obscene gesture at Brunel as he disappeared. Around him, papers lifted into the air, were held for a moment in the rain and then drifted to the cobblestones.

Mme Adam appeared at Brunel's elbow. She caught his attention by punching him in the side. 'Are you going to shoot him or not?'

Brunel showed her his pistol, the cylinder flipped out. She could see that it was empty.

Brunel asked the Deputy Prefect, 'What's he stolen?'

The Deputy shrugged, but another policeman answered. 'Photographs. He's been loading that wagon all week. We wondered what he was up to.'

Air and Space

When Elise left Flavie's apartment, shortly after one o'clock, she waited a few minutes on the lower floor, then crept back to my door. The light switch is on a timer, so she made the return journey in the dark. I considered ignoring her, but she knew I was inside, having caught me spying at the window. We spoke in whispers in the dark of my hallway. She told me that nothing had happened between her and Flavie. *Didn't I believe her? Did I want to smell her?* She muzzled up to me and I took a pace backwards until I sank into the coats and jackets on the rack behind the door. Elise was telling the truth; I could smell Flavie's cologne but not the smell of sweat or sex.

Elise asked if I thought she was a liar. I told her, 'I know you're a liar. I've just seen you crying out of one eye and winking to me with the other.'

'That's true,' she said. 'And when all that drama builds up inside, you need a release. Do you want to help me out?' She had her arms around me, her breath in my ear. 'Do you want to help me out of these clothes?'

We came very close to kissing but I broke away saying, 'I think you had better leave now.' How often in a life can one say that? *I think you had better leave now.*

Elise did leave, but only because she could not start a fight without alerting Flavie. She told me, 'You know you're going to regret this,' and she meant it. I could hear the menace in her voice. But I found myself staring at her mouth, and especially at the gap between her two front teeth. I must have noticed this before, but it had barely registered. Now it seemed to have a physiognomical significance, to hint at something dark.

It was three days later before I got a chance to spend time with Flavie. It came at a cost. I had to devote my Saturday to escorting a school group around the Air and Space Museum at Le Bourget. Flavie had volunteered me as a favour to Marguerite Galperin.

The school day starts early in France but Flavie had brought along a flask of black coffee to get me up to speed. The bus to Le Bourget found every reason to crawl, even though the rush-hour traffic ran in the opposite direction. But we made it to the museum in time to see Marguerite Galperin herding sixty-odd children off the school coach. She was almost one hundred metres away, at the far side of the car park, but there was no mistaking the red head rising above the eight- and nine-year-old kids. I felt Flavie's growing agitation. I still have no idea what is so devastating about Marguerite but it is clear that she is not meant for me. I could never be attracted to Marguerite Galperin. Flavie could never be attracted to me. Elise could be tempted by either of us, but only in the service of other desires: to wound, maim and spread misery over as wide an area as possible. Marguerite has the best possible position because she is outside the game, oblivious to the whole galaxy of intrigues that orbit around her. At that moment, I wished I was out of it, too.

Except, of course, Marguerite does have a weakness. It was so obvious that I almost didn't see it. I had come on the school trip as Flavie's fake boyfriend, providing a heterosexual alibi. But it was not Flavie's reputation I was protecting; no one cared about her sexuality. It was Marguerite who was trying to keep her private life from becoming a factor in her day job. The way Marguerite rushed across the car park only confirmed it. She was anxious and she was over-compensating, thanking us too effusively.

This strained cheeriness continued as Marguerite introduced us to the other staff members and parent volunteers. We were a mixed bunch, we responsible adults; one wore a hijab, another was a pensioner. I stood out because I was the only man. I wondered if this alone gave the game away: that Marguerite was trying too hard, and too many people were already suspicious of her sexuality. But that was far from being my primary worry. I was scared that, as the only man, I would attract all the macho kids; all the macho little boys followed by all the coquette little girls. And in the end, I would have the bad kids group.

I worried too soon. Marguerite clapped her hands and the children gathered into nine pre-arranged groups. Mine was the balloon group, identified by the children's hand-drawn badges. Other groups included: Concorde, biplanes, satellites and helicopters. All of a sudden, I began to get a good feeling about the day. I liked the badges, I liked the multiple-choice worksheets. I bought a pair of aviator sunglasses for my son Evan from the museum shop as Marguerite collected our tickets. Everything would be fine.

I had always intended to visit the Air and Space Museum for research. Two important battles were fought on the site: one over the weekend that Brunel spent imprisoned in the Prefecture, and another, repeat attempt at Christmas. I wanted to see the lay of the land, and I wanted to visit the museum to learn more about balloon technology. But it is impossible to make detailed notes while supervising seven young children, so I left my notebook in my pocket.

We stood and watched a working miniature model of a hot-air balloon, invented in France, 1783. The children ticked it off their worksheets. Moving deeper into the museum, I found a poster advertising a daredevil balloon display by Nadar, but the children had no interest in old posters and even less enthusiasm for a wooden valve, as used to control the hydrogen or coal gas inside balloons at the time of the siege. I might have been in charge of the balloon group but the children were more attracted to the beautiful and fragile biplanes that were suspended from the roof of the next hall. This was criss-crossed with steel gantries that took us right up beside the aeroplanes. The kids loved it, banging their feet to make the steel sing.

Flavie was on the far side of the hall, clearly in a panic that one of her group would throw themselves over the gantry rail. I was more confident around children. And because my spoken French is about equal to an eight-year-old's, once my ear was tuned to the kids' accents I found I was more relaxed with the language than at any time since I had arrived.

Marguerite Galperin smiled as our groups collided at the foot of a staircase. She asked if the children were behaving themselves. I told her, it was no problem, I was good with this age group. 'I have a son.'

'Is he this age?'

'He was. Five years ago.'

'Oh. Then you don't see so much of him?'

'No. He lives with his mother and her husband. But I do see him.'

I hate sounding defensive over this issue. But Marguerite has a soothing manner, and though I suspected that she had picked it up in a non-judgmental training session it was welcome. I smiled back and moved on, calling my group together to check on their worksheets, making sure we were all on the same page.

The Air and Space Museum is built on a vast plain to the north of Paris, not great for modern infantry battles, but perfect for airport runways. The museum occupies the site of the original Paris airport, and the old landing strips are largely intact and dotted with exhibits. As we walked under the wings of a Mirage fighter jet, one of the two black kids in my group asked if I knew how to fly. I told him that I didn't know, I had never tried. Did he think he could fly one?

'No problem.' He nodded vigorously, liking the idea. Then he asked, 'What did you do in the army?'

'I'm English. We don't have to join the army unless we want to.'

'Didn't you want to?'

'Yes, I wanted to. But I wanted to do other things more.'

'What?'

'Hang out, meet girls.'

The answer satisfied him. For the next task on the work-sheet, we had to sketch the shark grin painted on the nose of a Thunderchief. The outline was ready printed on the work-sheet, they only had to fill in the teeth. I flipped ahead a few pages and saw there was a question about the Spitfire on display in the next hangar. I decided I would give them a lesson in the superiority of British engineering, rivet by rivet.

Across the runway, Flavie looked harassed. One little girl had hooked on to her and would not let go. This slowed Flavie down. She had to drag the girl with one hand and constantly crane her neck, scared that her group would run into trouble around the next corner. I caught her eye and waved. She smiled back, but it was a wild kind of smile.

I caught up with Marguerite Galperin by Concorde. We had to stand in a queue to take our turn inside the aircraft and I was surprised that the children were so patient, that Concorde had a romance for them when they were a quarter of a century younger than us. I had no idea if the children appreciated its history or what I felt was its very real mystique. Or whether they were simply intrigued because one caught fire and crashed last year and the whole fleet of planes had been grounded.

One of my girls asked, 'What kind of aeroplane hit the Twin Towers?'

I did not know. I guessed all four were Boeings, but whether they were 757s or another model, I could not say. Oddly, I remembered the flight numbers: Flights 11 and 175 hit the World Trade Towers. Flight 77 hit the Pentagon. Flight 93 came down in Pennsylvania.

'Who planned it?' she asked. 'The Americans or the Jews?'

I was caught completely off-stride. I wonder if I would have been less surprised if one of the Muslim kids had asked the question. Sophie was white French. I had no idea where she developed her confidence that 9/11 was a conspiracy. It had to be her parents' opinion; she was too young to have understood any of the revisionist theories that had begun to be peddled in newspapers and on chat shows.

'Neither. It was Al-Qaeda.'

As I answered, I looked over at Marguerite, wondering how she would handle the question: a left-wing Jew and a supporter of the Palestinians.

She crouched down with a smile. 'There's a lot of evidence, Sophie. If we look at it all calmly, the evidence against Al-Qaeda is convincing. There is no reason for us to blame anyone else.'

She handled the question so well that I felt guilty for doubting her. We exchanged shrugged smiles over the little girl's head, but had no time to analyse the issue. The queue had begun to move. We were entering Concorde.

Concorde prototype 001 is a real cigar-tube shape. The effect is emphasised because there are no seats to break up the space. The walls are filled with instrument panels, sealed behind plexiglas. The ceiling is so low, it is only possible to stand up straight at the centre of the aisle. And the aisle is so narrow, even the children had difficulty pushing past each other.

I turned and said over my shoulder, 'Flavie thinks a lot of you.'

'Oh, Flavie is great. She is so alive.'

'Yeah.' This sounded inadequate. After a pause I added, 'Moving to a strange city, I've been lucky to have her as a neighbour.'

'That was good luck.'

'Yes.' I saw a chance to move the conversation along. 'Except when she was arguing with her ex-girlfriend Elise.'

Marguerite tensed. We were in a bottleneck caused by a group of aeroplane enthusiasts. These bespectacled men were so fascinated by the different instruments that as they tore themselves away from one bank of dials, they were instantly ensnared by the next. I turned again.

'Have you met Elise?'

'I've known Elise for years.'

This was news to me. They were so unlike each other, I would have thought they were incapable of existing in the same space.

'I didn't know that.'

'An old friend.'

'A *friend*?'

She looked away, but I had got the message. And with it, Marguerite lost all the advantages I had ascribed to her. She was no longer on the outside of the game. In fact, she was a key player – not like me, stubbornly hanging in, allowing myself to be manipulated by Elise.

'You were lovers?'

'I can hardly talk about it here.'

The kids were banging on the plexiglas screens, impatient to get moving. Marguerite looked away from me, raising her voice as she told her group to calm down. The aircraft enthusiasts continued to coalesce over the instrument panels and hold up everyone else. Perhaps they pictured themselves on the early test flights, breaking the sound barrier, watching the needles and gauges as they registered the stresses on the fuselage. I imagined the needles myself, quivering on the red, as Marguerite grew more and more uncomfortable. It was my decision now, whether to push or whether to leave it.

I said, 'I'm sorry.'

'That's okay.'

'It's just, Elise, you know. She is putting Flavie under a lot of emotional pressure. Manipulating her, even lying.'

'I will not talk about this. Please don't let the children out of your sight.'

I looked down the cabin. My kids were getting away. I should have gone after them but I wanted to know more. As the kids escaped, the crush in the cabin eased, simultaneously relieving the pressure I was putting on Marguerite.

'Have you spoken to Elise recently?'

'I'm sorry. Let me through.' Marguerite was agitated, but she was also determined. In a second, she had pushed me to the side and squeezed away. She was halfway down the aisle before I could take stock. She was so thin that every gap became an escape route.

The aircraft enthusiasts became aware of events around them – I made them aware, physically pushing them aside. It was like swimming through modelling clay, not easy but possible, as long as I kept my strokes long and strong, gouging out lumps as I went.

I shouted instructions to my group, telling them to wait at the foot of the stairs. They were bunched together like a circle of anoraked pixies when I got there, but there was no sign of Marguerite.

'Come on.' I started across the hangar.

The conspiracy girl, Sophie, said, 'I'm not ready.'

'What's the problem?'

'I haven't finished the question on Concorde.'

'We can do it later. Hurry up.'

I reached the door to the next hangar and held it open. This led to the Arianne rocket. My group gazed up, their mouths open.

'We'll come back to it,' I snapped. 'Keep moving.'

I made herding gestures with my hands as my eyes swivelled across the hall, searching for any sign of Marguerite. I had a horrible premonition of what I was about to do. I saw a train wreck coming. But I had to get to the bottom of this.

These exhibits were devoted to space travel and in a darkened corner, inside a cube, a film was playing of the view of earth from a satellite. An orange line broke across the horizon, flowing like molten metal and then bursting over the earth's rim. As the light expanded, I saw Marguerite's silhouette. She stood at a bench, behind her sitting kids.

Silently, I directed my group to the spare benches. And then I crept towards Marguerite.

'Here you are.'

She turned to me, her voice reduced to a hiss. 'Listen, James.

If I wanted to air my personal life, do you think I would have asked Flavie to bring a boyfriend with her? Flavie said you would be considerate. Is this your idea of considerate?'

Even in this dim, reflected light, I could feel her stare. I dropped my eyes and muttered, 'Sorry.' I could be the eight-year-old. But I was not done. Not quite.

'It's just that Elise is using me, too. Don't you think we should stand up to that bitch?'

'No. I have to respect Elise, too. What do you do to your ex-lovers? I respect Elise and she deserves no less.'

I could not quite absorb her message. But then Arianne's booster rockets fired, lighting up Marguerite's face in all its freckled innocence.

'You love and respect Elise?' I said. 'How stupid are you?'

A face of freckles, innocence, sadness and hurt. I had gone too far. I wondered if the next word out of my mouth would be an apology or a question. A third group of kids had entered the cube, jostling their way on to the already crowded benches. They were too boisterous, falling over each other as they fought for space. I moved in closer to Marguerite, and as I moved I found myself swaying aggressively, bristling with irritation.

'I mean it: how stupid are you? Elise is fucking with you, fucking with Flavie and coming round to my apartment to fuck me behind everyone's back.'

These new kids were out of control, leaping and pushing each other. And I was feeding them, via my aggression, although I doubt any of them understood the actual words. I turned, gathering myself, getting ready to bring them back in line.

Flavie was right behind me. There was no doubt, she had heard every word.

The Battle for the Hôtel de Ville

Babette might have rejected him but as they shared an umbrella, the pressure of her body against his arm gave him hope. The rain swirled around them, scattering the remnants of the crowds to the very edges of the square. A few hours ago, there might have been demonstrations. Now, Flo's supporters huddled close to the walls of the buildings surrounding the Hôtel de Ville, standing beneath awnings or porticoes while the unlucky ones held newspapers over their heads.

Babette pointed upwards. 'He's back again.' Brunel followed the line of her finger. The light was fading but Flo was recognisable at an open second-storey window, his long hair flying in the wind. He was the main attraction, yet he had to struggle to hold his place as faces reared above his shoulder or appeared beneath his arm. There had to be as many people inside the building as outside in the square. Some waved to the crowd, others made lewd gestures behind Flo's back.

As Flo's voice rang out – 'My loved ones, citizens, my friends' – the crowds unwrapped themselves and surged forward into the heart of the square.

'My friends. Your fervour infects us all, we feel it pulsing through the walls of this building. It brings blood to the centre and fires the heart of this great Republican endeavour.' A rousing crescendo, followed by a diminution. 'My friends, Metz has fallen. Now we hear that Trochu's negotiator, the weasel Adolphe Thiers, has come fresh from sucking the Kaiser's cock to persuade us to surrender. We, the sovereign people of Paris. Surrender! I have released Trochu with orders to tell this cur that Paris will never surrender. Never!'

Flo was glossing over events. He had not released Trochu at all. President Trochu and Prefect Adam had escaped from the building, helped by the chaos of Flo's endeavour. Since their escape, Trochu and Adam had been holding a closed council in the Tuileries to hammer out a plan to bring the city back under their control.

'We feed off your energy,' Flo continued. 'We feed. We drink deep.' This brought cries asking how deep Flo had drunk. The laughs seemed to create a response; Flourens flung an arm out of the window, perhaps a salute. But then a sheet of paper appeared, flickering as it tumbled through the dusk. Flo was throwing another ballot list to the crowd.

'Who will lead us? We have the names, they are your men, driven by your energy. Give them your voice, citizens of Paris, because with your voice, the world receives its clarion call: liberty, fraternity, equality.'

The paper was caught by a young man in a National Guard hat and oilskin coat. He fumbled, trying to unfold the piece of paper before an older man snatched it from his hands. In a strong, clear voice the old man read out the details of Flo's cabinet.

'President and Minister of War: Commandant Gustave Flourens.'

There were both cheers and laughter – yes, give Flo both jobs, keep him out of mischief.

'Minister of Works: Dorian.'

The name of Dorian could always be relied upon to raise a cheer, just as it had when he appeared at the Comédie Française with the aeronaut, Nadar. There was no hint as to whether Dorian had put his own name forward but it was doubtful; he was still a hostage with all the rest of the ministers who had failed to make a break with the Prefect.

Brunel asked one of the demonstrators, 'How long has this been going on?'

'All afternoon. They're still working on the cabinet.'

The Hôtel de Ville was linked to the Napoleon barracks across the road by a subterranean passageway. Trochu and the Prefect believed that neither Flourens nor any of the other Red leaders knew of the tunnel's existence. After long and fractious debates, they had agreed that only the tunnel offered hope of a swift end to the insurrection.

Brunel and Babette found Adam in the barracks' inner courtyard, a middle-aged banker-like figure holding a rifle, trying to impose his authority on the uncomprehending Bretons. When he caught sight of Babette and Brunel, he broke out of the circle, surprising Brunel by greeting him with an extravagant embrace and thanking him profusely for protecting Madame Juliette, his wife. Brunel would have protested, but all at once the Prefect was hissing in his ears: 'Is it true you speak Breton? They're claiming they don't understand me but I don't trust them at all.'

'Yes. I speak Breton.'

'Thank God. If these bumpkins start shooting, it will be a massacre. Someone has to make them see sense.'

'I'll do my best, sir.'

'Christ. This is going to be a new ordeal.' The Prefect rubbed his hands together, drying them before he turned to greet Babette. 'You came with Captain Brunel? No one saw you enter?'

Babette reassured him. 'No one paid the least attention. Who would hang around the back, here, when Florence is putting on such a great show at the front of the building?'

Even in his nervous state, the Prefect managed a short grin. 'That man loves the sound of his own voice. All the time he held us hostage, he stood on top of a table talking his gibberish. But, thank the Lord, if there was any semblance of order, I doubt we would have got out. They are tiring, and we have the element of surprise. I think the chances are good that we can find deliverance without shedding blood.'

The Prefect had been waiting for nightfall, reasoning that the crowds would drift away even more quickly after dark. But now there was a new deadline. In the past half-hour, word had come from Porte Maillot that General Ducrot was on the move, and that he was bringing field artillery and machine-guns to deal with Gustave Flourens' insurrection. This would be the only chance to attempt a peaceful end to the coup.

Babette had been intrigued by the idea of a secret tunnel. She approached the entrance, marked by a brazier. As dusk slumped down, the orange coals glowed brighter. The Bretons gathered around, holding paraffin lamps.

It was time to go.

The men queued as the lamps were lit, one by one. Brunel hung back, unsure how the words would sound when he told Babette that he wanted to see her again.

He said, 'You're not looking for romance, I know. But you're going to find me standing outside your restaurant.'

'Let's leave this alone, monsieur. Don't begin to pin your hopes on me.' Her face looked bright despite the dismal evening. 'Let me know when you are back safe. I'll be waiting for word.'

The Prefect drew close. 'We need to move. Get your lamp.'

Brunel turned to look back as he started down the steps, but he was deep inside the pack of Bretons and didn't see her leave. The echo of their feet on the stone drove him on, pounding down into the cellars.

Edmond Adam was at his shoulder. 'I'm grateful that you volunteered for this, Captain. After the way Trochu treated you, you would have every right to refuse.'

'Why would I refuse? Flo stages a mutiny and then makes speeches about patriotism; I want to knock his head off.'

The intensity of his response caught the Prefect by surprise. 'I thought you and Flourens were friends. The Prefect lifted his paraffin lamp. He appeared to loom out of the dark as a greenish-orange mask. 'If Auguste Ducrot arrives before us, this will become a bloodbath. Do you want that?'

'If the army doesn't break out of Paris in the next week, we lose everything. This is no time to start a civil war.'

'If we gun down Flo's men, we are more likely to get a civil war. Paris will be ungovernable. That is a stone certainty, sir.' Edmond Adam swung the lamp so close to Brunel that he felt a burning at his cheeks. 'I want your word that you will do nothing to inflame the situation. You are under my command here, not Ducrot's.'

'Yes, sir.'

Brunel wondered if he ought to give the Prefect a hint of the thousands of insults that the Bretons were heaping on the heads of Flo and all Parisians in general. It was a fact: the Prefect was in trouble. He was leading a hundred armed men who loathed everything about the city and its people.

'Translate for me,' Edmond Adam said. Then lifting his voice, 'Let's understand each other. We are here to re-establish discipline, and I want discipline from you.'

Brunel repeated his words in Breton, translating as faithfully as he could.

'This is the plan. I have two battalions of dependable Nationals at the front of the building and they will push their way in through the main gates. That is our diversion. The rebels have been losing men all day, they are tired, they are bored – most likely what they really want is a drink. The insurrection is fizzling out and all we need to do is piss on the embers.'

Deep in the tunnel, lamps aloft and rifles in their hands, the Prefect asked, 'How do you think my speech went down?'

Brunel told him, 'Fine. You did well,' though the Prefect had won the most credit by placing himself at the front of the column. Brunel crept beside him, his revolver in his hand.

As they reached the door to the cellars of the Hôtel de Ville, Brunel tested it. It was stiff. He whispered to Edmond Adam, 'You push, I'll go through first.'

Brunel braced himself. As Adam pushed, Brunel released all the energy in his body and he was through, swinging his firearm on three shocked men crouched around a paraffin burner. Brunel kicked one in the head and easily covered the remaining two with his pistol.

Adam was out, pattering across the shadowy expanse of the cellar towards the stairs to the ground floor. The Bretons spread out behind him, keeping in good tight formation.

Whispering in Breton, Brunel reminded the first man, 'Whatever happens, only fire on command. Pass it on.'

'What if they shoot first?'

'That's their funeral.'

Edmond Adam was at the foot of the stairs. Brunel rushed to catch up with him. As his eyes adjusted to the dark, he began to notice groups of bewildered men lumbering in the shadows. And these men in turn were only just beginning to grasp that the flickering lamps belonged to a hundred armed men. There was a flare of panic – a voice started shouting. One of the Bretons broke into a sprint and rammed the butt of his *chassepot* into the shouter's mouth.

Brunel gave the command to go.

They charged the steps two at a time, making no effort to muffle the sound. The lobby of the building was so crowded that there was scarcely room to lift an elbow, but the Bretons burst from the cellars with such speed that the force carried them forwards. And as their momentum slowed, they cleared the way by battering through the crowd, using their *chassepots* like fighting staves. Brunel used his revolver, clubbing anyone who didn't clear out of his path. Edmond Adam was just as ruthless: they needed to reach the main staircase before the rebels gathered their forces.

Flourens' men appeared on the balustrade above them. The staircase became the site of a seething rippling panic as those trapped between the guns of Flo's Tirailleurs and those of the Breton Mobiles tried to find escape routes, flailing up or down the stairs. A few showed their courage by diving out over the stair rail, finding themselves borne on the hands of the crowds below them. Brunel hoisted a boy over the edge with his left hand while he levelled his pistol with his right. Among the rifles aimed at him, he recognised the feeble *tabatières*, the standard issue to the Belleville Nationals, but also Spencers and

Remingtons – the rebels had evidently got their hands on one of the caches of American civil war rifles that had been brought into the city before the siege.

Edmond Adam started bellowing, 'Hold your fire.' Brunel turned to repeat the order in Breton and saw their phalanx snaking through the crowd at his back, bristling with rifles like a spiny lizard bursting from the depths of the cellar.

'Hold your fire. We are going to end this peacefully.'

Brunel relayed the Prefect's words and faced forward again, to see how the situation struck the men above them. Perhaps Adam's plan might work. The slightest bit of imagination would make it plain to everyone that the alternative would be horrendous.

'We are going to talk this out.'

'How will you do that, sir?' someone yelled. 'You are already dead.'

'Look outside the building. Look down to the square. You are surrounded and outgunned.'

Brunel pictured General Ducrot arriving with his heavy guns or training his *mitrailleuse* machine-guns on the Hôtel de Ville.

'I'm coming up,' Adam shouted. 'I'm coming to talk.'

'To hell with you.'

'With respect, no. To hell with you.'

Every rifle in that great lobby could have been a living thing. They swung back and forth with each line of argument and bridled at every insult.

'Where is Flo?'

A voice, hoarse from shouting yet almost languid, emerged from the ranks above. 'I am here, Monsieur le Préfet.' With the voice, the face rose up. Flourens was tall enough to appear to float above his men. 'You want to talk, I've been doing nothing else all day. I think I've damaged my throat.'

His hand appeared, holding the neck of a brandy bottle.

'I'm authorised to negotiate by His Excellency President Trochu.'

'Then negotiate. What's your best offer?'

'Free elections and an amnesty for everyone here today.'

Flo paused. He rocked back on his heels, disappearing for a moment so that it appeared he might have fallen over. But then Brunel saw that he was conferring.

The wait grew.

'What's your answer?'

'Patience, sir. I'm not alone up here.'

A messenger had been sent to a distant salon. But finally a rumble began and heads began to nod; something like assent had been conjured out of the masses. Flourens straightened and cast his eye over the lobby, a bubbling lumpy stew, a porridge of heads. He noticed Brunel and nodded. But when he spoke, he addressed everyone.

'We have lived through a crisis, my friends. We faced the abyss of surrender, the ignominious fate that the traitors brought down on to Metz. We learned of decisions made in the dark that would condemn us to servitude. We, slaves? Citizens of France, who alone in this world know the true meaning of freedom? The sacred home of liberty, reduced to silence? No! Paris has found her voice. We accept the offer of free elections.'

The Plan

President Trochu downgraded his promise to hold free elections; instead, he offered a plebiscite, which brought a swift vote of confidence in his government. It was only when he reneged on his second promise and issued warrants for the arrest of the rebels that Edmond Adam resigned as Prefect of the Police. The Mazas prison soon filled with the leaders of Red Paris; only Gustave Flourens avoided capture. Brunel's preparations for the break-out often took him to Belleville, where the factories were retooling to provide parts for the Marsouins' field artillery. Each time he travelled there, he wondered where Flourens might be hiding. The tenements provided a myriad of bolt holes, cloaked by the smoking chimneys and drowned by the constant clank of the presses in the iron and steel works.

Brunel's horsemanship was poor, so he took to riding on a munitions wagon, driven by Aspirant Barclay, now his permanent driver. The young man often reminisced about the meal they had eaten at Chez Babette, and the girl – Murielle, wasn't it? – who had served them. So, one day, Brunel suggested they stop at the restaurant on their return to camp. Barclay could speak to Murielle, and he might also mention that Brunel was waiting outside.

Barclay looked doubtful. 'And what do you want me to do? To speak to Madame Hébert on your behalf? Bring out food?'

'Let's see how it goes.'

That hour outside Babette's restaurant introduced Brunel to all of Babette's regular customers. General Vinoy rolled by, accompanied by two adjutants wearing the glowing white tunics and burnished helmets of the Lancers. The men, Brunel knew, were brothers – nephews of the old general. The younger nephew nodded in his direction but Vinoy showed no sign of recognising Brunel. It was understandable, they had only seen each other briefly since that first meeting at the Comédie Française. Now that General Ducrot had supplanted General Vinoy as commander of the Second Army, Vinoy no longer attended meetings of the Chief of Staff.

It was possible that General Vinoy did not even recognise Brunel, who was lounging against the canvas of the munitions wagon. But when Zizi Hébert glanced over as he entered the restaurant, it was Brunel who almost failed to recognise him. Not that the hairdresser had changed much in the past week; the difference was all in the uniform. Zizi had joined the National Guard and was wearing a modified version of the National's uniform – modified not out of personal vanity, but because his quartier had voted to wear red trousers to distinguish them from other battalions. The trousers were fancy, but the uniform was still vastly more sober than those of General's Vinoy's nephews.

Brunel had been standing outside the restaurant for more than twenty minutes before he realised that Christian was staring down at him from a window above. This was uncomfortable, but Brunel bore it for a while. He now knew something of the family's story. It was true that the marriage was over. Babette and Zizi had separated, and while Christian worked with his father at the Maison de Worth it had made sense that they also lived together. Only after Zizi enlisted in the Nationals had Christian moved in with his mother.

Charles Frederick Worth's mansion was now in the process of being converted into a hospital. Brunel wandered down to the square and watched as a steeplejack skimmed across its roof, decorating the tiles with bright red Geneva crosses. As he was returning to the restaurant, hoping that Christian had tired of staring at him, he almost walked past Edmond Adam, who touched his arm and coughed. 'What a surprise to see you in the city, Captain Brunel. Is Porte Maillot getting too quiet?'

'I am waiting for my aspirant, Monsieur Adam.'

'Here? Chez Babette? Either your aspirant's a millionaire or this is another part of your campaign to win Babette Hébert.'

'I am waiting for my aspirant,' Brunel repeated, stubbornly.

'Then perhaps you saw Babette's husband in uniform? It amazes me how many people are ready to join the Nationals and defend their homes. Everyone has friends or family in uniform, and they all resent General Ducrot's judgement that they are not fit to fight the Prussians.'

Adam sounded bitter but he was tired of the politics of the siege. 'You don't think it is ironic? Instead of Ducrot's break-out, we fight among ourselves.'

'I will not speak about Ducrot or his plans, monsieur.' Brunel could hear the strain in his voice. Edmond Adam had touched a nerve. With each passing day, Brunel saw that the break-out faced new delays and he could not explain why.

'Fine,' the older man said. 'But take a look at the city. Trochu has won his plebiscite, so he's secure. Flourens is on the run, but he's won too. He's shown that if the war is not fought the way Paris likes it, there will be trouble.' Edmond Adam took hold of Brunel's arm; his grip was not tight, not insistent, but gentle. 'Come dine with me. And not Chez Babette. I have even less time for Joseph Vinoy and his family than I have for Auguste Ducrot. Come to Brébants with me.'

'I'm sorry, sir.' Brunel could see Barclay approaching from the alley, smacking his lips after the lunch that Murielle had given him in the restaurant's kitchen. It was now two o'clock and Brunel had promised to pass by the Post Office and pick up the latest intelligence reports for Admiral de la Roncière, ahead of a full conference with the Chiefs of Staff at five-thirty that evening. 'I wish I had thought about lunch, but now I have left it too late.'

'Another time, perhaps.' Edmond Adam started moving off,

but he turned back. 'You know, I wouldn't normally add insult to injury by following political advice with romantic advice. But the way you're pursuing Babette, you look as though you're searching for signs of weakness, not signs of affection.'

Brunel would have objected, but he already spent long nights at Porte-Maillot interrogating his faith that Babette would eventually welcome his attentions.

As he and Barclay rode to the Post Office, the young man offered his own opinion. Perhaps Madame Babette was keeping him at arm's length because of her son.

'Is that what you think?' Brunel asked. 'Or were you told?'

'It's what Murielle thinks. Me, I just don't understand women.'

When they reached the Post Office, Barclay remained outside with the munitions wagon. If had wished he could have waited in the reception, but he was not allowed into the great hall where the carrier-pigeon messages were deciphered. Brunel had once tried to describe this space, beginning with the darkness. The windows were blacked out with paper and covered with heavy drapes. This was more than a precaution against spies; the messages could only be read in the dark. The hall was lit by the flicker of the magic lanterns that projected the micro-filmed messages on to the walls. It was an extraordinary sight, the rows and rows of clerks working in the dark, each in charge of a lantern as they transcribed messages on to paper while, above them, these dancing loops of film, orange-streaked across the Post Office walls, seemed to burn as hot and bright as the furnaces of Belleville.

The Chiefs of Staff were growing nervous. The harder General Ducrot pushed for his break-out, the more space was given to other voices, especially those who argued that no plan would work without the support of the forces outside of Paris. A few weeks ago, Brunel would have said that General Ducrot was capable of driving any argument through, no matter what the opposition. Now he was less sure. There were times, even to

Brunel's ears, when the strategy they had worked so hard to hone sounded like vainglorious bluster in Ducrot's mouth. The General continued to fight his corner, but as the disquiet spread among the other Chiefs of Staff, he was like a man raging against fog or smoke, he wanted to face down his opponents, but their fears were so vague, they could not be smothered or stifled.

In these circumstances, Brunel was hardly surprised to find Ducrot in the pigeon room. There was no one the General trusted to bring favourable news of the army Léon Gambetta was raising in the Loire valley – he had to see the details for himself. And rather than wait for the clerks to do their work, he stood above them, making them speed through the reels of photographs. They had to keep twisting the film through the lantern as he chewed on his cigar, barked insults and read the messages straight from the walls.

General Ducrot had thought the break-out had been set for the week beginning 13 November. But at the meeting of the Chiefs of Staff that evening, President Trochu declared that it must be pushed back another seven days. Brunel expected Ducrot to be apoplectic, but the general left the meeting after making only the briefest protest. The situation was growing so tense that Ducrot thought it was better to accept a delay rather than to push for a date and see the break-out abandoned entirely.

Brunel did not return straight to his quarters. He had made up his mind to revisit Babette's restaurant.

It was not so late, but it was far from clear whether the restaurant was open. Brunel tapped at the door and when Murielle appeared, he asked if she had a table, telling her he would be dining alone. She was flustered and admitted they were expecting a party later. But she was also concerned that Brunel would not be able to afford his meal. Brunel told her not to worry – it was his problem if he was bankrupted by the menu.

General Vinoy's two nephews arrived as Brunel was finishing his soup, the only course he could afford. The brothers were dazzling in their white uniforms, and although they were not drunk they had been drinking. The older called for wine before he had even chosen a table. In moments, more of their friends arrived – evidently, this was the party that Murielle had warned him about. They numbered about fifteen, many of them in uniform, Zizi among them.

The last person to arrive was General Vinoy. As he cleared the threshold, everyone rose from their seats to applaud. Brunel also stood. He clapped his hands, wondering what on earth was happening – what could they be celebrating?

The younger of Vinoy's nephews, Gilles Furet, had seen Brunel often enough to know his position within General Ducrot's circle. He came over, saluting. 'A pleasure to see you, Captain.' He was nervous, yet excited. 'May I ask you to join us, sir. We have a place for you at our table.'

Across the room, Murielle was suddenly squealing, literally jumping up and down with delight.

Brunel asked, 'What's happening?'

'The greatest news. France has won her first victory. The road is clear for the armies of Paris and the army of the Loire to join up.'

This was excellent news, and it came out of nowhere.

'You're surprised, Captain Brunel?'

'I'm glad.' Brunel allowed himself to be taken by the arm. 'How did the news arrive?'

'A messenger crossed the lines – I think the first man to do it since yourself.'

A wine glass found its way into his hand and now Gilles Furet was spilling champagne into it. Murielle was also doing the rounds, making sure everyone had a drink ahead of the toast. Even Babette had appeared; she, too, was holding a glass. Brunel tried to smile at her. This was it – a victory – the start of the break-out.

General Vinoy raised his glass. 'Gentlemen, ladies, to Orléans.'

Brunel was confused; his first thought was that the toast was to the Orléanists, the party of the monarchists. But everyone lifted their glasses and repeated: 'Orléans.' Brunel began to realise that they were drinking to the city.

Brunel whispered to Lieutenant Furet, 'What's happened – has Gambetta's army captured Orléans?'

'That's right.' Furet smiled back. 'What will General Ducrot say to that? We can forget his plans to run off to the Atlantic coast. We are for the direct route. Route One to the south.'

'A victory is good. But it will not affect weeks of preparation.'

'Don't be sure, Captain.' Furet had his arm around Zizi's shoulder. 'What kind of army are we if we can't seize the day?'

Flavie Goes Missing

I was poaching a lunchtime egg when Jean-Luc phoned, convinced that Flavie was missing. I had not seen her since the visit to the Air and Space Museum, but I had not considered that she had actually disappeared. By the time we had sifted the evidence, there was nothing left in the pan but a hard yellow pellet and strings of frogspit in a millimetre of water. I dumped the lot in the swingbin and got right back on the telephone. Over the next few hours, we called as many of Flavie's friends and workmates as we knew. We continuously returned each other's calls. We rehashed what we knew and by three o'clock we were certain that Flavie was a missing person.

She had not spent a single night in her apartment in the past three weeks. I knew this for certain; I had kept a vigil. I was often awake and nearly always at home, what else would I do? I was missing her – in a dumb dull way – but I was not yet worried. I assumed that she was continuing to show for work at the salon; I had a string of rebuffed telephone calls to prove that. Now I learned that she had not been to work for more than a week. I called Elise, who knew nothing, not even unsupported gossip. She admitted that she and Flavie had argued fifteen or twenty days ago and had not spoken since. She promised to call Flavie's parents in Montpellier. Then I telephoned Marguerite at her school. Marguerite was taking a class but the headmistress's assistant promised that she would return my call within the hour. While I waited, I tried putting in a call to the salon. This time they spoke to me; Jean-Luc had already made five calls, which seemed to have spooked them. It appeared that Flavie had arranged to take time off work, but nothing more than a long weekend. Now she was gone longer than they had expected and there had been no further news.

Jean-Luc appeared as I was coming off the call from Marguerite. He could see that I was shaken, and not because Marguerite had been unpleasant towards me. She was far nicer than I deserved. Her cool politeness quickly faded into anxiety when she understood why I had called. She had not seen or spoken to Flavie since the museum visit. Until now, Marguerite had been faintly concerned – now she was genuinely worried.

It turned out that Jean-Luc had a few secrets of his own. He had taken to dropping by the salon every few days. Ten days ago, he had met Flavie for a drink after work. She had told him she was staying with Marguerite – which we now knew was untrue – but he had not seen her since and her unexplained absence from the salon had begun to worry him. As he was telling me this Elise called back to tell us that Flavie was not with her parents either.

Jean-Luc said, 'We should call the cops.'

'Okay.' I reached for the phone. Then stopped. 'Will you do it?'

'Why?'

'You're a lawyer, you deal with the police all the time.'

'But they never like me.'

'Well, my French isn't good enough, so you've got no choice.'

We came up with another plan. Flavie's window lay open and although it was impossible to climb from my window through hers, it could be done from the apartment of the neighbour on the other side. The pair of us crowded at the neighbour's door to explain our idea. Jean-Luc told her we would be looking for clues – for instance, whether Flavie had packed for a journey before disappearing. The neighbour did not take much persuading; she was also disturbed by Flavie's disappearance.

I got out on to the window ledge, reaching across to Flavie's window with one hand as I searched for somewhere to grab hold. When I found my grip, I snaked out a leg and stood on the steel bar that ran across the casement. This was it; now I only had to decide whether I would go or not. I glanced downwards. I had a vision of falling and Jean-Luc trying to grab my belt as I went, the momentum carrying him after me like the streamer on a kite.

Jean-Luc said, 'I wish I didn't look down.'

'I wish I didn't, too. Okay.'

He counted *un, deux, trois*. On *trois*, I swung myself out and around, dropping through Flavie's window with the slinky grace of a sack of potatoes.

Jean-Luc ran to Flavie's front door, followed by the neighbour, who was not going to let anyone traipse over Flavie's apartment unsupervised. As I let them through the door, I noticed a spare set of keys hanging from a hook beneath the coat rack. I slipped them into my pocket, in case I needed to return to the apartment, then joined in the search for evidence of Flavie's safety.

The obvious place to start was the wardrobe; the problem was, it seemed as full of clothes as it could possibly be. Flavie kept her shoes in the original boxes, stacked on top of it. If any were missing, I would not know. We stood staring, the three of us in a line, but we didn't confer. Soon Jean-Luc was off, sniffing around the main room; he walked with his hands behind his back, led by his nose as he looked at the ornaments and the pictures on Flavie's shelves.

He stopped.

'Have you see this before?' He pointed to a photograph in a dull aluminium frame.

Jean-Luc spoke to me but it was the neighbour who stepped forwards. I had thought this small round woman was a little older than us but the more time I spent with her, the more likely it seemed that she was younger. She was married, she had a husband and children, and despite having a son myself, I tended to see anyone with a family as older than me.

The neighbour held the photograph and, in French, expressed

surprise that Flavie should have framed such a strange picture. I walked over and as the reflected glare of the table lamp dissolved away, I saw a glossy scrap of paper torn from a magazine: a photograph of Marguerite Galperin wearing a white jumpsuit and waving handfuls of long green, bushy stalks. I assumed it was taken at a protest against genetically modified crops, and found it oddly touching that Flavie had cut out the picture and framed it. Odd. But touching.

There was a red envelope on the table, addressed to Marguerite. Jean-Luc turned it over and shook it theatrically to show that it was empty. My eye drifted to a waste basket in the corner. The torn fragments of a letter lay in the bin, the same colour red as the envelope. It was easy to reassemble it, beginning from the bottom and the words, 'I still love you,' above Flavie's signature. Flavie was writing, begging for another chance and insisting that she was not a frivolous person. She loved the profundity of Marguerite's commitment to life and the most important issues.

We read the letter twice, looking down on the fragments assembled on the table. It was written out of a desperate love. The three of us – Jean-Luc, Madame the neighbour and myself – were left reeling.

After the neighbour left, Jean-Luc and I continued to discuss the letter in the little bar across the street. It was not the words but the emotion that most struck him, the desperation with which Flavie begged for another chance. Jean-Luc admired Marguerite but, like me, failed to see her sexual allure.

Jean-Luc wondered why Flavie had never sent the letter. He thought it was a worrying sign; she must have felt the situation was so hopeless that it was no longer worth struggling. It was not a suicide note. But it could be read as a final, desperate act. As we talked, Elise called on my cellphone to tell us that Flavie was not with her parents. Then and there we decided we had to call the police.

We lodged Flavie as a missing person. I secretly believed that my behaviour at the museum was the catalyst. No doubt Marguerite felt that as long as Flavie could indulge such a cruel and stupid friend, she would never make a perfect lover.

At four in the morning I found myself wide awake. I had gone to bed early and had fallen asleep almost immediately. God knows why – how one's mind can do that, shut down when it should be thinking. But three hours later I woke, certain that I would not sleep again. So I began writing. And as I wrote, I began to think that the date on the letter made no sense. It was dated the night before we went to the Air and Space Museum, not after. That put me in the clear, from one point of view. But it proved again that I was so far out of the loop. I was utterly insensitive to the state of the relationship between Flavie and Marguerite.

The Attack

The army camp stretched away before him, a maze of blue-black shadows against the charcoal night. Only Ducrot's pavilion stood out, shadowy figures moving within a soft creamy glow. As Brunel entered, the silhouettes resolved into the generals of Paris, standing over the model of their capital. Seeing the whole city like that, shrunk within its walls and laid out on a table, it was possible to imagine picking up the army and moving it from one side to the other, but only for the length of time it took to process the idea. One by one the generals began to raise hypotheses, apologetically, as though this was only a thought experiment, a distraction from their real business. The Orléans road would lead them past the Châtillon Heights, which was dominated by the Prussian guns.

Ducrot pointed to the eastern flanks of the city and ran through the statistics: 'We have four hundred heavy guns, eighty thousand men and equipment, fifty-four pontoons.'

The original plan had called for pontoons to cross the Seine north-west of the city at Épinay-sur-Seine. They were now tempted to head across the Marne, to the south-east of Paris – so they would still need the pontoons. Ducrot used his baton to sketch a route, from Porte Maillot, cutting across from the Champs Élysées down to the quay on the river. From there, the pontoons could be towed under steam the ten or twelve kilometres upriver to where they were needed.

'Is that possible?'

'Not in less than a fortnight. And only if we use every horse in the city.'

Another fortnight would take them to 28 November, by which

time the Prussians would certainly have deployed their forces from Metz. But there were worse problems: Admiral de la Roncière reminded the generals how high the river would be by late November. It was rising every day, the current growing ever stronger. The pontoons were hard enough to control as it was; how much worse they would be in winter floods.

There was a consensus: they were never going to get to Orléans. Any route they cared to choose, they would face disaster. Yet they were going to do it.

Paris never stopped celebrating. As the fever of victory at Orléans took hold, Brunel realised how depressed the city had been since his arrival. Now it was exploding with life, and moving the army seemed a part of that: a spectacle designed purely to entertain the citizens. There were so many thousands of men and equipment on the streets. The boulevards were filled with wagons; the perimeter railway was working twenty-four hours a day. The Seine was a steaming mass of barges and gunships.

Up until this moment, the army had been like a dark star that had played upon the moods of Paris without ever entering fully into its life. Almost every man in the city had signed up for the Nationals and was drawing his daily pay of one and a half francs. As the men of Paris drilled together, debated strategy or argued over the choice of leader, they began to imagine they were fighting the war alone. The decision to keep the professional army separate from the Nationals encouraged this delusion. Now that the army was on the move, many saw it as coming to the aid of Paris, even as the unification of two great forces. And so the abandonment of the Normandy plan for a disastrous strike to the South was reinterpreted as a triumph; worse, as a triumphal procession. Paris came out of its houses and apartments to watch and, once out, began to swarm. The parks and public squares were filled with battalions of Nationals. Every concierge in the city was claiming to have once been a drill sergeant. They leaned on canes, shouting orders,

keeping the men tight, while sipping cheap brandy from medi-
cine bottles. As night fell, the battalions would disperse to the
cafés, or buy in bottles of absinthe and return to barracks. This
was how they learned their fighting spirit, singing songs all
night about Madeleine from Bobigny with a fanny like a bucket.

Brunel would gingerly step his horse across the cobblestones.
The nights were dark, the street lamps were never lit and any
window could surprise him with a half-burst of a song. In the
flickering of a candle or a paraffin lamp, a dozen or twenty
drunken men in improvised uniform would be laughing or
crying. Not all of their songs were filthy. There were also ballads:
a young heart waiting, a bright eye crying, a leg lost on a battlefield.

The differences between the city's districts were never so clear
as when the National Guard were out on the streets. Those who
could afford it had their uniforms tailored. The most popular
regiment by far was the Zouaves, so much so that it had long
ceased to be an Arab regiment and was now full of wealthy young
men dressed as Arabs, while the real Arabs served in the Turcos
regiments. The Zouaves' popularity was reflected in the designs
chosen by the battalions from the western arrondissements,
who copied or improved upon the Zouave uniform, increasing
the size of the pantaloons or the length of the tassel on the fez.
In Belleville, by contrast, it was rare enough to see a man in
matching tunic and trousers. Many would march up and down
in their everyday clothes, topped with a random military cap
or even a helmet.

The central arrondissements were not solidly either bourgeois or working class; the divisions varied from quartier to
quartier. There were sales assistants from the department stores,
stall-holders from the markets, old working-class families who
were holding on despite the rising rents. Then there were the
Freemasons who joined the battalions closest to their lodges;
there were the Jews in the Marais. And, especially, there were
students. The 1st arrondissement was filled with students, not

only from the provinces but from every country across the globe, including the émigrés and refugees from nationalist movements in Eastern Europe. Pass by one of the cafés on the edge of Les Halles and you heard nothing but Polish songs: Patrysja from Poznan with a cunt like a nosebag.

The Nationals now had to be incorporated into the battle plans. President Trochu had insisted upon this and General Ducrot had accepted it without a fight. It must have pained Auguste Ducrot to indulge Belleville, as he saw it, rewarding it for its rebellion. Yet the compromise would bring the Belleville Nationals under the control of professional soldiers and, as he said, 'That is something.'

The one thing that did not change was the role of the marines. They were still going to set out from St Denis to attack the village of Épinay-sur-Seine, but whereas they had once been the key element in the attack, the wedge in the door that would allow the army to break out of the city, they were now merely a diversion. The best justification that General Ducrot could offer for this was to say: 'The Prussians have their spies. No doubt they knew we were planning to break out towards Normandy. If the marines attack Épinay, they might believe it's still the plan.'

'General, yes. But if they have any spies, they'll have noticed the city has been turned upside down. It's clear we are striking south, not west.'

General Ducrot did not respond. The greater part of his task had become organisation and he did not seem to be looking further forward than the planning – as though he knew the battle would be a disaster.

If anything St Denis was in greater turmoil than Paris. The troops that the marines were relieving had not yet left the town and their supply wagons jostled for road space with the equipment of both the Marsouin and the Bigors, as the marine gunners were known. St Denis' children crowded down the streets to the station to watch the marines unload shells for their howitzers and mortars. The shells were brought on flat-bed trucks at night, pulled along the rail track by horses. The biggest guns were already in position, dug into earthworks or placed on the town's walls. There would be four days of shelling from St Denis, then they would attack. A simple plan. It was now the 23rd; they would attack on the 29th.

The retiring commander of St Denis had recommended the view from the top of the cathedral, and Brunel took to going up there, at first with one of the priests and then, as the barrage began and the Prussians returned fire, on his own. On the night of 24 November he saw a balloon leave the city, skimming under the clouds before it rose and disappeared. One of his men later swore there had been two balloons. That would have been reckless when the Prussians were scouring the city for any indication of the coming attack. Then, on the 26th, the gates to the city swung shut, like a semaphore indicating that something was about to happen.

Although visibility was often poor that week, it was never less than three kilometres from the top of the cathedral, giving Brunel a clear arc across the entire northern front, from Épinay-sur-Seine to Le Bourget. The previous commander of St Denis had seized Le Bourget from the Prussians and held it, though only for twenty-four hours before the Prussians took it back. Brunel had read the reports, and the local Francs-Tireurs – the militia of St Denis – could confirm the details. The Prussians attacked the town along a broken line, playing tag across the battlefield as they ran forward, always covered by fire from their rear. Brunel had heard reports of the same tactic being used in the American civil war, but this was the first clear and successful example of it in Europe. The Prussians needed to move rapidly across a battlefield because the French rifles were so efficient. Although the *chassepot* was similar to the Prussian needle-gun, it had a much better seal on the breech. With no loss of gas in the chamber, the concentrated force of the ignition gave the *chassepot* a range of fifteen hundred metres, three times that of the needle-gun. The Prussians needed to cover those fifteen hundred metres as quickly as possible, and every time they broke into the open they needed strong covering fire.

Brunel stood at the top of St Denis Cathedral, his back to the new slate spire that the Emperor had placed on the ancient tower. He turned from Le Bourget towards Épinay. Against the roar of the present barrage, Brunel superimposed an image of his Marsouin on the move, swarming across the farmland in packs, emerging out of the hedgerows and over the stone walls, appearing without warning, always covered by fire. Brunel recalled how easy it had been, at first, to pick off the Saxon soldiers as they had attacked Bazeilles. Brunel had set himself up in one of the foremost positions in the village, an inn that had been built to greet travellers off the highway. As the Saxon line attacked, it kept to its rhythm, monotonously feeding in from the left, and once he had found his range Brunel just kept picking them off one by one.

He thought of this, not because he was sorry for the Saxons he had killed – if anything, their early setbacks might have encouraged the Saxons' later brutality. He was thinking of the Parisian forces, their own Nationals. No one in the army command believed they would hold under fire unless they were in close formation. There had been no attempt to train them to attack in broken lines. All of that drilling, up and down the city streets, shoulder to shoulder, that's how they would move across the battlefield. It was how they were going to die.

The level of the Seine was rising, as Admiral de la Roncière had predicted, and the meadowland was soft underfoot. Brunel imagined Zizi Hébert struggling across a sodden field on the other side of Paris, mud streaked across his new uniform, Prussian bullets raining down on him. The needle-gun was not as good as the *chassepot*, but it was a lot better than the *tabatières* that the Nationals carried. Once Zizi was within five hundred metres of the Prussian lines, his comrades would be collapsing around him, step by step. Given the wrong circumstances – a poor attack, poor ground, untrained men stuck in the open – a battalion of a thousand men might see 60 or 70 or 80 per cent of their men dead within an hour. It had already happened in America.

The Saxons at Bazeilles had soon changed their tactics, softening the defences with shells before a second attack. Atop the cathedral, Brunel looked down on Épinay. The French marine gunners had been shelling the village almost continuously for three days. The return fire was fierce, and the Prussians had the better field artillery. But field guns could only fire along a flat trajectory and the elevation of St Denis meant that the marines had the advantage of plunging fire. They also had their howitzers and their mortars, lobbing shells over the front line in great arcs. The buildings at the edge of Épinay were smashed to pieces, reduced to craggy tombstones wedged upright between great piles of rubble. During the day, the devastation was largely hidden behind a rolling, pounding cloud of dust. But at night, fires burst out of the dark, and the gunners could see their work. Then a shell with a too-short fuse would burst in the air above Épinay, and in one moment the village was lit in a spotlight, a hell of black and red and graveyard teeth.

Three days of shelling, gunfire and explosions. Throughout this time, Brunel continued to return to the cathedral. Admiral de la Roncière found him there on the eve of the battle, not in the tower but in the darkness of a side chapel among the tombs of the Kings of France, sitting with his head bent.

The admiral made the sign of the cross to the small altar and took a seat, breathing a prayer in soft wheezes. He had been sitting there for almost ten minutes before Brunel turned round and saw him. He tried to leap to his feet, but the admiral stopped him with a hand.

'You know something, Captain Brunel, I had taken you for a Protestant.'

Brunel was still half dazed, unable to see the reasoning behind the question. 'I am a Protestant, sir.'

'But you spend all your time in the cathedral, sitting in the dark, head bent in prayer. Is that not what you are doing?'

'Oh.' Brunel shook his head to rouse himself. 'I was just gathering my thoughts.'

'What is it about the men who fought at Bazeilles? You're all so quiet.'

Brunel could not see any clear answer but said, 'It was a defeat, sir. What's there to brag about?'

'Yes. But you're all so ponderous. Even when you are here, you're not here.'

Brunel only nodded, which perhaps proved the admiral's point: the marines were fast sinking into silence. But the truth was that there was too much going on inside his head, which was why he was sitting alone in the dark. He turned, only now noticing a clutch of candles flickering on spikes. The admiral must have lit them. Ahead, on the altar, the crucifix was made of wood. Brunel had not thought about it before, but now he grasped that it was a replacement. The priests must be losing confidence if they were no longer putting out their best silverware.

'People talk because you're a mystery. But as long as you deliver, they have nothing to complain about.' The admiral put a hand on Brunel's shoulder. 'Will there be any reason for complaints after this battle?'

'No, sir. I promise.'

At six o'clock in the morning, Brunel was making his way along a network of trenches to a copse less than half a kilometre from the first buildings of Épinay. As dawn came, he and his men sheltered beneath trees that shook with the force of the French barrage. This thunder of guns could activate something inside of you, find the spaces inside your body and set up reverberations. Brunel realised his jaws were set tight and he wondered how long he had been standing there grimacing. He always tried to relax himself in front of his men, so that none of them ever caught his mood. There were forty men alongside him. All along the trenches were other small parties, heads down as the shells raged above them. The Prussian guns were pounding back, the biggest of them hitting the walls of St Denis behind them, the field artillery smashing into the earthworks and sending great sprays of soil into the air.

The signal to charge came – not a bugle, as there was too much noise for it to be heard, but two flares that streamed up from the walls of the town. Brunel's men were on their feet, firing across the battlefield as the corps to their left started running. They advanced fifty metres, then took cover and Brunel shouted out his order. His men charged.

The fields were firm enough underfoot. With no backpacks, the men could almost have been flying. The surge of energy took them eighty metres across the ground, rifle fire covering them from their left and shells criss-crossing the sky. Then they were on their faces behind a ridge, lying on their stomachs, taking aim and firing, then calmly reloading. They were so close that they could see the Prussians, even the spikes of their helmets. Then the men they had overtaken were hot-footing past them, shouting as they went, bayonets flashing.

'Hup!'

Brunel's men were on their feet, lungs filled. The helmets ahead of them had disappeared, the Germans taking cover as French rifle fire bit into the brickwork and plaster. They breached the outskirts of the town, diving for cover in people's gardens. Brunel was conscious of a man falling. His eyes darted back. One of his own men lay on his face though it was impossible to say if he was dead or injured. There was no time to think about it. His men were inside the walls and working as a team. Their target: a merchant's house with a stone arch that led to a stable and courtyard. Brunel saw it ahead and signalled. If they took the house, they would control the approaches to the town and overlook one of the biggest of the Prussians guns.

Brunel led the charge. The outline of Prussians appeared from the depths of the courtyard, guns flaring, answered by Brunel's party.

Part Two

Christmas 1870/2001

Hospitals of Paris

On the eve of the battle, Zizi had held a farewell party at Chez Babette that they could not afford. Babette had remained in the kitchen all night, ignoring the calls from her husband and his friends until almost the very end. Then she had washed her face, untied her bandanna and smoothed out her hair. When Murielle advised her to apply a little make-up also, she had said, 'Who do you think would be impressed?'

'That's not what I meant,' Murielle had replied, 'but, for that matter, they don't all prefer men. Two of them are fighting over me and I wasn't even trying to be charming.'

As Babette walked out of the kitchen, they had stood and saluted. Happy, drunken men, faces red with the alcohol, with excitement and anxiety. And, with the exception of Freddie Worth, they had all been in uniform. Zizi had looked so much the part, tall and slender with a moustache that framed his laughter lines. He had never been a great drinker. While other men tripped over their toasts, or stuttered to a halt during a funny story, Zizi always kept to the same pace, charming or encouraging, listening or prompting, laughing when necessary. Of the twenty men around the table that night, Zizi had been one of only three serving with the Nationals. Yet no one would have thought that he was new to soldiering; he had looked more than the equal of the other guests, the Zouaves and the Hussars, tied up in braid and tassels, the Dragoons, struggling to find room for their coal-scuttle helmets beneath their chairs. Even Zizi's current lover, Gilles Furet, who was undeniably sweet and certainly dignified, did not have the sweetness and dignity of Zizi.

His charm had served them well – Zizi had attracted investors to their restaurant and brought in customers once it had opened. It had accomplished many other things too: he had often brought Babette to the brink of despair. Yet that night, as Babette had worked in the kitchen and Zizi had entertained his friends in the dining room, she had focused on his part in the creation of their restaurant. She had also focused on suppressing her rage that he had become so profligate that he was ready to launch himself into battle and do it in such style that he risked bankrupting them.

Then she had stepped out of the kitchen, seen Zizi in uniform and felt a sense of desolation as cold and wide and unbreakable as a winter at the end of the world. Zizi was going away, and all his sweetness would count for nothing. He had looked like a perfect soldier, but only a month before he had never even touched a rifle.

Christian had not eaten with his father, rather waiting until he would be called when the brandy was passed around the table. When he appeared, Babette had wondered – again – how adolescence could have made his face seem too small for its features, leaving his nose and ears out of scale and alignment. She had reached out to touch her son's arm in what she hoped was sympathy, although it only emphasised the distance between them. Zizi had walked over to fold his son into his arms, holding him for over a minute, his eyes tightly closed. When he opened them, they had been bleary with tears. Babette had hovered at the side, waiting for her turn, and Zizi had pulled her into a three-way embrace.

That was a week ago.

Babette was not sure how long it would be before she became used to living with her son. Christian slept badly every night. Babette heard him turning in his bed – which proved that she was also sleeping badly. When she met him in the corridor, before dawn on the fourth day of the battle, he looked bewildered.

She asked whether he needed anything, but he shook his head and blamed the cold for keeping him awake.

It was not only the nights that were cold. As Babette made her regular trip to buy newspapers and to read the notices outside the National Guard headquarters, she felt the cold clawing at her skin. The papers crowed about a victory at Épinay-sur-Seine, and were full of speculation about General Ducrot's main offensive across the Marne: of small wins, rumoured defeats, and calls for new ideas and new leaders. But there was never any concrete news, and no up-to-date lists of casualties were ever posted outside the National Guard headquarters. And so the only certainty was the bitter cold. Babette tried to imagine how the soldiers survived without blankets or tents. Everything had been planned around a swift attack and they had now spent a week on the battlefield.

The next job was to visit Roos, the butcher. Yesterday, the meat had arrived with a note, demanding that Babette come and see him first thing in the morning. She had to go. She could not pay his bills, so she could hardly afford to ignore his summons.

Babette was crossing the Place Vendôme when she heard the rumble of wheels – an ambulance was arriving at the Maison de Worth. Since Freddie Worth had turned his building into a hospital, hundreds of other private hospitals had sprung up across the city. Freddie Worth might have been the first to realise that the Geneva Convention would protect his property but the idea was soon taken up by the city's hoteliers, the proprietors of the department stores and even the owners of some private mansions. At least Freddie Worth had invested in hospital equipment and hired a real doctor. The ambulance was a converted removal wagon, painted white and marked with a cross. When Babette saw the stretchers carried out of its back, she ran across the square and followed the ambulance man into the lobby.

Freddie Worth was leaning over the balustrade of his mezzanine, smoking furiously as he watched his American doctor at work on the patients below. When he saw Babette, he yelled down: was there any news of Zizi? Babette shook her head; she had hoped that he might know something. When she asked the doctor all he could say was that, as far as he knew, the Nationals were still in the field. He looked exhausted; he had left Paris three days ago to set up a field ambulance in a village near the front and looked as if he had not slept since. When the cease-fire was declared, he had brought the worst of his patients back to Paris and they were nearly all cavalry men.

Babette had not known about the ceasefire. 'When was that called?'

'Last night, Madame Hébert,' the doctor said. 'If you get down to the quayside in a couple of hours, you'll see the injured coming back on the boats.'

It was now ten o'clock. Babette mouthed goodbye up at Freddie, who asked her to wait a moment as he wanted to walk her back to the restaurant. As Freddie edged down the stairs, the doctor told her the reason for Freddie Worth's cigar. 'He's scared of infection – someone told him that smoking wards off diseases.'

Babette had heard the same thing. 'But fire does kill germs, doesn't it?'

'It has to be a lot hotter than cigar smoke.' He pointed to his patients, lying on their camp beds throughout the ground floor. 'The problem is that everyone wants their rooms warm and stuffy, but that's how diseases like it, too. Most of these new hospitals are so rank, you could cut your finger and I promise you would be dead before you reached the door.'

It made sense; diseases were alive, they would flourish in the warmth, hide in the cold.

On the way back to Chez Babette, Freddie asked whether she had heard from the butcher.

'What do you know about that?' she demanded.

'I heard that you couldn't pay, that's all.' Freddie was one of the restaurant's backers, but he was also Zizi's closest friend.

'Why are you having problems, anyway? Other people are making money – the Brébants are making it hand over fist.'

'The Brébants aren't throwing parties – and they don't have backers to keep sweet.'

'What's the problem with having backers? We like to make profits.'

'That's true. But mostly, you like free food.'

'You can't put the whole blame on my waistline. The butcher might have been more sympathetic. But then you egged on that Marsouin to steal his cow.' Freddie could be sly; he rarely ignored the temptation. 'How are your relations with the marines, anyway? Have you heard from him recently?'

'Don't start, Freddie.'

He rolled his eyes in mock innocence. When he realised she was not going to say anything else, he added, 'Well, you're going to have to speak to your marine captain again. I heard the butcher wants vengeance, not money. I don't know if that counts as good news or bad news.'

By the time she left Freddie, Babette felt as though a ball of nerves were ravelling and unravelling inside her stomach. She gathered her composure as she walked down the alley beside the restaurant, taking a last deep breath as she pushed through into her kitchen. Murielle was standing inside the door, as though she had been lying in wait.

'The butcher sent word: he wants to know where you are.'

'Tell him my husband is lost on a battlefield and I'm trying to find him.' She grabbed her laundered apron and her clean bandanna from the shelf where they waited ahead of each shift.

'Do you actually want me to send that message? Or was that a joke?'

'Yes. No. Just send someone with my regards and tell him that because of the ceasefire, I'll be there first thing in the morning. Actually, go yourself and try to get eight birds off him, a side of beef and all the pigs' trotters he's prepared to part with.'

Babette spent the morning walking her kitchen, checking the temperature of the ovens, the quality of the bread that had arrived from the bakers, the readiness of the bouillons and the reductions. She heard the comments and the complaints of her staff, ranging from the quality of spices that seemed to have been bulked out with coloured plaster to accusations of bullying; one of the sous-chefs had threatened to roast a younger boy over a hotplate. Babette told the boy to think of St Lawrence, patron saint of cooks, who was martyred on a gridiron.

While she worked, she sent out messages. To keep the boy from a roasting, she sent him to the Prince Eugène barracks to see if anyone from the regular army had news of the Nationals. She sent Christian on a similar mission to the Napoleon barracks. Both boys were back in an hour to tell her that the telegraph from the front was down and there was almost no communication with the troops on the ground. Both brought back rumours that the Belleville battalions had scattered on the first Prussian barrage, but where they had scattered to no one could say for sure.

Murielle returned from the butcher's with a brace of pheasants so green they looked as if they had been hung down a leper's trousers. The butcher had also sent a message: if Madame Hébert wished to stay in business, she had better be prepared to receive him tomorrow morning. Babette noted the message and sent Murielle straight back out, to the home of Lieutenant Gilles Furet. The news from his household was grim: they had received a report on the first day of the battle that his battalion had been cut off in a diversionary tactic led by his uncle, General Joseph Vinoy. There had been no further news in five days.

At midday, Babette and Christian were waiting at the quay by the Pont Neuf, watching the dead and injured carried into Paris. The boats were moored four and five deep across the river. The ambulance men passed the stretchers from boat to boat, over the sandbags that reinforced the bulwarks and on to the quay. Babette stared at one man, twisting in pain while his shattered leg remained uncannily still. His bandages were so sodden with water and blood, and his wound was so poorly dressed, that the splintered bone was clearly visible. Babette wondered how the medics could be so slapdash. But when she saw other wounds, dressed just as badly, she learned that the wounds had frozen in the night while the men lay on the battle-field and that they had only begun to thaw on the steamboat back to Paris.

Babette was convinced that Zizi would be among the wounded. She and Christian waited for hours, yet by the time it grew dark there had been no sign of him at all. Christian began to believe that they had missed him and wanted to make a tour of the hospitals. There were so many that Babette did not know where to begin but Christian insisted he would check them all. She watched him set off up the quay, towards the Palais de l'Industrie, then turned towards home.

It was past midnight, the restaurant was closing early – there were no customers – and Babette was only waiting for her son to return. She was standing at her door when she heard noise from the National Guard headquarters in the Place Vendôme. When she went down, she found the lights there were burning so bright, one would think they were celebrating a victory. Babette stopped an old sergeant on the steps of the building and asked, 'What's the news?'

He grinned from out of his white beard. 'It's Flo. I cannot tell you how, but they've managed to get hold of him. I wouldn't like to be in his shoes.'

Gustave Flourens had been in hiding for almost a month, though, like everyone else in Paris, Babette knew that he was in Belleville. He was safe just as long as the police were reluc-tant to go on house-to-house searches through the tenements.

'They've arrested Flo? Where did they find him?' she asked.

'I don't know, love. With his men, maybe. That's what I heard.'

Babette started pushing her way into the lobby. If Flo was

with his men, then perhaps he had been fighting at the front. The headquarters was packed full of old windbags, smoking and talking, as though someone had called for a national college of concierges. At the end of a corridor, where the cloud of tobacco smoke was thickest, they were waiting outside a door. Waiting for another glimpse of their prisoner.

Though the question was redundant, she asked it anyway. 'Is Flo in there?'

'That's where he is, right enough,' a man answered her, his pipe still clenched between his teeth.

'Where did they find him? Was he in Belleville?'

'No. He was with his battalion. I'll say that for Flo, he's always prepared to get stuck in. Not that it does him or anyone any good.'

'Have the Nationals returned, then?'

'Most of them, love. Most of them. Those that can walk, those that can't. And those that came back in boxes.'

There was a draught, a signal that the door was opening. The crowd surged forward as the crack widened and the doors swung back. Gustave Flourens was inside, sitting on a chair and surrounded by the old officers who had been brought out of retirement to run the Nationals. Flo's long red hair was matted with blood and his nose was flattened to his face. Babette assumed that these were his war injuries. Then she saw that his hands were tied behind his back. It took just that long for her to understand his predicament. One of the officers slammed a fist into Flo's face. They were taking turns administering the beating.

Babette ran back across the Place Vendôme. As she pushed through the door of her restaurant, Murielle grabbed her.

'Take a second, madame. Get your breath back.'

The image of Flourens's head bathed in blood came back to her.

'The Nationals are back. Zizi must be back,' she said.

'So are the marines, madame. Captain Brunel is in the kitchen.

I didn't know what to do – so I gave him a bowl of the game soup.'

She allowed him to finish the soup before she pushed him out of the rear of the kitchen. The alley was blocked by a dray horse, its lips twisted back over its teeth. Brunel resisted, telling her to take it easy – didn't she know that you had to be wary around spooked horses. Babette kept pushing. 'You promised you would help me.' At least he kept moving.

Her plan had been to tour the hospitals until she found Zizi. But Brunel persuaded her it was a waste of time; they didn't even know if Zizi was wounded, let alone which ambulances had taken the Nationals. It would be far better to find members of Zizi's battalion. They began at a club close to Les Halles that catered for the porters from the market. There was no work, the markets were closed and the porters had joined the Nationals, but the Red Club was still popular.

Babette took a seat at a table while Brunel made a circuit of the men in uniform. A newspaper lay on the chair by her table: *The Awakening*. A tag beneath the title declared that the editor was Citizen Charles Delescluze. It was unlikely that he did much editing; as one of the rebels of 31 October, Delescluze had been locked up in the Mazas prison for the best part of a month. The front page of the paper showed a cartoon of General Auguste Ducrot riding through the Arc de Triomphe, waving the proclamation that he had posted around Paris on the eve of the battle, in which he declared that he would return either victorious or dead. The bubble out of his mouth read, 'Always read the small print, my friends.'

There actually was some small print along the bottom of the drawing. As Babette squinted to read it, a tall student type slipped in beside her and read it aloud: '*Either victorious or dead or neither*. Not much of a joke, unless one likes logic. Fairly prophetic, though.' He tapped the masthead. It was dated 27 November, five days ago. The day the battle began.

The student introduced himself as Jules Bergeret. In his tour of the club, Brunel had missed Bergeret, who was wearing army trousers with an ordinary jacket. The trousers and the jacket showed signs of dirt and mud, despite an apparent attempt to brush them clean.

'Tell me, Monsieur Bergeret, did you fight in the break-out?' Babette asked.

'I did.' Bergeret motioned to the waitress as he spoke. 'What will you have, mademoiselle?'

'Madame.' She corrected him just as Brunel arrived at their table. So then there was another correction to make: Brunel was not her husband, but he was helping her to locate him.

'Is there a man named Georges Hébert in your battalion?'

'The hairdresser? Yes, of course. He's a great guy.' Bergeret sucked in his cheeks. 'But we got separated.'

'Do you remember where you last saw him?'

'That's a question. It was along the Seine, past the point where it splits into the Marne. I know that much because we were stuck there for twenty-four hours before we got the signal to advance. It was a disaster, all crammed shoulder to shoulder, like they told us. The Prussians were picking us off and we could barely see them. That's when we split.'

Brunel said, 'I spoke to a man over there who thought he saw Hébert at Charenton.'

Bergeret shook his head. 'That's where most of us ended up, after we pulled back across the river. But I was there for three days and I don't recall seeing Hébert.'

'You were there three days? Why? Was there no new offensive?'

'Nothing. We just sat there. I think General Ducrot was too embarrassed to do anything else. His plan had fallen through and he had nothing up his sleeve. All he could do was postpone the humiliation. You know, I saw Ducrot and he wasn't even trying to put a brave face on it.'

Father and Son

I stood on the mezzanine above the main concourse of the Gare du Nord, squeezing a paper cup of black coffee. Everything worth drinking had disappeared with my first sip and there was nothing left to look forward to but the cold grounds. My son was arriving on the Eurostar, which was running five minutes late according to the revised time posted on the TV screens. Below me, the other train-greeters stood at the end of the platform behind a shiny rail. I wanted to go down and plant myself among them so that Evan would see me, a smiling, safe father. But that's a tough role to play. Then the train appeared and I ran for the stairs, looking wildly for a bin so I could lose the paper cup.

These things are never as bad as one expects. Evan was smiling the moment he saw me. In twenty minutes, we were inside Chez Casimir, my second-favourite bistro, chatting and sharing a beer. I had got Evan's age wrong, thinking he was thirteen years old. When he told me he was fourteen, I realised I had miscalculated the year his mother and I broke up. I admitted, yes, fourteen was old enough to have a beer with a meal.

I asked if his mother was as relaxed about the change of plan as she had seemed on the telephone.

Evan said, 'She's not fussed. She told me to learn French.'

'In five days?' It was 19 December and he was going home on the 24th. 'How's your French now?'

'Crap.'

I left Sally when I started working with the World Bank. She and I were never married, so we were never divorced. But she is married now. Evan has a two-year-old half-sister named Ava whom he is tremendously proud of. When I asked, 'How's Ava?' he told me, 'She is *so* advanced.' The kind of bragging one normally hears from parents, although he was smiling as he said it.

As we ate, I asked, 'Are many of the parents separated at your school? I mean, is it common?'

'There's a few among my friends.'

'Your friends? Is that because you have things in common?'

'I don't think so. They're just my friends. They're a good laugh.'

This scared me. Anyone who is a good laugh at fourteen is a delinquent.

Then Evan caught me by surprise by saying that he had just split with his girlfriend. He said it was mutual and there was no one he was particularly interested in. I replied that I had been single for about two years. There was no one on the horizon.

'But I thought I had to come to Paris because you were having girlfriend trouble.'

'No. A girl who's my friend has gone missing. I didn't want her to come back home and find there was no one around.' This sounded inadequate. I had changed the Christmas plans of my entire family because of someone that Evan must have realised was a relatively recent acquaintance. So I said, 'All of her other friends have commitments they couldn't get out of. Actually, I have to go and see a couple of them tonight. I hope that's fine with you.'

Elise was spending Christmas with her parents in their holiday home and Marguerite was going to Jerusalem. Jean-Luc had already left for a holiday in Thailand, though he was emailing every day to see if I had any news of Flavie. There was none, no sign of her at all. This was why I was seeing Elise and Marguerite, to tell them face to face before they left the city.

It was only a short walk to Elise's apartment, though it's all uphill to Montmartre and it began to rain on the way. I looked around for a taxi but Evan said he didn't mind. He took a knitted hat out of his rucksack and pulled it low over his brow. I jokingly asked if he had another for me to wear. It turned out that he had. So we were father and son, walking through the rain in matching hats. Though I pulled mine off when we reached Elise's door.

She said, 'You.'

'You knew I was coming. You gave me the door code.' I held out the scrap of paper on which I had scribbled the access number for her block.

'I forgot. I'm not dressed.' She was wearing a dressing gown with a feather collar; this was at nine o'clock in the evening but Elise does not really work, calling herself a freelance but leaving the details vague. Her family is quite wealthy and money does not seem to be a problem. As I leaned forward to greet her, she noticed Evan. 'Who's he?'

'My son. Evan. Elise.'

She sent us into the living room while she went to make hot chocolate. Neither of us had asked for chocolate but Elise said we needed to be fortified, which sounded ominous. I took Evan to the window and pointed out the Basilica of the Sacred Heart. The basilica was built to commemorate General Clément Thomas, commander-in-chief of the National Guard during the siege and the man responsible for arresting Flourens in the middle of a battle and dragging him back to Paris. General Thomas was killed in a riot on the site of the basilica in March 1871, perhaps by Gustave Flourens himself. Elise is absolutely the last person who should partake in a significant moment in revolutionary history. But her apartment is terrific.

The butte of Montmartre is one of my favourite parts of Paris, where the streets hug the steepest part of the hill, criss-crossed by a maze of steps. The evening rain had made the trees heavy and the leaves showed up a luscious dark green in the spotlights that illuminated the path to the basilica. A little lower down, there are a few cabaret bars where drag queens perform lip-synch routines to old French songs. I once visited one with

Flavie. She had claimed that it wasn't really her thing, she was not gay like *that*, but if I had never seen one we should go, it would be fun. It was. Brigitte Bardot was played by a huge, fat man. I had noticed him earlier, standing in the street wearing a Hawaiian shirt. Seeing him again, emerging from behind the stage curtains in a dress and blond wig, I almost fell off my bar stool.

Evan seemed entranced. He nodded towards the church. 'That is beautiful.'

'It's at its best in the dark,' I replied and whispered, 'I'm sorry for dragging you round here.'

'That's okay. But what's up with this Elise woman?'

'I wish I knew. Flavie has odd taste in women.'

'Oh. She's a lezza?' Evan's voice rose. I shushed him quickly as Elise returned with the hot chocolate.

'Have you heard anything new?' she asked.

I shook my head. Flavie had been missing for a little over three weeks now.

'And were the cops any help at all?'

'No, not really. I don't think they are doing anything.' Elise rolled her eyes, as though we could expect nothing else from the police. I said, 'I showed the police a letter Flavie wrote. She sounded so desperate that I thought it might be significant.'

'A red letter? All torn into little pieces?'

'You already know about it?'

'Of course. I tore it up. What kind of letter is that? Flavie dumps me, and the next moment she is writing begging letters to another woman. She may not have any pride, but I do.' Elise threw herself back on her sofa, sending warm flesh quivering beneath her dressing gown. 'And what does Flavie see in Marguerite anyway? I fucked her and she was no fun. Even worse than you.'

I am certain that I blushed. I know I grimaced as I nodded towards Evan.

'Please, Elise. Not here.'

She ignored me. 'I think we spent two nights together before she bored the ass off me.'

Elise was so crude that it took a moment before the revelation hit me. 'You only spent two nights together? Marguerite described it as a relationship. She said that was why she could not date Flavie.'

'Well, it's quite right. Why should Flavie go sniffing after my exes? Would you sleep with your sister's husband? Or with your father's mistress? It's the same thing. And when I told Marguerite that, she promised that she would respect my feelings.'

'You know you're insane? Why have you gone to so much trouble to wreck their relationship?'

'You think I'm insane? I'm not the one who likes to play disappearing tricks.'

'Are you saying that Flavie makes a habit of disappearing?' As far as I knew, Elise had never suggested this before. 'For three weeks? Without saying anything?'

'Maybe not three weeks. But it's not the first time.'

I had instructions to call Marguerite Galperin at nine-thirty sharp. She had told me she would know by then if she could get away from a meeting to see me. I did not want to make the call in front of Elise, so I went to the bathroom to do it and risked leaving Elise with my son. When I returned, I discovered Elise fully dressed, wearing make-up and ready to go out.

I had to make up an excuse, so I told her, 'I'm sorry. I'm spending the evening with my son.'

'It doesn't matter. I'll be as quiet as a mouse.'

'That's not the point. And it's certainly not true.'

'I'm coming with you. I don't want to stay in on my own. What's the matter? You think I am not frightened about Flavie? I am worried sick.'

'I don't know what you think.'

'No, you don't. You don't ever know. You know Flavie for ten minutes, you are so desperate to fuck her that you worm your way into her life and now there is a drama, you get to play the big hero. Who do you think you are? The knight riding out to save her? You know how ridiculous you look? And all you really want to do is squeeze out her real friends.'

'Bloody hell, Elise.' I shepherded everyone towards the door. 'Come on, then. Let's go.'

The rain was still coming down hard. As we crossed the road, Elise tossed me her car keys. 'You drive. I don't enjoy it so much when it's dark and wet.'

The rain sluiced across the windscreen, so heavy that the wipers could not cope with the volume. Elise took the front seat, so I had to conduct my conversation with Evan via the rear-view mirror. I told him, 'You know, it's not true that your grandfather has a mistress. Elise was making a hypothetical comment.'

'I know,' he said. 'I didn't believe her.'

We were again passing the Gare du Nord when Elise told me to stop. She had seen the glint of a *tabac* and wanted to buy herself cigarettes. We watched her stride across a puddle, umbrella in hand. And then I had a thought: what was to stop us from escaping?

We abandoned the car and ran.

As I fed our tickets into the Metro gate I knew I would regret it later, Elise would make sure of that. But it was worth it to share that wave of exhilaration with Evan. He was laughing so hard, the tears were running down his face.

I hope that I am making Evan sound well adjusted. I certainly believe that he is. But I also think he is not particularly happy. He has some acne problems, not disfiguring but embarrassing enough. He is physically awkward and his hair is tufted up with so much wax that as we waited for Marguerite in a café, I wanted to turn him upside down and do the parquet. His unhappiness comes from teenage insecurity; I was similar at his age. But when I see it, I feel all the more guilty that I am never around.

Marguerite did not keep us waiting long. She had been at

a final meeting of her group, the Civil Mission to Palestine. She would fly out in the morning for a two-week fact-finding visit.

She said, 'I thought Flavie would reappear before I went away.'

'What about a number and a contact address, so she can contact you when she does?' I asked.

'Tell her to use email. I don't have a contact address. I will probably be in East Jerusalem for a few days but after that, who knows?'

I remember once, six years ago, speaking to Evan from a hotel room in East Jerusalem – that was our first Christmas apart. Evan must have been eight years old. He asked what I would do that day and I told him: see the Baby Jesus and Yasser Arafat. I had been invited to mass at the Church of the Nativity by a friend, a local doctor who also taught at the university. This was the Christmas of 1995, the year Arafat returned from exile. So the first year that I missed a family Christmas, I was in Bethlehem with Yasser Arafat, though I only glimpsed him from a distance as he gave a speech from the roof of the basilica. The coincidence, that Marguerite would also be spending Christmas in Palestine, would not be lost on Evan. I remember that he cried during our telephone call.

'By the way,' Marguerite added, 'I wanted to thank you for all your contacts, James. I would have thanked you earlier, but you didn't make it easy for me.'

As she said that, I thought, now you're just being patronising.

I offered Evan my bed but he opted for the floor. I thought that he was not sleeping well and a couple of nights later I woke and realised the television was on. So I got up and sat with him.

'What are you watching?'

'Just news. I couldn't find any other English channels.'

He was watching the news channel, BBC World. Tony Blair

had announced he was dragging his whole family to Egypt to meet President Mubarak. The next story moved to Palestine and the news that the Israeli Government was refusing to allow Yasser Arafat to travel to Bethlehem at Christmas.

I told Evan I was making a drink – did he want one to help him sleep?

'Coffee?'

'How's that going to help?'

'Beer?'

'I was thinking of camomile tea. But I guess I could make hot toddies.'

I hoped the toddy would medicate him to sleep, though mine was purely recreational. As we sat and drank them, we could have talked but instead I passed him a copy of *Pariscope* and told him to check the cinema listings for a film we could see in the morning. Preferably one in English, unless he was serious about working on his French. He started reading out the choice: *Curse of the Jade Scorpion* by Woody Allen; *Storytelling* – Todd Solondz; *Mulholland Drive* by David Lynch; *Bully* – Larry Clarke; *Osmosis Jones* – the Farrelly brothers; *Zoolander* with Ben Stiller; or *Harry Potter and the Sorcerer's Stone*. It was an odd variety and I had no idea what Evan would choose.

Then, as he reached the end of the list, he said, 'I think your friend's lights are on.'

The Zoo

The butcher brought his own coffee to Chez Babette and gave Murielle elaborate instructions on how to prepare it. Then he sat sipping it on one side of the table while Brunel and Babette sat on the other, like junior supplicants at court. He looked exactly what he was: the new king of Paris.

The name of his shop, La Boucherie Anglaise, suggested a corpulent Englishman, with beefy whiskers and a round belly. In fact, Roos was rather dark and small, a hyperactive businessman. When Babette described him as the most powerful man in Paris, Brunel said, well, there were few other candidates left. But Roos' kingdom lay beneath the city, in its cellars. This underworld contained his fattening pens, his dairy farms and his abattoirs. Even his stables. It was rumoured that the racehorses he had bought for slaughter from impoverished members of the Jockey Club were being kept alive in these cellars and would re-emerge after the war to race again under new names. Although Babette had become ingenious in her attempts to waste as little food as possible, the restaurant still produced bins of leftovers, scraps and peelings, which were collected late at night by the butcher to feed his animals. Perhaps somewhere, a racehorse was being fed on cabbage stalks and gristle.

Brunel finally tired of watching the butcher drink and asked, 'How is the coffee?'

'Excellent. All these people saying there's not a bean left in Paris, what do they know? They should ask me first.' A pause. 'This is a beautiful restaurant, definitely one of the top three or four, and Babette herself doesn't have a peer. But the restaurant is in trouble and I need a favour. So, fine. Let's work together.' The butcher spread out his hands. 'Of course, Babette owes me a great deal of money. Supplies are poor and there's a limit to the amount of credit I can extend her. But there's an alternative. I need help slaughtering livestock and I want you to do it.'

'Me? I'm a soldier, not a butcher. I admit there's only a slim difference these days but I'm not the man for the job.'

'I think you are. And as you stole my cow, you owe me.'

'What kind of livestock?'

'The zoo is selling off all its animals. The more exotic species present certain problems.'

Brunel waited.

'The elephant, for instance.'

'How would I know how to kill an elephant?'

'How? How would I know? I've never done it either. But I hear about the army's new machine-gun and, I think, everyone is so fascinated – perhaps they would pay to see one in action.' The butcher smiled. 'Here's the deal. You figure out the best way to kill the elephant with a machine-gun. I'll sell tickets.'

The search for Zizi had grown more upsetting the longer it had gone on, and when Christian came running into the restaurant, claiming that he had found his father in La Pitié-Salpêtrière, Babette thought that someone was playing a cruel joke on the boy; La Pitié-Salpêtrière was the women's hospital. But it was true. As far as they could discover, Zizi had been knocked unconscious by fragments of a shell as it shattered on the frozen ground. Whoever had brought him into Paris had dumped him at the first hospital they came to. It was likely that Zizi's saviours were among the scavengers who descended on the battlefield after the conflict. But at least they had taken Zizi back with them.

As Zizi returned to consciousness, the nuns began to fear the effect he would have on weak females. Freddie Worth sent his ambulance to the hospital, and when Babette saw her husband he was installed in his own room in the Maison de Worth. Zizi's face was thinner and his skin was yellow but his head injuries were hidden beneath thick white bandages. She imagined the damage beneath this swollen turban with dread. When she spoke to Zizi, he answered in halting sentences, interrupted by tremors in his voice that were matched by the shaking of his hands. When she told him that Brunel had agreed to put on a show for the butcher, Zizi said, 'Well, Captain Brunel is the cause of the problem with the butcher.'

'He's not the reason I can't pay his bills.'

As she said this, it sounded like a reprimand and she felt guilty. But even Christian, who was so dazzled by his father, knew that Zizi had brought them to the brink of bankruptcy.

The butcher had turned the elephant house at the Jardin des Plantes into an amphitheatre with the addition of banked seating. The tickets that he had had printed stated clearly that this would be a charity event: Pollux's own contribution to the war effort, as though the elephant had volunteered. The butcher was not making any money from the event, which he viewed as part of the marketing campaign to boost the price of the meat.

When Babette arrived, the seats were empty, the audience still on their way through the soft fresh snow that covered the gardens. She watched from the wings as Brunel talked with the veterinarian surgeon, stage centre, while Pollux stood a little apart, swinging his trunk from side to side. There was something mournful in the slow sway, but elephants always look mournful. Babette dared herself to be hypnotised. She tried to blot out the voice of the vet as he gave details on the thickness of the skin and the best kinds of cartridge to use to kill the animal, and explained that he would have favoured a heavy calibre and a head shot.

Brunel said, 'That's going to be impossible. The gun isn't accurate enough, I can't try to aim for the head.'

The elephant had an enormous head – how could he possibly miss it? At the edge of the stage, in what Babette supposed would be the orchestra pit, Aspirant Barclay was lifting the *mitrailleuse* out of its coffin-like box. It was a huge weapon, twenty-five barrels bound together and mounted on a carriage. Brunel and Barclay had borrowed the gun from Porte Maillot, but they had needed one more man to operate it and were too embarrassed to call in a detail of marines. It was Brunel who brought in Jules Bergeret, the student they had met in the Red Club. The young man claimed to have had experience with the American Gatling gun, the original model for the *mitrailleuse*. It turned out to be theoretical experience. Before the war, Bergeret had worked part-time as a bookseller's clerk and had seen technical drawings of Gatling's weapon. But Bergeret was bright enough, Brunel said. He and Barclay would manage.

The *mitrailleuse* was operated by turning a handle, at which the twenty-five barrels would fire in sequence as they revolved. Barclay and Bergeret tinkered with the elevation, trying to fix the sights on the spot where the vet had indicated that the heart lay. The butcher had managed to get both the light and the heating in the elephant house turned on, when the garden had been cold for so long that the unheated greenhouses were filled with the dead remains of rare plants. Up above Pollux's head, gas jets burned to illuminate the auditorium. Babette was certain that the audience would find the whole thing barbaric. Yet the feeling was growing that a drama was about to begin.

The vet's eyes were bright and his voice grew tighter as stage fright took hold. He had almost forgotten the most important thing. 'The butcher wants you to keep the trunk intact.'

Brunel said, 'He is going to be unlucky. Unless the keeper can get it to stand on its back legs with its nose in the air.'

The keeper stood to the side, holding a bamboo cane. He had not said much – anything at all in fact – in the past hour.

Brunel left the surgeon and went to crouch at the pit to give his last instructions to Bergeret and Barclay. Their faces were hot and red, their eyes twitching as they listened to Brunel and nodded.

The butcher had justified the spectacle as a demonstration of the Genius of the French. He had his keywords. *Think Patriotism! Think Morale!* The *mitrailleuse* had been a national secret until well into the war, and though everyone knew about it few civilians had seen it in action. The butcher fed on the willingness, still, to believe in victory, even after the terrible defeats of November. General Ducrot was said to be a broken man; President Trochu had had no option but to sack him. Léon Gambetta's army of the Loire had been smashed. All Paris had left were its hopes. But as the clatter of a crowd finding its seats died away, and the full auditorium settled, a curious silence began to take hold. Babette saw how the people looked from the gun, with its multiple barrels and its huge cranking handle, across to Pollux. Still swinging his trunk.

The butcher appeared at Babette's shoulder. 'Almost show-time. Shall I go and speak to your friend?'

He said friend, but the way that he said it actually meant lover. Which they weren't. Brunel was a taciturn man, who showed no obvious pleasure in or talent for the process of seduction, but he was more than willing to keep pressing on. And Babette could not pretend she had not played her part; with little thought and nothing like deliberation, she had set him a series of tasks. Sit and suffer a bad shave. Go find me a cow. Murder an elephant.

She watched as Brunel straightened up, stretched. He turned and looked in her direction and started walking across the stage.

'I didn't notice you there. I thought you had decided to stay away.'

'No. I was here. I've been looking at the animals.'

She saw him half formulate a question – that it seemed a strange time to take a trip around the gardens. But as he opened his mouth, he looked from her to the butcher and guessed the truth.

'You were shopping?'

There was no inflection in his voice. But in that moment, she understood exactly how he saw her. She had painted him as a kind of brute. But she was the one who had brought him here. And she was the one calculating what she could do with the dead animals.

'So what's going on the menu? Penguin pie?'

'Seabirds are too oily. Penguin pie would never work.'

Neither of them smiled.

It was time for the machine-gun demonstration.

Barclay stood ready, braced on the handle.

Even the butcher began to have second thoughts. 'This will work, won't it? I mean, it's scientific. What better way could there be?'

Brunel shrugged. 'I don't know.'

'Well, what method would you have chosen? Firing squad?'

'I don't have a method. When am I going to need to kill an elephant?'

Babette took a last look at Pollux. Was it a happy animal? It certainly didn't look like it, up on the stage with two short lengths of chain manacling its back feet.

Brunel walked back across the stage. She heard him shout an order to Barclay. On his command, Barclay would start cranking the handle. Bergeret stood ready with another firing block. Twenty-five barrels. Twenty-five rounds in each block. Fifty bullets ought to be enough to kill anything.

Brunel reached inside his shirt and removed his pistol. 'One shot. Ready.'

Brunel aimed between the elephant's front feet. He fired, the elephant reared up, seeming to scream, but if there was any noise it was drowned by the racket of the *mitrailleuse*. A spiral of fire and smoke ripped out of the turning barrels. The elephant seemed to dance behind a spray of blood. Then the gun fell silent and the elephant was falling.

Bergeret was reloading as Pollux slumped to the stage. The elephant hit the ground and the whole building shook. There was a hush, all the more profound because it followed the explosions of the machine-gun. Then Pollux started cycling his legs.

Barclay was feverishly trying to alter the elevation of the gun, now that the elephant was on the floor. Bergeret looked towards Brunel for direction; were they going to keep firing? Brunel lifted his pistol and put four bullets between the elephant's eyes.

Finnmark Etc.

Flavie answered her door and I had a split second to take the temperature of her smile – it seemed cool to me.

'Sorry to call so late. I was worried and I thought if I don't speak to you now, I'll worry all night.'

'I'm fine. Just back from holiday. See?'

She pointed to the suitcase. She hadn't yet unpacked.

'Do you need anything?'

'I'm fine.'

'Not even milk?' I wiggled my hand in the direction of my apartment, trying to imply that I came from a world rich in dairy products. The gesture drew Flavie's attention to my front door, where Evan was standing.

'Who is this?' she asked.

'I'm Evan. I'm his son.'

How it happened, I am not sure, but within moments she and Evan were sitting on her chaise longue and I was exiled next door, preparing a fresh batch of hot toddies in my kitchen.

Flavie told us she had run away to Finnmark, the land where Scandinavia and Russia touch under the hem of the Arctic Circle. Silently, I wondered if her chill was an after-effect of the arctic winter. Yet she warmed to Evan. And there was no doubt that she was calmer, more self-possessed. Perhaps the vastness of the dark and the cold had put her problems into perspective. After all, what did she have to worry about? She was in love with a woman who was idealistic and selfless, yet also priggish and who did not love her. And she had little else in her life apart from her work, her intrusive neighbour and a psychotic ex-girlfriend.

As I handed out the brandies, I asked, 'What did you do all day? Is there any light at all in December?'

'Of course there's light. That's why I went. There's the aurora borealis.'

Evan said, 'I want to see that. I really want to see it.'

'It's beautiful. And it's what I needed. I was getting so upset with everyone. Work is fine but I thought that owning my own salon would give me freedom and it just doesn't feel that way. So, I went to the travel shop and bought myself a package cruise – one pre-paid spiritual experience. And now I am fixed.'

We had already had about ten minutes' worth of conversation. All of it quite hectic, as I told her how worried I had been. No, how worried everyone had been: Marguerite, Jean-Luc, Elise, the neighbour. But she seemed to see it differently, that she was allowing everyone else to upset her and that was what she had needed to fix. I was surprised that she chose to fix it through a New Age pilgrimage.

'You're fixed?' I said. 'There was nothing to fix.'

'There's always room for a miracle.'

Evan said, 'The aurora borealis isn't a miracle. There's a scientific explanation for it.'

'I know. I have a leaflet that explains it.' She warmed her hand on her toddy. 'But, you know, what does the science explain? If you see a kaleidoscope of lights dancing across the sky, there is no reason in it. So when you ask yourself, "What does it mean?" you either say "electro-magnetic forces and ions" or you ask yourself what it means to you. What does it do to your place in the world?'

'Eh?' I said.

'I was so unhappy,' she continued. 'I was even crying all the time. I told myself, I could go get myself some therapy or I could do something different. So I went to see God's handwriting.'

This easy admission of depression disturbed me almost as much as her weird idea of a cure.

'Are you sure you're fine?'

'Yes, sure.' She turned to Evan. 'Your father thinks I'm crazy. What about you?'

Evan switched immediately from scepticism to understanding. 'I know what you mean. The aurora borealis isn't really God's handwriting. But if you can put yourself into a new and amazing place, then it can free your mind and make it easier to get closer to God.'

'See, Evan understands but you don't.'

What was I supposed to understand? How my son had suddenly come to spout theology, for instance? I doubted he had the low cunning to try to bullshit Flavie, but I was just as certain that this was not the voice of a fourteen-year-old. More like a sixty-year-old hippy. I could accept that I knew nothing of the working of Flavie's mind, but I didn't want to admit that I didn't know my son either. Better to believe I had passed through a fold in time–space and landed among familiar-looking strangers, with strangely warped minds.

I bit my tongue; it seemed better to stay quiet.

Right up until the moment, three seconds later, when Evan said, 'That's why I started going to church.'

'When the fuck did you start going to church?'

'Two years ago. I'm an altar boy now. I'll be serving communion at the Christmas Eve service at the cathedral.'

'You're an altar boy! I didn't know you were even confirmed. Or baptised for that matter.'

'I did both kind of together, about two years ago.'

'You're a Born Again Christian?'

Evan was looking uncomfortable. 'I just did it through my school's prayer group. There's nothing special about it, just Church of England and stuff. It was just something that I wanted to do.'

He looked so vulnerable that I willed myself to be calmer. 'Don't your parents have to be around when you're baptised?'

It may have sounded like a question, but I knew for a fact

that the parents do have to be involved. Which means that Sally's husband must have stood in for me. Leaving me shut out and uninformed. But Sally knows that I don't believe in God, so she probably thought there was no point in involving me.

'It was no big deal,' Evan said.

'Getting baptised is supposed to be a big deal. Especially when you do it of your own free will.'

'Well, okay, it was. It was a big deal back then but it's not now. Mum and Mike aren't interested in religion, they were just humouring me. I think the only reason I'm still going to church is because I am an altar boy. It would be too boring to sit through a service if I wasn't serving. Most of the time I'm thinking of something else. But then there are moments . . .' He trailed off, ending with a lame, 'Like me and Flavie were saying. Like at the Christmas service last year.'

Flavie was nodding vigorously, as much to give Evan courage as to agree with him. 'That's exactly what I mean, when you put yourself in a strange and beautiful place, you are free to think a little differently. You sometimes see the spiritual side of everyday things that everyday life keeps hidden.'

At bottom, it was the way that I had been excluded that upset me. I knew that I must not lose my temper so I excused myself and took a few moments in the bathroom to calm down. I told myself, it really was no big deal; it would not be a big deal to Sally and certainly not to Mike. Two years ago, Evan was just hitting puberty, the age for bar mitzvahs or confirmations. Religions are at their most attractive when we are at our most vulnerable.

As I came out of the bathroom, I said, 'We're going to the cinema tomorrow, Flavie. Do you want to come?'

'What's the choice?'

I ran through the list of films that were playing in English. Flavie screwed up her face. 'I don't know. I would like to, but listening to English is so hard, I get tired. Those films sound difficult.'

'*Zoolander* and *Harry Potter* sound difficult?'

She said she would think about it.

This time, I was the one who had difficulty sleeping. I was too annoyed. But as I watched the patterns thrown on to the ceiling by the occasional passing car, I also began to reflect on Flavie's disappearance and the spiritual meaning she had given to the aurora borealis. It was possible to interpret her trip as a symptom of a renewed thirst for life rather than depression. But even that line of thought put more emphasis on the blackness of the cloud, rather than the glint of its lining.

Evan woke to the sound of my modem. I had given up trying to sleep and was writing an article on the German Federal Bank's concerns about the weakness of the Euro. It wasn't until the third paragraph that I revealed that the Germans were questioning the quality of the paper used to print the notes, not the currency's financial strength. We were only nine days away from Euro-Day and the English newspapers were ready to buy any kind of scare story. It was such easy money, better than printing my own Euros.

Evan made coffee for me and cracked open a can of coke for himself. I noticed him slip a headache tablet out of my bathroom cabinet and realised that he had a hangover, a warning that I should watch what he drank more carefully. As we took our breakfast, he asked questions about Flavie.

He was smitten. He asked what time I thought we should call to see if she had made up her mind about the film.

We saw *Harry Potter and the Sorcerer's Stone*. Evan had read the book three or four years ago and though he had outgrown boy wizards, the combination of Christmas, movie hype and his own nostalgia meant that he was happy to go. Especially in the company of Flavie.

I ordered three Cokes in the cinema lobby, and as we waited for the film to begin I asked Flavie if she had visited Berlevaag while she was in Norway.

'I think the cruise boat may have stopped there; it's just a concrete ferry terminal, isn't it?'

'I don't know. I thought it was a collection of coloured houses on the edge of a fjord.'

'Oh? Maybe past the terminal. It was so cold, I didn't leave the boat that night. Why? Do you know it?'

I shook my head. 'It's the setting for the story "Babette's Feast". In the film, she goes to Jutland in Denmark but the original short story is set in Norway.'

In the dark of the cinema, the two-and-a-half-hour running time of Harry Potter gave me plenty of time to think about 'Babette's Feast'. There is a theological dimension to Karen Blixen's story that I have never understood. Or, rather, that I regard with the same cynicism that I lent to Flavie and Evan's account of their spiritual experiences. The villagers of Berlevaag, all devout Lutherans, achieve a moment of grace as they eat the fabulous meal Babette prepares for them. Each time I read the story, it strikes me that the villagers buy their grace too cheaply, although it serves to make a contrast with Babette's own story.

What always affects me, and unfailingly pricks me each time I read 'Babette's Feast', is the story of Babette herself. The grand mystery of why she chose to settle among these people. Why has she inflicted this dull crowd, with their hard, cold life, upon herself? But also, having put herself through this punishment, what consolation does she receive by spending her own money, a huge lottery win, on a luxurious feast that these simpletons only barely appreciate? Babette explains that she wishes only to stay true to her vocation as a chef; her pleasure lay in cooking the meal. But if she had simply left boring bloody Finnmark, she might have found a job where she could cook a feast every day of the year. The lottery win that she spends in one go, on a single meal, is the only money that she has or could ever expect to receive. The point of the story, surely, is not that Babette finds grace in following her vocation, but that she wilfully condemns herself to lifelong penury.

Once the money is gone, Babette will never be able to leave this arctic wasteland. She exhibits a stoical acceptance of the hardest of lives far in excess of the real puritans who surround her. The Norwegian dullards find grace. They find it too easily. But Babette never will. The central mystery remains: what hubris, what pride, what crime, drove her to this? What on earth did she do in Paris?

I got up, leaving Flavie and Evan in the dark. After a visit to the toilet, I stood at the back of the cinema and located the backs of their heads. I calculated there was about an hour of film left so I slipped back into the foyer and bought a coffee.

Flavie and Evan claimed insights into great transcendental experiences, yet they were happy watching Harry Potter. As far as I could make out, Potter's appeal is that he looks weak but is actually very, very strong. Who wouldn't dream of such powers? This is Christ's appeal; he appeared weak though he had all the power in creation. But at least with Christ there is a little bit of mystery; why didn't he use his powers to save himself?

Just as I was finishing my coffee, Flavie came through the cinema doors. I waved but her head was bent, staring intently at the screen of her mobile telephone. She disconnected a call and redialled, all the time walking across the foyer and not once lifting her eyes. I would have called out but I did not feel I could intrude.

As she headed out of the foyer, I realised that Evan was now watching the film on his own. I hurried back into the cinema and dropped into the seat beside him.

'Where's Flavie got to?' I whispered.

'I don't know. She started to get fidgety and began playing with her telephone. Then she ran out.'

I wondered who she might be calling – and immediately answered my own question. It could only be Marguerite.

'What's the matter?' Evan asked.

'Neither of us told Flavie that Marguerite was spending her holidays in Palestine. Flavie's probably only just found out.'

'We have to follow her.'

He was already out of his seat, though the film was nowhere near over.

The Second Battle of Le Bourget

It was 21 December 1870 and twenty degrees below freezing as the Marsouin surfaced on the plain of Le Bourget; Brunel felt the cold like fish-hooks in his face. This was President Trochu's first campaign, now that he had assumed direct control of the Paris forces, and Brunel's part in the action was essentially a reprise of a failed action in October. The Marsouin, alongside two battalions of Breton Mobiles and another of the local Francs-Tireurs, had set out from St Denis under a supporting barrage from the marine gunners. Once they had seized Le Bourget, President Trochu's forces would sweep out of the city in a great, torrential break-out.

The barrage from St Denis received an immediate answer from the Prussian guns within the town, then from rifle fire as the Prussians picked out the colour of the French uniforms. Brunel knew right away that they were going to suffer heavy losses. He pressed on.

His troops faltered on the outskirts of Le Bourget. Brunel was at the head of a detachment pinned down in a simple stone building, a storehouse that looked as though it had once formed part of a farm on the site. The Prussian forces were concentrated in the taller buildings to their front and left. Brunel's men kept up their fire, supported down the line by fire from behind walls and whatever other cover the town's outskirts afforded. A corps of the Francs-Tireurs tried to make it across the open space in a frontal assault. Brunel's forces stepped up to twelve shots a minute, their rifles wreathed in steam as they tried to weave a canopy of fire over the exposed Franc-Tireur fighters. It was not enough. At Brunel's signal a detachment of

Marsouin broke cover, drawing fire to give the men a chance. They were cut down and beaten back, slipping on the icy grass and mud, but it gave the Francs-Tireurs time to find cover.

They could hear the sound of heavy guns from deep within Le Bourget, hurling shells above their heads and into the plain. Brunel assumed the Prussians were firing on the President's army coming from the south. If so, then Trochu was moving too early; he was supposed to wait for a signal that victory in Le Bourget was imminent. Brunel imagined the effects of the shells on the advancing troops, the steel splintering into razor shards on the wide frozen plain and then scattering to tear the soldiers to pieces. Brunel could do nothing but signal down the line to bring another corps forward as they fought for a footing in Le Bourget. By the time darkness fell at four o'clock on this late December afternoon, they had barely crept past the first line of gardens.

For the third time since the war began, the Marsouin were attempting to fight their way through a town, through houses, gardens, even living rooms and bedrooms. It had happened in Bazeilles, then three weeks ago in Épinay-sur-Seine. Now again in Le Bourget. Brunel wondered if every war would be like this: an end to battlefields proper as fighting erupted in towns and villages and cities. He believed that Paris would be next. He was in no doubt that the Prussians would soon break into the city. This assault had certainly failed.

A lieutenant from the Francs-Tireurs approached Brunel. His battalion had taken part in the last assault on Le Bourget. Brunel had been amazed to learn that it was made up of journalists and print-workers, but they knew the area and showed irreproachable bravery as well as some signs of discipline. So when the lieutenant asked Brunel for his orders, Brunel asked him what he believed they should do. They moved to the upper storey of the last building they had taken, creeping through the dark. Behind them, the plain was lit by the bursting shells, crawling with packs of tiny figures. There was no cover out there.

The Franc-Tireur said, 'I heard it's your fault we no longer have an army outside Paris, is that true?'

'I heard that rumour,' Brunel said. He had thought, at first, that it was another story put about by a politician to blacken his name. But now he feared it was accurate in every respect.

As far as he could make out, President Trochu had tried to downplay the failure of the November break-out towards Orléans by emphasising the Marsouin victory at Épinay-sur-Seine. Gambetta received the news via balloon messenger and because he had never heard of the village, he opened his map and alighted on the town of Épinay-sur-Orge on the road south from Paris. The victory was an unexpected triumph but Gambetta welcomed it; it meant that Auguste Ducrot had succeeded in breaking through the Prussian lines. Gambetta immediately split the army of the Loire in two and sent a force to link with the non-existent Parisian forces at the wrong Épinay. In this weakened state, his entire army was destroyed.

The lieutenant said, 'If you got us into this, maybe you're the best man to get us out.' He nodded towards the buildings ahead, where the presence of the Prussians prevented French troops from advancing. 'We need to dislodge those bastards.'

Brunel pointed to the nearer, much lower buildings. 'I've got marines and Mobiles all along there.'

'It would be better if they weren't there at all and we could fire straight through them.'

Of their field artillery, only the howitzers could hurt the enemy troops. Their guns and the *mitrailleuses* were effective only at point-blank range – and the chief obstacles were the buildings being used for cover by their own troops.

Brunel saw the solution. 'We'll blow them. In fact, we'll burn our whole position. We aren't going to take this town by digging in, we need to clear fields for our artillery.'

'You're going to burn down the whole sector?'

'Why not? At least Trochu will know where to bring his troops, if he ever gets them across the plain.'

As the houses went up, one by one, the battle in their sector froze. The marines dynamited the stone buildings, cracking them open to expose the wooden structures inside. Incendiary mortars touched off the wood and flames sprang up into the winter night.

'They're going to think we're insane.'

Brunel watched the fires spread. 'That's good. No one wants to fight an insane enemy.'

The Prussians had fallen silent. Brunel imagined them fleeing from their own rooftop positions as the fires from the nearby houses spread to their buildings. And in this silence, Brunel's field artillery cranked up again, using the fires for cover as they began beating a route into the city.

The Franc-Tireur lieutenant, a journalist, was already imagining the headline: CAPTAIN BRUNEL, THE BURNER. He was smiling, he was so pleased with himself.

As they forced their way deep into the town, their progress was lit by the buildings that they were torching. But by the time night took hold, it became clear that President Trochu would never reach them.

Their retreat was lit by the percussion shells from the German Krupps guns. The flashes of light momentarily brought into resolution the silhouettes of the stretcher-bearers, all dotted across the plain, before disappearing again. The Francs-Tireurs led the way back to St Denis, carrying the wounded. The Mobiles and the marines covered the rear. The dead stayed behind, waiting for the ceasefire to be collected and buried.

They actually stumbled over Trochu's army on the long flat plain of Le Bourget. The ground was frozen solid but Trochu had given orders to dig trenches and secure their positions. It was lunacy. The temperature was dropping even further and these soldiers, many of them untrained Nationals, were not even scratching the surface. Brunel heard one of his Bretons curse the stupidity of the Parisians; these cunts were all crazy, what did they think they were doing? When Brunel next tripped over an officer, he demanded to know what was the idea. Surely Trochu could not force his men to freeze through the night on an icy plain? But, like General Ducrot before him, President Trochu was too scared to return to Paris only hours after he had set out. It seemed that he was determined to hang on until morning and delay the moment when he would have to admit that the attack had been a disaster.

The officer was only a kid, and close to despair. 'I can't even drive a tent peg into this ground. It's like iron.'

The wind came sweeping down from the Prussian lines, cutting across the flat plain like death's own scythe. There was nothing in its path, nothing but men scrabbling to take cover in the slightest dip in the ground. Frozen puddles were shattered with the butts of rifles and soldiers made their beds among the splinters. Of the three thousand casualties from the battle, a thousand were cases of frostbite. The majority of those who died that night were drawn from Brunel's forces. Long after the next day's retreat, when the ambulances were allowed out under the Geneva cross, they brought back almost three hundred corpses and there were even more marines missing.

As Brunel waited in St Denis, he made up his mind to send word to Babette that he was safe. They had seen each other only once since the slaughter of Pollux and it had been clear, then, that the death of the elephant had altered their relationship, if that was an appropriate word for a state of constant tension. The intensity was gone now, with an elephant corpse in the way. So there was no reason to send Babette a letter, except that he still spent every moment that he was able to think, thinking about her.

When her reply arrived within the hour, he was caught off-guard. It was easy to forget that these battles were being fought so close to Paris and not only that a great city lay at their backs but that a kind of life flourished there. There were still charity performances at the theatres, still newspapers and debates, still cabaret shows, readings, lectures. The celebrities of the siege would appear at the cafés or the music halls. If they were in prison, like Delescluze and Flourens, then they continued to issue proclamations from their cells.

Brunel broke the seal on Babette's letter. Every word was carefully spaced and laid out, flexing off invisible lines in supple curves. It was impossible to believe that she had created this letter within the hour; she must have written it on some previous night, in the hope she would have an opportunity to send it. It was a love souvenir, and one so poised that Brunel barely knew how to read it. He believed that the only authentic words were those that leapt from the breast to the lips. If a statement must be flattened on to paper, then it had to be swift and direct. So how could he believe this letter?

He hunched over her words in a kind of terror. He tried to read without reading, extracting her main points without noticing the ornamental settings. And once he had discarded everything else, he was left with the news that she was concerned, and that she wanted him to visit her as soon as possible.

Chez Babette I

The lights in the kitchen were low. The boy who separated the food scraps for the butcher lay asleep on a chair, huddled close to the wood stove. Brunel crept past him, turning . . .

He froze. There was a figure crucified against the back wall. It was monstrous, green and horribly swollen. He couldn't catch hold of his breath. He tried, his mouth open. He was conscious of a tic-like clicking inside his jaw. He took a single step, forcing himself forward as the first cold flush of fear receded.

It was a turtle, at least eighty kilograms in weight, hanging by its back fins. As his eyes grew accustomed to the dark, Brunel realised that it was hanging upside down, a fact that was not immediately obvious because the head had been severed. A tin bath lay beneath the turtle, half filled with a green sludge.

Light from a candle jumped and slid across the shell, bringing Brunel's reflection into brief flickering life – along with another, more vivid figure, standing at his shoulder. He turned. Babette was holding a lamp beneath her chin and the light brought a demonic cast to her features. Her eyes and lips appeared huge in a face that was divided by the heavy shadows of her brow and her broad nose. Her mouth broke open into a smile and her teeth . . .

Brunel staggered. She caught him.

Upstairs in her bedroom, she fed him soup. Not, she swore, turtle soup. That was being prepared for a Christmas feast. Her crucifix swung on its chain around her neck, moving in and out of the shadows.

'When did you last eat?'

Brunel tried to think. He had eaten that day. He knew that

he wasn't starving. He remembered a piece of boiled meat, served in its own broth. But that had been the previous day. He told her, 'You know, I came as soon as I could.'

There was a pillow beneath his head. He was wrapped in clean sheets. Babette looked beautiful, her face open and clear, framed by hair that had slipped out of its high knot. The mask he had seen in the kitchen, caught in burning paraffin, had dissolved without trace. What was it? That tribal mask, floating out of the same sea that brought the turtle.

'I sent the note three days ago.'

He knew. 'Where did you get a turtle?'

'It was fished out of the Seine.'

She smiled down at him, only confusing him. She brought another two spoonfuls of soup to his mouth before he made the right set of deductions.

'It came from the zoo? Was that my prize for killing an elephant?'

'What do you mean, your prize? What do you want with a giant turtle?' She shook her head. 'Anyway, it's on loan. I make the soup, the butcher lets me keep a few litres, and the rest is returned to him, along with the shell.' She lifted the spoon again to his lips but paused. 'The Nationals returned two days ago. Where were you?'

'I had to stay until we accounted for the last man.'

'What about me?'

'What?'

'I needed to account for you. I needed to know where you were.'

The night after the battle had been as cold as any Babette remembered. In her anxiety to know the worst, on her last visit to see her husband in Worth's hospital, she had watched an amputation. The Lord only knows why. But it was only the amputation of a toe. The blackened stub was what she remembered, lying in the doctor's enamel dish, etched with frostbite. She had hardly dared look at Brunel's toes as she undressed him.

'Did you hear me?'

His eyes flickered open. Then closed again. On the edge of sleep, between the dead of the battlefield and the crucified turtle, he was becoming confused. Once, caught in a mid-Atlantic storm when he had fought for seven straight days to keep his grip on a stair rail below decks, he had been as exhausted as he was now. But this time his exhaustion was amplified by failure; it became harder and harder to believe that any new offensive might crack the enemy.

After the Cinema

Since Flavie had arrived back in Paris, she had repeatedly tried to call Marguerite but had always been routed to a messenger service. She persevered but assumed that Marguerite did not want to speak to her. Then as she was watching the film, her phone began vibrating and she missed a whole series of calls. She became convinced that Marguerite was trying to get in touch with her – that there was an emergency. Which was when I saw her running across the cinema lobby.

Evan led me across the pavement as Flavie snapped her phone shut.

'I should have told you,' I said.

'Marguerite is in Palestine!'

'I know. I'm sorry I didn't mention it.'

She shook her mobile phone in fury. 'So I found out from Jean-Luc.'

I had emailed Jean-Luc that Flavie had returned. I had not expected him to become so excited that he would call her repeatedly until the vibration of the telephone gave her a dead leg. Four out of the five missed calls were from Jean-Luc. The last was 'caller withheld'.

Flavie said, 'This other missed call. Do you think it might be Marguerite?'

'It could be,' I said. 'Marguerite was going to buy a Sim-card from the local phone company once she got to Palestine.'

I suggested that we look on the internet and see if Marguerite's new contact details were posted on her group's website. This quickly became Evan's job, our technical expert, Q to my Bond. We were racing against the clock, which gave our mission an added frisson; Evan needed to leave for the Gare du Nord in a couple of hours to catch the last possible train to make Christmas in Coventry with his mother, his baby sister and Michael.

Evan set about finding all the sites linked to the Civil Mission to Palestine. While he skipped from page to page, Flavie hovered at his shoulder, ready to dial any numbers he came across. She kept dialling but contacted only dead lines or Arab-speakers who could not help her, who had never heard of Marguerite. And time was ticking away. The five o'clock train from Paris would arrive at London Waterloo at seven o'clock. Evan had to change stations for a connection to Coventry, arriving at nine forty-five. Assemble for midnight communion at Coventry Cathedral, 22.30 hours.

He called me over to the screen and asked if I recognised any of the names of the Palestinians working with Marguerite's group. It was four years or more since I had worked in Palestine, so I was surprised that I did recognise the name of someone on the web-page of a group called the International Solidarity Movement, a nephew of the man who had invited me to mass at that other Christmas in Bethlehem. Evan told me to try calling my friend, while he began subscribing to all the news-groups associated with Marguerite's group.

When Nadim answered the phone, he assumed that I had called for an end-of-year catch-up, and though I tried to be brisk, our conversation quickly took a sideways detour. Like me, he was spending Christmas away from his family: he had sent his wife and two young boys to stay with in-laws in America. Our common loneliness kept us talking. And with the situation in Palestine having deteriorated so much, there was a lot to talk about. The year or so that I had spent there was the quietest since the Intifada began in the late 1980s. Peaceful in the sense that there was an absence of violence – but it was also a time of inertia and friction. The only signs of efficiency were in the Israeli settlement programme that was throwing up housing estates with heart-stopping speed.

For a while, a couple of us Western advisers had shared an apartment in Ramallah, the administrative centre of Palestine. It was very much a nine-to-five, four-day-week experience, four days because my flatmates and I began taking long weekends to cover the three different Sabbaths. To escape the tension we spent most of our free time in Israel, and as it became increasingly difficult for our Palestinian colleagues to cross through checkpoints we tended to hang out solely with our Israeli friends and colleagues. Over the course of a year, I learned to scuba-dive in Eilat and to crew yachts in the Mediterranean, one of the most pleasant experiences one could imagine, until you return at dusk and realise that the dancing lights on the shore-line are the huge shanty towns of Gaza's refugee camps.

Flavie put her head around the door to see how I was doing, and found me laughing and joking with Nadim. She was sick with worry about Marguerite while I was cracking jokes: that is how it looked. I got the number of Nadim's nephew and wrapped up the call, then apologised to Flavie as I explained that I was trying to be efficient. It's just not possible to ask a Palestinian a question, get an answer and hang up.

I called Nadim's nephew. I got the information. I hung up.

'Sorry,' I said, handing Flavie the number of Marguerite's mobile.

That was it. In moments Flavie was talking directly to Marguerite. I looked at Evan and told him, good work. He was looking anxiously at the kitchen clock: his train left in forty minutes.

We made our holiday calls to my parents on the race to the station, upsetting just about everyone involved. When I next spoke to my mother, I had to apologise all over again for cutting her off mid-sentence. I tried to explain that passport control was about to close, I had to get Evan on his train, I had no choice but to end the call in a hurry. But my mother had the last word because she was the one in the right: we should have called earlier and not left it until the last moment.

When I got back to my apartment, Flavie reported that Marguerite was safe and well, dismantling roadblocks and planning a candlelit march from Bethlehem to Jerusalem. I had remembered to buy food after seeing Evan off, and so Flavie and I had our own Christmas feast, eating roast duck and drinking jasmine tea from the Chinese supermarket.

Chez Babette II

When Zizi shook him awake, Brunel saw the shaved head, the blood-stained gauze, and threw himself out of bed, scrabbling for his pistol before his brain registered what was happening. Zizi looked terrified. He was holding a gown, saying, 'I've come to shave you.'

'Why?'

'You have to look good. You've been invited to General Vinoy's banquet.'

Brunel saw his uniform hanging from the back of the door. It was pressed and laundered.

Zizi said, 'You get the best shave when your face is still asleep.'

'All of me is asleep. What time is it?'

'It's midnight. Mass will soon be over and everyone will be here.'

'Why aren't you with them?'

'I didn't feel like it this year.'

'What about Babette?'

'She hasn't been to midnight mass since I've known her, and I've known her since she was fourteen. She always works at Christmas, so she always misses mass and makes amends the next day.' Zizi had laid his tools out on the dressing table. Soap whisked to a foam. A neat pile of white towels. As he sharpened his razor on the strop, he said, 'Is it too uncomfortable to have her husband bring a razor to your neck? I would have sent Christian but another guest needs the full works. He's a redhead and, worse, he's got a full beard and psoriasis so it's difficult to tell where the skin ends and the hair begins. Christian's going to be some time.'

Zizi had lost a lot of weight and the bandage that held the dressing to his wound made his head look misshapen. While he could still be described as handsome, it was a deathly kind of beauty.

Zizi warned Brunel, 'It could be a strange night tonight.'

It was strange already.

'How so?'

Zizi was bent over the enamel bowl of hot water that stood on the washstand. 'It's not the night for a celebration, is it? But General Vinoy wants everything perfect – and since I've been spending a little too much money recently, we cannot afford to turn anyone away.'

Zizi picked up the razor again. A tremor passed through his hand and sent a quiver through the blade. Zizi tried to mask it by plunging his hand back into the bowl but it was too late.

'Are you all right?'

'Maybe a little too much war; at least for me, my friend. But I'll be fine.' Zizi flashed a smile, covering up so well that he seemed absolutely relaxed. 'I'll go and fetch my son. He can finish you in a second and, while he's at it, I can cover for him. I'll click the scissors behind the other guy's head and he'll assume that I am strimming away.'

The restaurant was hung with greenery and drapes so full and so luxuriant that as Brunel descended the stairs he felt as if he was falling through a forest canopy. The air was spiced; candles burned beneath dishes of perfumed oil, filling the room with the scent of cloves. More candles lay down the centre of the table, their flames reflected in the buttons and brocades of the soldiers' uniforms as they rose to greet Brunel. Brunel saluted his host General Joseph Vinoy, then turned to General Clément Thomas and Admiral de la Roncière, the man who had become his mentor. Then he attended to the ladies, the priests, the junior officers. Finally, he came to a halt.

There were two empty seats at the table and Brunel did not

know which one was his. He was left dangling, waiting for a sign, then he heard the yapping of a dog and hoped that this was not it. Another dog joined in the yapping, then two Pekinese emerged from beneath the arms of a tiny woman. The seat beside her was free but Brunel continued to hover. To his left, someone made a joke – asking if the Pekes were saluting Captain Brunel or guarding Mme Cordier. The woman answered in a warm purr that both Héctor and Achille – lifting each dog as she announced its name – were confused, poor things. They were shaken up by their journey into Paris. She had encouraged them to bark at Kraut officers; now they were slow to recognise his nobler French counterpart.

A woman asked, 'But if they bark indiscriminately at both French and Prussian officers, surely they would have given your brother away?'

'Oh, my dear, of course not. Gaston was clinging to the roof of the carriage. My little darlings ride inside with me.' She tufted the hair sticking straight up from the head of Achille. 'Anyway, I doubt my boys saw through Gaston's disguise. With his great beard and his long hair, he hardly looked like officer material. Nor smelled like it, to be honest. Sleeping in a stable was taking the search for authenticity a little too far, in my opinion.'

Everyone laughed. Brunel would have joined in, but he had very little idea what they were talking about. General Vinoy's eldest nephew, Henri Furet, who sat on the far side of Mme Cordier, took such energetic delight in everything she said that Brunel assumed they were lovers.

Mme Cordier smiled up at Brunel. 'I believe you are placed by me, sir.'

Brunel bowed, said his thanks and took his seat. The nearest dog sniffed at him through its squashed nose.

Gilles Furet sat on the opposite side of the table, beside the wife of General Thomas. Then came Admiral de la Roncière, who shot Brunel an encouraging smile. As Brunel smiled back, he felt the tightness of his skin, fresh from its shave. There was a priest on the admiral's right-hand side, breaking the alternating male-female order. Maybe that was a necessity. Among the twelve guests there was another priest and a couple of other young women, wives or mistresses or sisters, Brunel could not tell. He finished surveying the table, ending with Mme Cordier. That brought a jolt. She was staring straight at him, with an arched eyebrow and an amused look on her face.

Mme Cordier demanded confirmation: was it true that they had something in common? Brunel doubted it, but asked, 'What is that, madame?'

'We both had to slip through enemy lines to be here. I drove through on the Versailles road this morning. Can you imagine the palace at Versailles filled with Prussians?'

Brunel had to admit he could not – but then he had never been to Versailles. One of the priests declared that the thought distressed him. He mentioned a certain Father, apparently the confessor to the Empress Eugénie, although the name meant nothing to Brunel.

'I often visited Versailles in his company,' the priest said. 'But the memory is soured, now that I imagine the Prussians sleeping top to tail in her bed.'

'There's an image,' replied Mme Cordier. 'But let's not dwell on it. At least, the Prussians allowed me to visit my Henri. I could thank them for that.' Mme Cordier's fingers briefly skipped across her lover's arm. 'Despite the fact that I told them I was frightfully unimpressed by their cannons. They insisted that I must be terrified. I said, must I, really? I probably wasn't paying attention. Achille was barking so, he must have drowned them out.'

Amid the laughter, Brunel heard Gilles Furet praise the amontillado. Brunel had already realised that the wine was special; it floated across his palate and fanned the back of his throat with the warmth of toasted nuts. He took another sip. He had hoped Christian's shave would invigorate him and it had, but the effect was wearing off. Brunel was drifting away when Mme Cordier, sensing this, pulled him back with a hand on his arm.

'But you entered Paris disguised as a farmer? I really feel left out. My brother was dressed up as my coachman, you came as a lonely cowherd. What kind of disguise might I have adopted, do you think?'

'Are you easily disguised, madame? I imagine you would stand out.'

'Aren't you gallant, Captain.' Now her fingers danced on Brunel's arm, until she heard the sound of boots on the staircase. 'Ah, here's my sweetie, Gaston.'

Everyone around the table rose. The man was clearly a soldier, though he was in civilian clothes. As the other soldiers saluted him, Brunel followed their lead. He had enough wits about him to realise that this was Mme Cordier's brother: a tall blond man with traces of red in his sweeping moustache. There was no beard; Christian had shaved him of his disguise. Nor was there any trace of psoriasis. After Zizi's description of the man, Brunel might have expected his head to be nothing but a flayed piece of red flesh. Either Zizi had exaggerated, or he and Christian knew how to soothe the angriest skin.

Mme Cordier's brother was greeted as a general as he moved around the table to take his seat, each man giving him a secondary bow to complement the initial salute. The women got kisses, on their hands or on their cheeks. And Brunel realised, at last, that he recognised this man: General Gaston de Gallifet. He had fought at Sedan and taken part in the surrender. If he had now smuggled himself into the city, then he must be ready to fight and break his *parole* just as General Ducrot had done.

Gaston de Gallifet took the last seat. After a last burst of noise, the table began to subside into coughs and murmurs, then these also died away. The curtain was about to rise. Murielle arrived with a tureen of turtle soup, helped by one of the sous-chefs. Brunel sat and waited; when the green liquor was served, he lifted his spoon and simply let it swivel between his fingers. The gasps of appreciation around the table did nothing to encourage him. When Mme Cordier next spoke to him, he gave her his full attention, grateful for the distraction.

'Did you really drive a cow all the way through the German lines?'

'I abandoned the cow on the road. If anyone had warned me that fresh milk was so rare, I might have brought it all the way into the city.'

'A gift for our clever Babette?'

Her praise for Babette merged with the chorus around the table, everyone swearing that the turtle soup was a wonder, a genuine creation. Brunel turned the handle of his spoon again and let the thick green liquid fill its bowl. At last, he lifted the spoon to his mouth. There was something familiar here; he had eaten sea turtle before. But this soup wiped away his memories and replaced them with an elaborate fantasy – where the sea turned to cloud and the cloud dissolved on his tongue.

In the next lull, Brunel found himself having to explain his cowherd disguise to General Clément Thomas's wife. She listened to his story, told jointly between Brunel and her husband, and ended by saying, 'They could have made use of the cow in Belleville. Without any milk, the youngest children don't stand much chance.'

'Except that their fathers would have killed the cow for a steak supper before the babies ever got close to it.' This was Henri Furet. 'I warned Mme Cordier not to visit Belleville. Or if she did, to leave her dogs at home or they'd be on someone's table this Christmas.'

A young woman declared, 'I could never eat a dog,' just as another voice – General Vinoy himself – declared that he had tried dog only yesterday at Brébants.

'All it requires is a sauce.'

General de Gallifet laughed out loud at this. 'Dog, my general? Are you barking?'

'Tomorrow, sir, you dine with me siege-style: rats, cats and puppy dogs.'

'I'll hold you to that.'

The laughter segued into a debate over salt; there was virtually none to be had. Then there was a discussion of prices; someone had seen cat on sale for twenty-five francs a kilo. Rats had reached fifty centimes each. The butcher Roos was capitalising on the fashion for novelty meats. There were crowds outside his shop, looking at the flayed elephant's trunk hanging in the window, though at seventy-five francs a slice.

Henri Furet said, 'We have the lieutenant to thank for our fresh supplies of elephant meat.'

Brunel looked up, trying to guess the man's motive in introducing this dismal piece of information.

Brunel enjoyed a few moments of silence as the next course was served. He had thought he would be unable to eat the turtle soup – but now it was gone and he was staring down at nests of caviar eggs, cradled on pancakes in the Russian style. Again, he was filled with doubts and listlessly scraped a few eggs on to the back of his fork. It was only when Mme Cordier nudged him that he realised General Vinoy was speaking directly to him.

'Your troops made a valiant effort at Le Bourget.'

'I was proud of them, General.'

'You engaged the enemy, while Trochu never even saw them. Ain't that right, Gilles?'

Gilles Furet had been peering towards the back of the restaurant. He whipped around as his uncle spoke.

'Yes, sir. The fog was so thick, our men had nothing to aim at. The Prussians only had to keep tossing their shells over, and they tore great chunks out of us.'

'I thought Captain Brunel lit your way?'

'That was glorious – the whole of Paris has toasted the Burner in the last few days.' The young man grinned happily at Brunel. 'Though it came too late for us. By the time Le Bourget was ablaze, half our line had disappeared back to Belleville.'

General Vinoy said, 'Tell me, Captain Brunel, was Trochu well advised to sack Auguste Ducrot?'

Vinoy had to wait a moment for a reply – Brunel was stopped dead by the caviar eggs as they ripened silkily in his mouth, to contrast with the briskness of the buckwheat. He had to force himself to swallow, wanting only to leave these flavours coursing across his palate.

Finally, 'Sir, I believe General Ducrot would no longer provide effective leadership.'

'Is that your opinion, Captain? It's no secret that I had my differences with him. He threatened to resign if he did not get command of the Paris forces. I was left with a choice, split the army or swallow my pride. But you've done well from your association with Auguste. Are you an ambitious man, Captain Brunel?'

'I would not say so.'

Admiral de la Roncière leapt to his defence. 'You do not know Captain Brunel very well, Joseph. He's one of those honest men who takes more pride in a job well done than in receiving the credit for it.'

Brunel wondered if this was an accurate assessment, but he let it pass. As he finished his caviar and blinis, he let many false words pass. He wondered why Gilles Furet had been so disparaging of the Nationals when his own lover had fought in their ranks. Many of the diners knew of Gilles Furet's relationship with Zizi – indeed, the reason that Furet kept looking over his shoulder was that Zizi was hovering in the passageway, anxiously smoking a cigar, and each time Murielle brushed through the curtains, Zizi and Furet exchanged stolen looks.

General Clément Thomas took up the theme of the Nationals' reliability. 'The difficulty is countering the influence of the Red Clubs – that's been the struggle from the beginning.'

'And we pay them for their disloyalty.' This was Mme Thomas, who was swiftly backed up by another of the women, declaring that only the women and children were suffering. 'The men get their army rations and their franc a day to spend on alcohol. Once they are drunk, do you think any of them cares how their families survive? We laugh about feeding on cat meat. In Belleville, the children are living on biscuits of bonemeal and cardboard.'

Brunel ate boiled salted mutton every day; it was monotonous but there was no sign that the mess was facing shortages. The idea that children could be living on biscuits – inedible biscuits – would have been difficult to absorb at the best of times. When he was surrounded by such luxury, it was impossible.

'I read an article in a Red newspaper today,' Henri Furet said. 'The writer declared himself for drunkenness and against discipline – arguing that if our troops were sober at Sedan then so much for sobriety. He believes in the passion of the ordinary man, wherever it comes from, even out of a bottle.'

Mme Cordier flared up. 'I would very much like to meet the writer of that article, Henri. I hope I would have the strength to make him eat his rag. What does he know of Sedan?' She pointed to her brother. 'Gaston led a cavalry charge into the Prussian guns. After the first, when General Ducrot asked whether he thought he could do it again, what did you reply, Gaston?'

'I told him, as often as you like, sir. As long as one of us is still on his horse.'

The table applauded him. The young general shone his bluff smile about the table. 'On our third sally, the Prussians rose up to give us a standing ovation.'

Brunel had heard this story many times before – it was part of the growing legend of Sedan, though he had not seen it happen himself because he had already been taken prisoner. He only saw these generals later, when they too were led into captivity. Yet when Henri Furet led a toast to General de Gallifet's squadron – 'Everywhere renowned as the bravest at Sedan' –

Brunel lifted his glass. He agreed that the cavalry were as brave as the Marsouin. Just more stupid. This thought inevitably led Brunel to Bazeilles and only the clinking of a glass brought him back to the table. There would be a second round of toasts, led by General Vinoy. Even now, he was rising to his feet to speak.

'It is true. We are fortunate to have General de Gallifet here, allowing us to toast the hero of one of the few valiant moments of last summer's debacle.'

A new wine was being served, the yellow label of Veuve Cliquot that even Brunel recognised. The entire company lifted their glasses and toasted General de Gallifet once more. The wine had barely passed Brunel's lips when General Vinoy continued.

'But we have one other hero of that summer with us. Our guest the Burner fought at Bazeilles.'

Brunel heard the name echo around the room. He understood: this was why he had been invited to General Vinoy's Christmas feast. Babette had led him into one circus, where he entertained the crowds by machine-gunning an elephant. Now here he was again, at the centre of a more select assembly. He was the hero of Bazeilles, live and dangerous. The faces of those lifting their glasses to him, smiling in the candlelight, looked genuine. But, Brunel knew, they had a very different perspective on the world. So what did they want from him? What did they think he could do for them?

He raised his own glass in thanks and brought it to his lips. The champagne in his mouth simultaneously echoed as it erased the caviar: its dry-biscuit taste reminding him of the buckwheat pancakes, the bubbles of the eggs. Brunel began to understand that there is a certain kind of sensual experience that no longer takes place on the material plane; its natural homeland is the world of dreams.

As Brunel returned from the lavatory, he looked towards the kitchen, hoping for a glimpse of Babette. Instead, he found Christian waiting for him. Brunel returned the boy's smile.

'How are you? Are you all right?'

'I'm fine, sir. How's the meal?'

'Good. Very good. Everyone's enjoying it.'

'You and General de Gallifet are the guests of honour. And General Vinoy paid ten thousand francs for this party.'

'Ten thousand francs?' Brunel thought he had misheard. 'What was ten thousand francs?'

'The meal.'

This was an enormous sum of money, five times Brunel's annual wage. Christian was quick to add, 'For all twelve guests, of course.'

Brunel looked through the curtains that led back to the restaurant and all the people gathered for this meal. Maybe he ought to be flattered that the general had assumed his loyalty would cost so much. Brunel did another calculation: twelve guests meant eight hundred and thirty francs each, or forty-odd louis. Was that the equivalent of a year's wage for a skilled man? It was definitely in the area.

'Sir, are you going to take charge of the National Guard?' Christian asked.

'General Thomas commands the Nationals. Why would I do it? I'm a Marsouin.'

'General Thomas would not appear on a battlefield, sir, he's only a quartermaster. They were talking about it earlier.'

'Not to me.'

'Sir, if you do assume command, can you refuse to take the 125th?'

It took a moment before Brunel realised the significance. 'Is that your father's battalion? You don't need to worry, your father won't fight again.'

'He says that he will.'

When Brunel returned to his seat, he found a new dish had been brought to the table: small birds, perhaps quails or, he wondered, small pigeons? They were encased in delicate pastry shells. He turned from the plate and picked up his champagne glass, smiling at General de Gallifet across its brim. The smile hurt him, but it was returned easily, swimming out of the warm glow of candlelight seen through crystal.

'I must say, it is a great relief to see you, General. Are you hopeful we can break the siege?' Brunel asked.

Gallifet shook his head. 'Alas, I'm not here to fight, Captain. I gave my *parole* to the Prussians.'

'My brother does not break his word as easily as other men.' Mme Cordier's voice had risen. What had seemed an attractive purr now had a dangerous edge. 'From what I see of Paris, we would have been better off if General Ducrot was also a man of honour and kept his word.'

'When Auguste Ducrot gives his word, you have to ask: what's his agenda?' said General Vinoy. 'His word has no value in itself; it's there to be bartered or sold. He gave his word to the Prussians and broke it. So what? He swore to the mob that he would bring them victory, or die on the battlefield. He let them down, too.'

Brunel felt compelled to speak. 'Sir, with respect, the break-out to Orléans failed because the plan was forced on us at the last moment.'

'Yes, it was forced on us. And we were forced to use the National Guard. The new politics demand that the multitude must have its voice. Well, if the mob wants another go, we will have to indulge them. But let us make sure that this is the very last time.'

'What do you intend?'

'Trochu and Ducrot thought they could handle the mob. They allowed the Nationals to elect their own officers and drink themselves stupid. They gave them rifles that are twenty years out of date, as the British do with their Hindu troops. But the truth is, the mob is in control and why?' He stared around the table. Everyone waited for his pronouncement. 'Commanding men can never be a career. It's the highest duty and responsibility, and that's too much for one person to bear. The gift to command can only come from a tradition. But now we have generals thinking first of their careers, and threatening to resign when they don't get the top jobs. They forget their first duty is to the honour of their regiments and to France. Well, Auguste Ducrot lost. He played to the mob and he lost us the war. Now it's time to start behaving like officers again and getting our priorities right.' Vinoy seemed to have finished his speech, but he was only playing with his timing. 'And fuck the mob.'

The table laughed.

Brunel looked at the pigeon on his plate; the pastry didn't represent a shell. It was a coffin. 'It is true, General Ducrot was forced to use the Nationals. But not because he wanted to – because they wanted to. They may be the mob. But I've seen their newspapers, I've seen them training, I've even seen them in their clubs. They don't think the war is lost. They are still ready to fight.'

'Yes – drunk on absinthe and reeling from their leaders' speeches, they think they can achieve anything. Well, let's give them a last chance. They know you, Captain Brunel. After Le Bourget, they know that you fight to the last. How would you like to make colonel?'

The offer came with a flourish. A few weeks ago, Brunel was a lieutenant. He had been a marine for almost twenty years; now his career was suddenly in the ascendant. But he knew what he was being asked to do.

Vinoy spelled it out anyway.

'The mob are going to get what they want. Let's just make certain that it's the last time. We are not fools, soon we will have to make peace. When that time comes, we do not want the Nationals overconfident, still full of piss and fire. We have to knock that out of them.'

I Cook

Flavie and I threw a great New Year party. She hosted the dance floor and I provided the chill-out rooms and buffet. In the landing between our apartments, we draped swathes of material in imitation of a Bedouin tent, partly as a reception room to welcome our guests, chiefly to symbolise the fact that Marguerite, the guest of honour, had arrived home from Palestine. She looked rather dazed as she stepped through the curtain, accepting the oyster that I opened for her and the glass of champagne that Flavie put into her hand. Dazed but pleased, as she told us it all looked beautiful. She didn't look bad herself, in a slinky floor-length dress and with her long red hair styled so that it fell as a curtain across one eye and spooled on one shoulder like an expensive scarf.

She said, 'Happy New Year.'

'Forget New Year, this is a welcome home party for you,' I said.

She laughed it off, though Flavie insisted that it was true. 'Why would we lie? I didn't even realise it was New Year until James mentioned it this morning. Welcome back, darling.'

Flavie had invited all the girls from the gay bars, May and Louise and Héloise and Harry (a woman), and up to thirty others whose names I don't think I ever knew. Elise arrived with a new girlfriend who was young enough for everyone else to mutter disapproval while, at the same time, begin to feel rather old.

I was glad to see Jean-Luc, just back from Thailand, though he stood over me in my own kitchen, criticising my technique as I rolled out thin cuts of beef between greaseproof paper, and told me that I should have prepared this dish much earlier because carpaccio must be chilled before it is served.

I said, 'You can't cook, you French twit.'

'I can eat,' he replied, picking a stray piece of the carpaccio off my rolling pin. 'And on the whole, I am impressed.'

I was doing the catering as research, either cooking or preparing those things that did not need cooking. I had learnt to open oysters with the tip of a small knife. I had arranged a stack of *fruits de mer* and rearranged it when I failed to achieve unrestrained superfluity, a dizzy lobster leering over the heads of the langoustines like a lecherous drunk. I had made a Russian and an Arabic salad, both incredibly time consuming because the ingredients had to be cut up so finely. There was no turtle soup and no birds encased in pastry coffins, but I did serve individual Yorkshire puddings that I intended to be cradles for the slithers of carpaccio, my one attempt at an original dish. I guess no one can learn how to cook in a week, but I think I faked a good banquet, using ready-made ingredients, hours of preparation and a steaming credit card. The most ambitious element was the roast suckling pig. I spent days reading and rereading the recipe, comparing it with others until I decided it was a possible project.

The pig occupied one side of the table, the lobsters the other. As Jean-Luc and I stood at the table admiring it, he put an arm around my shoulder and said, 'Magnificent. Roast pork, beautiful shellfish; who would have thought the guest of honour was Jewish. No one's going to accuse you of being kosher, my friend. Your Republican credentials are beyond reproach.'

'Oh, fuck, I forgot. Is she going to be offended?'

I looked around wildly and found Marguerite just ten feet away in the chill-out room, my bedroom. Elise and her young girlfriend were also there, reclining against my futon. In fact, of the ten or so people scattered around the room, only Marguerite seemed unable to recline – she was irredeemably stiff. But as I approached, I found she was speaking with lucidity and fervour, describing her fortnight in a Palestine full of violent settlers, teenage soldiers and indomitable refugees. She was explaining that the Palestinians had been asking for United Nations observers for years but Israel would not countenance any international intervention. Marguerite's civilian volunteer force was created to fill that gap.

Elise said, 'So you're there to replace the United Nations? I thought you were anti-global; isn't the UN a global organisation?'

Marguerite refused to rise to the bait. 'I believe the world should not be run for the benefit of international corporations, so I have to imagine transnational bodies that will regulate business.'

Elise rolled her shoulders, creating the impression that a body like hers demanded constant and fine adjustments to be kept happy. 'And are the Palestinians being persecuted by big business, do you think?' she said, as she settled down, one arm draped around her young girlfriend. Then she turned to me. 'Perhaps we should ask James the economist?'

'Don't drag me into this, Elise. I'm the cook.'

'But you must have an opinion. Is international business a bad idea? Is it persecuting the Palestinians?'

I wondered if there was a way to banish Elise from my apartment. I certainly didn't have the party-host skills to police her behaviour. So I said, 'The food is ready, but it's not very kosher, I'm afraid.' I threw an apologetic grimace to Marguerite. 'Is that okay? I just didn't think.'

'Of course it's okay. It looks delicious,' she said, linking my arm with hers. 'Let's eat.'

As we moved to the front of my buffet, I groped for a bit of conversation and began telling Marguerite that I once had an argument with an Israeli who attacked every organisation with 'World' in the title, beginning with the World Bank and ending with the World Wildlife Fund. I said, 'I guess you could say he was anti-global.'

It was supposed to be a funny story, but Marguerite replied, 'But you worked for the World Bank.'

'Yes and that explains why he hated them,' I said. 'But I had nothing to do with the World Wildlife Fund. He believed that if history had taught the Jews anything, it was that each time they were put in a weak position they were less than a step away from the gas ovens. And so, because no one cares about the Jews except for the Jews, Israel has a responsibility to never surrender its power to any higher body. And, he said, that goes for the World Wildlife motherfuckers.'

Now that I had finished the story, I was no longer sure if I was joking or trying to illuminate Israeli society. Marguerite gave me a half-smile – about fair.

When I lived among Israelis, I spent my time almost exclusively in right-wing circles. After all, I was advocating free-market ideas and presenting them as solutions. I was selling the idea that trade demanded openness, openness guaranteed communication and communication meant freedom. And I really believed this, as did my Israeli friends. But they had other views that I slowly grew to understand, concerning the whole area of Israel's relationship with the international community. There was a growing conviction in Israel that they were being patronised by older nations in their constant calls for Israel to live up to international norms. They believed, rather, that Israel was at the vanguard of a new understanding of international politics. The onus was not on Israel to grow up, but on the rest of the world to abandon the fanciful dreams of world order and the hope for international law, and to accept the reality Israel lived under. Israel's reality was the question of security, which even then was synonymous with the phrase 'war on terror', which had emerged in the early 1980s and included everything from the Israeli bombing of Beirut to its policy of assassinating foreign nationals. One of the big stories from my time in Israel was the almost comical bungling of an assassination attempt in A mman. The Israeli assassins were discovered to be travelling on illegally acquired Canadian passports. Canada lodged an official complaint. I don't know what happened next. The affair seemed to fizzle out.

My experiences in Israel had been part of the reason that I lost interest in economics. I was offering the Palestinians a blueprint for a functioning, market-run, civil society. And the Israelis I met – admittedly a small circle – were genuine in their wish to see Palestine adopt these proposals and enter a new age of market-led peaceful prosperity. But the core issue for Palestinians was national liberation and there was no enthusiasm among Israelis to see this achieved. The Palestinian reality, the military occupation, was eclipsed by the Israeli reality, the need for security. And among the Israelis I met, the only security tool that they were willing to accept was the absolute right to do what they wanted, whenever they wanted, wherever they wanted, unconstrained by any norm or any outside body.

How does that sound? Does it sound as though Marguerite and I could thrash out a line on the Middle East in a spirit of comradeship and accord? At least we were beginning to bond, that night. She liked the lobster and the Yorkshire pudding, and if she avoided the pig, well, so did everyone else. It was undercooked.

By one o'clock in the New Year, we were all dancing in Flavie's apartment. I had one eye on Flavie and Marguerite, and when I watched them dance together, it was difficult to believe they would only ever be friends, not lovers.

Elise pulled me to one side, whispering in my ear, 'What do you think? Will Marguerite stay the night?'

'You're incorrigible, Elise. This evening is supposed to put an end to all the mind games.'

'I'm just speculating.'

'Not looking for new ways to cause trouble?'

'Why should I care? Have you noticed my girlfriend? Isn't she hot?'

'You're very lucky, Elise.'

'You know I'm talking about sex.'

'I know.'

It was a relief to find Flavie and Marguerite, later, standing together as they waited for the toilet in my apartment to become free.

Flavie said, 'You know James has this fantastic beautiful son who sends me emails and tells me all about England.' And turning to me, 'I can't believe he's yours. He's so responsible and grown up.'

'Only a couple of years younger than Elise's girlfriend.'

'Happy 2002.'

As we clinked our glasses together, I reflected that I was more than halfway through my tenancy. Soon I would be going and letting Ben have his apartment back.

The End of the Republic

Brunel left his horse with his adjutant, Barclay, and entered Château d'Eau on foot. This was the rendezvous point for the battalions from Belleville, as well as those from Buttes-Chaumont, from Montmartre and the rest of western Paris but, down at street level, there was no way to discern the separate battalions. It was bubbling chaos, filled with jostling elbows, backpacks, rifle butts and bayonets, rank with the smell of mouldy wool, sweat, tobacco and so much alcohol that the air seemed to shimmer. Brunel looked up at the buildings that surrounded the square, each one plastered with political posters, and chose the local burlesque theatre, distinguished by its large wraparound balcony, as the best vantage point. He needed to climb above the crowd to get a true picture of his army and its organisation.

There were far more than the forty thousand Nationals he expected. The crowds flowed out of the square in every direction and included wives, girlfriends and children, together with all kinds of wagons and omnibuses, forming motley caravans that stretched the entire distance to the smokestacks of Belleville. Looking down on this rolling mass, Brunel could see individual battalions grouped together, forming loose balls about the square. The height also gave him a sense of the crowd's restless energy. He remembered the morning that he first arrived in Paris; it was in Château d'Eau that he and Barclay had had their run-in with Flourens. In spite of Flo's talent for rabble rousing, that day was nothing compared to the spectacle now laid out below him. These people were starving and they were drunk; so, right there, Brunel found two reasons for their mad chattering exuberance. But that hardly began to explain their willingness to fight.

He rejoined Barclay and told him to keep hold of his horse; he wanted to ride on top of one of the omnibuses. As the bugle sounded, Brunel stood on the open deck and waited for the battalion commanders to respond. He won their attention and swung his raised arm: forward. They were ready to roll out. From atop the bus, Brunel felt as though he was floating above the crowd. The truth was that he only wanted to avoid riding his horse. The hard frosts of December had given way to freezing rain and though the weather was dry so far, he was certain there was black ice underfoot. He was not going to risk falling in front of the army he was supposed to be leading.

He would almost say that he was delivering the Nationals, rather than leading them. On the way to Porte Maillot, they would pick up another ten thousand Nationals from the central arrondissements; then, when they joined with the regular army, they would be divided into columns for a three-pronged assault on Versailles. Brunel would command only one of these columns, and his authority derived from General Vinoy. Brunel was under strict orders to keep his men out of the city centre on their way west and, especially, away from the Hôtel de Ville. He chose a route that curved above the city centre on the new Boulevard Haussman. There had been trees, saplings really, lining this avenue. They had begun to disappear in early November, and at first it had looked like vandalism – the saplings were snapped off at the height of the steel cages that surrounded them. But then the scavengers became professional. They tore down the cages and cut the broken stumps off level with the paving stones. Now that the stocks of gas and paraffin and firewood were gone, old women and young children could be glimpsed among the crowds, digging into the ground with bread knives and pokers, trying to prise out whatever remained of the trees' roots. They reached the unfinished Opera House to find its wooden cladding had been stolen, exposing the scaffold skeleton that held the massive dome aloft.

The battalions of the 1st and 2nd arrondissements came marching around the Opera House and halted, waiting to join the procession. The cheering became deafening, as the Belleville Nationals welcomed these new battalions into their ranks. They were cheered back in their turn, by their comrades and the masses of well-wishers thronging the streets. Brunel stood with his hands on the omnibus rail and found Zizi, Lieutenant Georges Hébert, sitting astride his horse at the head of the 125th. In the month since Christmas, Brunel had seen Zizi a number of times, as he had seen the commanders of all the National Guard battalions, but he had never asked Zizi why he had campaigned so hard to take command of the 125th. Zizi knew that this battle was intended only to teach Paris the wisdom of surrender, yet still wanted to fight.

Once, just once, Brunel had asked Zizi about Babette. This was a fortnight earlier, after the Prussians began shelling the city from the Châtillon Heights. Zizi assured him that Babette was safe. Since then, three or four hundred shells had been fired into the city every night but none had landed north of the Seine, so Brunel had not asked again. Anyway, he had other connections to Babette and to her restaurant. Barclay was seeing Murielle, for instance. Although Brunel did nothing, he often found himself rehearsing a confrontation with Babette. He would demand to know: was she happy that she had delivered him to General Vinoy, gift-wrapped, at a Christmas meal? He imagined her turning on him, asking why he had been so compliant if he found the general's offer so offensive. Each time he played their argument through, she remained proud and unapologetic. In truth, however, he had no idea what she would say. What kind of woman was she, betraying a dark and unpredictable humour as she served the generals of Paris a Christmas meal of little birds, each one laid out in an individual pastry coffin?

Barclay guided his horse out of the ranks and picked his way to the roadside where Murielle was waiting for him. The girl allowed herself to be hoisted off the ground for a kiss that ended in smiles, though her face shone with tears. There was Zizi, leaning out of his saddle to embrace Freddie Worth and Christian.

Finally, a pace to the side, he found Babette, her dark eyes like saucers in her pale face. She was staring at him, and as the procession had stalled he could do nothing but sit there, on top of a bus, under her gaze.

It was night when they left Porte Maillot. There was no moon, and as the rain gathered strength the vast field of tents was almost invisible. The regular army had been spirited away to reinforce the forts, leaving only forty thousand professional troops to match the fifty thousand Nationals taking part in this mass sortie. The Red papers had been clamouring for what they called a 'torrential attack'. Day after day, they had extolled the indomitable energy of the Parisian masses. They would soon find out how effective this energy could be when it was not backed by experience or training.

Brunel was now riding on a munitions truck, containing ten *mitrailleuses* in wooden crates. As he reached the river, word came that no one had removed the barricades on the bridges. This slowed the whole army to a painful crawl, marching three abreast. Brunel's wagon just scraped through, and that was achieved only by unhooking the horses and manhandling the wagon around the obstructions. Brunel was leading the foremost troops. Over the course of the night, ninety thousand men would have to navigate their way through these barricades in pitch darkness and heavy rain.

Brunel had stared at this landscape so often, both on maps and on models in General Ducrot's now empty pavilion. After the break-out to Normandy was abandoned, many alternatives had been laid before the army council, but only one was ever dismissed as outright lunacy: an attack south-west towards Versailles. And now that was what they were going to do, using mostly untrained men. The plan was to strike in three columns along the Versailles road. Brunel, on the left-hand side, sheltered beneath the fort at Mont Valérien, behind the monumental system of earthworks and trenches that the French had built as defences. His troops drew courage from their sheer scale. Once they moved into the open, they would be facing row after row of entrenched Prussian positions. It was six o'clock, the time scheduled for the attack, when General Vinoy appeared, at the head of a regiment of Zouaves whose command he had gleefully assumed from General Ducrot. Brunel's column would engage the Prussians head on, while Vinoy hoped to outflank them with his Zouaves. Like Zizi, in his way, Vinoy was planning not simply to survive, he expected to find glory in certain defeat. But while Zizi lacked the experience to rise above the pointless and vainglorious, Brunel had to assume that Vinoy knew what he was doing. He had remained in the army through monarchies, republics and empires. He would surely not want his name tied to a debacle, even one that he had planned.

As he rode over to Brunel, General Vinoy saluted and shouted down, 'Good hunting, Colonel. Ready to saddle up?'

'Yes, General. Are the other columns in place?'

'There's no problem with the centre. Can't say there is any news of Auguste Ducrot, but no doubt he will catch up.'

General Ducrot had been placed in command of the right-hand column, the only one comprised solely of regular troops. Ducrot had the furthest to travel to get into position, and he had been the last to leave. Yet even with all the handicaps – the state of the bridges, a night of driving rain that had thawed the roads and turned them to thick mud, the moonless dark and the hundreds of carts and buses of the makeshift ambulance processions that blocked the roads – even with all that, it seemed suspicious that Ducrot was still not in place. Brunel found it hard to believe that the general had got lost deliberately to spare his men the ordeal that awaited them. But it seemed possible.

The Nationals, laden with full packs containing tents and spades, clenched their *tabatières* in their hands. As they waited for the signal, the Prussian guns roared out behind them in a continuous, random shelling of civilian Paris. Brunel hoped the sound would galvanise his troops better than any speech he could make. There was no sign the Prussians knew of the imminent attack. If the Nationals could move before light, they might do some damage.

The signal came: a cannonade from Fort Valérien. Vinoy and the Zouaves swung out to their left, to be swallowed in the thinning darkness. The National Guard began moving. Brunel was back on his horse; Barclay mounted to his side, making sure that both their horses remained close together as they kept pace with the line. Brunel had abandoned the old battle orders: that the troops had to maintain physical contact with the men to each side. The Belleville battalions believed passion would win out. Brunel doubted it but allowed them to charge freely, knowing they could hardly do worse than inch towards the enemy at the pace of the slowest man.

With speed and surprise, they soon overran the forward enemy positions and harried the Prussians out of their trenches. But these positions were lightly defended and within the hour, as the dawn mist dissolved in the weak sunlight, Brunel knew they had failed. The enemy had dropped back, and as the Nationals were drawn into these deeper positions the enemy blazed down from their dirt ramparts. As the Nationals had attacked in disorder, they now found themselves in disarray, strung in loose groups across the battlefield. Many rushed to find cover, diving for the abandoned Prussian trenches and foxholes. Others turned to run from the battlefield. Watching them, it became easier to understand the accusations constantly laid against the Belleville battalions: that they were always too quick to run, claiming that they had been betrayed. The problem was that they had no idea how to fight a retreat. Brunel looked at the backpacks that lay scattered across no-man's land. He could have wished the men were in less of a hurry, that they had at least kept their supplies with them.

Yet there were signs of skill. The 125th were in retreat, but Zizi or his second-in-command was keeping them moving with discipline, ensuring they provided cover for their comrades as they went. A number of the Belleville battalions had found secure positions and, safely entrenched, were returning fire with a will. And where the Versailles highway began, one battalion was even pressing forward in deliberate broken lines. They were checked by the huge dirt and wood barricade across the road but they succeeded in fighting their way to cover, right at the critical point for any successful attack.

Brunel dispatched runners to summon the field artillery, so they could return enemy fire. But he was told that the artillery was still held up in the many kilometres of traffic jams and no one could predict when it would arrive. At the front, they had nothing but the *mitrailleuses* that Brunel had brought with him, and despite Barclay's pleas Brunel refused to use them. They would be useless anyway. They were at their best when gunning down tight formations of the enemy. They could never tear apart these defences, or clear a route for a fresh attack.

Barclay said, 'What else do we have? They are better than nothing.'

'They're good for making a noise, but the Prussians already know we are here.'

Brunel remembered the jagged line that the machine-gun bullets had cut in the carcass of the elephant, which had kept rearing and dancing as the bullets sprayed across it. There was no point using the *mitrailleuse* here, across more than a kilometre of battlefield with the enemy out of sight.

'What does our colonel the Burner suggest?' Barclay asked.

'We have dynamite.' He pointed to the forward troops, beneath the barricade on the Versailles road. 'Let's get dynamite over to them and see if they can blow a path for us.'

The morning lengthened, bringing both danger and embarrassment. Most of the troops that had run from the battlefield had returned and were now huddled in the Prussian-built trenches, under Prussian guns. Brunel learnt that the battalion that had advanced furthest along the Versailles road was the remains of Gustave Flourens' own skirmishers. Brunel summoned his commanders together – and it was Zizi who volunteered to take the dynamite to their position. When the detachment moved off with the crates of explosives, Brunel was relieved that it also contained Jules Bergeret, the level-headed student who had helped slaughter Pollux.

Brunel and Barclay began to rally their troops for a second attack, if it should prove possible to sweep through the barricade as Zizi and his men blasted it open. Brunel ran along the trenches and found a vantage point, focusing his field glasses on the crack and smoke of rifle fire as Flo's men tried to provide covering fire for the group of figures with the boxes of dynamite. The wait grew longer until Brunel could almost believe he had missed the explosion. But he would have seen something, cascades of earth as a passageway emerged from the dust.

Barclay said, 'What's wrong? Why aren't they blasting that thing up?'

'The dynamite could be frozen.'

'Is that possible?' When Brunel assured him it was, he added, 'Surely there must be some way of warming it?'

'Short of putting a match to it?'

The struggle to light the dynamite continued into the afternoon. The situation was ridiculous, but it was made worse when President Trochu appeared on the slopes and began urging the troops up out of the trenches.

Trochu saw Brunel and hailed him, shouting, 'Horse killed, Colonel?'

Brunel lied, snapping out, 'Yes, sir.'

'Find yourself a fresh steed, Colonel. Let's have at them, and let the Lord judge our valour.'

With no sign of progress on the highway, there was no reason to launch a fresh assault. Trochu's aim was barbaric: to force more men into the line of fire. Yet he was doing it on horseback, within range of the enemy guns. There were reports from all along the front of generals gone insane. General Vinoy was said to be deep behind the Prussian lines, fighting with his Zouaves in the heart of St Cloud. Now there was word that General Ducrot had appeared six kilometres to the north at Malmaison and was leading his men from so far in front that they were struggling to keep sight of him. Finally, there was the twit Trochu, shooting off his mouth and riding around in circles. The generals demanded that the mob face reality, but took solace in a dream world of chivalry, glory and this bizarre word, élan.

Brunel decided the time had come to rescue the troops trapped on the highway under the enemy guns. He spurred on his Nationals in a race against the twilight, directing two battalions on to the Versailles road to provide covering fire for a retreat. These were the 125th, Zizi's own battalion, and the 109th, one of the most able of the Belleville battalions. As dusk fell, their *tabatières* blazed. Red and orange flares hung in the air. The battle was fought in frozen moments, like glass plates fed painfully slowly through a magic lantern. Out of the emptiness came indistinct forms that became figures, then men.

Brunel's eyeglasses picked up flickers of faces in this gloom, with expression of relief, or exhilaration, or simply the effort of running as fast as possible. Among them came the wounded, carried on stretchers or helped by an arm slung about their shoulders, the rest hobbling their way to safety. A kneeling figure signalled for a horse, then stood as he swung a wounded man over his saddle. In the flashes of gunfire, Brunel caught two split-second images, one as the man flexed and the other as he crumpled. The two images created their own narrative: he was hit by a bullet, arched in shock and then fell beneath his horse's feet.

The man was Zizi. There was no doubt in Brunel's mind. He flew across the seventy metres of frozen ground, his boots shattering the earth below him. The horse was gone, carrying with it whoever lay alive or dead across its saddle. The man left behind, that was Zizi. Brunel knelt beside him and hoisted him on to his shoulders.

The *mitrailleuses* came into their own in the dark, peppering the night sky with flame-red lightning and filling the battlefield with a skittering noise. This was what the Prussians would remember, as the sound swirled in echoes through the ravines of Buzenval, down to Versailles: an explosive rattle, as fast as the telegraph, each beat as loud as any cannon. Behind this barrage, this spectacle, the Prussian forces did not realise that the French were leaving the battlefield. Brunel had at last allowed Barclay to deploy the machine-guns. A division of only twenty men, led by a seventeen-year-old, had succeeded in providing the cover that allowed almost fifty thousand men to slip away.

Brunel always tried to bring his wounded home. When they were risking their lives for such stupid reasons, he was more determined than ever. But getting them off the battlefield was the least of his problems. The road to Paris was still impassable. The wagons, the buses, the improvised ambulances and supply vehicles formed a solid jam on the narrow country roads.

After pressing a medical officer to make a series of assessments, and to identify those that were beyond hope and those that could be safely left for a ceasefire, Brunel struck across country with six hundred men, carrying fifty stretchers in relays. Zizi was among the wounded; Brunel had ignored the medical officer's advice that he was unlikely to last until morning. The night would be long, and there could always be a miracle.

They abandoned the road and followed the rail tracks to Paris. Where a rail bridge crossed the main road, they looked down and saw the field artillery that had never reached the battlefield. It was clear that there was no point in rejoining the road; it was jammed all the way to the Bois de Boulogne. So they kept on the railway lines, crossing the Seine further north on the rail bridge.

It was dawn as they reached the city walls, twenty-four hours after the attack began. Overnight, they had covered a distance twice as wide as the city itself. Of the fifty wounded, ten had died. Zizi was among those still holding on. The wound in his shoulder was messy. It seemed certain that the shrapnel had done more damage than they could see, or hope to repair. There was a danger, too, that the jogging of the stretcher might loosen the shrapnel, freeing it to tear away more of his insides. But he had lasted the night, and if one put a finger to his lips one felt the warmth of his breath.

Brunel led the men to the hospital at the Maison de Worth. Once there, he would go to the restaurant with the news. If Zizi was going to die, he would have everyone that he needed close by. It was early. There was a nurse awake at the hospital and soon an American doctor appeared, cutting off a yawn as he saw how many patients he had just received. Brunel did not doubt that his men would be well cared for, but there was something in this half-asleep city that was so out of step with the world he had come from that it seemed like an affront. On the morning after such a huge defeat, wouldn't the city be awake and waiting for news? Even the headquarters of the National Guard opposite Worth's looked deserted.

On a whim, he walked into the National Guard headquarters and began moving from room to room. Standing at the second-floor window, he looked down on his men sprawled below in the Place Vendôme. Brunel was tired enough to drop to the floor himself. He could have dismissed them but because he had forgotten to give the order, they were making themselves as comfortable as they could.

An old colonel appeared behind him, alerting Brunel with a cough. He had seen the men outside and wondered where they had come from.

Brunel told him: the battlefield, where else?

'I thought everyone was trapped there.'

The old man held a telegraph. He passed it over to Brunel,

who read that President Trochu was asking the Prussians for a three-day amnesty to clear the battlefield.

That was the moment when Brunel realised that his men, those six hundred Nationals strewn around the square below, were the largest force in the whole of Paris.

Part Three

Two Sieges

Babette and Brunel

The banging at the door came to her through a layer of sleep so thin that she thought she had not slept at all. She pulled herself out of bed, finding her room and the corridor beyond – in fact, the entire building – shockingly cold, and it was only through a step-one, step-two system of recall and deduction as she searched for a warm robe that she realised why. There was no wood for the stoves, so no heat. The restaurant had never been cold before.

The banging came from the rue de la Paix. She pulled open the door and found Brunel standing there, palm up, mid-strike. The last time she had seen him, he was riding to war on a double-decker bus. The city had not stopped shaking with cannonfire and explosions since then and she had made a point of blaming Brunel for every tremor.

'Madame Hébert, I've got bad news.' He spoke in a slow, calm voice. 'And there's no easy way to deliver it.' He offered his arm. 'Your husband is seriously injured. We should hurry to Monsieur Worth's hospital.'

A series of images came into her mind of Zizi, variously crippled: leaning on crutches; his head freshly swollen with bandages; sitting in a chair, wheeled across the floor. Then she realised what Brunel really meant: Zizi was dying, he might be dead already.

She reached out – Brunel was right, she did need his arm. As she grasped it, she heard the clatter of feet on the staircase, a cry of 'Papa' and found herself pushed off-balance by Christian.

'Where have you taken him?'

Brunel said, 'He's in Worth's hospital.'

The boy had squeezed his way between them and the door. Now he swung his shoulders violently, as though they were holding him back, and set off at a run down the street. Christian had somehow got hold of an army greatcoat several sizes too large, and it flapped like a sail tied to a broken mast. Under the coat, he was wearing only the clothes he had slept in. Babette found a man's coat hanging from the hook in the back corridor – lost property – and pulled it over her robe. Then she stepped out beside Brunel.

The soldiers milling around the reception rooms barely made an impression as they parted to clear a path for her. She swept through the first ward. All of the beds were occupied. Babette kept her eyes fixed ahead, but the images seeped through of men in disarray, their uniforms filthy, lying on top of the unmade beds. Then there was a sharp right-hand turn and she was in the next room. Ahead of her, Christian and Freddie and Freddie's American doctor stood around a bed. They made way for her, and she found herself staring at a bloodless head on a coarse cotton pillow. It was Zizi, though she felt she was still seeing the world through the gauze of sleep. It would take another effort of logic to make sense of the scene: how could Zizi have become so *damaged* in less than two days? His skin had gained a tight waxy look that made his moustache seem fake, too big for this shrunken head. His eyes were closed. Babette had never before thought how close-fitting an eyelid was to an eyeball, that it didn't so much protect the sleeping eye as emphasise the impossibly bulbous swell.

She asked, 'Has he woken?'

Freddie replied: he was not sure this could be called sleep.

'But he's not dead?'

Christian turned on her with anger. 'No, he's not dead.'

The doctor said, 'We can keep him comfortable and continue to watch him. If he shows any sign of recovering his strength, we might think about doing something with the wound.' The doctor was holding a galvanised spray can, similar to the one

Zizi used for hairspray though the doctor's contained disinfectant. He lifted it up as he said, 'For now, we can keep the wound clean.'

'Have you done anything else for him?'

'He's not strong enough, Madame Hébert. I don't want to do anything that risks giving fresh shocks to his system.'

The doctor appeared ready to move off, having given her all the information he could. She nodded her assent and he was gone, leaving just Freddie, Christian and herself. They were the three people who most loved Zizi – he had his boyfriends, but they were his whole family. Zizi had no doubt about that though Babette often questioned her role in it. Too many of his friends saw her as the girl who had rolled up in Paris on Zizi's coat-tails – a childhood friend or, worse, childhood mistake, rather than the mother of his son. Zizi's fifteen-year relationship with Freddie Worth held far more significance because it had come to define both men in the eyes of those who knew them. If Babette ever gave voice to her insecurity, Zizi would deny that she was extraneous in any way. He would say that passion never lasts, any more so with Freddie than it had with her. But, he would say, the most vital relationships feed off the deepest roots and without doubt the most crucial people in his life were her and Freddie and Christian.

It never really sounded plausible to her, and standing around Zizi's deathbed could hardly improve her feeling of loneliness and isolation. The word 'deathbed' slipped into Babette's mind without resistance, leaving her feeling both guilty and nauseous. This was a deathbed. That was her thirty-two-year-old husband, dying in it.

'Freddie, do you think it would be better to put him in a private room?'

She asked for her own sake, because she felt self-conscious. Zizi was no longer capable of being bothered by strangers. Christian chimed in, however, asking how they could leave him in a room without any heating. It was freezing in the ward.

Freddie put his arm around Christian's shoulder and explained that it was supposed to be cold. 'The doctor says it's good for the blood, or something.'

Worth stretched out a hand to Babette. She took it and squeezed it but let it drop.

The morning passed with no change in Zizi, nor between the three of them. They agreed that someone should remain at Zizi's bedside, but as they shared this task Babette began to become conscious of the activity around her. And not simply in the hospital. She went up to the balcony and, despite the cold, stood and looked down into the square at the men under Brunel's command. They were queuing outside the doors of the National Guard headquarters and, after a few minutes of watching, she realised that they were receiving rations of cold meat and bread. She wondered where the food could have come from – had the army kept back supplies? When the student, Jules Bergeret, appeared on the balcony, she got her chance to ask.

'It was requisitioned, Madame Hébert.'

'You mean stolen?'

'Absolutely not, madame. To say it was stolen implies that it was ever someone's property. And it was not. It was requisitioned, lawfully or at least in full moral right.'

She refined her question. 'Was it locked up in anyone's premises?'

'Yes. In the butcher's, but Colonel Brunel told us to kick in the door.' Bergeret smiled. 'Your place was declared off-limits, if that's any comfort.'

He also told her that the bread had been stolen from a bakery in the Place Madeleine. But it was only when Babette went down to the National Guard headquarters that she discovered Brunel's most audacious action. He had sent a detachment of men to cut the telegraph lines between the city and Fort Valérien, ensuring that anything that happened within Paris would not reach the ears of its generals. Babette walked from room to room in the headquarters, but Brunel was nowhere to be seen. She found a Polish officer showing a group of Nationals how to strip a *chassepot* rifle and asked him what was happening – were they planning a *coup d'état*? He told her that she ought not to worry about that.

'You're not answering my question,' she insisted.

'I am, madame. A *coup d'état* is not something you should worry about. We are several steps closer to Prussian rule than a revolution.'

When the Red posters first began appearing across the city, Babette had heard one of her customers countering their demands for a more representative Paris government by arguing that they would be better off ruled by King Frederick of Prussia than King Flo of Belleville. She wondered if this really was now the choice.

Early afternoon dimmed and dusk brought the resumption of the Prussian barrage. As the shells hit the Left Bank, the sky was splashed with sparks and flares. Every so often, the sparks would ignite a building and the skyline would dance with flames. Babette had been sitting at Zizi's bedside with Freddie Worth, but she found herself so frustrated by the sight of Freddie's huge fat head, bent in grief, that she went back up to the balcony. In the square below, lanterns danced around the great column in the Place Vendôme. Brunel had reappeared and was now gathering his forces.

She thought there must be close to six hundred men. Perhaps a third came from the central arrondissements and nearly all of these were young students like Jules Bergeret or refugees like the Polish officer she had seen giving rifle instruction. The rest came from Belleville or similar areas and included a large number of Gustave Flourens' men. Brunel gave the order and marched them out. She knew where they were heading: the Mazas prison, where Flo and Delescluze and the rest of the Red leaders were imprisoned. They were certain they would meet no opposition. There was a contingent of Breton Mobiles stationed in the

Hôtel de Ville, but they would avoid alerting them by marching along the Left Bank.

Brunel's route would take him through the scene of the Prussian bombardment: the craters left by shells, the wall sheared away from the theatre at the Odéon. The Salpêtrière hospital had been hit so often that great gouges were bitten out of its walls, exposing collapsed floors and abandoned wards. That night, the shells fell at the rate of around one a minute.

It was dark in the ward, and to sit in that dark and hear the moans, even screams, of the wounded would have been dismal enough, but to raise one's eyes and see Christian, that was heartbreaking. Everything he suffered showed in his face.

Babette heard Freddie's footsteps and stood, beckoning him to a corner of the room.

'We have to call a priest.'

'What will Christian say, if he thinks we are giving up?'

'We don't have a choice, do we? We can't wait for him to die.'

Freddie had been crying, the tears filling the doughy ripples beneath his eyes. After a long silence, he nodded – but asked her if she would be the one to tell Christian. He volunteered to fetch the priest.

Freddie returned with the Archbishop of Paris. It was an act of desperate flamboyance, but also a heartfelt tribute to a friend. No doubt, it had cost him a fortune, but Freddie was a great patron of the Church, despite suspicions that he was not even a Catholic.

As the archbishop performed the last rites, they were joined by those patients who could rise unaided from their beds. Surrounded by these men, Babette understood that Zizi had been a soldier, and his comrades wished to honour him as a hero.

He died in the early hours of the morning. Freddie immediately began promising Christian that he would plan the greatest funeral. It was strange talk. Babette wondered that Freddie was not conscious of his bad taste, but she realised he was babbling, not knowing what else to say. Christian was too shaken to reply but he pulled himself away from Freddie, and when Babette found him again he was standing on the balcony upstairs.

She said, 'Whenever you want to return to the restaurant, I'll come back with you.'

He told her that he wasn't ready to sleep. 'I just wanted to be on my own.'

'I'd prefer you to stay with me. Can't we comfort each other?'

'I don't know.'

Christian had maintained a deep anger towards her ever since she had told Zizi that he had to leave the family home. Of course, as Christian grew older, he began to understand why she was unable to live with his father and the anger would dissipate. But it would keep building in secret, and finally it would spew out again. What could she do? Arguing with him wasn't going to help. So they sat in silence. That's how they remained until almost an hour later when soldiers started filtering into the square below. They were evidently Brunel's men, returning from whatever they had been doing that night. There were so many fewer, little more than a hundred, that Babette's first thought was that they had lost numbers in a fight. But when she and Christian went downstairs, they learned that Gustave Flourens' men had returned to Belleville where Flo was celebrating his release from prison.

She found Brunel at Zizi's bedside. She did not know how long he had been there. He turned almost the moment she reached the door to the ward, strode over and offered her his condolences.

'Lieutenant Hébert fought as bravely as any soldier I've known. We can't afford to lose men like him.' He stopped, but she could think of nothing to say in reply, so he went on to ask about the funeral.

'I don't know anything about that,' she said.

'I spoke to Monsieur Worth, he said the funeral will be this morning.'

'No.' There was a clock on the salon mantelpiece. It was two in the morning. 'Are you sure? When did he tell you that?'

'Just now, as the Sisters were laying out the body.'

Babette had purposefully avoided looking at Zizi's body, which was why she had failed to notice that it was no longer clothed in uniform but dressed in white. She knew that this ought to have been her job, but it seemed that Freddie had chosen to bring in professionals.

'It's sudden. It is too sudden.' She halted. 'I think I need to speak to Monsieur Worth.'

'He said he wants to act quickly, because he's afraid the Prussians will soon enter the city.'

'Is that going to happen? I thought you were trying to stop that?'

February

I felt my life slipping into another gear throughout January and February but I did not know what it meant. Work was changing. Journalists were prepared to travel abroad again, so I was fast losing my advantage as one of the rare English-speaking hacks in Paris. And there was much less work, too. The launch of the Euro had been so smooth, it was a struggle to find enough disaster stories to sell to the British press.

The changes in work ought to have left more time for my book. But it was New Year, and it felt like time to take stock. The catalyst was Evan's leaving. I began to miss him in a helpless and wounded way. That had to change. I composed a letter to Sally and emailed it to her at work, where it lay waiting in the wires until she switched on her computer after the holidays. I could search out a copy from the files on my laptop, but it wasn't so eloquent that it deserves a second life. I simply told her that I had enjoyed Evan's stay at Christmas, and if she had any ideas how I could be more a part of his life I would welcome any suggestions. She wrote back, appreciating the sentiment and suggesting that, short of moving to the Coventry area, she didn't have a clue. She told me to speak to Evan directly and ended by reminding me that Evan loved me very much.

I have always spoken to Evan at least once a week by telephone. And we both used email. But most of the time, we simply laid down markers. Now I had to find a way of moving up a level. I had no idea how I was going to do it. Then Flavie saved me by persuading me to buy a digital camera and brighten my ordinary emails by attaching electronic pictures.

By taking the photographs, I found myself stepping back

from my life: there were a lot of pluses. Flavie lived next door. I had a great apartment, in a district that I had begun to love. I even had friends. I sent Evan photographs of everyone I knew. Jean-Luc, mid-rant over the speech that President Bush made that month, naming Iran, Iraq and North Korea as the 'axis of evil'. I sent a picture of Elise, her lips in a moue as she blew inappropriate kisses. Even a photograph of Marguerite, looking both prim and sweet, simultaneously. I also sent photographs of the most interesting-looking food in the Chinese supermarket.

Evan and I were doing well. And everyone else was happier too. Flavie and Marguerite were seeing each other, with Elise's grudging approval. Elise was dating teenagers. Jean-Luc had lost his court case but was becoming famous. And Marguerite was planning her next visit to Palestine. It was scheduled for the Easter vacation and Flavie was torn between pride and out-and-out anxiety.

I was maintaining my own link with Palestine, emailing the Palestinian doctor, Nadim, since we had renewed our friendship over Christmas. We still had one thing in common: he was missing his family, though his situation was worse. When Nadim sent his wife and two kids abroad, it was supposed to be a temporary measure, but that February an Israeli missile strike on the local government offices near his house blew out all his windows and stripped the tiles off his roof. Nadim wrote the next day to say that he was waiting for a municipal work crew to fix the damage, but he told me that he could not imagine ever bringing his family home.

After speaking to Nadim, it seemed a good idea to count my blessings. This was my last month in Paris: it was time to look around and connect before it was too late, so I took a break.

Fittingly, nothing much happened to Paul-Antoine Brunel during February 1871. He was in Sainte-Pélagie prison.

Brunel was arrested the day after he freed the rebels of the October insurrection. This was the 23 January and it would be another month before Gustave Flourens repaid his debt and broke Brunel out of prison.

Brunel had done much more than simply cut the telegraph wires and storm the Mazas prison. He ransacked the Napoleon barracks and stole the arms. He made sure that the Government could not escape in the balloons laid out on the station platforms of the Gare du Nord by pouring acid over them, leaving them in smouldering tatters. He strung three of the *bateaux-mouches* across the Seine and mined the boats. He did everything possible to stop President Trochu and General Vinoy from surrendering, either in person or by messenger. Yet despite these strenuous efforts, and his fervent belief that France was not yet defeated and the resistance could continue, he did not attempt to mobilise a full-scale insurrection.

There are later journal entries where Brunel regrets he did not move sooner. But he felt unable to do anything more until Zizi had been buried. Brunel was taken from Babette's restaurant during the funeral supper. General Vinoy's troops surrounded the building and, once Gilles Furet, one of the mourners, had informed Brunel of his position, he chose to surrender quietly.

The Birth of the Federals

In all her visits to the Sainte-Pélagie prison, Babette had tried to prise a promise out of Brunel that he would stay with her when he was released. The night that Gustave Flourens gathered together his battalion and broke him out of prison, Babette sat in the window of the restaurant until dawn without knowing whether or not he would appear. It was a few hours after first light when he tapped at her door and accepted her offer of breakfast.

She sat across from him as he ate, watching his face for every sign of displeasure or pleasure. Christian waited with a coffee pot, hidden behind the drapes in the passageway, and as Brunel finished his cup the boy slipped into the room without even disturbing the curtain material. Afterwards, she asked Brunel if he wanted to wash: she had prepared a guest room on the second floor. Not her room. She was not yet certain what she was doing. She knew the direction she was taking but felt the route was so unclear that she could still turn aside at any moment. The bowl of steaming water was the pretext; she also offered him a razor and shaving soap. It would be just like the first time he visited the restaurant. She had made it seem like a joke and he had accepted it as though it was one – even putting on a grim smile.

They were each beginning to realise how nervous the other was.

There were at least two reasons why she had chosen to take him to a guest room. Two or perhaps more. She wanted to give the pretext some weight, of course, so the washbowl had to be placed in a neutral space. But if things did go further, she did not want it to happen in the bed that she had once shared with

Zizi. Beds are wire and horsehair boxes, padded cells for memories. Sometimes they absorb too much and those memories cannot be allowed out again.

The guest room might be a neutral space, but it was not an innocent space. It was used by the diners who chose not to go home at night, who wanted to continue the night with their companions. It was the kind of room where things happened.

Brunel had stripped to his waist. There was something dogged about the way that he did it, as though he had decided that, if she was inviting him to undress, then he would press on and do it. She remembered the last time she had seen him like this, four months ago, and the satisfaction she had felt when she realised how self-conscious he was. It had been easy to use this timidity against him.

She saw Brunel eye the razor and brush, and deadpanned, 'Do you want me to try again? I might have been practising.' He shook his head and picked up the blade, his eyes trained on hers via the mirror hanging on the wall, and continued to bounce glances at her as he shaved. She bounced one back, miming a growl as she flashed her eyes. His hand slipped. Blood showed through the soap on his face.

Babette started laughing.

It was the laughter that loosened him up. Only a touch and only slowly. He put down his razor and turned around to face her. Their eyes met, and then he looked away again, grabbing a towel so that he could wipe the soap off his face. She laughed again. She stepped forward. They kissed.

There was something in the idea of holding a near-naked man when she was completely dressed. Her fingertips trembled as they read the pulse of his body. The shift as nervous energy turned to sexual energy right beneath her fingers. Their mouths were so tightly pressed together that, as she pulled away, their lips parted with a smacking sound and sprang back into a grin. She hooked her fingers into his, so that they were laced together – then she pulled him towards the bed. There, in an awkward and tender confusion of kisses, their caresses took them into the surprise of sex.

She crouched on her haunches, out of sight behind the screen, still reeling from shock at the pleasure he had brought her. She began to speak with a freedom she did not entirely feel because she wanted to keep things warm. She also wanted to distract him from the sound of what she was doing: peeing, douching, washing. She didn't want him to lie there, puzzling over every splash. But most of all, she wanted him to know that she wanted to be back in bed beside him.

'What did you do all night? Couldn't you have sent word that you were coming?'

'Would you have liked me to send a boy over in the middle of the night, warning you to get ready because I was on my way?'

'Telling me to change the sheets on the bed?'

She could hear the skip of a smile in his voice. 'I wish I'd had the confidence.'

'Even though I kept visiting you, asking you to come?'

'Especially then.'

The last thing she did before she stepped from behind the screen was to smooth a perfumed cream along her arms and her breasts. There was no light in the bedroom apart from the naked flames of the fire in the grate. But as she was a child of the Mediterranean, her skin had been tempered in sunlight – the fire brought out a glow that the winter had not managed to kill. The cream burnished it with memories of lavender and hints of neroli.

She hovered midway between the fire and the bed. 'Do you know why I kept asking you to come and stay with me?'

'I thought perhaps you were frightened. You didn't know how I would react when I found out your son had betrayed me.'

She had been willing Brunel to guess the truth and to admit it to her – she wanted the relief of knowing that everything between them was laid out in the open. But she had not estimated the pain or the embarrassment she would feel.

'You knew it was Christian? How?' she asked. 'Until he told me, I had blamed Vinoy's nephew.'

On the day after Brunel's arrest, Christian confessed that it was he who had brought Vinoy's men to the restaurant the night he was imprisoned. Since then Babette had been terrified of what Brunel would do when he got out of Sainte-Pélagie.

Brunel said, 'I saw him leave the funeral party, and when he returned I saw him waiting at the window. But Christian had asked me not to lead his father's batallion. He knew the assault would fail and he believed I would only bring more bad luck.'

'I'm sorry.'

'Don't be. You know that's not why I am here.'

She knew. As they replayed their games over the razor, she had felt a shift in the balance of power.

'What do you think of me now?' she asked.

'Now? What do you mean: now, at this moment?'

'Yes, at this moment. Now that you've had me.'

'I think that you want me here, in your bed. Am I mistaken?'

'No. You are right.'

'You want me here?'

'Yes.'

'Then let's forget everything else.' He held up the edge of the sheets. 'Come back to me.'

She crossed the room slowly, took the corner of the bedsheet and slipped in beside him, holding his gaze as she folded herself into his embrace. Brunel moved his legs so he could trap her feet and warm them on his skin. He smelled of fresh soap and clean linen. She wrapped her fingers in his hair and dragged him forwards until their tongues met.

She had closed her restaurant immediately after Zizi's death. Over the following month, she had let all of her staff go with the exception of Murielle. Since Christmas, the most elaborate thing she had prepared had been the meal for Zizi's mourners – which had cleared her stores of every last thing they possessed.

It made sense to close the restaurant. By the time the armistice with the Prussians was agreed, even the butcher was out of food – thanks in part to the looting carried out by Brunel and his men. But since the general elections were held on 8 February, supplies had begun to flow back to Paris. There was a humanitarian shipment from Britain, followed by others from the French provinces. But Babette saw no point in reopening. Her previous clients had fled Paris for their country estates at the end of the siege. Then, once Brunel came to live with her, she had no choice but to keep the restaurant closed. Brunel's meetings continued day and night and the restaurant was surrounded by General Vinoy's spies.

Brunel was astonishingly indiscreet for an escaped prisoner. He came and went through the front door of the restaurant, determined to prove that he was untouchable. He was seen so often in the neighbourhood that within a week he had become a local phenomenon. People would point him out as he strode by with his two lieutenants, Jules Bergeret and Wroblewski, a Polish officer who, Babette learned, was a minor nobleman wanted by the Prussians in his own country.

The three men would talk late into the night with the battalion commanders of the disbanded Nationals, trying to persuade them to speak out against the peace terms agreed by the new French Government. The meetings lasted so long that often the only times that Babette could speak to Brunel came when they were alone in bed.

One evening, ten days after his escape from prison, Brunel was brushing down his blue coat while Babette lay in bed. She told him to leave it, she could give it to Murielle.

'I doubt that. When I ask her to do anything, she throws me a dirty look and walks away.'

'You're lucky. She never stops talking to me. And she looks so petulant that I thought she was pregnant.'

'Pregnant? By Barclay?'

'She's not – she is only lovesick. I promised her I would ask if you knew where Barclay was, or what he was doing.'

The Marsouin had been posted to Fort Valérien, just outside the city. Brunel asked, 'Do you think Murielle understands that Barclay and I are now on different sides?'

'She's finally realised. Though she was a little slow, considering that she is living in the rebel headquarters.'

Brunel was amused that she could be so oblivious to her surroundings. Yet one might think he was the ignorant one. He had plunged everything Babette cared about – her son, her home, her restaurant, even stupid Murielle – into the centre of an anti-government conspiracy without once asking how she felt about it.

Brunel had been in gaol during the general elections of 8 February 1871. The National Assembly was convened in Bordeaux because Paris remained vehemently opposed to the peace terms accepted by Adolphe Thiers, the one-time chief negotiator and now the new President of the Republic. Adolphe Thiers quickly confirmed Joseph Vinoy as the head of the army, the only general of the siege with no personal responsibility for any disaster. The Parisian delegates, headed by Louis Charles Delescluze, walked out of the Bordeaux assembly in protest against the peace treaty. Delescluze was still technically an escaped prisoner, and after he refused to recognise the assembly a warrant was issued for his arrest.

Paris was full of these wanted men. Louis Charles Delescluze could not be charged for voting against the new government, so he had been charged instead with the break-out from the Mazas prison. And once the charges were laid against Delescluze, then they had to be laid against every man that Brunel had released that day. Overnight, Raoul Rigault, the police clerk, achieved a kind of notoriety as the one name on the wanted list that no one recognised and everyone asked about.

Like Brunel, these men soon began to appear openly around the city. Eventually they found their way to Chez Babette. As the number of conspirators grew, along with the spies following them, Babette saw the change in Murielle. She finally woke up to what was happening under her nose: the disappearance of all those Hussars and Lancers, to be replaced by Federals, as the Nationals had taken to calling themselves since their dissolution. The adoption of the name 'Federals' comforted Babette, and helped her to reassure Murielle. She knew that the Federals had won the American civil war, and that they stood for Republican ideals, for the Rights of Man and Liberty, Fraternity and Equality. Still, she felt more secure when General Vinoy withdrew to the École Militaire, south of the river, leaving Brunel and Wroblewski to hold sway over the 1st arrondissement.

Lovesick Murielle actually began to relish her new level of celebrity in the quartier; wherever she went, she was asked about the late-night meetings that everyone knew were being held Chez Babette. All things considered, Babette saw she had no reason to worry about the girl. Christian was more of a problem. He was working full-time in the restaurant, but walked around with such a blank face that there was no way of telling his opinion of the men he had to serve. As Babette's relationship with Brunel deepened, she knew there was nothing she could do to appease a serious-minded, judgemental fourteen-year-old, still in mourning for his father. Then again, on the one occasion that she asked Christian how he felt about the changes in the city, he told her that he did not believe his father would ever have voted for surrender.

These defenders of France's honours, however, these Federals, they made an odd bunch.

Jules Bergeret and Raoul Rigault

Jules Bergeret and Raoul Rigault were the youngest members of Brunel's circle. They were treated as runners, responsible for bringing the battalion commanders to negotiations, and they used charm and flattery, appealing to self-interest, patriotism or ideology. Both were committed Reds, though in very different ways. Bergeret embraced the movement with optimism; he believed it was inevitable that a fairer society would soon emerge and he wanted to be part of the process. Rigault, in contrast, saw war as an inevitable stage in human history; it was proof of the dark forces that must shatter this world before the better one could emerge. This extreme pessimism might have crushed another man, but it filled Rigault with energy, making him seem all the taller, his hair wilder. He was fantastic at dealing with the most nervous and reluctant of the battalion commanders. He would arrange to meet them at burlesque theatres, telling them they might as well see a show before they got down to business. Anyway, he would ask, who's going to be watching the audience with naked women on stage? As the strippers took their bows, Rigault would lead the commanders out the back of the theatres and into a waiting carriage. When they arrived Chez Babette, the carriage would slip down the side alley and Rigault would bring the commander in through the kitchen door. No matter how late they stayed talking, Christian would stay awake to serve them, as tirelessly as an automaton. And Raoul Rigault would make sure that Murielle had the commanders' names, so that she could spread the gossip around Les Halles, and everyone would know the name of the latest recruit to the side of the Federals.

Louise Michel

Louise Michel arrived late one night, though not via a burlesque show. It seemed impossible that a woman so modest and so austere could be so fond of Raoul Rigault, but she was. She doted on him as though he was a younger brother who could do no wrong, even when he was caught in the act of doing it. Like Rigault, Louise Michel believed that the world was moved by a terrible and destructive force, yet she had an unshakeable faith that this force would leave the poor and the pure of heart unscathed as it passed over the city. This was her religion. It ought to have seemed crazy, but after the winter they had just lived through, the Reds were not alone in believing the world had gone so far towards hell that nothing could make it worse.

Brunel was stunned to discover that Louise Michel controlled the largest arsenal in the city. He came into the kitchen to ask Babette if she would step into the dining room and meet this woman, but then made her pause in the passageway so that they could both stare at Louise Michel through the curtains. She wore her hair scraped back and plaited tight, and dressed like a schoolmistress, in black from throat to toe. But rather than a shawl, she wore a National Guard blouson on her shoulders, and there was a *tabatière* slung over the back of her chair. Later, when the meal was served, Babette discovered that Louise Michel was a reluctant eater. She was unable to enjoy anything, but would try to compliment the cook by saying that her mother would like it, it was just the kind of thing that her mother loved to eat. 'Next time,' Babette said, 'bring your mother with you.' Even then, with that hint of a reproach, Louise Michel didn't take offence – she just apologised again.

Louise Michel had gathered several hundred field guns and dozens of *mitrailleuses* in the square on the butte of Montmartre. The armistice agreement had allowed the Prussians to hold a victory parade down the Champs Élysées, followed by a symbolic two-day occupation of the city. When news of the Prussian occupation had hit Paris, the Nationals rounded up all their heavy guns and dragged them to Montmartre to keep them out of enemy hands. Since then, the guns had remained in the care of Louise Michel. Now that the Prussians had set up their camps outside the city walls, all along the northern outskirts of Paris, Louise Michel was afraid that Vinoy would try to seize the weapons for his forces.

Walery Wroblewski and Gustave Flourens

Walery Wroblewski and Gustave Flourens were ostensibly motivated by the same thing: they were fervent believers in national liberation. But Wroblewski's aims were more transparent. He wanted to kill Prussians. Every Prussian dead weakened that country's grip on Poland. Every Prussian force tied up in the fight for France brought Polish liberation closer. In contrast, Flourens believed in liberation in general, romantically and flamboyantly. All his military experience had been gained as a volunteer in the interminable war of Greek liberation. It seemed like a stroke of providence that he could bring his skill and passion to the fight for liberation in his own country.

When Flourens appeared in the restaurant, Babette found herself angry on Brunel's behalf. Flo had taken a month to free Brunel from Sainte-Pélagie, and he only took the risk then because he had nothing to lose – his name was on the list of wanted men. When Babette challenged him, Flo turned to Brunel and asked him if he bore a grudge. When Brunel said it was no skin off his nose, Flo told Babette, 'We all suffer in the cause of freedom.' Then he helped himself to another slice of cold ham.

Flourens had been sentenced to death that day, *in absentia*. This seemed to annoy him more than anything. He was demanding, where's the legality, where's the justice, in that? 'The heart of a democracy is the right to be judged by your peers,' he declared. 'It doesn't lie in the ballot box, it lies in the fellowship of its citizens, in those who speak and those who listen. Am I right?'

They spent that evening listening to Flo's complaints against General Thomas, who Flo claimed had broken his nose. There was no doubt that his nose was broken; it was twisted at about twenty degrees from the perpendicular. Babette squinted across the table, measuring the angle against a candlestick and trying to keep from yawning. She had made the mistake of admitting that she had caught sight of Flourens shortly after he was taken into custody, and so he had stayed half the night until she agreed that he had probably taken the worst beating of anyone, at any time. Now that the National Guard headquarters had been shut down, Flo declared that it was lucky for Thomas that he had cut and run. If he was still in his office, he would be dead for sure.

Louis Charles Delescluze

Louis Charles Delescluze was the last to arrive, standing wheezing in the doorway of the restaurant as he demanded to know if this was the residence of General Paul-Antoine Brunel. It was the first time that Babette had heard Brunel described as a general and she was unable to tell whether the old man was being ironic. For the past month, Delescluze had shown no interest at all in the events Chez Babette. Instead, he had toured all the *mairies* in an attempt to get the city's twenty mayors to establish a Commune of Paris and, on behalf of its citizens, reject the government's surrender. His arrival at the restaurant showed that he had failed.

It was early in the morning and Brunel was still in bed. Babette sent Christian upstairs to wake him. Although it took Brunel less than ten minutes to appear in the restaurant, Raoul Rigault was there before him, telling Delescluze that he happened to be in the neighbourhood, 'When I heard you had come to negotiate, Comrade Deputy.'

'Negotiate what?' Delescluze was asthmatic, which was why he was out of breath. Rigault was panting so hard that he might have run from the other side of Paris. 'In fact, who are you?'

'I was in prison with you, Comrade Deputy.'

Delescluze showed no sign of recognising him. He took a seat and, between asthmatic breaths, spoke directly to Brunel, making what he called a simple request. He wanted Brunel to call an assembly of all the Federal commanders; if the mayors refused to call for a commune, Delescluze would look to the only other elected representatives in the city. After all, the battalion commanders had all been elected by their fellow soldiers during the siege, so they were the most representative democratic body in Paris.

Brunel held up his hands, admitting frankly that he might be stupid but he didn't see Delescluze's point at all. 'I'm not trying to reform local government – I'm trying to build an army.'

'But to what purpose, Citizen? We need to be clear about our political objectives. What are we fighting for?'

'To liberate France. Declaring a commune is not only a waste of time, it sends out the wrong signal. We are not fighting for Paris but for the whole of France, for Alsace and Lorraine and everywhere else under the Prussian heel.'

Rigault had also taken a seat. He said, 'Let me try to find a way through this, Comrades; maybe we are not so far apart. Now that our Comrade General Paul-Antoine has revived the army, then surely the commune already exists.'

'How does the commune exist?'

'We all agree, taken en masse, the Federal commanders constitute the only democratically elected body in the city. And if a democratically elected body exists, we therefore have the formal conditions for a Commune of Paris. Now then, Comrades, let us recognise that whatever exists formally will necessarily exist in practice.'

'Necessarily?' Louis Charles Delescluze stared at the younger man in disbelief. 'Where is the necessity?'

'It's a matter of dialectics and the Will, Comrade.'

Delescluze looked from Brunel to Babette. 'Can either of you explain what he's talking about?'

Babette had already learned that arguments about dialectics and the Will could continue all day and into the night. She stood up, telling the men that she had to return to work. As she was leaving, she heard Delescluze arguing that if no assembly was ever called, then far from having an elected body Paris had nothing but government by generals, and as far as he could see Brunel was free to do whatever he wanted.

Babette kept only one of her battery of stoves burning these days and she ran the kitchen single-handedly, with Murielle and Christian on call when she needed them. Otherwise, the pair were left alone to manage the dining room.

She checked on the pots simmering on the range before stepping outside to her store, which was now replenished. She was running what amounted to a private Red Club, and she no longer charged for anything she served – but neither did she pay for anything she received. Wroblewski and Bergeret were in charge of distributing relief supplies in the quartier, and they simply brought whatever she needed.

As she re-entered the kitchen, she found Raoul Rigault with his head in her biggest pan, inhaling the fumes from the stock as though it was eucalyptus oil and he was suffering from a head cold. When he heard Babette rap on the stove top with her knife, he came up, smacking his lips. 'Damn, it smells so good. I can't wait for tonight.'

'If there are any more dialectics, you'll be eating at home.'

'I knew the old fool wouldn't understand a word, but I was playing for time. You have to make Paul-Antoine understand, we cannot afford to call an assembly. Suppose the twits in the Federals ignore Delescluze, and refuse to declare a commune. What then? What legitimacy will the war have? We don't need another talking shop, we need to move.' He brought his fingers to his lips. They were brown with the jus from the pan. 'If any talking needs to be done, let's keep it between ourselves.'

She was on the side of war – she believed in war, she wanted more of it. When she and Brunel lay in bed, it was all they talked about, that and nothing else, how to fire up the war again. Brunel listened as she relayed the opinion of Rigault, but surprised her by flatly disagreeing. He thought that an assembly of the Federal commanders could be a good idea, a show of strength. His greatest fear was that the Federals would only be willing to fight in their own neighbourhoods. If he could bring them together, it could help forge a common purpose. It would almost certainly scare General Vinoy into a reaction. Brunel was convinced that there was no way of taking the war back to the Prussians without first dealing with General Vinoy and his government forces.

The Federal commanders met and did nothing but form a

committee. Yet, sure enough, two nights later a division of government troops and several thousand gendarmes appeared in Montmartre to round up Louise Michel's guns. Despite another direct plea from Louise Michel, Brunel again refused to send her any men. It seemed a brutal decision, but he argued that the soldiers had brought so few horses that they would be unable to take the guns anyway.

As the night wore on and Louise Michel continued to wrangle over the guns, Jules Bergeret surveyed her position and returned to the restaurant to report that the government forces were surrounded by a crowd of several thousand spectators, who were jeering and laughing at them. Then news came that Louise Michel had arrested a General Lecomte; she sent a messenger to Brunel, asking if this was a decisive victory. Brunel doubted it; he had never heard of Lecomte. It was only when a report came that General Clément Thomas had been abducted from his home by a group of Federals that Brunel knew the time had come to act; General Thomas was a dead man, and once a general was killed France would be in a state of civil war.

Babette went down to the square in front of the Hôtel de Ville. There was a crowd of thousands gathering to show their opposition to the government and the peace terms. In the middle of this mass, Babette saw with her own eyes how much the character of Paris had changed. There were so few of the old bourgeoisie left in the city that the 1st and 2nd arrondissements were as Red as Belleville. There was a rumour buzzing across the square that a couple of Vinoy's generals had been lynched up in Montmartre and their bodies were being dragged through the streets. She was certain the rumours were true, as she had so much faith in Brunel's assessment of the situation.

Walery Wroblewski was to lead a force against the Prince Eugène barracks, Brunel led an assault by the 125th on the larger Napoleon barracks. When Babette heard shots from the far side of the Hôtel de Ville, she knew the attack had begun. The gunfire sent panic through the crowd; most people thought they were coming under fire from the machine-guns mounted in the windows above them. As the square filled with screaming, everyone began running to find cover. The panic all but drowned out the fight at the barracks, the true source of the shots.

For almost twenty minutes, there was nothing in the square but windblown litter. Gradually the crowd began re-emerging from the arcades to the north of the square and then up from the quays to the south. Every time there was the crack of a rifle, figures would duck and then straighten but the shots were so intermittent that the crowd grew bolder.

Then a volley began . . .

Babette looked at the roof of the Hôtel de Ville. There were men lined along the parapet, firing into the air in celebration. The crowd in the square soon realised they were in no danger. They were a little slower in grasping the significance of what was happening.

Brunel emerged on the roof. Babette knew it was him, even before his men started cheering his name. He paused, and the crowd below took up the chant: *Vive le Commune, vive Brunel*.

There was a flagpole up on the roof. And on it a banner was sniffing the breeze, unfurling slowly as it found its strength.

Brunel raised his fist and the crowd surged forward, continuing to chant: *Vive la révolution, vive le Commune*.

Vive General Brunel. Across the river, General Vinoy was pulling his troops out of their quarters at the École Militaire and heading for Versailles. Brunel had captured Paris in barely an hour, with few shots exchanged.

Bethlehem, April Fool's Day, 2002

I woke early on Good Friday, 29 March 2002, just to stare at my half-assed packing of the night before. Ben had allowed me an extra few weeks in his apartment as he rounded off his contract in Colombia with a Latin American vacation. But after the Easter weekend he was returning to Paris and I had to go. When Flavie began banging at my door, telling me to turn on the satellite channel, the news came from both sides at once – in English and in French. The Israelis had invaded Ramallah. Marguerite Galperin was under siege.

Between the TV news and our snatched telephone calls with Marguerite, we learned that the Israelis had brought their tanks right into the centre of the city. Marguerite's accounts were peppered with the sound of gunfire. Flavie screamed, 'Oh my God, oh my God, are you staying down? Can you get out of the city?'

Far from trying to escape, Marguerite was insisting on staying right where she was, at the heart of the invasion. She was working with the ambulance crews of the Palestinian Red Crescent Society, riding in the cabs in the hope that the presence of 'internationals', as she described herself, would deter the soldiers from shooting. I stood so close to Flavie that the telephone was sandwiched between our ears and I listened to the fraught pitch of her voice as Marguerite cried, 'Get the story out, there are ambulances being shot at, there are people dying.'

Marguerite never found much time to talk to us and we got only fragments of the story of her day. When Jean-Luc heard, he started calling contacts in French newspapers and telling them that a French-Jewish woman was under fire in Ramallah. Flavie asked if I could call British newspapers or, better, write something myself. But I knew that no British papers would be interested in Marguerite's story – I needed to know if there were any British volunteers with her.

By the evening, we had a new shock. Marguerite was inside the presidential compound, trying to negotiate the removal of injured and elderly men from within the building. Flavie remained in my apartment because I had satellite, and we had a sleepless night. As morning came, we heard a report that a Jewish peace activist had taken breakfast with President Arafat and was said to have announced she would stay in the compound until the end of the siege. We flipped channels, trying to find confirmation of the story. Instead, we learned that there was a gun battle at a downtown mall in Ramallah. I squinted at the screen and tried to recognise the building; there were no downtown malls when I lived in Ramallah. The building looked brand new.

By the next evening, the latest pictures from inside the mall showed eleven bodies in the blue military uniforms of the Palestinian secutiry service, all lying face down, apparently executed. The pictures switched back to the presidential compound where the reporter announced that the Palestinian President had received an ultimatum: he must leave the compound and surrender or be shelled. CNN had managed to get a news crew into the building. In a candlelit interview, Arafat said he would not move. If the ultimatum was serious – and why would it not be; we could hear the noise of shelling outside – then they were about to kill him. I could barely grasp what I was seeing: the assassination of a nation's leader live on television. As for Flavie, she might be about to see the killing of the woman she loved. In the gloom of a building with every door and window sealed with sandbags and barricaded with furniture, we saw members of Arafat's police force, government ministers, etc. The camera panned around and found Marguerite, sitting a little to the side, hollow-eyed as the powerful camera light threw a giant shadow of her on the pock-marked wall.

Flavie sat upright and told me she was going. She was going to Ramallah. 'Where is it?' she asked. 'Is it close to Jerusalem?'

I looked at my room, at my suitcase standing ready to be packed. I said, 'If you want, I'll go too.'

Her eyes widened; she had been holding on to her tears for the past day and night. 'You will go with me?'

We touched down in Israel early the next morning: Easter Sunday. I had faced questions at Ben Gurion airport before, but never for very long. Now that groups were arriving from around the world and attempting to get into the Palestinian cities, the questioning was tougher, but Flavie and I had cooked up a story and she stuck to it with a fervour that I found difficult to match: we were Christians, we were going to attend mass in the Church of the Holy Sepulchre in Jerusalem. I was sweating and digging a key into the palm of my hand when the official handed us back our passports and nodded in the direction of our bags. We were free to enter the country.

We could not reach Marguerite on her mobile. Everyone that we managed to speak to told us that there was no way into Ramallah. Even Marguerite's own Civil Mission had no suggestions, though they assured us that Marguerite was safe and well and determined to sit out the siege; perhaps her presence had already deterred the Israelis from destroying the building. When Flavie asked why Marguerite's phone was switched off, they explained that she was saving her battery now that the Israelis had cut off the electricity.

We took a *sherut* to Jerusalem and toured the Palestinian taxi rank at Damascus Gate. Every driver confirmed that the Israelis had sealed all routes into Ramallah. There were estimates of as many as four hundred tanks inside the city, barely six miles from where we stood. When Flavie asked, what do we do? I had only one idea: if I could get a press pass, then perhaps we would be able to negotiate our way through the Israeli lines.

Sunday is the start of the working week in Israel and there was a small queue of journalists inside the plasterboard-shell office at the Ministry of Information. There was no sign of the Press Officer and, inevitably, everyone was discussing Israel's next step. Did they intend to kill or deport the Palestinian leadership? Almost everyone who could be described as part of the Palestinian Government was trapped inside the presidential compound in Ramallah. If the Israelis did destroy it, was that part of a wider strategy? Or were they only intending to hit hard and pull back, as they had done in November and February? The fact is that no one had a clue. Flavie could only listen anxiously; it was clear that her head was swimming as she tried to assess these options, calculations that she had never thought she would have to make.

A Scottish journalist asked if this was her first application for a press pass. She pointed at me and said, 'He is the journalist.'

I admitted it was my first time. 'Is there anything I should know?'

He told me that the Israelis were only accrediting reporters from rolling news organisations. The policy, as he described it, was called 'bang-bang': make sure the focus is on the attacks and the response. He said, 'Do you think they want anyone to take a wider look at this mess?'

I had a problem. 'I'm a business journalist.' I showed him the press pass I had been issued in France.

He smiled as he handed it back. 'So what are you doing here with your fancy business journalism credentials?'

'Trying to get into Ramallah.'

'You don't stand a chance. None of us does.'

I thought he was probably telling the truth. He was certainly right about the press pass. When the Israeli official showed up, I was turned down flat. But I was offered a press kit anyway. It consisted of a leaflet in the form of FAQs about Israel and a CD-ROM on Palestine.

As we were leaving, a couple of journalists started making excited telephone calls, swiftly copied by others. Something was happening, and as I questioned them I got a confused story of peace protesters breaking into the presidential compound. Back on the street, we made our own call to Marguerite's organisation and found that it was true; a party of twenty international protesters had run between the Israeli tanks and made it into the compound.

'That's what I came to do,' Flavie said. 'How do we do that?'

The woman on the other end of the phone repeated that we could not get into Ramallah; the protesters were already inside the city when the Israelis struck. But Flavie was desperate; there must be something she could do?

The woman advised her to go to Bethlehem. All the new protesters were being sent to the Star Hotel, Bethlehem, to do training in non-violent direct action. They could not take anyone on any protest who had not done the training. Flavie spelled out the name and number of the organiser for me, but I knew at once who it was: Nadim's nephew, the person from the International Solidarity Movement who had given us Marguerite's number at Christmas.

The hills around Bethlehem are shorn of their olive trees and scarred by spiral roads, as though squeezed by giant serpents. All this was done by a handful of private contractors, backed up by the army. Up close, there are no pioneers building their own homes. What you see are clouds of concrete dust, military checkpoints, bulldozers, razor wire. The image in my mind was of the Paris defences of 1870. The French dug trenches and built defensive earthworks, by far the largest anyone had seen up until that time. Within months, they had changed the entire landscape in preparation for war. The West Bank looked as I imagine the area around Fort Valérien to have looked, especially in the grey weather, when days of rain had left everything slick with mud. The Israelis justify their presence in the West Bank, in part, as a defensive strategy. The West Bank is their trench. And so the landscape is turned into a panorama of war.

As I clawed the shekels out of my pocket and paid our taxi driver, there was a moment when I saw myself as a sniper might. It was not a fanciful thought; we were in sniper territory, at the highest point in Bethlehem, faced by an Israeli settlement. I dropped my hand and collected my change. Ahead of me, Flavie was squeezing through a roadblock and running for the waving figure of Nadim, waiting with his car. The Israeli army was not allowing any vehicles in or out of Bethlehem, so we could only take a taxi as far as this hillside roadblock. It was surrounded by coils of razor wire but there were no soldiers. As I followed Flavie between the concrete blocks, I stepped into a puddle deeper than my shoes.

Nadim started the car almost before I was inside. 'What the hell are you doing here?'

He already knew, so repeating it would not help. I asked if Flavie had introduced herself.

Nadim shook hands over his shoulder as he gunned his car down the hill, explaining that the Israelis had announced a curfew. As far as he knew, there were no Israelis around to enforce the order. But it had the effect of clearing everyone off the streets.

The emptiness around us combined with the weather made everything twice as frightening. It was spring and the clouds were so low and black that we could not see the jet fighters overhead; we only heard the explosions as they broke the sound barrier. The weight of the Israeli tanks used in the February invasion had fractured the sewers beneath the roads. After the rains, raw sewage had swilled on to the streets. We had arrived in this dark, wet, close, foul atmosphere, to join a group of peace protesters in non-violent resistance. It seemed they were our only hope of reaching Marguerite.

As we stopped at the hotel, Nadim said, 'I'm coming in. I know I shouldn't, but I am. I need a drink.'

'It can't be like this for ever.'

'Of course it can. It can be like this for ever, no problem.'

His nephew George greeted us at the door with hugs, though they had already seen each other twice that day, at mass in the morning and then over Easter lunch with their in-laws. The lunch had been abandoned after twenty minutes, once the curfew was announced.

When Nadim left for his hospital, George introduced us to the other fifteen protesters in the bar, and told us that there were many more around Bethlehem. A decision had been made that, as the Israelis might invade in the night, the protesters would be better staying in the refugee camps rather than the centre of town. Nadim was not so sure. He thought the local militiamen would gather in the centre, away from their homes, so any fighting was more likely to take place around Manger Square and in front of the Church of the Nativity.

George said, 'Do you think they will stay out of the church this time?'

Nadim shook his head. 'I don't think so. Not a chance in hell.'

Almost half of the people in the bar were American, including a couple of strongly pacifist Christians from the Midwest, a gangly Jew from California and an elderly Jewish woman from New York who was a veteran of the American civil rights movement. Among the English, there was a Quaker and a woman who had been involved in the Greenham Common protests in the 1980s, as well as a college lecturer and a solicitor. I had no idea whether they were representative of the people we would meet.

There was no invasion.

I woke in our shared bedroom to the sound of Flavie talking to Marguerite. I don't think the call lasted long; the battery of Marguerite's mobile gave out. But Flavie had established contact. She was shaken; talking to Marguerite had only made her aware of how dangerous the situation had become. It didn't help that we came downstairs to find the television showing Israeli troops praying beside their tanks on the road outside Bethlehem. It was Monday, 1 April, and all the protesters, those in the camps and those in the hotel, were going to come together to debate a response. I reminded Flavie that we needed to do our non-violence training, but Flavie said she needed fresh air; could we step outside?

We ended up walking down to Manger Square, via the steps by the souk. There was a kind of gaiety; the air was full of roasted chickpeas, deep-fried falafel and barbecued meat. But the shopkeepers were nervous. Children stared down from the apartments above the souk, and if we smiled at them they flashed victory signs back at us. But their parents were clearly keeping them off the streets. Flavie took pictures with the digital camera I had brought as a communication aid with Evan. It made me feel guilty; I had not told Evan that I was going to Palestine.

As we approached the square, we started to see the fighters with their guns slung over their shoulders: M-16s for the security men, AK-47s or replicas for the Tanzim militias, and a few old rifles and even Lee-Enfields scattered among the rest. There were similarities between Paris in 1870 and Bethlehem in 2002. This was one: the motley collection of defenders, drawn from all political parties, from families and other factions. I didn't know if these different groups had anything like a common chain of command. What was certain was that they were far more poorly equipped than the Parisians. Nadim and George estimated there were between fifty and a hundred armed men in Bethlehem, a town of twenty or thirty thousand people. They had no howitzers and certainly no heavy guns. They possibly had home-made mortars but their propellants would be as primitive as those available in 1870. Before the invention of high explosives, there was only black powder. The Palestinians could probably buy or steal this – stone-quarrying is one of the country's staple industries – but they were unable to obtain explosives, unless from the Israelis, so they would have to make

their own from fertiliser, petrol and other kitchen and indus-
trial products.

The men gathered in groups in Manger Square. There was
evidence that they were sleeping there: bedrolls, rucksacks and
blankets. But the surroundings had more to surprise me. The
last time I had visited Bethlehem, the square was a dilapidated
car park. Nadim had told me that the town had been renovated
and restored for the millennium celebrations. If I had visited
fifteen months ago, he said, I would not have believed the feeling
of optimism. The square had been repaved with white stone,
and where the old police station used to stand there was a new
Peace Centre, a gift from the people of Denmark. Along the
back of the square, like a stone backdrop, there was the Church
of the Nativity, its ancient walls dominating the area.

By the time we returned to the Star Hotel, the meeting had
begun. George was getting to his feet to give a short speech.
He began by admitting that he did not know what would happen.
'If the Israelis decide to get rid of the current leadership, in
whatever way they may choose to do that, then this will be a
completely open conflict. I don't think any of us can predict
what will happen.' He advised us to be very careful about what
decisions we made and ended by saying that, in his opinion,
Bethlehem would be invaded that day or, more likely, in the
early hours of Tuesday morning. Then he gave the floor to the
foreign volunteers.

Flavie and I were plunged into the art of group decision-
making. It was a system that allowed everyone to speak, and
decisions were arrived at through consensus rather than by
voting. It took a long while. Our party had swollen to around
fifty, and it grew even larger when we were joined by representatives of the Italian and Belgian groups that were also in the
town. But after a great deal of talking, it was agreed that we
would march up to the army lines. The idea was to keep pushing
the message that there were more than a hundred foreigners
scattered around Bethlehem.

We were marching to the summit of the hill where we had met Nadim, only yesterday. As we climbed, an Italian with a clarinet played the song of the partisans: *Oh partisan, take me away, for they have to bury me. Oh partisan, take me away. Bella, ciao, Bella, ciao, Bella, ciao, ciao, ciao*. We clapped our hands as we marched and sang. Just level with the Orthodox Church, a tank appeared around a corner. Or, rather, not a tank but an APC, an armoured personnel carrier. I was learning the new terminology. It had sandbags piled on its front and in it was an Israeli soldier in sports sunglasses, aiming his rifle at us.

The demonstrators had appointed two negotiators to speak to the soldiers. This pair, both English, stepped forward and with diffident English gestures indicated that they wanted to converse with the man in the tank. When the bullets came, biting into the asphalt at their feet, they jumped back. Everyone looked at one another without knowing what to do.

The soldier fired another couple of rounds.

Flavie and I had not done the special training, so we had deliberately kept to the back of the crowd to watch what others would do. I don't know if they were prepared to be fired on, but they kept their lines tight and proceeded in what seemed to me to be a dignified retreat. The soldier fired again. Bullet fragments and chunks of road flew up ahead of us. I saw a Palestinian man with a camera go down; he was wearing a helmet and flak jacket, both with the letters TV marked in white tape. He staggered back to his feet; I could see the backs of his jeans were torn and he was bleeding through the denim.

To my left, a couple held a sheet with NO OCCUPATION written in black pen. They had been in my eye-line for most of the walk, their banner jiggling and flapping because the material was too light. It was flapping wildly now. I realised that the man had let go of his end and was clutching his hand as blood seeped through his fingers. I could feel the panic growing inside me. As long as I remained within the crowd, I neither communicated it nor gave in to it.

We went on backing down the hill.

The APC rumbled on towards us, the soldier continuing to fire at the ground or at the walls of the buildings to create a rattling smoke-cloud of shrapnel and stone dust, dirt and chunks of asphalt. Spaces kept opening up and I found myself pausing so that the lines would catch up with me and I could fill any gaps. After a few such manoeuvres, I was in the first row, linking arms with a bearlike American on one side and a skinny Swede on the other. The American kept nodding grimly, I don't know why. His weight and strength kept the line steady as the bullets bounced and shattered in front of us.

The soldier turned, lifting his rifle in the air. A crew with the letters BBC on their flak jackets moved forward to film, but he lowered the rifle and sent a volley of gunfire to drive them into a side street. He continued firing down the alleyway where they were crouching. I could see the legs of the female TV reporter as she sheltered behind a big four-wheel-drive vehicle. I was thinking: why is he going so mad at the BBC, is he insane? Does he want to kill a BBC reporter?

To my right, a woman's leg lifted up in the air and it flickered through my head that the shoes looked familiar. Then as the leg descended, Flavie's face popped into view. She was crying out in pain as two men carried her to a waiting ambulance.

Parade Day

Brunel took a deep breath before he stepped up to the podium. The Committee of the Federals' Commanders sat in front of him, one from each of the twenty arrondissements of Paris, gathered together around the table in the great debating chamber of the Hôtel de Ville. Behind these men stood the city's political leaders and anyone else with the power or the influence to push their way into this first assembly of a Free Paris. Brunel knew that he was not appealing to the committee alone, but beyond them to Louis Charles Delescluze and his Jacobins, and all of the other more or less organised factions: the Blanquists and the Anarchists, the Socialist Internationalists, the Italians and the Poles. Then there were the street leaders from the different quartiers: the gangsters, the loan sharks and bar-room heroes. Among these was Gustave Flourens, wearing a hat so large and flamboyant that he could only have stolen it from a museum.

All the talk, thus far, had been on the possibility of negotiation, and whether the government of a defeated France might be ready to strike a deal with a Paris that was still willing to fight. Brunel believed there was no chance, and as he stepped forward he knew he had to make everyone understand this. He gripped the side of the podium and let the noise in the room rumble on, like a wagon braking and slowing, until there was near silence.

'Citizens. Comrades. My name is Paul-Antoine Brunel.' He coughed and began again, gaining confidence as he went. 'I have never made a speech before. This is a first. But I had to do it. The decision we are about to take is as great as any decision made anywhere, at any time in man's history. We are going to war.' He paused, just long enough for the crowd to register his steady gaze. 'That is not the decision. War is unavoidable. Our decision is this: will we fight to win? We are a poor army, Comrades, small, ill-equipped and untrained. But at this precise moment we are greater than our enemies, and if we don't keep moving we throw that one advantage away.'

He had not only written the speech, he had practised reading it aloud. Babette had listened and made suggestions. Whenever she failed to understand a phrase, Brunel mouthed the words over and then abandoned them. He had tried to conjure sonorous phrases, aiming for a speech in the style of Gustave Flourens: the martyrs' blood cooling on the cobblestones; the Prussians hammering at backs that had not broken during a siege, that would not bow nor break, that would rather die than allow Joseph Vinoy and Adolphe Thiers to auction their future from their salesroom in Versailles. Babette had said, why do we have to attack, why do we have to do it now? That's what you have to make them understand.

And that was what he was trying to do. 'You are soldiers and I want to talk to you as soldiers. These past six months you have learned that soldiers cannot defend a city. First Metz fell, then Strasbourg and finally Paris. Last night, Vinoy fled before us. His forces are retrenching in Versailles but his next step will be to occupy the forts and the siege will begin again – and this time it will be Frenchmen against Frenchmen, those traitors against we patriots.'

Babette had asked him: did you really know that Paris would fall? Is soldiering as easy as that; you look so many moves ahead and know exactly what will happen? He told her: perhaps a better soldier would have seen another possibility. But once the plan to strike out for Normandy was abandoned, he could see no other outcome. At Le Bourget, he had been guilty of the most terrible wishful thinking. He could never again do that to men under his command.

As Brunel spoke, he tried to keep to a steady pace, like a councillor giving a report. 'There will be no negotiations between us and the traitors in Versailles. Vinoy will not forget that two of his generals were lynched last night. But that's not why he won't talk to us. He will not negotiate because he knows he can win. How will we defend our homes, our neighbourhoods, our city? We can stockpile provisions and armaments, build barricades, defend the heights and the main water supplies. We can make him fight for every square metre of ground. But we will be defeated. You know that. You know that defenders always end as martyrs. I love and respect you as soldiers who are ready to fight and to risk your lives. But don't you want a chance of surviving?'

He looked up, just as he had practised with Babette. He counted silently through his next pause. 'Do you imagine there's another roll of the dice? That, maybe, we will fight them to a standstill? Don't believe it. Adolphe Thiers has already handed Alsace and Lorraine to the Prussians, and promised them five billion francs on top. To safeguard a deal like that, the Prussians will give Vinoy whatever he needs, including Krupp guns and shells. If it ever looks as if we might have victory, we will face Vinoy and the Prussians together, dynamiting us out of our homes, dragging our bodies into the streets.'

This was as close to rhetoric as his script got. Brunel read to the bottom of the page and his fist clenched around the piece of paper. He could feel tears pricking, but not because what he had written was so powerful. It felt piss-weak, there on the page, read out line by line by someone playing at being a politician.

'I fought at Bazeilles,' he said. 'We tried to defend the town, and we failed. When people hear that I fought there, they ask what it was like. I try to tell them it was bad but I doubt I ever make them understand just how bad. Bazeilles is a small town, with a single main street, built on the meadow plain between two rivers. It's not difficult to defend: climb into any upper window and you see the enemy coming over the bridges and rolling slowly across the flat land. We put our first line of troops at the outer limits of the town, and we halted them for a time. With the second attack, they brought their big guns into the fight, and when the fusillade came we moved back into stronger buildings with higher walls. The enemy attacked along the main street. They had no choice, there was no other route into the town. We had snipers in every building along the road. It doesn't get any easier than that. And yet we held out for just one day. One fucking day. You'll hear people say that we could have held it for longer. There were bad orders, generals contradicting other generals. All that's true. But it's not why we failed. We failed because we could not win. The enemy came and they beat us down, house by house. They shelled and burned their way through the town. I saw men throwing themselves off burning roofs. I saw three-storey buildings collapse and knew that men were buried in the rubble and that I could do nothing except keep fighting a retreat, all the way up the road to Sedan. The people who lived in Bazeilles, the townspeople who had fought alongside us, were left behind. You know what happened to them. Every one of you has heard what happened. They were dragged into the square, they were lined up along the walls and they were shot. I was there, I was injured and I was trapped, I saw it happen. But I was wearing a uniform so I was only taken prisoner. The rest were shot as unlawful combatants, fighting out of uniform. What would they be wearing? They were shopkeepers and farmers and merchants, they wore aprons and smocks and business clothes. But without a uniform, the rules of war say they are turncoats and traitors or spies. So shoot them. And if they start to twitch, walk over again and keep pumping in the fucking bullets until they stop.

'That is what is coming, you can be certain of it. Vinoy's forces are weak. Yesterday, he didn't have enough horses to remove the guns from Montmartre or enough men to defend his barracks or his arsenals. So he ran. We have one chance. We attack Versailles tonight. In one stroke, we get out of Paris, leaving us free to take the war back to the Prussians, on open ground, while we simultaneously destroy the only body prepared to make peace with them. We move tonight. Or we die here.'

Brunel folded his papers to signal that he had finished. The audience had listened in silence. He hoped that meant he had won them over.

He looked up. A delegate was already on his feet.

'If I understood the Comrade General, he is telling us to leave Paris and go gypsying across the country. Why would we do that, right after we spent six months starving to defend our city?'

Brunel overrode the murmurs of agreement. 'I am telling you that if we attack Vinoy while he is still at Versailles, we will turn the tide of the war. If we leave him, we are dead. All of us: the people in this room, the ones standing outside singing whatever revolutionary hymn they are singing . . .' – Brunel could not make out a word – '. . . and their wives and their children.'

The first person to speak out for Brunel was Louise Michel, crying, 'Listen to the Comrade General.'

Brunel felt another few seconds slip away. If no one else came to his aid, he was certain that he was sunk. He looked to Flourens, leaning against the wall with his hat flapping in the breeze from the window. If Flo spoke, then perhaps he could carry the meeting.

It was too late, Louis Charles Delescluze was climbing out of his chair. 'The Comrade General paints an interesting picture: a mobile commune, as liquid as oil, slipping around the country and everywhere fighting the Prussians. Imagine us, we Parisians, roaming the country like the Bedouin of Algeria, pitching a city of tents wherever we go.' Delescluze was such a fine orator that his asthma, which would have hindered anyone else, was a tool to him. He used it like a pair of bellows, gathering a reservoir of air in wheezes, conserving his breath in quiet phrases and building power until he could deliver it as needed. 'The only weapon the people have is their solidarity, and solidarity is built from the ground up, brick by brick. Solidarity is part of the city, and Paris has survived today because of our splendid solidarity. We are here today, Comrades, undefeated and we will remain undefeated as a city. As long as the political realm is strong, then nothing can defeat the people.'

In exasperation, Brunel shouted, 'An army can defeat the people.'

'The Commune of Paris must come first, otherwise why are we asking them to fight?'

'For France.'

'This is no time for sentimental nationalism. The Emperor was French; the monsignors, the marquises, their *maquereaux* and all the other mountebanks are French. We are not fighting for a patriotic fancy; in this room we have Citizens Dombrewski and Wroblewski from Poland, Citizen Cipriani from Rimini. I see among us both Hungarians and Russians, Citizens Frankel and Dimitrieff. If Paris and its citizens stand for anything, it is rationality, not the narrow nationhood preached by the ex-Emperor and his toadies. Yes, we fight for the greater glory of France. But we fight for the glory of a land ruled by its people, the true homeland of civilisation.'

Delescluze was ending his speech to applause. Brunel realised that the motion would go to a vote and there was nothing he could do to impede it.

Each time he returned to the restaurant, he felt the shock of a cold kitchen. The memory of the searing heat and the steam was so fresh that to find this freezing, empty space had something of the horror of a bombed-out city. He passed on, through to the restaurant, where he found Babette with a broom in her hand, sweeping the corners of the staircase. She looked up and saw from his face that he had failed. She dropped the broom and ran to hold him. There was dust in her hair and so he pushed his nose deeper, where traces of her old perfume still lingered.

'What happened?'

'They voted to call fresh elections.'

For the second time she asked if he could really see so many moves ahead, step by step. 'Are we certain to be defeated?'

'I don't know. I think . . . what I think now . . .'

He stalled. When he held her, it was possible to be quiet. Her warmth took the edge off his anger and his frustration. She allowed him to be silent, when elsewhere silence seemed symptomatic of his inability to move this stupid and stubborn city. But although she soothed him, he was never quite at ease. She trusted him to continue the war and he was far from justifying her faith.

The result was that the Federals' Committee had voted to hold elections for a Commune of Paris, and to dissolve itself. It was only as the committee members raised their hands that Brunel saw that this had always been the real political battle. All those men standing behind them had good reason to crowd into the debating hall. They were there to intimidate the committee and make them doubt their right to take the decisions that the city now required. Not one of the leaders of the political parties had a seat on the committee; they needed a wholesale reform to the political structure of Paris if they were to exercise any power. To them, Brunel was the advocate of the status quo, the man who wanted to postpone change and keep faith with the ramshackle system of battalion commanders.

It was no wonder that the only person to give him a hearing was Louise Michel, who would gain nothing from a political reorganisation. As a woman, she could not be elected. But when she managed to prise her way back into the debate, her speech argued that an army should be dispatched to Versailles immediately to assassinate the heads of this vile defeatist government. She demanded that the committee either lend forces to Comrade General Brunel or employ her as a special agent at which she would swear, here and now, to kill the traitor Adolphe Thiers and General Vinoy, too. And she did move the debate, but only backwards, to Delescluze's contention that they represented civilisation – they could not stoop to assassinations and murder. They congratulated themselves that the elections would prove to the world that Paris was very far from being ruled by the mob.

The lynching of the two generals dominated the election campaign. It was the single biggest news story in the outside world, and the wellspring of all anti-Paris propaganda. Many inside the city felt they should not wait for the end of the election; in the interim they must disavow the killings of Generals Lecomte and Thomas and produce evidence that the Federals had played no part in the murders. Thiers and Vinoy used these deaths to claim that there was no law in Paris, just the free flow of psychotic impulses. They drew quotes from the Red magazines to prove that Paris had given itself over to the mob: a polemic that stated that no one should ever repudiate the spontaneous actions of the masses, the energy source and foundation of all revolution.

Yet many of the shrewdest minds in the city doubted that there was anything spontaneous about the murders. The bodies of the generals were riddled with bullets fired from a *chassepot*: a dozen for Lecomte, more than forty for General Thomas. As the Federals were still armed with *tabatières*, the evidence suggested that the regular army troops may have turned on their own generals. There was, however, another explanation: that one of the city's better-armed battalions had formed an impromptu death squad.

Late at night, in Babette's restaurant, Gustave Flourens denied the accusation.

'Where were we, Rigault?'

Rigault shrugged. 'We were here, we were there. We covered the city, we agitated, we probed.'

'Damn it, Rigault. We were on the Buttes-Chaumont.' Then to the table, 'Don't listen to the cunt, he's drunk.'

'I'm drunk?' Rigault raised an eyebrow. 'I believe I have my wits about me.'

Wroblewski and Bergeret were sitting alongside them, Brunel opposite and Babette across the room on a settee.

Bergeret said, 'So what are you saying, Flo? You condemn the murder of General Thomas?'

'What do you want me to say? The man was a crook and a scoundrel, a drunken quartermaster, puffed up on power.'

'So it was justice?'

Flourens appealed to Babette. 'Do you believe I orchestrated the lynching of Generals Lecomte and Thomas?'

'How much effort would it take to organise?' she replied. 'I am sure you could manage it.'

'Well, of course I could do it. But possessing the ability to do something is not the same as actually doing that thing in practice.'

Brunel remembered something that Raoul Rigault had said. Almost spontaneously, a paraphrase came to his lips: 'If the formal conditions exist, then it will necessarily exist in practice.'

'What kind of rubbish is that?' Flourens looked as though he had been slapped. 'Where do you even get an argument like that?'

'It's dialectics, it's all the rage.'

'It's diarrhoea.' Flourens was regaining some of his composure. 'I'll prove it to you. What are the formal conditions for a grand military parade? One: an army. Two: an upstart drill sergeant. But are you ready to bet on your ability to deliver, Comrade Sergeant-Major?'

'I want to start a war, they ask me to organise a party.' Brunel slammed a hand on the table. 'The morons. But the parade will be ready.'

Brunel would organise the parade that marked the end of the elections and the inauguration of the Paris commune. He could not escape the feeling of bitterness, each day, as he went about his job. The plan was that all of the city's troops would march past the Hôtel de Ville. Many of the candidates for the Commune hoped this show of strength would persuade the Thiers–Vinoy Government to negotiate. Brunel knew this was a hopeless fantasy. But he agreed to organise the parade, to tighten his bonds with the city's commanders and, through them, instil the troops with a readiness to fight.

And if he was organising a parade, it was better to do it properly. Hundreds of maps of the route were printed, marked with the spots where the different battalions would gather, and from where they would join the grand march. These were distributed to the battalion commanders in a series of meetings held at the National Guard headquarters, and it was here that Brunel outlined his view that every soldier needed to be sure of his role in the greater design. Battles were won on the ground; the troops had to learn that they owed the army the best of themselves, not just their obedience, but their intelligence and their initiative.

The stage designer from the Comédie Française was hired to build the stage outside the Hôtel de Ville. The largest and most heroic bust that could be found in the imperial art collection was decorated with a Phrygian cap to form the centrepiece. It would stand against a backdrop of red banners that hung the full height of the building. Against all this, the retiring chairman of the battalion commanders' committee would proclaim the Commune and hand over power to its new, elected assembly. Federals placed around the square would raise their rifles as cannons fired on the quayside and a marching band entered playing the Marseillaise, leading the two hundred battalions that Brunel could muster inside Paris.

As the Federals' Committee prepared for its last days in power, Raoul Rigault inveigled his way on board as the delegate for the Paris police. Through this, the organisation of the police force was brought under the new civic authorities and Rigault achieved his ambition: he was installed in the headquarters of the Prefecture, surrounded by his photographic records. His chief task, however, was to organise the practicalities of the election: the security of the polling stations, vetting the officers that would bring the ballot boxes to the count, printing the election lists and the ballot papers. He visited Brunel at his office in the National Guard headquarters and asked whether there ought to be a grand reception after the parade. And if so, should it include a banquet?

'Either a banquet, or a buffet. Which do you think would be best?'

Brunel said, 'Are you asking me as the city's chief choreographer, or as the friend of Babette Hébert?'

'Both. There's no shame in being a dancing master, now that we are all dancing to popular tunes. But your closeness to Babette is a definite advantage.'

Brunel said he would not speak for Babette, but as it was evening, he and Rigault walked to the restaurant together. Earlier in the day, there had been a small demonstration in the Place Vendôme by a group calling itself the Friends of Order, opposed to the Commune and the forthcoming elections. Rigault joked that they must be close friends as there were so few of them. By his estimate, a hundred thousand people had left Paris for the countryside and these were the remnants, the aspiring bourgeoisie who could not afford to close their businesses any longer. Or perhaps, as Rigault claimed, they were the ones who had never received an invitation to a country estate; they were only doing all this hysterical demonstrating out of pique.

The demonstrators were long gone; Jules Bergeret had dispersed them with just a handful of troops. The only sign of a disturbance was the increase in the number of Federals stationed around the square, and the scraps of paper that the demonstrators had left behind, blowing around the foot of the Vendôme column.

Brunel picked up one of their leaflets – it promised there would be further demonstrations. Rigault looked it over and nodded; he had information that the Friends of Order were planning a second demonstration in the morning, bolstered by a senior officer representing the government in Versailles.

Babette found herself in the Place Vendôme as the second demonstration kicked off. Freddie Worth was fitting her with a dress for the grand parade. It was scarlet. He told her: no one was going to mistake her for a Red Virgin but was she sure she wanted to make such a strong statement? Well, she was part of it now. She would be on the stage during the march past and had agreed to provide the food for the evening reception.

Another of Worth's clients, a young American, was turning in front of a mirror, lit by the strong sunlight through the window. The weather had been poor for so long that feeling the warmth of the sun on one's shoulders was a surprise and a delight – or so the young woman said. The open window brought the noise of the street right into the salon. Slowly, it became clear that something was happening; a crowd was approaching from the direction of the Opéra. It was just as Raoul Rigault had predicted; the demonstrators were returning in greater numbers, marching into the Place Vendôme from the rue de la Paix.

Babette and the American girl went out on to the balcony. Freddie accompanied them, speaking in English as he explained to his young client who the demonstrators were. They were carrying placards this time, but with the same message: they were for peace and they were unarmed. The American recognised one of the marchers and waved excitedly. She did not know the older man at the head of the procession.

Freddie said, 'I think he's an admiral. Is that right, Babette?'

She nodded. 'It's Admiral de la Roncière.'

Jules Bergeret had gathered his troops in a line across the square, their backs to the Vendôme column as they faced down the demonstrators approaching from the rue de la Paix. From the balcony, Babette saw that the leaders of the Friends were now trying to push back against the crowd, struggling to demarcate a no-man's land between themselves and Bergeret's men. Jules Bergeret himself stepped forward into that space, holding up a piece of paper and reading from it. There was no way of telling what he was saying. His other hand was lifted in a futile signal to halt. The demonstrators were still being pressed forward by the force of the crowd behind them. Babette looked across to the guard headquarters; sure enough, Brunel was there, gazing downwards, as though at a cabaret act whose antics he did not understand. The sight of the elderly admiral, struggling to keep his footing on the pavement, drew no response. When disaster came – as it would, as it would – Babette knew that Brunel would do nothing to save the admiral.

Bergeret dropped his hand. Immediately, there was a shot. It echoed around the square and for a moment the sound of the explosion appeared to separate into layers: explosion, retort, peal. Then came the volley . . .

The Federals fired a first round into the crowd. There were screams as men fell. A second round of shots came. The pressure from the rue de la Paix dropped as the crowd shook itself into fragments. In moments, a dense throng was reduced to bloody red clumps. There were only sporadic shots now, as the few protesters remaining in the square tried to carry away the dead and the wounded.

Babette was only one of the many people to question Brunel later about that day, but she had more opportunity than most. What she most wanted to know was whether he had given Jules Bergeret specific instructions to shoot at the crowd.

Surely, she thought, they had spoken about the tactics he would employ.

Brunel's face lay in profile, lit by the bedside lamp as he stared at the ceiling.

Babette said, 'You loved Admiral de la Roncière.'

Brunel did not answer for a full minute, but she could tell that he had heard because he was nodding all the while. She also knew that he had two messengers running relay from Val de Grâce to keep him informed about the admiral's condition. The old man was only said to be out of danger on the evening of the fourth day, just as the polls closed.

'I've brought him years closer to the grave, I'm certain of that,' Brunel said, eventually.

Babette could take this literally, as an admission that he was personally to blame. Certainly, he always took the blame in public, both for the admiral's injuries and the eleven dead demonstrators. But as the senior officer, he was also punctilious in defending Jules Bergeret, which could be taken as a sign that he was in no way culpable, as the senior man always covers for the junior.

She eventually asked, 'Do you regret what happened?'

Babette expected another long pause. But he answered quickly, 'No.'

'You don't regret it at all?'

'I wish they hadn't marched.'

'I doubt anyone will try it again.'

'No. Which is why I don't regret it. Let them stop to think for a second, they know a war is coming. And when it comes, there is no third position. All they could ever do is weaken our resolve, which strengthens the enemy.'

It made sense. But it did not alter the fact that Bergeret had shot at an unarmed crowd. Not that Jules ever admitted that that was what he had done, claiming always that the first shot could not have come from his men. At least, there was no conclusive evidence. In any event, who really believed the Friends of Order to be unarmed? Who thought those canes were for gout or the umbrellas for protection against the sun? They were swordsticks and nearly every man carried one.

The day of the election count was the warmest yet. By four o'clock, the afternoon sun was both bright and low, turning the red of the banners outside the Hôtel de Ville a flaming scarlet. Most of the newly elected members of the Commune Assembly were in place, sitting on tiers of banks with their wives or their lovers, who held up gloved hands to shield their eyes from the sun. With that gesture, the women all appeared to be saluting simultaneously. Babette was among them, wearing the red dress that she had had to complete herself after Freddie Worth fled the city. She had been given a central position, beside an empty chair that was waiting for Brunel. Gustave Flourens sat a little to her side and Jules Bergeret and his seventeen-year-old girl-friend a little to her rear.

Brunel took a last look from the roof of the Hôtel de Ville. Using field glasses, he began at his left where his cannons lined the Seine, ready for the salute. He turned through one hundred and eighty degrees to Château d'Eau where the battalions would merge and march down the rue du Temple to halt in the square below him. It was time that he took his seat.

As he was making his way down the staircase, Raoul Rigault hurried to catch him.

'Are you disappointed?'

'That today is over? No, I'm glad. I never wanted to be a party planner.'

'But you do it so well. There's been nothing like this since the days of the Emperor.'

Rigault had made an effort himself. His hair was oiled so that it was almost flat and his beard had been trimmed. His spectacles were also new, with smoked lenses that hid his eyes.

Rigault continued: 'You know that people were comparing you to Louis Napoleon – and your mistress to Eugénie.'

That brought Brunel up short. 'Who the hell would say that?'

'Who, indeed? Jealous bastards. Just because your old lady has style and can fill a dress. But, I tell you, there were a lot of relieved faces when they realised your name was not on the election lists – even among those who were trading on their closeness to you, just to get themselves elected.'

'I'm a soldier, not a politician.'

'Each to his own. I thought you were smarter though. I thought we were playing the same game.'

'I thought so, too. These elections have lost us a month. I thought you were going to back me to continue the war.'

'What could I do? Once they decided on the elections, it was a whole different game. It wasn't enough to get into the Prefecture, I knew I also had to get myself elected. Otherwise, some son of a bitch would have come along and chucked me out, too.'

'I didn't know you were on the election list.'

'I was a late addition.'

Rigault was also the election officer, so it could not have been difficult for him to get votes. Brunel offered his sardonic congratulations and was about to continue down the stairs when he stopped short.

'Who's been chucked out?'

'You, of course. You left yourself wide open. Now the two-faced bastards are saying: how can the Commune be led by a general who does not represent the people?'

'Who made the decision?'

'You scared them, Brunel. You're too efficient, too glamorous, too bloody Napoleonic all round. Your only mistake was giving that speech and allowing them to debate. Once you put yourself up for discussion, you legitimised the whole talking shop.'

'I asked, who sacked me?'

'It's the wrong question. Ask yourself, who are the new commanders.'

Brunel noted the plural. 'Who are they?'

'Flourens and Bergeret. Come on, did you really think either of those were going to play second fiddle to you? If it is any consolation, Flo is almost as sick as you. He never saw the challenge from Bergeret and he can't believe that he's only joint commander.'

The War Hotel

Flavie was barely conscious of the invasion. For two days and nights helicopters swooped around the hospital and descended on the city centre. There was the constant rumble of the tanks, the shelling, the night sky lit up with tracer fire. The intensive care ward lay on the third floor of Bethlehem hospital, and as I cowered by Flavie's bed and held her clammy hand, I wondered why they could not have put us in the basement.

A surgeon was able to open her up and stop the internal bleeding before stitching her back together again. I should not say stitched; she was stapled. There was only one entry wound, a sign that she was hit by a fragmentation round. The nurses lent me the bed beside her. I felt guilty as a healthy man in a hospital bed. But there were only two other patients in the ward. As Nadim had predicted, the local fighters had taken refuge in the Church of the Nativity, so casualties in Bethlehem were limited. And because the Israelis did not allow the ambulances to move around for the first three days of the invasion, nearly all were fatal. There were eighteen deaths, I believe, almost all of them in the smallest of Bethlehem's three refugee camps, which lay on the Israelis' route into the city.

Flavie came out of her drugged, shocked daze after four days and the first thing she did was ask to speak to Marguerite. I brought her a mobile phone and left her to it.

Over the next week, I started to do ambulance shifts as a committed volunteer of the International Solidarity Movement. There were now fewer peace protesters available to do the work. Many left on the third day, escorted out of the war zone by their embassies, and those who stayed were living inside the refugee camps. As long as the Israeli APCs dominated the roads they were unable to get to the hospital. George, Nadim's nephew, gave me some training in negotiation techniques and I began riding around in the ambulances as a 'human shield', for want of a better word, to deter the Israelis from shooting at it. Whenever the soldiers stopped us, I would step forward to negotiate. They never once spoke to me; they only gestured for me to move back and put my hands in the air. They did the same with the driver, while the third member of our crew was made to lift out all the equipment and prove that we were not smuggling weapons or explosives. If we were returning with a patient – almost always dialysis cases, for some reason – they had to lie on their stretcher in the road.

The weather had improved since the invasion and standing in the road with my hands above my head was both frightening and tedious. But it allowed me to see the landscape behind Bethlehem in the weeks after the spring rains. What had appeared to be desert suddenly bloomed with grass, so green that the rolling hills reminded me of a miniature version of England. Except that, every twenty yards along the road, an Israeli flag had been planted.

It was a lot less pleasant inside Bethlehem. There had been no refuse collection for so long, and as the weather grew hotter the city began to stink. The largest of the refugee camps decided their rubbish had become a health risk, so they burned it. That day, the town was filled with the after-effects of the bonfire, stinging our eyes and leaving an acrid taste in our mouths.

The APCs moved much faster than one would expect, leaving deep track marks in the hard surface of the road. As the siege wore on, the troop movements settled into a pattern. We could even predict the times. When the tanks and the APCs ended their shifts, they fired off a few rounds from their heavy machine-guns. All the houses along the main north–south highway had their water tanks shot up. The telegraph poles were shot up from top to bottom. The gunners also took aim at the loudspeakers on the mosques, especially during prayer call, and had destroyed the statue of the Virgin Mary on the roof of the maternity hospital where Nadim worked as a paediatrician.

Yet, apart from the gunfire and the explosions as the Israelis toured the city, blowing up cars, it was so quiet that it was easy to forget that Bethlehem only appeared to be deserted. The houses were filled with families, but they stayed away from the windows and kept their blinds shut. It was a surprise to see anyone, like the man on his roof trying to repair a water tank that was riddled with bullet holes. The solar panels next to it were beyond help.

After working a shift, I would return to Flavie with bright stories: of the Bedouin family who insisted on feeding me when I picked up their tattooed grandmother for kidney dialysis, or my descriptions of the verdant hills. I made the Israeli target practice sound as though it was a joke; perhaps it was, in their minds. I glossed over the occupation because Flavie was so unsettled. She had nothing to do but wait for her staples to be removed, and she wanted to leave the hospital.

'I am taking up too much space.'

It was not true. There was still no demand for her bed. Desperately sick people preferred to stay home rather than risk travelling. Flavie's real problem was that she was embarrassed by the care being lavished on her. She was being treated as a hero. She had taken an Israeli bullet.

The nurses at Bethlehem General adored Flavie. They loved her for herself and for her injuries and for the telephone calls that she swapped with Marguerite Galperin, who was entering her third week inside the presidential compound in Ramallah. Flavie did not feel she deserved this special attention, admitting she felt like a fake. When she persisted in talking about moving, I told her, 'I'll go back to the hotel and see if I can get our old room.'

The past few days had been so quiet that I decided to walk to the hotel. It was no more than five minutes away. But as I reached the junction on the main road, I heard the familiar rumble of an APC. I crossed hurriedly, unsure where the sound came from, and huddled into the gates of the maternity hospital. The APC appeared around the corner and the gunner on top saw me, exposed in the street. I lifted my arms high above my head so that my T-shirt rode up and showed there were no weapons in my trousers or explosives around my waist. As the gunner saw me, he fired into the roadway, raking up a shower of tarmac. My stomach began to turn over and over but I took a breath, determined to swallow this upsurge of dread. I wanted to face death without flinching. I made sure he could see my eyes and only wished I could see his, but like all the soldiers he wore sunglasses.

He only had to raise his aim and he would fire directly at me. But he didn't. He gestured angrily, get off the street, and the APC drove on.

The maternity hospital had steel gates, monitored by a CCTV camera. They began to open automatically and I stepped through them, grateful for the shelter, when I saw Nadim running towards me. He was shouting, 'You are crazy, what are you doing out here?'

Nadim had been sleeping in his office at the maternity hospital since the night of the invasion. I don't know if he had acknowledged it to himself, but it was clear to me that he had abandoned his house. He had once told me that it was not a home if his family were not there. But now that the house next door had been seized as a District Command Centre and was filled with Israeli soldiers, he had another reason to stay away. He was extremely concerned about his elderly neighbours, Mr and Mrs Obeid, who he presumed were still inside the house. A week earlier, a group from the International Solidarity Movement had negotiated access and had spoken to the couple for a few minutes. The army had restricted the Obeids to a single room at the back of the house, and the couple had declined the negotiators' offer to try to win their release. As Nadim said at the time, they had nowhere else to go. At least he had the hospital.

As he led me up the hospital driveway, he continued to berate me for my stupidity. He pointed to the stump of the statue of the Virgin Mary on top of the hospital chapel and said, 'If they shoot at the Virgin, why are you safe?' It was a rhetorical question, but I answered it anyway.

'It's just an inanimate object. This isn't a religious war.'

'It's not about religious tolerance either.'

As he gave me tea, he said, 'Who do they respect? Not even President Bush.' This was a reference to a news story that had broken that morning. Israel's Prime Minister had rejected a US demand to get his forces out of the Palestinian cities, a demand that President Bush had relayed through a television soundbite, saying, 'Now means now,' as he jabbed his finger in the air. It had taken a couple of days for Israel's Prime Minister to make his response, again at a televised event, an Israeli cabinet meeting. He had said he was staying until operations were over. Nadim said, 'How will it be over? You know, this isn't war.'

'It's not?'

'When we talk about war, we imagine it breaks out and finally it ends. This is different because this lasts for ever. The default position isn't peace, the default is war. They reset the dials.'

At the hotel, at night, I finally got to be alone with Flavie, playing spoons in a double bed. On her first night out of the hospital, I wore my thickest pair of trousers to muffle any erection. But I found that massive abdominal scars are a passion killer. Palestinian medics are supposed to be among the finest at dealing with shrapnel wounds and maybe they are, but they are a long way from keyhole surgery. And this was only an examination; six pieces of shrapnel remained in Flavie's guts. I lay spooned around her, my arm curled over to rest in the space between her breasts and her knees without a single erotic thought, worried only that my hand might brush her bandages. After the first two nights, I began wearing my boxers.

The hotel was now filled with TV crews. Whatever we watched on television, they had filmed from the panoramic restaurant at the top of the hotel. Yet, though we were surrounded by CNN, the BBC and others, we soon learned that the most important news channel was Bethlehem TV; not for the pictures, but for the live feed that scrolled across the bottom of the screen. I remember watching a programme on the Apollo space mission, taped from the Discovery Channel, while Nadim's nephew George read out the news that a sixteen-year-old boy had been shot as he escaped from the Church of the Nativity, and that the army had abruptly cancelled the lifting of the curfew that had been promised for the next day.

I started work in the hotel kitchen as a dishwasher. The hotel had no staff and the journalists could legitimately claim to be busy, so I volunteered. I thought, what the hell. The days were long. Flavie was not supposed to spend much time on her feet, yet she also needed moderate exercise. She took to walking around the hotel corridors, one hand pressed against her stomach. She was on one of her walks when a barrage balloon appeared above the Church of the Nativity. She came and dragged me to the restaurant windows. I had to jostle for space with all the cameramen but then I saw it, a silver Zeppelin, hovering above the basilica. The balloon was thought to have a remote camera on board to spy on any movement within its open courtyards. As Israel invaded, the fighters had been joined by some hundred or more youths. Speaking to George, who had the mobile number of a kid inside the church, we learned that there were probably as many as two hundred men and boys inside, not counting the priests and the monks. Some were injured, one badly, and all of them were out of supplies. The courtyards inside the church contained freshwater wells and lemon trees, which the men had stripped to eat their leaves.

On the surface, this siege was very different to any that had gone before. What could be weirder than the sheer amount of information available to us: we spoke to the boys in the church; Flavie spoke to Marguerite every day. We had rolling news channels and internet access; we spoke to family and friends at home. We even knew the minds of Presidents and Prime Ministers.

I was now communicating regularly with Evan, and when Jean-Luc somehow managed to copy an email to me, him and Flavie with a link to *Le Monde* newspaper that described the protesters here as 'terror tourists', Evan was so angry that he campaigned to have *Le Monde* removed from sale in Coventry. I spent a lot of time worrying about the effect my presence in Palestine would have on him. In an earlier email, when he had said he was proud of me, I half wanted to accept his pride, half wanted to disown it. I felt a fake, as Flavie had with her nurses.

Yet, despite our access to the outside world, nothing about sieges had really changed. There was the same fear, generated by the absence of the enemy, always faceless, always somewhere out there. We did not know them, we rarely saw them, and we had no idea what they would do. There were no laws to restrain them. In 1870, the Geneva Convention was a novelty. One hundred and thirty years later, it had no meaning at all. Flavie was shot by dumdum bullets; the ambulances in the hospital forecourt were peppered with bullet holes and one of them had been crushed by an Israeli tank. Medics had been shot and killed in every Palestinian city. Settlements continued to be built as Palestinians' homes were blown up. All these acts were outlawed by the Geneva Convention.

The enemy was faceless and unknowable. The closest that the Israeli Prime Minister came to evoking a strategy was to say that the war was ongoing, that it had objectives but that these had not been completed. I started to look for clues as to what the Israelis might intend and remembered the leaflet that the press office had given to me. It addressed the reasons for the occupation of Palestine, though avoided using the word. It talked instead of the natural expansion of Israel and its new settlements; of the belief of religious Jews that this land was given by God to the Jews alone; of the existence beneath the territories of strategic water and mineral supplies; of the problem of security raised by the terrorist groups operating from inside the territories; of the need to defend Israel's borders from hostile nations. What struck me was the hypothetical tone of the list. The various reasons were presented as possible explanations for the continuation of military occupation. There was no suggestion that one ought to accept all of them; indeed, many were contradictory. How could a housing estate be a defensive measure against a foreign enemy? The list was pick-and-mix; some reasons were religious, some were strategic, some were tactical, some were unintelligible.

This hypothetical tone turned the terrain into an abstract space in which Israel could always conjure up a new possibility.

We were under siege but that was because we saw the world as civilians. From the Israeli army's viewpoint the city had already been erased. They saw their borders not as a line but a zone, an amorphous grey area that resisted definition, that simply slid across the land and ignored all existing landmarks. A city could be three, four or five thousand years old; it did not matter. To the army commanders, this was a perfectly clear field of fire that they could roam over at will in their tanks and helicopters and fighter jets: their dream theatre. To the building contractors, it was simply the best kind of real estate: free and unregulated. To the army recruits, it was a blank sheet of paper, to shoot like the targets at a rifle range . . . or to wipe their arses on.

I had forgotten about hunger, the chief weapon in a siege. Or rather, I thought about it only when I considered the conditions inside the Church of the Nativity, but I had not thought that Flavie and I would become hungry.

But then the hotel ran out of food. It began with our portions growing smaller. I wanted to telephone the hospital and ask an ambulance to bring Flavie more food. She was their patient. She was due to return to the hospital in a few days to have her staples removed; they would not want to see her half starved. But Flavie refused to ask for help; it had been her decision to leave the hospital. She had been released into her own care, and her hunger was her responsibility. She had the example of Marguerite, whose food rations varied wildly, depending on conditions at the presidential compound so for two days we lived on crisps and biscuits.

Then the Israelis announced they would lift their curfew for two hours.

When the streets filled, the people seemed to come from nowhere. A great crowd gathered around the nearest super-market, jostling to be let inside. On the outskirts of this crowd, I turned towards the end of the street, where the closed zone around the town centre began. The families that lived in the souk were forbidden from leaving their homes; to glance in their direction was like looking at a force field in a science fiction movie. There was an invisible barrier and, beyond that, there were empty streets. There was nothing sophisticated about the barrier, however; it was maintained by the Israeli snipers in the buildings above us.

The queue to get into the supermarket was so chaotic that Flavie opted to sit in the street, scared that her staples would pop in the crush. After half an hour, I was allowed to squeeze inside with the few hundred other shoppers. I had wanted to buy snack food that we could keep in our room but the customers were packed tight and the few shop assistants were unable to move around the store, so I found I had to clamber behind the delicatessen counter to cut and weigh my own sausage and cheese. Then I was trapped, and had to serve other customers for thirty minutes until someone was prepared to relieve me. I came away with a carrier bag of everything one might need for a sandwich, apart from bread. Because the curfew had lasted for so many weeks and was only ever lifted for a few hours, even if the bakers were able to get to work they had no time to warm their ovens.

When my old ambulance crew appeared at the hotel door an hour later, I fantasised that they were bringing us emergency baguettes. Flavie waved to them – she was friends with all the staff from the hospital. Then Nadim's face appeared. He had become so worried about his next-door neighbours that he had persuaded the ambulance crew to help him check up on them. But the ambulance was not enough. He felt that he also needed a human shield.

'If you're the best protection around, I'll take you,' he said. 'Perhaps you will finally get a chance to negotiate.'

'Maybe they only speak French,' Flavie said. 'Better that I come, too.' It was unlikely, but she refused to be left behind.

We travelled on the back roads, at one point going through a private garden and across a building site via a hole made in the garden wall. Bethlehem was now filled with these makeshift routes, as the highway was dominated by Israeli APCs. This brought us to the back of Nadim's house, which was rather sheltered, lying in a dip below the level of the road. The Obeids' house stood above it, throwing a long shadow across Nadim's garden. The upper-storey windows were barricaded with mattresses – a sign that it had been used by Israeli snipers. Nadim's information, gleaned from Bethlehem TV, was that the soldiers had abandoned this position. He told us that a local reporter had sneaked over a few days ago but found no sign of the Obeids.

'But they didn't see any soldiers either,' Nadim said.

I pulled back the ambulance door, my passport in my hand to prove I was a foreigner, when Flavie said, 'I'll come with you.'

'That's crazy. You hobble everywhere, holding your insides together. If there's a problem, how are you going to run away?'

'Can you run faster than a bullet?' she asked, opening up a

pause that she knew I could not fill. 'Fine, it seems that speed is not the priority.'

In the end, all five of us went, Flavie and I holding our passports in the air. At the gate to the house, we stood absolutely still for almost a minute. When there were no shouts or shots, we took a pace forward and stopped again. When I felt my heartbeat had slowed and my palms dried out, I asked, 'Everyone ready?'

We went inside.

The entrance led to a large salon. Every inch of the carpet was covered in broken glass and ornaments, crumpled sports day trophies and trampled family photographs. The TV had been thrown on its side in the centre of the room, the screen smashed. But it was not the TV that caught the eye; it was the arc of human shit wiped across the back wall. The soldier had torn off a sheet of fax roll to smear his shit and the paper remained, stuck to a dried brown crust. There was another lump of shit on the leather settee.

We passed through into the kitchen. This had suffered less damage – only the refrigerator. The door stood open and the shelves had been pulled out, leaving a pile of rotten tomatoes, broken eggs and smashed Lilt bottles on the floor.

'So what do we do now?' Flavie asked.

Nadim pointed to a back room. 'They were supposed to be in there.'

There was no sign of them. Nor upstairs. We found food wrappers and cigarette stubs but otherwise the rooms were relatively clean. This was where the soldiers had slept.

As we were leaving, the ambulance driver found a prayer mat stuffed in the downstairs toilet. This upset him so much that we had to stand and debate whether we ought to take it, so that the Obeids never saw what had happened to it. We had not yet reached a decision when Flavie said, 'There is someone in the cellar.'

We strained to listen for any sound . . . and found it, a shuffling that came from the cellar below us but seemed to be drawing closer. It was the sound of slow feet struggling up concrete steps. The cellar door was locked but the key stood proud in the lock. A hands slapped on the wood and a weak voice said, 'Please.'

I turned the key and paused, but when the person on the other side failed to take the initiative, I grasped the door handle and slowly twisted it. An elderly man in a murky grey suit stood right in front of me. In the gloom of the cellar, there was an equally elderly woman in a dressing gown, looking up at us.

The Israeli soldiers had transferred the Obeids from the back room to the cellar because the door was lockable. They had then omitted to release the couple when they left. As far as we could tell, the Obeids had been down there for ten days. Mrs Obeid was in a frightful state, and could not even look at the damage to her property. She stumbled around, wailing, with her hands covering her eyes, until Flavie folded her into an embrace. Mr Obeid was simply ashamed. He walked around, trying to be stoical, but when he saw his prayer mat in the lavatory pan, he had to be helped out of the house.

The Obeids had survived because their chest freezer was in the cellar. They had a tin barbecue tray to cook their food, which filled the space with smoke. There was a toilet down there, with a washbasin, a cold water tap and even an extractor fan, so it could have been worse. Or so I told myself.

After we had taken the Obeids to Bethlehem General, we sat in the courtyard with the ambulance crews. Nadim cradled a cup of tea.

'You know that I have made up my mind. I will leave as soon as I can get a pass out of Palestine.'

'For a rest or for good?'

'For ever, I think.'

It was not my place to tell him that, if he left the country, there were very few people who could fill his shoes. I remembered what he had said, on the day we arrived, that war had become the default position, the Israelis had reset the dials. Nadim would have been two or three years old when the military occupation of Bethlehem began. He had lived under this occupation almost his whole life and even brought children into it. There must have been a time when he had expectations that he would one day see peace, but these hopes were gone.

His homeland had been erased. This was a world created for soldiers: there were no forums, no court rooms, no markets, just a pure battle-space. Brunel had failed to save France from defeat but his intuition that cities were indefensible, even irrelevant to armies that needed to move without limits, had been proved true here in Palestine. But it was the Israelis who had learned the lesson. And now I had a problem – how would I write from inside this space, when all the quarters where words, arguments and imagination had a value no longer existed. Because I had already made my decision, I had to include our experiences in any book I wrote.

Back in Prison

Gustave Flourens was captured as he emerged from an inn on the road to Versailles, having lost contact with Bergeret's forces the night before. He was beheaded in the street by a gendarme with a cavalry sabre. Jules Bergeret was shortly demoted from joint commander of the Federals and placed in charge of Fort Issy, at the head of Flo's old battalion, now rechristened the Blood of Flourens. The fort was under constant bombardment and Bergeret spent his command hiding from Flo's men and drinking alone in his office.

And Brunel was back in prison. His gaoler, Prefect Raoul Rigault, appeared fresh from his bath, wearing a bathrobe that fell open to expose a massive and hairy chest. He slid two photographs out of a file and after balancing two plates of rotten food on top of each other, he found enough room to lay them side by side on his desk.

Babette and Louise Michel took a step forward.

The first was a portrait of Brunel taken six months earlier. Babette saw the marks on his face, the results of her attempted shave. She saw the hollows of his cheeks and the firm line of his mouth with the *impérial* beneath it. The second showed Monsignor Darboy, the Archbishop of Paris, who was bare-headed with two days' growth of grey stubble spouting from a wan face. It was a much more recent picture, although he was unrecognisable as the man who had given Zizi the last rites. The archbishop had been arrested immediately following Flo's death. Rigault had sent a warning to Versailles that if any more of the leaders of the Commune were summarily executed, then he would begin killing his hostages.

'I feel like Pontius Pilate. Do I release the archbishop or do I release Brunel?' Rigault tilted his head as he spoke: first one way, then the other. The two men were in adjoining cells, deep below the Prefecture. Rigault continued, 'I ought to warn you, the stakes are high. The American Ambassador is demanding the immediate release of Monsignor Darboy. What's your counter-proposal?'

Rigault winked at Babette, making clear what kind of proposal would be acceptable. Or clear to anyone apart from Louise Michel. Rigault's antics completely passed her by.

'Why compare Brunel and the archbishop?' Louise Michel asked. 'There is no comparison between the archbishop and General Brunel.'

'Brunel is not a general any more,' Rigault corrected her.

'Maybe not,' said Louise Michel. 'But he remains our best general.'

Brunel and Louise Michel had mounted the defence of the village of Issy, on the south-western outskirts of Paris. In a dispatch from the front, Louise Michel had described the battle as 'enchanting': 'The battered building gleaming faintly in the night, our soldiers emerging in the silver moonlight, the red teeth of the machine-guns flashing on the horizon. It was so beautiful. I'm a savage, I love the smell of gunpowder, grapeshot flying through the air. But above all, I'm devoted to the revolution.' She and Brunel had fought at the head of an irregular force from Montmartre. When they were driven out of the village, they retreated to Fort Issy, where these enchanting machine-guns were positioned. They found the fort in disarray. The Blood of Flourens were barely holding on and Bergeret had disappeared.

Rigault said, 'If Brunel is our best general, then he knows how serious is his offence. The day after he abandoned his position at Fort Issy, it was overrun.'

'He was never the commander of Issy. And if you blame him for leaving the fort without a leader, then you ought first to blame

Bergeret, wherever he is. Or why not blame me? Brunel was fighting with my men; an autocrat might argue that he was under my command. If he can be blamed for not taking control of the fort, then the fault is doubly mine. I ought to be blamed, too.'

Now that he was being pushed, Rigault admitted that the charges against Brunel had something of a trumped-up air. But, he argued, Brunel had been arrested three times since his arrival in the city. 'If every previous regime has found him a threat, I'd be foolish not to be on my guard.'

It had taken Babette some time to recognise that beneath the sour fug of decay, sweat and stale cigarettes, it was this suite of rooms that Brunel had once occupied. The longer that she remained in this airless space with Rigault, the more convinced she became that his mistrust of Brunel arose out of fascination. Why else would he take his rooms, only to desecrate them? Food was scattered everywhere, piled on plates that doubled as ashtrays. Many people had gone crazy after the first siege, surrounding themselves with more than they could ever eat, keeping it heaped on tables and sideboards like trophies. After the disaster of Flo's and Bergeret's attack on Versailles, it was clear that a second siege was inevitable. This time around, the siege lines were so porous that smuggling flourished. But the fear remained that they could all soon be living on rats again. Raoul Rigault might have looked relaxed and happy, but that fear must have affected him. Otherwise, why had he seized these particular rooms only to turn them into this dark nest?

Babette found her tongue. 'Why is Brunel such a threat to you?'

'I don't say he is a threat.' Rigault inclined back on his sofa, scratching at his stomach through a gap in his dressing gown. 'But let me ask you a question, Madame Hébert. Can you honestly say that Paul-Antoine Brunel is not a violent and chaotic force who might further destabilise Paris in an attempt to seize power?'

'He has fought in every single battle, under all of the city's commanders.'

'Which more than proves he is capable of great violence. And, yes, he has served every commander, it is true. But that shows a kind of weakness, a lack of guiding principles.'

'No. No. You have quite the wrong idea of him.' Louise Michel sat down and crossed her arms, as though in protest. 'Brunel is an extremely fine commander and as fine a man as you, Raoul. He is just as great an asset to the revolution.'

Though Rigault insisted that he could not release Brunel, he could not refuse him visitors. Babette and Louise Michel crossed the police yard and descended below the waterline. These cells held Monsignor Darboy and the rest of the friars and Jesuits who had been rounded up on Rigault's orders. Brunel was in the last cell, at the higher end of the corridor. The height made it a little drier than the priests' cells.

Louise Michel looked away as Brunel and Babette kissed. Brunel was damp and cold after two nights at river level. Babette pressed hard against him. The kiss gave way to an embrace. When they finally broke apart, it was because Louise Michel could no longer keep silent. Perhaps she also sensed Babette's desperation. She raised her voice, swearing that she would have Brunel out of prison by the next evening. She had started to plan alternative petitions on his behalf, an appeal to Chairman Delescluze and who else? She tried to remember the names of the latest committee members, but she realised that she was behind with the news. During the time she had spent out at Issy, the leadership of the Commune had changed three times.

'Rigault is not being reasonable at the moment. He as much as said that your arrest has nothing to do with Fort Issy.'

Brunel sat on the stone lip of his bed, his hand in Babette's. 'The fort fell the night we left it.'

'But you were never in command.'

'I could have taken command,' Brunel said. 'Who would have stopped me?'

'I wish you had seized power,' said Babette, tightening her grip; she meant that he should have taken the city when he had the chance rather than let the situation slide into pointless elections. 'But they cast you aside, and you don't owe the city anything. When we get you out of here, please, this time, let's escape.'

'It would be the best thing,' he admitted, shrugging. 'But I don't change my mind easily. And I always believed we should fight to the end. It doesn't really affect the situation, the question of how they treat me.'

Louise Michel persuaded the guard to withdraw with her into the corridor and give Babette and Brunel some privacy. Brunel asked after Christian. Her son had recently turned fifteen, and Babette knew two things about him: that he believed he was in love with Murielle and that he intended to fight when the city fell. So she told Brunel that she was worried about him.

'You should be proud of him, too.'

'That doesn't help me – hearing it from you.'

It was a poor note for them to end on. They sat in silence, hand in hand, until the guard knocked and reopened the door.

As they were leaving the Prefecture, Louise Michel stopped Babette and said, 'You have to understand, Raoul Rigault is a good man. He gives the city hope. He would not deprive Paris of its best general, in such dangerous times. It's against his nature.' This caught Babette off-guard, but it was part of Louise Michel's gaucherie that she never thought to trim her views, no matter whom she was speaking to. 'Paris is on the point of collapse, but Raoul holds it together. He's like a Samson in reverse, he holds up the columns of the temple.'

There was only one column in Paris and that had been demolished the previous day, as an unwanted symbol of Napoleonic imperialism and militarism; a glorification of everything that had destroyed the nation. For a week beforehand, the Place Vendôme had been filled with sandbags to cushion the iron column and protect the sewers beneath the square. When it was eventually felled, the crash was heard across the city and beyond.

Babette was reminded of Louise Michel's words a few days afterwards. It was late, and she was sitting in her kitchen, drinking brandy and waiting for Christian to return. She was already quite drunk when she heard music in the warm-cool of the evening and, in a kind of mental hiccup, left the house and went searching for its source. As she passed through the Place Vendôme, she was caught in a moment of bewilderment. She had not realised to what extent the giant gunmetal column had dominated the square, and now its absence put the whole square out of kilter. The pin was gone, the city was unhinged, like a door that had slipped from its frame. Above her, the night sky was filled with a mix of fireworks and shellfire. Babette reached the square in front of the Tuileries and found couples dancing. Though it was dark, the lights above the orchestra and the explosions in the sky were sufficient for the musicians to read their scores and the dancers to find their feet. A woman stood at the front of the stage and sang in a honeyed contralto that wove into the sound of shelling from the captured forts at Issy and Valérien.

Babette thought that she might find Christian at the festival but she didn't see him. When she returned to the restaurant, he was not in his room, either. The building was empty. But it was while she was looking for her son, cautiously peering around the door of Murielle's bedroom, that she heard someone enter the kitchen. The intruder was not trying to be discreet. There was the clatter of steel on her work surface, as someone put down their weapons. Then the heavy footfall of army boots. Finally, a call and she recognised the voice of Paul-Antoine Brunel.

She ran down the stairs and he caught her. She was crying so hard that she could barely fit her mouth to his, and as they kissed, their faces slid against each other on the sheen of her tears, so that her lips were pressed against his nose, his cheekbone and then his jawline. She was embarrassed that she was drunk, and she blamed this for her loose grip on her emotions. Right up until she realised that Brunel was crying, too.

'Are we going? Are we going to leave?'

'No. We have to stay and fight. General Vinoy is in the city. We've only got a few hours left.'

He meant that Paris had only a few hours, but he could have been referring to the two of them.

Burning Paris

Brunel had been led from his cell at the Prefecture and taken straight to a war council where Louis Charles Delescluze offered him operational command of the Right Bank. Walery Wroblewski was already organising resistance on the Left, building barricades even as Vinoy's forces approached. Louis Michel was in her beloved Montmartre, visiting her mother for what she believed was the last time before she joined her battalion at the Buttes-Chaumont.

Babette asked what had happened to Raoul Rigault. Brunel told her that he had been courteous throughout and came away from the meeting with responsibility for his own sector: the Île de la Cité. He was now holed up in the Prefecture, planning to blow the bridges and start a new siege as chairman of his own island.

Babette washed quickly and followed Brunel to the rue de Rivoli where work had begun on Brunel's main barricade. She had passed this way a few hours earlier, and already it was transformed. The cobblestones had been torn up from the street and teams of men were working to stack them into a solid wall. Brunel planned for the barricade to stand over three metres high and cover the entire street, with spaces left for the muzzles of his cannons. A stream of carts hurried in relays from the Napoleon barracks, bringing shells as well as barrels of black powder. There were crates of cartridges and rifles stacked in pyramids, ready and waiting, hung with jackets as the men worked through the night in their shirtsleeves.

Brunel moved on, leading Babette around his defences. Progress at the barricade across the Place de la Concorde was even better than at the rue de Rivoli. And it was there that Babette saw her son. Christian was working hard, piling up sandbags to brace and protect the huge brass cannon. As she moved closer, she recognised the men around him, porters from Les Halles, clerks from the shops and the municipal offices, many of them veterans of the 125th, Zizi's old battalion. Christian was far from being the only youngster; many of the boys were also under sixteen. But she did not want her son there.

She took Brunel aside to plead that he do something. He tried to reassure her that there was no question of Christian fighting. There were barely enough rifles for the men. He pointed to the cannon, with its levers and wheels, and told her that only trained soldiers could load and fire those weapons. Christian was simply helping build the barricade, and that was all.

'We need all the hands we can get and your son's not stupid, he knows that. How can I send him away?'

'But once men start dying, what then? What if he picks up a rifle and starts fighting? What will you tell him?' she demanded. 'He has to be stopped now. Look at him, he isn't thinking, he's just terrified.'

She knew that Brunel would not turn her down. Before they left the Place de la Concorde, Brunel ordered the division commander at the barricade to send the boy away and a runner was dispatched around the quartier with the same message. All of the commanders knew and recognised the son of Babette and Zizi, and would turn Christian away if he reappeared on any of the barricades.

Murielle had enlisted as a *cantinière* at the local Masonic lodge. Babette signed up, too, and once equipped with flasks of soup and alcohol she began touring the area. There were three main barricades in this district, and the third lay directly outside Chez Babette, across the entrance to the Place Vendôme. If Christian turned up anywhere she was certain that it would be there. Yet as the night waned, she saw no sign of her son.

Vinoy's forces were massing at the Arc de Triomphe, consolidating their position but strangely reluctant to move. By dawn, they had squandered the advantage gained on entering the city. Brunel's forces watched them from their barricade at the Place de la Concorde, down the length of the Champs Élysées. The avenue was still shorn of trees after the terrible winter and the two armies stared at each other, separated by barely a thousand metres.

Babette was carrying fresh flasks, on her way to rejoin Brunel at the Place de la Concorde, when she heard the sound of marching and horses hooves ringing off the stones. But she could see no movement on the great avenue. It was only when the machine-guns started cranking out their fire that she grasped that the troops were coming from the quayside to flank Brunel's position.

Babette picked up her feet and ran for shelter. She recognised the sound of these guns, the deafening noise and the smell of burning that recalled the slaughter of Pollux. Once again, she saw the elephant lie thrashing on its back and feared for the men atop the barricades. But as she reached them, she realised they were leaping and cheering. The machine-guns were Brunel's; he had emplacements hidden along the length of the quay, and in the narrow channel between the buildings and the river they were devastatingly effective. Vinoy's column appeared like a fire serpent, leaping and rearing in the fire-cracker explosions and trying to turn in on itself.

In the midst of these soldiers, Babette saw the red hair of General Gallifet on horseback. He was wheeling about on the far side of his troops, trying to pull his men out of range as he ordered a retreat.

The enemy were driven back to the Arc de Triomphe. Brunel began the task of reorganising his position. He was so focused on his work that Babette could not interrupt him and he was the last to receive one of her flasks. When he took a pull, he didn't appear to notice that she had filled it with good brandy rather than absinthe.

'Have you won the advantage? Do you counter-attack?' she asked.

'No. I don't have the men. All I can do is draw Vinoy on.' He slapped the breach of the great brass gun that faced down the Champs Élysées. 'They won't attack front on, and they've just learnt that flanking won't work. They have no choice, they will have to come down from the Opéra. The next battle will take place outside Chez Babette.'

Babette continued to roam the quartier, combining her work as a *cantinière* with the search for her son. The barricade on the rue de la Paix stood one storey high and was defended with a heavy cannon. There was no sign of Christian, either at the barricade or in the restaurant, and so she returned to the Masonic lodge to refill her flasks and find Murielle – hoping that the girl might know something. So far Murielle had turned down all of Christian's advances; she was too careful of Babette to encourage the boy. But even this had failed to reassure Babette, who now worried that Murielle would take up with one of the local fighters and spur Christian into stupid acts of bravery. His father had set him a poor enough example.

It was late in the afternoon when rumours began that Raoul Rigault was executing his hostages. Within the hour, a runner from the Île de la Cité confirmed that the Archbishop was dead. Babette abandoned her work and spent a few hours in the church of Saint-Germain-l'Auxerrois, but her prayers were disturbed by gunfire. As night fell, she was back at the Masonic lodge serving soup from the kitchen. The fighting seemed to be all around her, although she was assured that it was coming from across the river, where Walery Wroblewski was defending the Left Bank street by street.

By ten o'clock she was threading through the groups that had gathered in the shadow of the barricades. There were a great many women, canteen girls and volunteer nurses. Babette finally found Murielle, but was disappointed when she claimed not to have seen Christian since the morning. Despite her worries, Babette found the mood at the barricades strangely reassuring, perhaps desperately so. Everyone declared that the Burner was wise to Vinoy; he had checked his forces at the Place de la Concorde, and he would break them on the next attack.

The mood changed as the quartier was shaken by a series of explosions, so powerful it was clear they came from within their own positions. Then fire began spewing from the centre of the Tuileries: the palace was in flames. Each spout of fire set off a new explosion in a chain reaction across the entire building. Speculation raged that Vinoy was using incendiary shells. Or perhaps he had agents planted in the area? But another rumour began to emerge: the Burner was living up to his name and he was ready to torch the city rather than lose it.

As the fire raged, the men came running from the barricades at the Place de la Concorde with the story of how the Burner had led them into the palace where they had doused everything in paraffin: chairs, curtains, carpets. Barrels of gunpowder were carried into the chambers and linked with their fastest fuses. They filled the *cantinières'* empty flasks with paraffin and stuffed rags in the necks. When the rags were lit and the flasks thrown in the palace windows, the explosions shook the sky. Sheets of flames rose thirty and forty metres, making an impassable barrier for Vinoy's troops. This was why Brunel had been so confident that the next attack would come from the Opéra. All along, he had planned to lure them down into the Place Vendôme, where he would command the heights from the surrounding buildings.

Babette returned to her restaurant, certain now that this was where she would find Christian. The solid barricade of paving stones outside Chez Babette faced another, improvised barricade at the end of the street, across the entrance to the Place de l'Opéra. It was constructed around an overturned omnibus and had been stuffed with sandbags and studded with pieces of furniture. As she drew close, she recognised her own tables and chairs, and then ex-members of her kitchen staff. She gave them soup and offered absinthe, only to learn that they had their own brandy, borrowed from her cellar. One of her old porters advised her to keep her head down; there were snipers in the scaffolding around the Opera House. This was confirmed in seconds, as bullets bit into the pavement ahead of her. There was a lengthy pause, in which a few bars of a whistled melody drifted down from a sous-chef in a Federals uniform, steadying his *chassepot* on the wheel arch of the bus. Then came a whole fusillade, pinging and screeching off the bus's metal chassis. Babette gasped and the sous-chef shouted down, 'You think that's a surprise? You didn't notice the Tuileries on fire?'

Her restaurant was entirely dark. There were hardly any lights in the whole district, and wherever light broke from an apartment she noticed that the window was criss-crossed with tape to protect against blast damage. Up above her, she imagined she could see shadows moving in nests among the scaffolds at the Opéra, but it was probably her imagination. It seemed unlikely that any sniper would be able to see her. And yet, despite the dark, she could sense the forces massing out there, between the department stores of the Boulevard Haussmann and the streets off the Place de la Madeleine.

She asked the porter, 'Have you seen Christian?'

'He was around earlier, Madame Hébert. So, I don't know. Perhaps in the restaurant?'

The doors were unlocked. The restaurant was empty – no tables, no chairs, no Christian. She called up the staircase and continued through the kitchen towards the back door. She called out one more time, but there was no reply so she left by the back alley.

Once again, she went to refill her flasks and tour all the barricades, although her instincts still told her that she would find Christian at home. The fire of the Tuileries hypnotised the whole district, but it was dangerous to linger. Vinoy's snipers would pick off any figures seen silhouetted against the flames.

Circling back to Chez Babette took less than an hour but the barricades were now under heavy bombardment. As she reached the street, she saw the men on the move, running from the entrance to the Place de l'Opéra where their bus-barricade was falling, to the stone structure outside her restaurant. In moments, the abandoned barricade was in splinters – soon it took flame. The fire dominated the street and gave the Federals time to breathe, check their weapons and reload. That was her own furniture on fire among the carcass of the omnibus, and by its light Babette saw Brunel. He turned one hand in the other, his brows drawn together by deep black lines.

As she was moving towards him, the sous-chef from the barricade stopped and asked if she was still looking for Christian. 'Because I thought I saw him running towards the Maison de Worth.'

All the time that she had spent returning to her restaurant to search for her son had been wasted. It was the Maison de Worth that was his true home. As she realised this, she turned and ran, sending her flasks jangling together. A howitzer shell landed behind her, the shrapnel tearing across the face of the street. The blast lifted her sideways and slammed her on to the pavement. Behind her, she could hear Brunel shouting her name. As she tried to get upright again, cascades of glass shards rained down upon her.

Brunel lifted her to her feet. She shook off his questions, only wanting to get to the Maison de Worth.

The door was open. Her voice echoed through the lobby and the salons beyond. She was answered by a spark.

A paraffin lamp caught light, illuminating the face of the boy holding it. It was Christian, sitting alone in the centre of the bare room. Tears ran down his face and his hands shook so much that he could barely keep his grip on the lamp. He was perched on a barrel, his feet swinging off the floor. Babette wondered why the boy had chosen to drag a barrel all the way from the restaurant. But then Brunel clamped a hand on her shoulder, swinging her to the side with such force that she almost landed on her knees.

Brunel was walking towards Christian, but slowly, his hands outstretched as he begged the boy, 'Wait, please.'

The barrel of black powder had not come from the kitchen, but from the arsenal at the barricade. Christian had brought it into the salon and he was shivering and crying as he prepared to counter the next attack by destroying himself and everything that surrounded him.

Brunel held out his hands palm upwards and stepped into the circle of light from Christian's lamp.

'I've got your mother with me.'

The boy looked relieved, as though he had never thought there might be another way out. Brunel took the lamp away from him. With his other hand on Christian's shoulder, he guided everyone out to the square.

The Church of the Nativity

After the Israelis shot a priest inside the Church of the Nativity, the army took over the restaurant of the Star Hotel to prevent any more filming. The TV crews soon packed up and left. Shortly afterwards, a crane appeared in Manger Square and a steel container was lowered over the basilica. There were rumoured to be remote-controlled rifles and heat-sensitive cameras inside. Once the hotel filled with soldiers, we also had to leave. But there was a fascination; this was the first time I had seen any soldiers up close since I had arrived. They were reservists so they were my age, fuzzily unshaved with spreading stomachs. It made me realise just how young the soldiers had been who searched the ambulances or cruised the streets of Bethlehem in their APCs.

We spent two more nights at Bethlehem General for Flavie to have her staples removed. The Obeids were still there for observation, so we became reacquainted. After we volunteered to help clean their house, they asked if we would like to move in with them.

For as long as Flavie's stomach had been full of staples, we had successfully shared a bed. I was apprehensive that things might change, but once we moved in with the Obeids the sharing stopped anyway. I think the Obeids might have accepted the arrangement if we had been a real couple, either engaged or possibly even boyfriend and girlfriend. But they already knew we were only friends and so they gave us separate rooms. I had no idea how to say, '*Actually* . . .'

And it was hard work. It was a long time before Mrs Obeid was even close to satisfied that her house had been disinfected. But eventually the days took on a different rhythm, shaped chiefly around mealtimes. Mrs Obeid cooked. The chest freezer in their cellar was good for another two weeks, though some food at the bottom was not of the best, having survived power cuts, defrostings and drenchings from the thawing food above. The Obeids watched Bethlehem TV, we watched satellite, and over dinner we would compare notes.

And somehow, maybe inevitably, my relationship with Flavie began to deteriorate. I could blame domesticity with the Obeids, or the end of the bubble of intimacy we had maintained in the hotel. But a clear faultline emerged when I began talking about booking a flight out to Paris. Flavie was adamant that she would not leave the country until Marguerite was free.

We had an argument, a symptom of underlying tensions, although it was real enough. It followed the French general election. The Socialist candidate had been knocked out of the final run-off by the National Front candidate. Flavie ended a call to Marguerite absolutely shaken. She told me that Marguerite had started crying; for the past month, she had been locked in a small, unhygienic building with several hundred middle-aged men, while the surrounding buildings were systematically shelled or bull-dozed. The only thing that sustained her was the hope that she might contribute to a better world. So what possessed her countrymen to vote for a neo-Fascist? What was wrong, she wanted to know, that people wanted to see a crueller, more divided world?

I said, 'You should have told her to ring Elise and ask her for an explanation.'

Flavie knew I was right, that Elise had voted National Front. But she said, 'Elise is not racist. You cannot make that kind of accusation.'

'She is not wildly racist,' I said. 'But that's not what I meant; she mostly wants to be nasty to the left. She thinks they are so sanctimonious that every time they open their mouths someone should slap them shut. They had all this time to turn the world into a nice place and they fucked up, so now they should shut up about it.'

'That's not what Elise thinks,' Flavie said. 'That's what you think.'

I was contemplating booking flights anyway, thinking that I might be able to railroad Flavie into returning. Then Nadim's nephew called, asking if we would volunteer to take food to the men trapped inside the church. I might have told him it was pointless, that this was the third attempt and each one so far had failed completely. But Flavie took the call and volunteered without consulting me. There was little time to argue; it took only twenty minutes to walk to the rendezvous. Within half an hour, we had filled our backpacks with food and memorised our route into Manger Square.

I had never got this far into the town centre before. Water dripped off every roof, from the shattered pipes and from the bullet holes in the water tanks. The stench of the meat rotting inside the refrigerators of the souk was close to unbearable. Every car we passed was a blackened hulk; colonnades were shorn away, statues ground to dust; the windows of the Lutheran Church smashed and its gift shop vandalised. And everywhere, Hebrew graffiti on the walls and spray-painted Stars of David.

As we reached the steps by the souk, we picked our way through coils of razor wire. The soldiers had never yet let anyone past the souk and I wondered why it had suddenly become so easy. I saw a protester peek round the next corner and recognised the skinny Swede from the day that we were shot at, as well as a tiny Jewish girl from New York. But there were nine or ten people that I had never seen before, proving that volunteers were still finding their way into the town. The woman co-ordinator got us into a huddle and repeated the plan. We would emerge in three columns, from three sides of the square, but only the middle column would enter the church. I had insisted that we could only join a decoy party. But perhaps I should have sensed something would go wrong. The soldiers were so lax. They had grown careless just as the protesters were getting organised. Our co-ordinator was in contact with the men inside the church via mobile phone. They knew we were coming and they had already removed the internal barricades on the church door.

The last calls were made. The three columns got into position. Someone slapped me on the back and I picked my way over a lump of concrete debris, turning as I did so to make sure that Flavie was safely over. Then our group gathered speed.

The two other columns lay to our left. We made eye contact and started running. We were right across the car park before we began hearing shouts in Hebrew and English from the soldiers. I expected to hear racing footsteps or even shots at any moment. Our route took us in front of the Peace Centre which the Israelis had long ago seized as a command post. It was now decked with Star of David flags. But we had caught the commanders inside off-guard, and the only soldiers who noticed us were lounging and smoking at the far side of the square.

The entrance to the basilica is known as the Door of Humility. It is so low that one has to bend double to enter. As we drew close the door began to open. And still there were no soldiers coming for us: we were the decoy column but there was no one for us to fool. I realised our plan was changing, but as I slowed down, adrenaline seemed to push everyone else on. I was halfway across the white stone piazza outside the basilica as the first member of our group ducked his head through the door. I looked over my shoulder for Flavie, just in time to see her streak ahead of me.

Some of the protesters dived for the open doors, others shielded them with their bodies. The last I saw of Flavie, her face was framed between the legs of the co-ordinator. I had come to a dead halt, simply staring at her, thinking: fuck. What now?

I picked the backpack off my shoulder and started swinging it. As I let go, it sailed in an arc towards the church door. I didn't see it land. At that moment, I was tackled. A soldier launched himself forward at waist height and I smashed to the ground. I recovered my breath as I was dragged away, one Israeli soldier holding each of my arms. I could not see the backpack, so it must have reached the inside of the church.

I was taken to the prison in Ariel settlement – a Jews-only city that barely existed in the mid-1990s. Even now it seemed to be little more than a prison and a technical college, surrounded by streets and streets of unoccupied houses. That's all I saw from the police minibus that carried me there. I was frightened, but I had four other protesters with me and we tried to keep each other focused. The guards were brusque and forbidding. They would thrust Hebrew documents under our noses and berate us when we refused to sign. Yet it was two days before they discovered I had a mobile phone inside my pants.

I doubt I will ever have any experience as crazy: Flavie was under siege in the Church of the Nativity, Marguerite was imprisoned in the presidential compound and I was in prison and we were all talking to each other. It was easy. I kept my mobile hidden and used it with care, curled up in my bunk bed and turned towards the wall. I even managed to buy a spare battery off an Israeli car thief.

I remember staring at the blank wall of airbricks beside my bunk, asking Flavie to describe where she was, and what she was doing.

She told me, 'I'm lying on a blanket and I'm so hungry that my head hurts. There was nothing to eat today, so we had leaves picked from the lemon tree, deep-fried to make chips. Now I have stomach ache, which makes my scar ache. But you know what really scares me? It's the thought that I'll be taken to prison at the end of this. I would be frightened to be anywhere near an Israeli, now.'

'You don't have to be.'

I told her that the guards seemed hazy about who we were

or what we were supposed to have done. The prisoners cared even less. The car thief had not even realised the prison was in the occupied territories until I told him.

That night, a man inside the church was shot and killed. Flavie did not know how; he had been walking beneath a covered walkway, which seemed to prove the theories about the steel container hovering over the basilica. As he lay dying, Flavie told me she had lit a candle. It made sense. She was in a church. She added, 'When this is over, I'll show you a picture. You left your camera in your backpack and so I made myself the official war photographer of the siege.'

This was good news. I thought I had lost the camera. I told her to keep it safe and reminded her of our conversation the night that she returned from Norway. We spoke about the importance of places with a spiritual resonance, and look at her now. When the siege ended, when she got back home, she could show her photographs of the Church of the Nativity to Evan.

That was when she told me she had a confession.

'I never went to Finnmark. I went to the Alps, to the ski resort where I met my first ever girlfriend. I should have told everyone, but it was personal and I never expected you and Jean-Luc to cause a major panic. So then I made up a story to tease you, because you were always reading *Babette's Feast*.'

'But the way you described the Northern Lights? I mean, why tell me all those lies?'

'I saw the Northern Lights another time, on a skiing vacation in Canada. Evan suggested I use them to embellish my story.'

'Evan knew you were lying?'

'We weren't trying to be horrible. I thought your book might like some colour and then I thought of the Northern Lights. And I also thought, if you use my description I would have left my own secret mark in your story.'

'I can do colour.'

'Yes, but I can do highlights.'

The End

There was a battle raging beyond the Place Vendôme. Brunel rushed Babette and Christian out of the square; Paris was falling, nothing could keep it together. Brunel's plan was to keep retreating, but when the barricade outside Babette's restaurant fell, then the rue de Rivoli would be his last redoubt. As they fled, Babette looked back at the buildings surrounding the square, to the balcony of the Maison de Worth and the windows of the National Guard headquarters. Brunel had snipers positioned everywhere. But when the Place Vendôme fell, those men would be behind the enemy's lines.

Babette had no choice but to allow her son to join the men on the barricades. Better that than allowing this child to believe that he could make a difference through a lone act, and to dream that his martyrdom might alter the fate of the city. But as they stood beneath the barricade, she made Brunel promise that if he ever saw a way to escape, he would not leave it too late.

'Take Christian with you,' she begged.

'We don't need to worry about that now.'

'We do.' She spoke to both Brunel and Christian. 'This is not a fight to the end. Do you understand me? You have to survive. Both of you.'

'We'll be safe. I promise.' Brunel wasn't even looking at her; his eyes were scanning the tops of the barricade, where his men crouched behind sandbags.

'Don't promise that. Promise me, if you get a chance to escape, you'll take it.'

'I promise,' he said.

She turned to Christian with the same question. He gave his word, too. And although she did not believe her son, she hoped that she could trust Brunel. If only she could find a way to give them an edge, to buy them the time they would need to get away.

She continued to work as a *cantinière* but not on the rue de Rivoli where her son was always in front of her, helping the gunners to stack shells or carrying boxes of ammunition. She made her way back to the Maison de Worth, the flasks of soup and alcohol hanging from her neck and shoulders.

The lobby was still deserted. Brunel's men were in the upper rooms. As she crossed towards the staircase, she looked towards the place where they had found Christian. The barrel of gunpowder was gone; only the lamp that he had been holding remained and, next to it, a flask. She walked over, picked it up and unscrewed the cap; the flask was filled with paraffin. This was how he had planned to ignite the explosive.

She was on the balcony when, across the square, she saw the barricade outside her restaurant fall. It was followed by an explosion and a wave of fire across the entrance to the square that swept up the buildings opposite, flattening and moulding itself to the façades then, almost as violently, being sucked back.

Brunel's men had checked the first assault but General Vinoy's forces were too great. They brought in their field guns and started blasting the men out of their nests. The first building to fall stood opposite the Maison de Worth. The next building tumbled soon after; the Federals were caught as they tried to run. The headquarters of the National Guard was on fire and Babette could see figures running across the roof, trying to find safety in the neighbouring buildings.

The balcony at the Maison de Worth made too tempting a target. As the National Guard headquarters was taken, the firepower seemed to turn en masse in Babette's direction, until the walls were in constant motion, vibrating to their foundations. Then, abruptly, one side of the building shattered. The blast carried Babette across the room in a shower of bricks and plaster. She lay dazed, and even as she came round she remained where she was.

She could not begin to calculate the length of the battle. If it had been fifty minutes or half the night, she could not say, it was nothing but an unrelenting barrage to her. She tried to remain limp, as though the softer her position, the less the battle could touch her. But her body became a conduit for every shock wave, the incessant thunder of the guns shaking through her until she was pounded flat and left numb. At last, she heard the now familiar cranking and spark of the *mitrailleuse*. Babette kicked back on her heels and found her feet. She began to look among the bodies that lay strewn around the salon. Some were dying and some were already dead. As she heard General Vinoy's men on the staircase, she flung herself on to a body and cowered, one arm gripping the corpse's blouson, the other covering her head.

When a rifle butt was jabbed into her spine, she registered the relative quiet before she registered the pain. The shooting had stopped. She flinched and the silence was broken by a shout that seemed to come from the depths of a locked room.

'This one's alive. It looks like a woman.'

'Another over here.'

'Bring them down to the square.'

She was kicked, and with the kick the first voice spoke out again, sounding muffled and distant. 'Get up.'

Her head was spinning, but she climbed from her knees to her feet. When the soldier swiped at her with his bayoneted rifle, she collapsed back against the wall. But he was not trying to spear her, he was aiming for the flasks around her neck. As the flasks clanked, he demanded, 'What's in this? Is this paraffin?'

'Paraffin? It's soup.'

'Show me.'

Her hearing had been damaged by the noise of the battle. The soldier had to repeat his order. She opened one of the canisters and emptied out the contents, the thin potato soup splashing on the floor.

'Open another.'

She poured out the contents of another flask, and as it sloshed at her feet she became bold enough to lift her eyes to the soldier who was commanding her.

'That's not soup. What's that? Is that paraffin?'

She nodded. It was the flask that Christian had left behind.

'So, who is this?' The soldier kicked at the body she had been holding when he found her.

'My lover. His name is Paul-Antoine Brunel.'

The corpse on the floor had lost half its face, and what remained was bloody and crushed out of shape. The soldier stared, and then conferred with others, who all came to stare at the body. Then Babette was hauled away, down the stairs and through the lobby. The Maison de Worth had been torn apart, the doors shredded and the walls perforated as easily as stiff cardboard. Vinoy's men stalked the debris, prodding at bodies with their rifles. Babette's dizziness returned; she felt her head wobble strangely from side to side, but when she tried to steady herself the soldier yanked her onwards. The front door was blocked by a pile of rubble: the remains of the balcony, which had been sheared clean off the building. The soldier dragged her across it. As he shouted, his voice seemed to boom out of a deep well.

'This one says she's the Burner's lover.'

Someone stared in her face. 'Is that right? Are you the Burner's lover?'

She didn't answer. But the first soldier said, 'She was holding on to a stiff up there. I had to prise her off.'

'Well, what did he look like?'

'Like nothing. He only had half a face.'

The square had been transformed into a depot. Horses were bringing in heavy guns; carts brought in shells and crates covered in army markings. Troops assembled, checking their weapons or looking around to take their bearings. The battle noise was carried on a black and acrid breeze. Babette hoped the sense of distance was not an effect of her damaged hearing. She wondered if the barricade in the rue de Rivoli still stood.

Beside her, someone again shouted, 'This is the Burner's mistress.'

'But I know her.'

She looked up. A tall man with red hair spoke from astride his horse, leaning over to look at her. It was General Gallifet.

'Lift up your face, woman. Let's see you.'

She stared him in the eyes.

'What's your name again. Roberts? Héberts?'

'It's Madame Hébert, General.'

'Babette Hébert. Yes, that's right. Lift up your hands, woman.'

Babette did not understand. The general repeated the command, this time with a new harshness. 'Your hands. Lift them up.'

She raised her hands, showing the palms to General Gallifet, who squinted, then asked her to turn them over so he could see the backs. He was looking for the tell-tale streak of black from the discharge of the rifle. Babette did what she was told and the general nodded, satisfied.

'Clean,' he said. 'Clean-ish. You've not been playing with guns, whatever else you have been doing.' He pointed his sabre at the flasks hanging over her shoulder. 'What's in the flasks?'

The soldier who had found her said, 'She had a flask full of paraffin, sir.'

Behind General Gallifet, Babette could see General Vinoy approaching on foot, surrounded by his staff officers. The news that Babette Hébert had been captured was relayed to him, along with the news that she had been found carrying paraffin. General Vinoy came over and peered at her. Behind him came Henri Furet and finally Zizi's lover, Gilles Furet.

A soldier was dispatched to fetch the corpse of the anonymous sniper from Freddie Worth's salon and Babette once again insisted that it was Paul-Antoine Brunel, the Burner.

'I thought he would be taller,' Gallifet said.

'You shared your Christmas with him,' Vinoy replied. 'Don't you recognise him?'

'Which chap was he?'

'He was sitting next to your sister, man.'

General Gallifet stared down at the corpse. 'Hard to recognise anyone without a face, sir.'

General Vinoy was already turning to shout orders at his nephews. 'Go and fetch that man from the London *Times* who we saw earlier, and the Kraut journalist with the moustache. Tell them we have the body of the rebel leader.'

Seventy-four-year-old Mons Brunel opened out the clipping from the newspaper and began to read. He was in the Fleet Street offices of the plump journalist Joseph Beddoes, who watched over him with the smug look of an amateur magician, confident that he had produced a wonder.

'What's it like to read an account of the discovery of one's own body, Monsieur Brunel?'

It was chilling. Brunel looked at the date, more than thirty years old, and then re-read the story. There was a lurid description of the state of the corpse, and the wild look of the woman that was found clinging to it, as the cannons raged around her and Paris burned.

Brunel covered his eyes, squeezing his temples with his fingertips before he looked back at the journalist. 'What did you hope to write when you discovered I was alive, Mr Beddoes? Did you really believe you had found a terrorist plot at the heart of the Royal Naval Academy?'

'I won't be writing anything, Monsieur. Yesterday afternoon, I was summoned to the editor's office and informed that you were once the schoolmaster of the Prince of Wales. We have strict rules on reporting stories concerning royalty. We never do it.' Beddoes blinked.

'Anyway, I found I was doubting my own story. I see that

Mlle Louise Michel is a revolutionary because she never talks about anything else. But you were a professional soldier. I don't see that you would have much in common.'

'We found common ground. But it's true, she was fighting for a revolution and I was fighting because I was ashamed that the army had fallen into the hands of men like Gallifet and Vinoy, who had surrendered before it was necessary. When there was, perhaps, still a chance that we could have turned the war around.'

Brunel knew that the journalist would recognise the names of General Gallifet and General Vinoy; both men were described in the article, striding across the Place Vendôme and stepping over the bodies of the dead.

Beddoes had laid his pad out on the table, but not yet touched his pen. 'But was there really a chance, Monsieur? How did it slip away?'

'I'd say there were one or two chances. Perhaps they were slim, but we failed to seize them – because the army lost all the important arguments to the politicians. One way or another, we were never ruthless enough. We failed to drive the arguments, or make the civilians dance to our tunes.'

'Do you regret that, now?'

'Do I regret not being ruthless enough?' It was the one question that Brunel was prepared for, because it was the one he had thought about the most. 'No, Mr Beddoes, I don't. Should I regret that I didn't kill more people, while promising that I would kill more in the future? Those aren't the kinds of regrets anyone wants. I have to hope for something better.'

'The article mentions a woman: your mistress. What happened to her?'

Brunel felt the weight of his years, the ache that began at his shoulders and travelled through his arms to his bony hands, clasping the handle of his stick. The heaviness inside his chest, the shallow rise and fall of his breath inside a frame that always felt too tight. The damaged bones of his thighs that ached as he sat and grated as he walked. Right down to his pavement-weary feet. But there was still enough life left in him, still a spark that could be fired up again.

He said, 'That's why I came back, Mr Beddoes. I was hoping you could tell me.'

'You never tried to find her?'

Brunel asked if he could sit. A chair was found, wheeled across the floor by an office boy and spun into place to catch Brunel. The journalist sat opposite and waited for him to begin speaking.

Brunel tapped the newspaper clipping. 'The day this article was published, I was fighting with a youth battalion.'

The battalion was known as the Lost Boys. When he took the bullet, they were fighting outside the Gare du Nord.

'I was shot in the thigh, the boys had to carry me to safety. We retreated as far as the rue Marcadet and they left me with a concierge in an apartment opposite the very last barricade. When that fell, the entire neighbourhood was herded into the street. I was certain that someone would give me away, but no one did. I had been handed a chance to escape: the people protected me, and the soldiers believed I was already dead.'

'What happened to the boys in your battalion?'

Brunel took a moment to answer. 'Most of the younger prisoners were sent to prison hulks in Brittany. Some were executed. Vinoy's men had this trick of examining your hands. If they thought you had fired a weapon, you were executed on the spot. But in those days, I used a revolver, and though my hands weren't exactly clean, I got away with it. Others weren't so lucky.'

Brunel had looked over at the remains of the barricade where Christian lay, his body draped over the sandbags. Whether he had been killed in the fighting or been executed afterwards, Brunel did not know. But he had promised Babette that he would try to protect the boy, and he had not.

Joseph Beddoes had just enough spark to see that Brunel was

holding something back. He said, 'Your mistress is described as a *pétroleuse*. The *pétroleuses* were tried and deported, but I could find no record of a Mme Hébert in the court records.'

'No. I think perhaps she managed to get away. I always hoped that she did.'

'But you didn't go looking for her?'

'No. I felt I could not do that.'

Berlevaag

I arrived back in London like any other released convict, by coach to Victoria station. I was even homeless, but only because I had tenants in my flat. I checked into a bed and breakfast and, alone in my room, began to get scared.

I could list the things that most terrify me; fireworks, aeroplanes and refuse trucks are at the top of the list. When the Queen celebrated her Golden Jubilee, the fireworks brought the war straight back into my bedroom and this time there was no Flavie to give me courage. Then the Royal Air Force staged a mass fly-past of every type of plane they possessed. Long before the end, I was shaking.

In the mornings, the dustbin trucks came rumbling down to empty the bins of the local restaurants and I woke thinking that they were APCs. And if I thought I would settle down after the Queen's fly-past, I soon discovered that even the normal level of London air traffic played havoc with my nerves and my sleep. I had to find somewhere else to live, but I surprised myself when I called Sally rather than my parents.

I moved into Evan's room in Sally's three-bed semi in Coventry. We shared bunk beds. Sally's husband had to get the second bunk out of the loft and reassemble it – no one had used it since Evan was twelve and used to have friends on sleepovers. He was now fifteen, and he had his mad dad sleeping above him.

I was reading on my bunk when Evan called me down to watch television. There was a documentary on the siege of Bethlehem. An Israeli colonel spoke directly to camera and claimed that his only aim was to conserve the basilica. I had Flavie's descriptions fresh in my mind; I knew the documentary-makers only had to move their cameras slightly to give the lie to the colonel's account. A little closer and they could show the burnt-out room where the Israelis had set fire to a medieval library, or around the side of the building to show the sixteenth-century door that they had blown up in an attempt to storm the church. They could even use the army crane to rise above the church and show the wooden roof and the stained-glass windows peppered with bullet holes. If I could have made the camera move by force of will-power, I would have. But all I could do was dig my fingers into Sally's sofa.

The documentary reached my point in the story. There was footage of the protesters taking food into the church. There I was, running across the piazza. And there was Flavie, overtaking me as the Door of Humility opened. I knew that there were no camera crews in the piazza that day. These shots were not taken by documentary-makers: there were no documentary-makers involved in the making of this film. This was TV made by an army.

But then, towards the end of the documentary, a series of still pictures were shown, taken inside the church during the siege. Evan and I leant forward, trying to see through the gloom for a glimpse of Flavie. The figures that emerged in the candle-light were all men, and after forty days they were thin with long beards. Evan asked, who do you think took these photographs? And I realised that it could only be Flavie, using my camera. When the documentary ended, there was nothing to indicate ownership of the photographs. I could not believe that Flavie had given her film to the army. She was still in prison in Israel, fighting a deportation order and determined to take her case right through the Israeli legal system.

The two sieges in Palestine ended simultaneously. It was a deal brokered between several states, and the result was that, in Ramallah, the tanks were pulled back to the edge of the downtown area, while in Bethlehem, everyone was taken into custody. So Marguerite was freed and Flavie ended up in prison. And now that she was intent on remaining in prison and fighting her case, Marguerite Galperin was staying at her side. She had taken an apartment in east Jerusalem and was visiting Flavie as often as she was allowed, liaising with her Israeli lawyers and trying to press for an official inquiry into the demonstration when Flavie was shot.

Jean-Luc was organising the French end of things, but he was also searching for a case that he could take to a court outside of Israel. This was why I called him. If the photographs had been taken with my camera, and were being used without permission, I wondered if the broadcaster could be in breach of copyright.

Jean-Luc was excited. But not because of the copyright case: he told me that copyright was bullshit. He wanted to build a war-crime case. 'However you look at this, the pictures came into their hands illegally. We call that looting, my friend. The TV company is profiting from a war crime. Which is great because we can sue in Europe.' I heard the scratch of a pencil as Jean-Luc took notes. 'Listen, James, I am hoping to speak to Flavie tonight, if she has a phone card. It's a nightmare, you know how Israeli prisons work.'

'I was in prison for less than a week,' I say. 'I signed the paper, remember.'

'Forget that, James. You have more responsibilities, it's different for you. So why are you blaming yourself?'

Because I had cracked.

Each day in prison, officials came and gave me a document to sign. Every day, I turned them away. Why would I sign a document in a language I did not understand? Then I decided to do it. There was no reason, no torture, not even undue pressure. I was just lonely. They had found my mobile phone a few days earlier and I was staring at the wall when I asked the warden if he could translate the document for me. Once he had finished speaking, I borrowed his pen and scrawled my name.

Within hours, I was on a plane to Britain, deported as an unde-
sirable alien and forbidden from returning to Israel for at least
ten years. Flavie stayed to fight but I had folded. If I could
change anything, it would be that. I wish I had stood firm.

I think of Flavie as I type these last few paragraphs. We are on
a ship in the Arctic Circle. Flavie is somewhere above me, on
the miles of white walkways of the deck, her face framed by
the soft fur of her parka hood. I imagine the boat stopping at
Berlevaag and the pair of us disembarking, walking down the
gangway to the quayside to find a little Lutheran church. And,
inside, in a display cabinet devoted to the history of the town
and the people that passed through, we find a letter in Paul-
Antoine Brunel's own hand, and next to it, a photograph of an
elderly couple. This is the evidence that I dream of finding: a
slender woman in a fisherman's woollen hat, a grey-bearded
man leaning on a stick. Their hands locked together, their
bodies turned towards each other.

The ship's horn blasts a jet of clear white steam into the air:
it seems to hang there for a moment, as crystals shaking to the
returning echo across the fjord. Flavie links her arm in mine
and asks how their meeting went. What would happen exactly?

'I think there would be food involved. Lots of it.'

'Would she still be working for those crazy sisters?'

'No. They were older than she was. I think they probably
would have died but they would have left a will that allowed
Babette to remain in their house for the rest of her life.'

'And so that's where they would live?'

'That's where they would live, in a painted wooden house
filled with the fragrance of pine logs burning in the stove, the
kitchen windows tinted with steam, while below them the fishing
boats dance in the harbour.'

The lights in the doorways of all these little houses glimmer
against the mountain backdrop. Flavie and I try to choose the
house, as we walk arm in arm along the quayside. How should

I explain our friendship? As a symptom of a kind of premature dotage? As a reflection of Brunel and Babette, already old as they walked along this same harbour a hundred years earlier, at the start of another century? If I imagine Brunel and Babette in their dotage, that might imply a kind of idealised, uncompleted relationship. I don't necessarily believe that Brunel and Babette would leap into bed together. But I don't want to end this without believing they would lead a life as full and as happy as any life could possibly be, in this frozen land where dreams are sketched by lights in the sky.

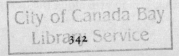

I have tried to credit my most important sources within the novel, but by far the most important was *The Fall of Paris: the Siege and the Commune 1870–71* by Alistair Horne. I would also like to thank Kay Quinn for the theft of her flat on the rue Marcadet.

The novel was read at different stages by a large number of people and I am more grateful than I can say, especially when early drafts were chaotic babbling polemics. So thank you to Robert Blincoe, Martin Delamere, Lesley Shaw, Carole Welch, Amber Burlinson, Jocasta Brownlee, Celia Levett, Matt King, Dea Brovig and especially to my beloved wife, Leila Sansour.

NICHOLAS BLINCOE

White Mice

Models are like white mice – they are cute, they all look identical, and they all sleep with each other.

Jamie and Louise Greenhalgh look more like twins than brother and sister. He is twenty and should be in college; she is twenty-three, a born diva and a desperately failing model. But as Louise drags him from Paris to Milan and back her career mysteriously re-ignites, and Jamie is suddenly the brother of Europe's most talked-about model. But then he learns what they are talking about . . .

'Hilarious, shocking and well researched . . . Blincoe is brilliant at depicting the double standards, neuroses and narcissism of the fashion world . . . What a treat.'
Henry Sutton, *Mirror*

'Blincoe continues to write books as up-to-the-minute as tomorrow's newspapers . . . an accomplished achievement.'
Thomas Hodgkinson, *Literary Review*

'A sleek, contemporary novel . . . Blincoe captures the fast pace, the insecurity and the mounting tension as showtime nears . . . If you want to know more about those creatures called models, Blincoe's your man'
Honor Fraser, *New Statesman*

'A dark tour de force which marks out Nicholas Blincoe as one of the most exciting talents writing in Britain today.'
Wayne Clews, *Attitude*

'References to pop culture and the fashion world are perfectly integrated into the characters in this assured thriller'
Christopher Silvester, *Daily Mail*

SCEPTRE